LU

DOCTOR WHO – THE NEW ADVENTURES

Also available:

THE NEW DOCTOR WHO ADVENTURES

ADVENTURES

LUCIFER RISING

Jim Mortimore & Andy Lane

First published in 1993 by
Doctor Who Books
an imprint of Virgin Publishing Ltd
332 Ladbroke Grove
London W10 5AH

Cover illustration by Jim Mortimore
Illustrated by Lee Brimmicombe-Wood
Phototypeset by Intype, London

Printed and bound in Great Britain by
Cox & Wyman Ltd, Reading, Berks

ISBN 0 42620 338 7

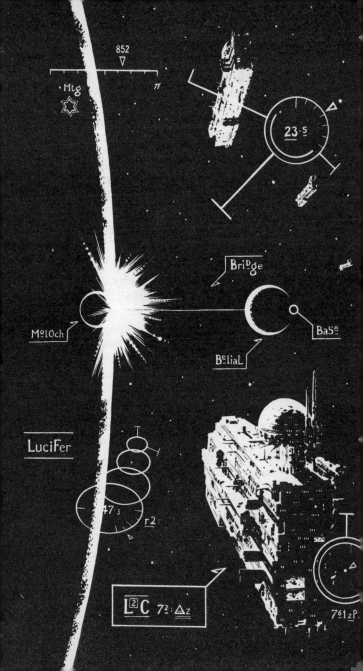

PROLOGUE

FALLING FROM GRACE

Though fallen thyself, never to rise again,
Live, and take comfort. Thou hast left behind
Powers that will work for thee;

Wordsworth – *Toussaint, the most unhappy man*

Yonder in the north there is singing on the lake. Cloud maidens dance on the shore. There we take our being.

Yonder in the north cloud beings rise. They ascend unto cloud blossoms. There we take our being.

Yonder in the north rain stands over the land . . . Yonder in the north stands forth at twilight the arc of a rainbow. There we have our being.

Tewa Pueblo Chant

Someone had once told Paula Engado that it wasn't the fall that killed you, it was the sudden stop when you hit the ground. At the time she'd found it funny.

She wasn't laughing now.

Tumbling uncontrollably through an atmosphere that was growing hotter and denser by the minute, her sense of humour seemed to have evaporated along with her starsuit's external sensors.

Tiny globules of sweat hung in front of Paula's eyes. She batted them aside with a twitch of her head. The stench of her own body was almost overwhelming, and she had to concentrate hard in order to read the suit's instruments. It was no use. Every single read-out, every single diagnostic, had crashed. Using the chin switches, she tried to pull some kind of exterior view from the infected software, but she might just as well have tried to walk back up to Belial. More angry than scared, she operated a manual control to peel back the first few layers of filters from the helmet visor, and finally managed to get a dim view of the storm through which she was falling: an atmospheric disturbance bigger than the distant Earth. The deep rumble of colliding pressure fronts filled her ears; flickering discharges of lightning illuminated the dead faces of the digital read-outs inside her helmet – further evidence, if it were needed, of the giant planet Lucifer's vast and complex meteorology.

Lucifer – the fallen Angel.

How apt.

Ignoring the safety regulations governing spacewalk protocol, Paula peeled back another layer of gold shielding from her visor. More shapes and colours leaped into focus. Through her reflection, she saw coils of gas rush past her helmet, churning sickeningly around each other before vanishing into the towering atmosphere above.

5

The starsuit suddenly seemed to be closing in on her. The miracle of modern science, which until now had surrounded and nurtured her, was becoming a claustrophobic prison in which the smell of plastic, sweat and burnt insulation was almost overwhelming.

Paula felt panic rise within her. She didn't want to die alone, thousands of kilometres from the nearest human being, beyond the reach of even her father's emotionless touch. She was facing her fear, but, unlike the Tewa American Indians of her grandfather's stories, *it* was defeating *her*. Desperately, she chinned the switch that should have dispensed a dose of tranquillizing drugs, but the autodoc software had crashed along with the main systems.

She closed her eyes and clutched at the solace of a remembered embrace, a stolen kiss. Then with a mighty effort she thrust the memory away. It was all behind her now.

The thought acted like a sudden blast of cold air: everything seemed to pull back into focus from the grainy world of terror. She was still shivering uncontrollably, although the temperature was hotter than comfortable. Blinking sweat out of her eyes, she looked out through the barely shielded helmet visor. Something was happening. If she peered hard she could still make out the multicoloured clouds and the thousand kilometre wide flashes of sheet lightning, but her visor seemed to be misting over. Everything outside was becoming blurred and confused. The colours were running together like a child's painting.

It was only when she felt the sudden warmth on her cheek that Paula knew she was crying, and with that realization all self-control fled. She beat senselessly upon the inside of her suit until her clenched fists were raw and bleeding, only to feel the joints in the sleeves begin to give way. The helmet visor cracked as the temperature rose sharply. Alien gases burst into the suit, blistering her skin and scorching her lungs. She clenched her eyes shut with pain, cutting off her last clear view of the dead internal systems displays.

As she died, Paula's mind fixed upon an odd trinket of philosophy that her long-dead grandfather had once quoted to her, the last thing she would ever consciously remember – a final, useless bead of comfort to ward off the inevitable.

Only in death do we find peace.

Only from death do we learn of life.

She choked the words aloud as a final goodbye; hurled them defiantly into the void; screamed them above the screech of rending metal, until Lucifer tore the breath from her lungs, the blood from the veins and the life from her body.

She died.

And the Angels came.

PART ONE

How art thou fallen from heaven,
O Lucifer, son of the morning?

Isaiah, chapter 14, verse 12

Silence.

The Adjudicator dimmed the worklight over Miles Engado's desk and studied the stacks of small crystalline blocks before him, piled up in towers like the cities back on Earth, ripe with false promise.

He sighed. So many questions; so few answers. Paula Engado's death. The antagonism of the staff. The unexplained arrival of this mysterious scientist with his uncoordinated wardrobe and his uncoordinated friends. The Angels. Where to start?

The Adjudicator let his fingers hover delicately over the opaque crystal blocks. He lifted one and fed it into the reader.

Although his movements appeared leisurely and unstudied, there was nothing random about them. The Adjudicator never did anything at random. Everything had a reason.

To find it, it was only necessary to look in the right place.

Chapter One

```
<LOAD FILE A153/X/23/2/2154>
<SETUP>
<RUN 35660>
```
'Ashes to ashes, dust to dust,' said Miles Engado, turning away from the group assembled amongst the cleared chairs and tables of the Belial Base refectory. 'Section Leaders to meet me in Conference Room One in ten minutes,' he added, and walked away.
```
<STOP>
<SET LINGUISTIC ANALYSIS = ON>
<SET SYNTAX = FULL>
<SET CONTEXT = FULL>
<SET MOTIVATIONAL ANALYSIS = ON>
<SET SUBROUTINES FREUD, JUNG, ADLER,
SKINNER>
<RERUN 35660>
```
'Ashes to ashes, dust to dust,' said Miles Engado, his voice catching slightly as he turned away from the simularity projector in the centre of the room. The rest of the small group assembled amongst the cleared chairs and tables of the Belial Base refectory stood transfixed by the replayed sight of Paula Engado's last moments, recorded by a remote drone which had followed her down into Lucifer's poisonous atmosphere. The drone had been too light and too slow to do anything but observe, transmit and finally be destroyed itself. As the tumbling figure grew a glowing tail of debris, then broke up into a shower of sparks, only Piper O'Rourke thought to put her hand on Miles Engado's shoulder. He patted it absently. In the glare of his daughter's death, the tears which silently

explored the creases and folds of his face glistened like comets.

'Section Leaders to meet me in the Conference Room in ten minutes,' he murmured, and walked away. Piper let her hand fall as her eyes lingered on Miles's back. The door to the refectory clunked into place behind him. Glances were exchanged all around the room.

<STOP>
<SET POINT-OF-VIEW = PIPER O'ROURKE>
<SET STYLE = 20>
<SET INTERPOLATION = ON>
<OPTIONS: (A) LIST ALL EMOTIONAL RESPONSES.
(B) PRIORITIZE EMOTIONAL RESPONSES>
<B>
<SORTING . . . PRIORITIZE AND LIST MOST PROBABLE RESPONSE>
<OK>
<RERUN 35660.1>

'Section Leaders to meet me in the Conference Room in ten minutes,' Miles added sharply, before shrugging off the woman's comforting touch and leaving the refectory. Piper let her hand fall as her eyes lingered on the tall, balding figure in the severely tailored turquoise tunic. He was a proud man, one who perhaps over valued dignity and restraint, but essentially a good man. Too good for her, perhaps.

Piper glanced around at the other members of the team who had turned out to mourn Paula and show support for her father. Practically the whole research staff was crammed into the circular refectory, one of the few human-built rooms on the Base capable of holding that many people. The only absentees were those on duty down on Moloch, together with Federique Moshe-Rabaan and the three newcomers.

Of the remaining twenty-five people, none were speaking, but then words were unnecessary. Everyone had their own way of coping with this, the Project's first death since its inception five years ago.

After watching one or two of her own support technicians begin to move the chairs and tables half-heartedly back into position for the evening meal, Piper wandered listlessly over to one of the windows which encircled the refectory. The windows had been a concession won by Christine LaFayette from Earth Government. Piper had sometimes wondered whether it had been the financial investment of Christine's mother in the Project which had spoken louder than her words. Whatever the reason, the site for the social centre of the Base was as near perfect as it was possible to get. Positioned atop the Base's central dome, the refectory commanded a perfect view both of the airless dark side of the moon and of the edge of Lucifer, the huge planet it orbited around. Lucifer's lurid atmospheric glow circled the horizon in a ring broken only by the irregular towers of the mountain ranges, the rock shaped by an abrasive atmosphere long since torn away. The Ring of Lucifer, as it had become known, cast a flat scarlet glare across the outlying regions of the base, and threw everyone's shadow towards the centre of the room. One or two of the staff considered the sight somewhat morbid, but Christine had insisted that the Base personnel needed to be able to look out on a real landscape once in a while, not a simularity of one generated by a neural net.

That was fine in theory but, gazing over the fantastic and disturbing landscape of Belial, Piper came close to admitting she would have preferred the simularity.

Ah, but you couldn't see reflections in a simularity, could you? You couldn't watch everyone in the room without being watched yourself.

Over on the far side of the refectory, Sam Russell, a middle-aged engineer in a padded foil suit, reached out to hold his wife Cheryl's hand as she sobbed inconsolably. Alex Bannen sneered as he walked past them, his ornate robes giving him the look of some sweaty Buddha. Only the diminutive, dark-haired Christine LaFayette was

15

actively studying everyone else in the room. But, Piper thought, as the Chief Psychologist responsible for the mental health of the team, that was her job.

Piper turned away. She felt distanced from their grief: cold and unreachable. She'd left Earth to escape a world disintegrating into a crazy mess of restrictions, paranoia and self-destruction. For a while, she had really thought she'd made it.

The simularity of Lucifer's turbulent cloud patterns flickered off just as Paula's last burning fragments, having used up the scant supply of oxygen from her suit, sputtered and died.

Piper jerked herself out of her reverie with an effort.

The nightmare view of Lucifer was replaced by a standard picture – a translucent view of Belial Base itself, with the main corridors and chambers shining pinkly inside it like the organs of some gelatinous alien life form. People began to move, drifting almost aimlessly around the refectory as if unsure what to do now the service was over.

Piper sighed. Her gaze travelled from the reflection of the room to her own image. Critically, she began to tug at the puffy sleeves and complicated thongs of her tunic, but her practised grooming motions died away as her gaze caught first upon the sapphire that had been surgically implanted on her left ring finger, and then on the blue veins which snaked across the backs of both hands. She straightened and did something which she usually avoided – looked at her face. Getting old was a funny thing. Paula never made it past her eighteenth birthday, but Piper would probably hit a hundred and ten before senility started to creep in. More, if she was careful. She certainly didn't intend to waste her life. She had plans. For after Eden.

Piper caught a cold glint in her reflection's eye. Age is making you hard, she thought. You've got too many years behind you, too many memories and regrets clogging up your mind. They're young. Death doesn't touch them the way it touches you. It's not breathing down their necks yet.

16

She pulled her gaze away from the familiar stranger that was her reflection and looked over to where Alex Bannen and Christine LaFayette were continuing an argument which had already flourished for years and seemed likely to go on forever.

'Look, it's obvious, right? All you've got to do is ask your mother for more financial support – that way the Eden Project gets a new lease of life and maybe we all end up winners.'

'I've told you before, Alex. Mother and I don't talk. Ever.' The faintest of French accents gently smoothed her vowels into soft shapes.

'Even though she bought you a place on the staff?'

Christine's voice became icy cold. 'Are you questioning my professional ability? Some people might think that merits a psychological checkup, and that could get you sent back to Earth.'

Bannen turned away in sudden embarrassment. Normally the Technical Services Supervisor was too fat, too loud, and just too much altogether. Piper had no time for him or his affectation of importance, so much larger in his own mind than in anyone else's when the mission began, and running dangerously out of control now. But then, sometimes, almost for no reason, the scientist would become like this: embarrassed, lonely, lacking in any of the social graces. At times like these Piper was tempted to feel sorry for him, but Bannen himself stifled any overtures of friendship. Piper had learned a long time ago that he couldn't handle them, and had stopped worrying about him. Now she simply found him irritating.

'You heard what Miles said,' she snapped, her harshness a deliberate attempt to shock them out of their argument. 'Alex, Christine. Let's go. The man's going to want answers and he's going to want them soon.'

Standing petulantly by the food dispenser, which of late had developed a tendency to drift around the refectory in search of customers, Bannen spoke. 'And how the hell are we supposed to do that without properly financed – '

17

Piper sighed. 'Alex, life's too short to listen to your whining.'

Christine rubbed her eyes tiredly. 'I'll go along with that.'

Bannen's face fell. 'Hey, look. We've all got our own ways of dealing with the situation, right?'

'Yeah, well, just show a little common sense in what you say, Alex, or we might suddenly find Earth pulling the rug out from underneath us,' Piper pointed out. 'If that happens, we're *all* on a long fall to nowhere.'

'And Paula thought we were so close,' Christine murmured. 'So close.'

Bannen spread his hands placatingly. 'Look. We're all fighting over the same pot of gold.' He turned to Piper and smiled in unconvincing friendship. 'Perhaps *you* can make her see reason. If we can't get more funding from somewhere, then the obvious thing to do is switch resources from LaFayette's area to mine. It's the only sensible thing to do. I mean, it's been five years and we're still not sure the Angels even know we exist!'

Christine sighed. 'I just don't want to argue with you any more, Alex.'

'This is neither the time nor place for this discussion,' Piper said. 'For God's sake, can't you both show a little respect?'

Bannen could not resist trying to get the last word. 'I'll bring it up at the meeting,' he said, 'and if Engado can't see the way ahead, I'm sure Moshe-Rabaan and the Energy Police can make him see the error of his ways. Earth Central can't afford to keep pumping money into the project for no return.' His face darkened. 'Nobody said we had jobs for life.'

'Great.' Piper breathed a sigh of relief. 'Now that we've all got that off our chests, let's stop behaving like juvenile simularities and give Miles the support he needs.'

Piper turned on her heel and began to walk towards the exit. After a sympathetic look at Bannen, Christine turned to follow. As the two women left the gallery, Bannen's face twisted into an irritated snarl. He smashed a fist into the simularity of the Base and gained absolutely no satisfaction at all when his arm passed harmlessly through the field.

<RUN ON 20>

The Conference Room was a small, enclosed space with neutral decoration and no windows to distract from its most important function: the exchange of information. Piper took her seat opposite Miles Engado thinking, as usual, how bare and characterless the room was. It was the one location on the Base where she felt truly uncomfortable. For a moment, as she sat, Miles caught her eye. Just for a moment. It was an exchange none of the others noticed, but that didn't surprise Piper in the least.

Miles seemed ready to speak. The room fell silent.

'The first thing I would like to say is – thank you for all your support. From both of us. As you know, Paula was very dear to me, the more so after her mother's – death, and I, I would very much like to express – ' Miles' words seemed to jam in his throat, 'my great – sorrow . . .'

Christine's eyes widened in concern. 'I move that this meeting be adjourned for twenty-four hours.'

Bannen spoke up. 'I object. If you'll forgive me, Coordinator. I know this is a trying time for you, but we *have* to find an explanation for the suit failure. We have a five person first contact team at the other end of the Bridge. Those people need our support. We can't risk any malfunction being repeated. The men and women on Moloch rely on us and their work is of paramount importance to the mission. We can't let them down.'

Piper felt like hitting the man. Bannen cared little for the safety of the mission, and not at all about Miles Engado's feelings. All he wanted was more money for his research, and that meant keeping the meeting going despite Christine's attempts to curtail it.

'Alex, Christine.' Miles's voice was completely under control. 'Our initial responsibility is to the mission. However, there is an agenda for this meeting, and I think we

19

should adhere to it. We will discuss possible causes of my daughter's death, accidental or otherwise, under the heading of "Any Other Business".'

Piper favoured Miles with a direct stare. She wished she could reach out and help this proud man. Ease his pain. Miles was precise and intelligent, and rarely showed any of his feelings. Although Christine, not she, was the psychologist, Piper could still tell how close to cracking Miles Engado was. It provoked a feeling within her that she thought had died with her husband.

'So,' the Coordinator continued, 'if there are no objections, I shall declare this meeting open. The minutes of the meeting will be abstracted from the neural network simularity records at a later date.' He glanced up at a tiny drone, no bigger than a twisted loop of silver tape, bobbing silently in the corner of the room.

'Now,' he continued, stroking the surface of the table before him, 'the first item on the agenda is the exploration of the aboriginal areas both here on Belial and down the Bridge on Moloch.' As his fingers moved, images appeared in bright primary colours, floating above the surface of the table. 'Piper, since this is your area, perhaps you would care to begin.'

'No sweat.' Piper's fingers caressed the touch-sensitive surface of the table. Pictures appeared in time with her movements: a real-time simularity of the huge gas giant Lucifer with its string of attendant moons – Astarte, Belial, Moloch and Demogorgon.

'There hasn't been a lot of progress since the last Team Leaders' meeting.'

The simularity suddenly expanded to isolate a section of Lucifer's outer atmosphere. Above it the two moons, Belial and Moloch, swung in geosynchronous orbit, one above the other, linked by the glittering neon thread of the Bridge. To Piper they resembled nothing so much as a dumbbell with unequal weights slowly tumbling through the void.

'Exploration of the chambers placed throughout the two moons, and of the Bridge which connects them, has

20

so far been proceeding slowly and without much success,' she continued. 'Apart from the operations of the Bridge itself, which Tiw Heimdall worked out two years ago, the functions of most of the other sites within the moon system remain unclear. Despite everyone's unstinting efforts, we still know nothing more about the aliens who built the complex than we did when we arrived. We don't even know if the Angels built it, or whether we're looking for a race who have since moved on. Sure we've found artefacts, hundreds of them. Alex's staff are busy cataloguing them even as we speak. But as to what they are,' Piper shrugged, 'well, even the neural net can't seem to help us. Take this for example.' She pulled something from a receptacle and held it up for general viewing. 'Jesus found this in the deadspace this morning. Is it a pen, a fork or a work of art? Analysis tells us it's made of high-grade tensile steel, but . . .' Piper bent and folded the device easily, like cloth. 'You see?' She passed the device to Christine. 'Perhaps the sociologists can make something of it. I can't.'

Christine took the object and examined it curiously, unfolding and folding it again several times. 'These things never cease to fascinate me,' she said. 'Their expertise in memory metals was certainly phenomenal. It must have led to a whole new way of thinking: a looser, more unstructured, more abstract philosophy.'

Alex Bannen snorted. 'Psychobabble,' he said, smiling as Christine flinched.

Piper's fingers made small, circular motions on the table, and the picture zoomed in again to show the two moons in more detail, locked into synchronous orbit. Belial Base, on the upper moon, was marked as a blue nest of tunnels on the side furthest from Lucifer. From it, the single orange tunnel known colloquially as the Pit passed completely through the entire moon, terminating in a small orange blob on the other side. From there, an orange line joined it to Moloch, the lower moon. Apart from a green outline, Moloch's interior was coloured completely in orange. The twin moons, one solid, one hollow,

21

continued their orbit, linked along an axis that, if extended, would join the centres of both moons to that of Lucifer itself.

Another brush of the fingers. New tunnels appeared, marked in red.

'In the last two weeks we've opened up a new system of galleries. Preliminary geodating places them at between five hundred and a thousand million years old. There's no atmosphere in there yet, so Cheryl and Sam Russell are trying to seal them and get an oxygen generator set up.' She paused. 'Strange that they'd fill the whole interior of Moloch with air and vegetation and a few hundred tunnels here on Belial with nothing but machinery.' She shook her head, dismissing the thought as one more insoluble mystery. 'And that's it. The rest you know.'

'Busy little critters, weren't they?' offered Bannen. 'Digging their tunnels and building their machines while our remote ancestors were still working out how to divide one cell in two.'

'Not so remote, in your case,' Christine murmured, just loud enough for Bannen to hear.

'We're no closer to finding out how the two moons are kept locked in their geosynchronous orbit,' Piper continued. 'I'm no astrophysicist, and I'm sure Alex will correct me if I'm wrong, but Moloch should be orbiting much faster than Belial, because it's closer to Lucifer. Somehow it's being held back.'

'By the Bridge?' Christine said.

Bannen smirked at her. 'We've gone over the mechanism with a fine-tooth comb. The equipment that locks each end in place is very sophisticated – bloody weird, in fact – but the Bridge itself is just an extruded monofilament woven into a tubular shaft. Nothing more sophisticated than a basic elevator. At the levels of tension those moons are generating, that Bridge should snap like a piece of old knicker elastic.'

'What about Moloch's hollowness?' Piper asked. 'Could the unusually low density be, oh, I don't know, holding it back, or something?'

'Don't be stupid,' Bannen sneered. 'Leave the science to me, dear.'

There was a momentary, embarrassed silence as all four of them looked at the simularity in the centre of the table. A small green ring could just be made out, sliding up the Bridge like a doughnut on a string. That would be the Lift containing B Shift, Piper decided, making their way back from Moloch to Belial, and a well-earned rest. As Head of Support Services, it was one of her jobs to organize the shifts around the seemingly random meanderings of the Lift. Sometimes it seemed that any time not taken up with designing, redesigning, streamlining, adjusting and rotating duty rosters for the Project staff was spent generating simularities of the Lift and trying to work out if there was any systematic basis for its movements, or whether it just shifted between Belial and Moloch on a whim and a prayer. So far only Tiw Heimdall seemed to have the faintest idea how and why the Bridge worked. The trouble with Tiw was . . . Well, he was just Tiw, and that was that.

As her thoughts gradually drifted back towards reality, Piper became aware that Bannen was still talking.

'. . . we're beginning to suspect,' Bannen was saying, 'that it's friction between Moloch and Lucifer's atmosphere that is slowing it down. We know that the moon is actually orbiting within Lucifer's atmospheric envelope, and its surface is markedly hotter than Belial's. Problem is, this raises more questions than it answers. If Moloch were subject to any degree of friction, however slight, over the length of time we are considering here that friction would have eroded the damn thing right away. And there's still the obvious question to be addressed: both the moons and the Bridge orbit well within Lucifer's Roche Limit, so why weren't they reduced to rubble aeons ago?'

Christine looked slightly puzzled. Bannen caught the expression.

'I know you're not an astronomer, Christine, but by all that's sensible, do your homework,' he snapped. 'No moon can exist within a certain distance of its parent planet without breaking apart due to gravitational stress. Moloch does. The implication is that the builders of these installations, whoever or whatever they were, physically moved Moloch to where they wanted it and then protected it for millennia from a basic law of nature.'

There was a longer silence as the four of them took in the significance of Bannen's remark. Piper watched Christine shrink back in her seat.

'And we're trespassing on their territory,' Piper said finally. 'Borrowing their bases for our own purposes. What happens if they come back?'

'We apologize,' said Bannen in a dry monotone.

'Thank you,' said Miles Engado, when it became clear that Piper had finished her report. She tried to catch his eye, but he either didn't see or wasn't going to respond. The Coordinator presented an impression of outward complacency. Piper wondered what emotions lay in wait beneath his calm exterior.

'Christine,' he continued, 'perhaps you could bring us up to speed on the next agenda item: the attempt to communicate with the Angels.'

The French psychologist drew a breath. 'Well, that's not a problem. I can sum it up in two words: total failure.'

'Would you care to expand on that?'

'There's not a lot to expand on. The original one-year programme of communications packages backed up with translation software and psychological interpretation washed out because the Angels shy away from any form of mechanical device.' Anticipating the next question, she added, 'We still have no idea why. As far as I'm concerned, there aren't many options left to explore. Our best idea for the past few months was to send Paula down in a shielded starpod to try and raise some sort of interest from the Angels. But for reasons I can't pretend to understand, she jumped the gun and tried to make a go of it in an ordinary star*suit*, with predictable results.'

She saw the pain in Miles's eyes, and flinched. 'Sorry Miles, clumsy of me.'

'Understood,' said the Coordinator, and gestured for her to continue.

'Progress on the artificial ecology programme can best be detailed by Alex and his pet scientist,' Christine said, waving dismissively at Bannen. 'After all, it's their baby.' She sighed. 'Basically, the bottom line is this: after five years, we still have no solid evidence that the Angels even know we're here.'

Piper grinned. 'I'll hang up an ideas box.'

'I've got one straight away,' Bannen said. 'Quit messing about and assign more money to the hard sciences.'

Christine leaned back in her chair and folded her arms. She sighed. 'You think you can accomplish more with spanners and scalpels than I can with the sensible application of proven psychological theory?'

'Sounds more like you need the application of a large dose of common sense to me,' Bannen snapped. 'If you can't get the Angels to talk to you then I'll breed you some that will. I have seventeen domefuls of artificial environment out there whose subroutines need careful adjustment if they're to be of any use.'

His fingers stabbed the table top, bringing to life a number of small blue dots scattered around the outlying regions of the base. 'I've re-created the planetary atmosphere in these domes. If Christine could overcome her reluctance to capture and dissect one of those creatures and provide me with a cell sample, I could be cloning and redeveloping Angel life forms in a controlled ecology before you could say "Jack Daniels".'

Miles Engado rapped the table with his knuckles. 'I take it you wish to begin your report now, Alex?'

'So far it's the only one to have yielded any results,' Bannen snapped.

'That's true, Alex,' said Piper, 'but we all know that your experiments are long term. You won't miss any vital information if you don't seed your precious arks for another six months or a year. Wait until the funds are rotated to your department. Not everything has to be done in seven days, you know.'

Bannen's fist crashed into the table. The simularity flickered, colours strobing across its surface. 'Every time we have these meetings, I hear the same line of crap,' he said harshly. 'Nobody's got the guts to terminate the unproductive research and channel the money to where it's needed!'

Miles quelled Bannen with a glance. 'I asked for a scientific report, not a shouting match. Please try to be more professional in your approach to the meeting. Nothing can be achieved with this attitude.'

Bannen looked sullen. 'Yeah. Right.'

'Please continue then.'

'I don't have anything to add on this subject.'

Miles sighed. 'Then what about your main function here – the analysis of the potential of this planet as a source of energy?'

'You know the answer as well as I do. You've seen my analyses. I suspect that all the super-heavy elements of the periodic table are here in abundance. They must be used to power the Lift and Moloch's interior sun. But we need the Angels to tell us where, and how, they're produced and stabilized, and to help us obtain samples. We have to communicate with them.'

Piper looked around. Nobody seemed to want to add anything to Bannen's comments.

Miles took a deep breath. 'Very well. In that case we will proceed to the last item on the agenda. Any Other Business.'

'Objection.' Bannen spoke the word as if he had been rehearsing it. 'We haven't finished discussing the reallocation of funds from Social to Technical.'

'Objection overruled,' said Miles calmly. 'There will be no reallocation. Despite the – setbacks – I'm happy with the status quo.'

Bannen's self-satisfied expression vanished like a burst soap bubble. 'I'll take this to Moshe-Rabaan,' he said, a whine creeping into his voice. 'She'll see things my way. She'll see how you're all just protecting your own interests.'

'You do that,' said Christine, a knowing smile crossing her face. 'Just be sure she doesn't think that your area deserves cutting more than mine.'

Miles continued over Bannen's protestations. 'Before I close this meeting,' he announced, 'I wish to make a statement. Paula's death has . . . Well, it has hit me hard. Getting through the next few days will not be easy for me. I will need all of you behind me.' His voice softened, and he met all of their eyes in turn. 'I would like to thank you all for your help so far. Christine, Alex.' Was it her imagination, or did his voice soften further, gain warmth? 'Piper – thank you.'

They all straightened in their seats and murmured embarrassed nothings. Piper was surprised to see even Bannen blush.

'But,' and Miles's voice was harsher now, 'I'm sure it's occurred to all of you that there are four possible explanations for Paula's death. The first is a technical malfunction on the suit itself. The second is carelessness on Paula's part. The third is some sort of action by the Angels, which implies that they might be more aware of us than we had thought. The fourth is Lucifer itself – an unexpected quirk of the planet or its atmosphere that caught Paula unawares.'

He looked around the table. 'The matter requires investigation. I have therefore summoned an Adjudicator from Ponten Six.'

He let the resultant uproar run its course for a minute before thumping the table and calling for quiet. The globes of the moons dissolved into a crazy patchwork of multicoloured rhomboids as the simularity projector was disturbed.

'You have just proved my point,' he said, as soon as it seemed his voice would be heard. 'We are all too close to the situation. If it was a technical problem with the suit which resulted in Paula's death, that falls to you, Piper, since it is the responsibility of Technical Support Services to maintain the suits.'

Piper felt the blood drain from her face. 'You can't – '

'Let me speak. If it was a personal fault, that's either down to the Base psychiatrists, and that means you, Christine, or Paula's family.'

He looked down at the table.

'And that means me.'

Christine chose not to respond to the potential accusation. Piper couldn't let the matter drop so easily. 'Look, we don't need any Adjudicator to – '

Miles lifted his eyes to stare her down. There was so much anguish in those eyes she found it hard to believe anyone could hold it all in without going mad.

'If it was the Angels who were responsible, well, that's down to you as well Christine, for not anticipating the possibility that they might turn against us. And if it was a climatic problem, an electrical storm or turbulence, you, Alex, assured us that Paula would be safe.'

Piper kept silent as the protests rose again.

'Of course, it's possible it could be Paula's . . .' Miles's voice cracked. 'Paula's . . .' He was unable to finish the sentence. A moment passed in silence. He stood up. 'Please understand that I am not trying to assign blame. I'm trying to indicate that we all have something at stake. We need an independent outsider to investigate the circumstances of Paula's death, to sift through the facts and decide which explanation is the correct one. An Adjudicator is completely independent.'

The profound silence that filled the room was broken by a bashful cough.

'Excuse me,' said a quiet voice, 'but you seem to have forgotten the fifth possibility.'

Miles Engado turned to look at the man who stood by the door.

'And what is that?' he queried.

'Murder,' said the Doctor.

<STOP>

<LOAD CURRENT FILE. SUBJECT: THE DOCTOR>

<NO RECORD IN BASE PERSONNEL>

28

<RECHECK PERSONNEL RECORDS. SUBJECT:
THE DOCTOR>
<CONFIRMED. NO RECORD IN BASE PER-
SONNEL>
<SEARCH FOR FIRST APPEARANCE: THE
DOCTOR>
<SEARCHING . . . FIRST APPEARANCE OF
THE DOCTOR:
FILE A151/X/19/11/2154>

Chapter Two

```
<LOAD FILE A151/X/19/11/2154>
<SETUP>
<SET STYLE = 75>
<SET POINT-OF-VIEW = THE DOCTOR>
<COMMAND INCOMPATIBLE WITH CURRENT
SYSTEM STATUS>
<LIST POINT-OF-VIEW OPTIONS>
<INTERPOLATED; ADDITIONAL PERSONNEL
ONLY>
<SET POINT-OF-VIEW = INTERPOLATED>
<RUN 34992>
```

The corridor was triangular in cross section and lined
with machinery. The floor was steeply concave, but covered with a mesh grille. Doorways led off it, each sealed
with a large slab of metal. The air was musty, as if something malevolent had crawled in there a million years ago
and given birth to shadows and silence and dust.

And then, perhaps for the first time in centuries, a faint
echo ran through the corridor; a sound like distant drums,
or perhaps a thunderstorm far away across a black sea.
The air in the corridor swung apart like a grimy curtain
to reveal a large blue box with a flashing light on top.
Momentarily the thunder crashed overhead, as if something infinitely heavy had come to rest.

The moment the doors of the blue box opened, and a
small, rather exuberant gentleman in a gaudy pullover,
tartan trousers and brown corduroy jacket emerged, the
atmosphere changed completely. Perhaps it was the white
Panama hat perched upon his head like a nesting bird;
perhaps the fact that beneath its brim, like two large,

round eggs, his eyes were bright and full of joyful intelligence. Whatever it was, the sum of all the individual details added up to a personality shining with the conviction that, whatever the situation, whatever the galaxy, it could be grasped as firmly and immediately as the crooked handle of his umbrella.

Twirling the umbrella like an old-fashioned propeller, the gentleman looked around, wide eyed, as if he couldn't believe his luck in landing exactly where he had. A corridor! Yes, but what sort of corridor? What was it a corridor in? Where did it lead? And what adventures were lying in wait for him at either end?

He walked jauntily over to the nearest door and pushed at it. Nothing happened. He looked around the frame for buttons or handles but there were none. He tapped it a few times with the handle of his umbrella. Still nothing. He tried to force his fingers into the gap around the frame, then suddenly withdrew them when he realized what might happen to them if the door suddenly opened. He tried humming a few bars of 'Chatanooga Choo-Choo' at it, but the door wasn't impressed. He sighed, and turned to survey the corridor. It glowed with possibilities. Should he go left? Or right? Perhaps he should try various combinations of the two?

Before he could even start to think about his next move, he discovered something very interesting.

The door was humming back at him.

He bent to listen. It wasn't humming anything recognizable – more a kind of monotonous, low-pitched vibration in the key of E flat minor with a sustained fifth than anything else – but it was recognizably a hum. And what did that tell him? The hum from a piece of heavy machinery, perhaps? A generator, maybe? Hmm.

E flat minor was his favourite key. A sustained fifth note was icing on the cake. The gentleman considered. Maybe the key to the door was a musical one.

Before he could wrestle the thought to the ground and force it to submit, somebody else left the large blue box – a young woman who wore a badge-loaded jacket over body armour of an unidentifiable material and lycra leggings tucked into military-style boots, and whose hair was pulled back into a severe ponytail.

'Incredible,' the girl said scornfully. 'With the entire universe to choose from, he finds another scungy corridor!'

The man turned.

'Is it deliberate?' she continued. 'Do you have some sort of Time Lord sensor in the TARDIS which automatically seeks out cold and dirty corridors to land in, Professor?'

'Ace!' the gentleman said, with a subtly hurt burr in his voice. 'I had hoped that your little holiday might have cured your innate cynicism. I see I was wrong.'

'Come on, Prof, the Spacefleet was hardly a rest-cure.'

'And how many times do I have to tell you, I'm not the "Prof", I'm the Doctor.'

'But that's not a real name either,' said a voice behind them. 'They're both labels. Why doesn't either one of you ever tell anybody your real name?'

The Doctor looked over Ace's shoulder at a tall, slender woman who had stepped out of the TARDIS. Her baggy jumpsuit seemed to have been woven from a nondescript material around a series of pockets and loops, and it was only the extravagance of her velvet waistcoat that stopped her blending in completely with the background. Slung across her shoulder was a portable instrument package. Her recently dreadlocked hair stuck out from beneath an old-fashioned baseball cap. She looked around curiously, as if she fully expected to find interesting things to look at, dig up, or otherwise poke her nose into.

The Doctor smiled. There was something faintly out of control about that smile.

'We all have our little secrets,' he said.

Ace looked away.

The other woman smiled sweetly. 'Point taken,' she replied.

Ace snorted contemptuously. 'It's still a corridor,' she muttered. 'No matter what you say.'

'But don't you see the positive plethora of possibilities implicit in the very existence of this corridor? There could be anything at the end of it. Anything in the universe – or beyond. Could you get back in the TARDIS, not knowing what was waiting for us?' He turned to the older woman. 'Could you, Bernice?'

'Hardly; it was me who wanted to come here.' She looked over at Ace, who was looking up and down the corridor warily. 'And Ace, as I recall, wasn't exactly averse to the idea.'

Leaving Ace with a slight frown marring her face, the Doctor set about the business of exploring the corridor. He took a few steps to his left, then hesitated. The corridor seemed to stretch to infinity ahead. He turned to the right, and headed back past Bernice, who watched him with growing amusement. He stopped again. If he went the wrong way he might miss all the action. If there was any. But which way was the wrong way? Was any way the right way?

'Eeney meeney miney moe,' he said, pointing alternately left and right, 'catch a Rutan by its toe. If it wriggles, let it go. Eeney meeney miney – moe!'

He strode off back past Ace and Bernice again. 'Come along,' he yelled over his shoulder. 'What are you waiting for?'

'Christmas,' Ace muttered bad-temperedly as she followed the Doctor.

<RUN ON 20>

Ace felt a hand on her arm. 'Are we looking for anything in particular?' Bernice said, drawing level with the younger woman, 'or is this more in the nature of a constitutional?'

Instead of answering, Ace glanced around, stared coldly at Bernice, and then increased her pace so that she was walking in front of the others. The TARDIS was a long way behind them by now. Gloomy and mysterious, and still lined with the hulking shapes of vast machinery, the corridor looked as if it went on ahead of them forever. Nothing, she knew, was more likely to arouse the Doc-

33

tor's curiosity. Ace was not so easily impressed. She could think of nothing more boring than walking for miles down some manky corridor. Except walking back again. She banged a clenched fist in frustration against the flank of a colossal piece of machinery. An echoing boom reverberated off into the far distance. Dust shivered loose from its years-old perch and trickled down upon her like dirty snow.

'Fascinating as this is, Doctor,' she said loudly, 'if I'd wanted to spend the rest of my life hoofing it around grimy spaceships for no good reason I'd have stayed in Spacefleet.'

Bernice stopped in the middle of the corridor and began to massage her calves. Ace walked on for several metres before realizing she was alone. She turned and stared impatiently at Bernice. The Doctor was leaning on his brolly at the archaeologist's shoulder, offering advice in a quiet voice. Ace looked away quickly, disturbed to find herself becoming angry without a discernible reason.

'I'm hungry,' she said in a loud voice.

'Yes,' Bernice agreed. 'Fascinating as this is, I'd much rather sink a pint.'

'Now listen to me both of you,' the Doctor said. 'This overstressed preponderance towards the absorption of purely physical nutrition has got to stop. Look at that piece of machinery you're standing by. Who knows what it is or why it's there? Feed the mind, ladies. Feed the mind!' And the Doctor gently tapped the top of his head with the umbrella handle to emphasize his point.

Bernice looked up with a tired sigh. 'It's – '

The Doctor touched her shoulder lightly. 'Why don't we see if Ace can work it out, Bernice? Perhaps it'll rekindle her sense of wonder. What do you think, Ace?'

Ace was looking at the Doctor with an irritated expression. Without pausing to study the device to which the Doctor referred, she said, 'It's an oxygen generator.' She pointed towards a universal junction about half-way up the device. 'Look at the convective flanges. And the line feeds. It's a museum piece, built around twenty-one fifty, which is just about the year we were aiming for.'

Ace suddenly fell quiet.

The Doctor sighed. Secrets, he thought grimly. He bent and dragged the tip of his umbrella along the floor, beneath the chassis. 'That the item in question is old, according to your rather solipsistic criteria, I will not call into question,' he said pointedly. 'But look here. This is packing grease. And here.' The Doctor tugged at some web fastenings around the device. 'Stowage, unsealed. This machine has obviously been packed for a journey and hasn't been used yet. So, far from being a dead place, this would appear to be somewhere awaiting the arrival of life. What do you have to say about that, then?'

'Don't patronize me. I'm not a kid, okay?'

'No. Of course you aren't.' The Doctor strode past Ace into the darkness. More slowly, Bernice followed him. Ace was forced to stand aside to allow them passage. She threw a piercing glance at the back of the Doctor's jacket wondering whether she should give it all up as a dead loss and head back for the ship. The Doctor waved his umbrella behind him in a peremptory gesture. 'Come along, Ace,' he called back along the corridor. 'Don't dawdle.'

Ace ran to catch up with the Doctor. 'I'm coming with you.'

The Doctor smiled. 'I hoped you might.'

Ace pursed her lips. 'Just so long as you realize I don't have to.'

'Of course, Ace. No question about it.'

They walked on.

<RUN ON 10>

Bernice strolled casually down the corridor, whistling chirpily to herself and occasionally stopping to examine the etched texture of the sloping walls, or to peer through the grillework down at the concave floor. Ahead of her the passage straightened. She stopped suddenly. Was she seeing things, or did there appear to be something hovering unobtrusively high up in the –

'What's that up ahead?' Ace asked suddenly, trying to peer around both the Doctor and Bernice.

'It looks very much like a door. And very much shut,' Bernice said.

'Maybe there's some food behind it!' Pushing past the others, Ace walked up to the door and gave it a swift kick.

Slowly, and to Bernice's astonishment, the door began to slide ponderously into the ceiling. The hiss of escaping hydraulic vapour swamped the creaks and groans of over-stressed metal as it slowly ground its way against the accumulated dirt of years. A few feet off the ground the entire device seized up, and something inside broke with a high 'plink!' Before the door could spring shut again, the Doctor jammed it open with his umbrella, pushed Ace and Bernice underneath, and leaped through himself.

He stood, examining a tiny spring he had picked up off the floor. He measured it against the size and weight of the door and shook his head. He was about to speak when the door suddenly clanged shut, neatly slicing his umbrella in half as it did so. Before he could quite come to terms with the sudden, shocking demise of an old and comfortable piece of apparel, he realized that the trouble hadn't stopped there.

'Professor!'

He turned. Ace was peering up into a corner of the room, where a small mechanical object hovered, looking something like a metallic knot in the process of being tied. Somehow the Doctor got the impression that it was peering back at her. And humming.

'Hmmm,' he murmured. 'E flat minor. So that was what it was.'

'What was what *what* was?' Ace asked, then frowned, trapped inside the tortured logic of her own question.

'My dear Ace, sometimes I think you do for the English language what Escher did for spatial geometry.' The Doctor leaned forward and his voice hardened. 'I am referring, of course, to the thing that's been following us.

It must have tried to get through the door before it closed, and given itself away by accident.'

'What is it?' Bernice asked curiously.

'It's a Peeping Tom.'

Ace's face twisted in sudden anger. 'You mean somebody's spying on us?'

'Yes . . . Or it could just be passively recording a document for somebody to experience later.'

He leaned closer and peered up at the ribbon-like device that twisted and turned before him. His eyes narrowed and his voice hardened yet again. Now there was real menace in it. 'I don't know about you, but I'm not so sure I'm partial to the idea of being peeped at.' Suddenly, and perfectly in character, the Doctor's mood swung back to the jovial. 'Still. It's rather a cute little bug really, don't you think?' The Doctor reached out a hand to pat the device. As he moved towards it, tiny air currents swung the device, lending it an appearance of alarm.

The Doctor smiled a predatory smile. 'Ladies and Gentlemen!' he proclaimed brightly. 'May I present; the Amazing Disappearing Doctor and Friends!'

Before the thing could react, the Doctor whipped a spray-can from his pocket and

<DATA ERROR>

blue paint back and forth across the

<DATA ERROR>

made their escape through

<DATA ERROR>

<PARITY CHECK>

bounced once or twice, then lay still

<UNEXPECTED END OF FILE>

<ATTEMPTED ACCESS OUT OF RANGE>

<SECTOR NOT FOUND OR FILE CORRUPT>

<STOP>

Silence.

The Adjudicator leaned back in his comfortable chair. With the file corrupt, the terminal had shut down, leaving the darkness surrounding him complete. He tried to relax, allowing a complex web of thoughts and associations to form within his brain. Cause and effect was the key here. But which was the cause and which the effect?

The Adjudicator crossed his legs and eased off one slipper. He spent a few minutes massaging his left foot. Was the mysterious Doctor right? Had the pressure and the loneliness got to one of the Base personnel? Was someone a killer? Piper's cynicism could be hiding a failure of nerve. Bannen was aggressive and opinionated, and that usually meant a lack of confidence underneath. Christine, the illegal daughter of parents rich enough to buy off the Energy Police, could well have problems fitting in with people from a lower class. Her nervousness might indicate something more than just social embarrassment. And Miles . . . Well, rigid structures usually broke easier than flexible ones.

He could feel a headache coming on. He hoped he wasn't coming down with something nasty.

Twenty-eight personnel on the base – not counting these new arrivals, the Doctor and his unconventional companions. Perhaps it wasn't such a good idea to rely on the simularity programs to deduce possible motives. How good did a machine have to be, to be able to correctly extrapolate five years of interpersonal relationships? Was it even really possible?

The Adjudicator replaced his slipper and began to massage his other foot. Five years alone together had certainly provided the staff with ample breeding ground for the kind of personality friction that was all too rife on Earth at the moment. Now, for perhaps the first time, the Adjudicator realized the scale of the problem that faced him.

He had the information he had requested, but it provided no answers.

Only more questions.

PART TWO

BELIAL

Faustus: And what are you that live with Lucifer?
Mephistopheles: Unhappy spirits that fell with Lucifer,
Conspired against our God with Lucifer,
And are for ever damned with Lucifer.

Christopher Marlowe – *Doctor Faustus*

Chapter Three

Bernice gazed unseeingly into her drink. Beyond the transparent panels which enclosed the refectory area of Belial Base, iron-grey rocks climbed towards a steep horizon in a series of shallow steps. Giant's steps, thought Bernice. Steps for seven-league boots. A flat red luminescence cast down from the lurid horizon gave the rocks a fantastic appearance. They seemed like mirror-smooth puddles of solidified light. Red ice. Black rock. Lucifer and its attendant environs seemed to be a place of stark extremes.

A babble of words and laughter attracted her attention back to the refectory. A group comprising some of the younger members of the Project Eden team – Jesus Delporto, Kosiana Kistasami, Lars Ulrich, Julie Ndema and Craig Richards – was playing cribbage. The big Russian woman, Anuskia Smyslov, sat watching them all with some bemusement.

Bernice sipped her drink, surprised to find the glass already almost drained. What in hell's name was the matter with her? Why was she so depressed? She didn't really think it had anything to do with Paula's death. I mean, she thought, it's not as if anyone else could have found out. Unless the Doctor . . .

A movement outside caught her attention. Two figures in starsuits lumbered ponderously out from beneath the protective canopy of an outlying area of the base: her friend Cheryl Russell and Cheryl's husband Sam. Bernice watched as they headed slowly for an airlock situated directly below her line of sight. Just before they disappeared, Sam reached out and took Cheryl's gloved hand in his.

Oh yeah, she thought, who does he think he's kidding?

Depression tried to settle on her, but Bernice wasn't having any of it. She walked over to a food dispenser, thumped it with her elbow, caught the drink that the machine hurled at her in alarm, and returned to her seat, peeling the plastic wrapping from the glass as she went.

'You do realize that damaging Earth Central property is an offence?'

Bernice froze, startled. A small man dressed in high-collared, floor-length black robes stood over her.

'Don't do that!' she snapped.

'Sorry,' he said, not sounding the least bit apologetic. 'May I sit down?' He pulled out a chair and sat without waiting for her reply.

'No,' she said, just for the hell of it.

'Thank you.' He smiled as if they'd known each other for years. 'My name is Bishop, but then you probably already know that.'

'I saw you arrive yesterday in that bijou little ship of yours. You're the Adjudicator, aren't you?'

'Yes, I am. And your name is Bernice, isn't it? Bernice Summerfield.'

'And it only took you a day to find out. I'm impressed.'

'I work fast, Krau Summerfield.'

Bernice looked at Bishop more closely. He was a small man. Small and unassuming. He could have been a bank manager on some outback planet, or perhaps a priest. His face was notable for its anonymity. She doubted that she would recognize him in a crowd.

'It comes in very useful,' he said.

She jerked guiltily. 'What does?'

'Looking ordinary. Nondescript.'

She rapidly reviewed everything she had been thinking, just in case.

'It's all right,' he said, and smiled again. 'I can't read your mind. It's just that everybody thinks that when they

44

first see me. Some of my closest friends don't recognize me at parties.'

Bernice wondered exactly what kind of parties a man like Bishop might attend.

'Fancy dress?' she asked, straight-faced.

He looked down ruefully at his flowing ebony robes. 'They come with the job, I'm afraid.'

She smiled. 'Not much use in a fight.'

'You'd be surprised what you can hide under here.' His face smoothed over, and she suddenly realized how flat and grey his eyes were. 'Who are you?' he asked quietly.

'Like you said, I'm Bernice Summerfield.' Her voice wasn't as calm as she would have liked.

'Yes, but who *are* you? You don't appear in the personnel records. You didn't arrive on any of the robot ships that drop supplies off here. You don't exist. Who *are* you?'

'I told you once. If you don't like the answer, you can whistle for another one.'

'Let me help.' He reached into his robes and pulled out a small blue object which he held out to her. 'Recognize it?'

'No,' she lied.

'Let me refresh your memory. It's a drone camera – one of a number which keep a permanent record of what goes on in this base.' He indicated a corner of the room, and Bernice noticed for the first time a tiny hovering shape that watched her without eyes. 'A permanent record,' he continued, 'which I've been watching since yesterday.'

He looked down at the object in his hand as if he had suddenly realized what it was himself. 'This one won't be doing much more recording – '

'Spying!'

' – for some time.' He leaned forward, his face absolutely blank. 'You, your friend the Doctor, and the woman Ace, appeared in the middle of a corridor in one of the newly-opened areas of Belial Base. I don't know how you've managed it, but in the intervening time you've got

45

the entire Base staff eating out of your hands. They seem to think that you've always been here. I know differently. Since you arrived, the security has become subject to an increasing number of corrupt files, and a member of the team has died. You destroyed one of the recording drones, at a cost of some thirty thousand adjusted ergs. Earth cannot afford thirty thousand adjusted ergs. Earth cannot afford you running around on this base like a deranged cybernetic waiter.'

Bernice favoured the Adjudicator with her coldest stare. 'Let me explain. I came in here for some peace, some quiet and, most especially, for a drink. I've got a lot on my plate at the moment. What I don't need is some jumped-up civil servant waving his inferiority complex in my face.'

Bishop leaned back in his chair. His face split in a totally humourless smile. 'Thank you, Krau Summerfield, for that little gem of advice. You've been most helpful.'

Bernice struggled to focus her anger. She couldn't seem to get a handle on Bishop. The Adjudicator was like an egg: seamless, smooth, unfathomable. The only way in was to smash through, but Bernice wasn't sure she wanted to go quite that far – yet. What was he thinking? Did he really believe that she, Ace and the Doctor could be responsible for Paula's death? She debated whether to confide in him about her own observations. But would he believe her? Or would he simply regard it as an attempt to deflect attention away from herself? Come to think about it, was she really that certain of her own theory?

Bishop was still smiling. He shook his head. Bernice couldn't tell whether he was answering her unspoken questions or not, but then she supposed that was the whole point. His whole manner seemed geared towards – well – inscrutability. He wasn't giving anything away.

'Let's get back to the point, shall we?' Once more Bishop assumed the offensive. 'What are you doing on this base?'

'Does the Base Coordinator know you're annoying everyone like this?'

'He requested my presence here. Please don't avoid the question. I repeat: what are you doing here?'

'Why should you assume that we're doing anything here?' an ironic voice interjected. Behind Bishop, the Doctor seemed to sway gently on his feet like a modestly-proportioned punchbag. Behind him, Ace slammed the door to the refectory and walked over to sit beside Bernice, crossing her feet on the table and leaning back with her arms folded behind her head.

'Hmph.' The Doctor gently slid Ace's crossed feet a short distance across the table and took a seat. 'My dear Adjudicator, I'm so very pleased to meet you at long last!'

The Adjudicator frowned. 'As I recall, our meeting is not scheduled until twenty-one hundred hours tomorrow.'

'I didn't come here to meet you. I came here to meet Bernice.' The Doctor thrust his head forward rather like an aggressive turtle. 'Privately,' he added pointedly.

'To what end?' Bishop obviously wasn't going to give up so easily.

The Doctor tapped the side of his nose. 'Would you believe a hot toddy?'

Casually, the Doctor beckoned to the food dispenser that had been hovering around waiting for an opportunity to serve them. As it slid up to him, he pressed a button and offered Bishop one of the two drinks which fell into his waiting hands. When Bishop refused, the Doctor produced two straws from an inside pocket and began simultaneously to drink from both containers.

'Hmm,' he murmured with raised eyebrows. 'Strawberry and oxtail. My favourites.' He took another appreciative gulp. 'You think there's something suspicious about us, don't you, Trau Bishop?'

Bishop just kept smiling the same enigmatic smile.

'It's all right,' the Doctor continued reassuringly, 'I can't read your thoughts. It's just that everybody thinks that when they first see us.'

Cheryl Russell moved with steamroller efficiency across the bleak, charcoal surface of Belial. Behind her came

Sam, slightly shorter than her two-metres-one-with-star-suit, and struggling to keep up with her power-assisted strides.

'Hang about,' mumbled Sam between wheezing breaths. 'I'm not half as young as I used to be.'

Cheryl tried to put a smile into her voice. 'But you look twice your age, so on average you're okay.'

Shift over, the married couple had taken leave of one of Bannen's domes and were moving purposefully back towards Belial Base's main airlock assembly. Bannen had put in a requisition for a pressurized tunnel four years before, and had renewed it at regular intervals, but Moshe-Rabaan had vetoed it every time. Miles might have been in charge of the project, but it was Moshe-Rabaan who allocated the energy to carry out his instructions. Some considered the cool, distant woman to be the real voice of Eden.

In the time since Paula Engado's death, tension had skyrocketed. Tempers had stretched to breaking point on any number of occasions, even between Sam and Cheryl. They had been married on the trip out from Earth, and until now Project Eden had been nothing more or less than a prolonged honeymoon for them. On Earth, with living space at an unprecedented premium, their records would have been stapled together in a memory bank somewhere and their living arrangements would have felt exactly the same as before: even married, their living space allocation would have consisted of only two rooms; there wouldn't have been space enough to swing a cat. Now here they were, two hundred and eighty light years from Earth, in orbit around a planet so big it made you dizzy just thinking about it. Okay so it was dark, cold and airless, the hours stank and so did the plumbing, but it was home now. A better home than Earth had ever been to them. Perhaps a better home than Earth could ever be, even if Project Eden were successful.

Sam shivered a little and adjusted the thermostat on his life-functions regulator. Sometimes the dark and the cold got to you out here. The Ring of Lucifer encircling

the horizon didn't help either. The damn planet was too
well named. Nowhere on Belial – even there, on the
dark side of the moon – could you escape its fiery gaze.
Anywhere you went, reflections from the planet's atmosphere overwhelmed the clear light of even the brightest
stars. He was glad to have Cheryl. She was, after all, the
reason he was there.

The Doctor and Bishop were head to head across the
refectory table. By now, other members of the crew who'd
come off shift had drifted in; the galley staff were up and
running at full steam and the food dispensers were rushed
off their null-grav units. Ace had become used to food
machines and ration packs, and was finding it strangely
hard to readjust. Her years in Spacefleet had affected her
more than she had thought. The clatter of cutlery and the
noisy munching of the off-duty roster were enough to put
any thoughts of sensible conversation in an early grave.
Ace wondered how the two could hear themselves talk
over the din.

At the moment, Bishop was still trying to sound the
Doctor out. Like many people before him, the Adjudicator wasn't really having a whole lot of luck. 'A chemical
analysis of the blue paint used to disable security monitor
five shows a high degree of magnetic alignment.'

'Yes, that's right,' said the Doctor, like a kid with a
beetle in a box. 'It's a clever little cocktail of my own
invention: a universally compatible software encoded on
magnetically aligned molecules of paint. Atomization
gives instant access to any hardware which isn't hermeti-
cally sealed. The program acts autonomously; all its
controls are built in. It's even colour-coded for easy
reference. Rather neat, don't you think? And such a
pretty colour!'

Bishop's bemused expression cleared. 'That would
explain how the other security file blackouts have
occurred. Software contagion can be dealt with. What
cannot be so easily explained is why the contagion was
introduced in the first place.' Bishop leaned even further

towards the Doctor, until their noses were only centimetres apart. 'Just what was it you didn't want anyone to see you do down there, Doctor?'

Now it was the Doctor's turn to look puzzled. He blinked rapidly as Bishop leaned back confidently in his chair. 'Other security file blackouts? On no. No, no, no, no, no. I took special care over mixing that batch. It was my favourite colour. And it was definitely non-viral.'

'The facts seem to indicate otherwise, Doctor,' Bishop said with some satisfaction. 'For example, you casually walked into Miles Engado's meeting and announced that his daughter had been killed by a suit malfunction that, you claimed, could only have been caused by a deliberately-induced software infection.'

'Hmm,' the Doctor mused, 'I can see how you could leap unerringly to the wrong conclusion – two and two making five, and all that. Still, it must have occurred to you that I wouldn't wander around incriminating myself unless I was a complete fool.'

'The thought had occurred,' Bishop said.

The Doctor leaned back in his chair. 'Two simple alternatives spring to mind, Adjudicator. Either your facts are wrong, or they are incomplete.'

Bishop rose to leave the table. 'Since evidence against you is still not conclusive, I will allow you the benefit of the doubt.'

The Doctor's expression was carefully neutral. 'But you'd appreciate us not leaving the star system without notifying you first, hmm?'

Bishop refused the bait. 'Thank you, Doctor. I appreciate your cooperation.'

The Doctor doffed his hat and smiled. 'You're very welcome,' he stated formally.

With a barely audible swish of ebony material, the Adjudicator left the refectory. Ace exchanged glances with the Doctor. 'Who pushed his button, then?'

'Trau Bishop is just doing his job, Ace.'

'Yeah, right. His job is obviously to upset everyone.'

'The Guild of Adjudicators has a long and interesting history. You should respect it.'

'We called them "ravens" in my time.'

The Doctor's eyes narrowed. '*My* time?' he asked.

Ace looked away. 'The twenty-fifth century.'

'What happens to them all?' Bernice asked. 'I wrote a couple of papers on Guild history. I'd love to know how it all comes out.'

The Doctor sighed, and gazed down at the table.

'A sad story,' he said. 'As Earth went through Empire and Federation, the fortunes of the Guild waxed and waned. Eventually, they became unnecessary. A thousand forms of local justice had sprung up. Every planet had its own laws, and its own police. The universe had passed them by. The Guild of Adjudicators had nothing to adjudicate. They degenerated into a reclusive order of assassins known as the Knights of the Grand Order of Oberon, dreaming of past glories and crusades for truth.' He smiled bitterly. 'I went looking for them once, to return something that was theirs. I couldn't find them.'

The Doctor glanced over at Bernice to check her reaction, but she didn't seem to have been listening. She gave the appearance of having furled all sails and battened down the hatches.

'You're upset about Paula's death,' the Time Lord observed casually. 'You were good friends, weren't you?'

Bernice looked the Doctor full in the face. There was so much in that face, she thought. So many layers of motivation, experience, understanding. Why did she see nothing in there for herself any more? Eyes that had beheld the birth and death of the universe met her gaze with steady recognition. Had he done what she thought he'd done? Or was she being melodramatic?

'Yes,' she said finally, bitterly. 'I was a real friend.'

Cheryl Russell heard nothing as the outer airlock hatch glided into its fairing, but the air movement as the lock pressurized and the inner portal dilated rocked her starsuit on its gyros. Have to get that sorted, she thought, and soon. All they needed to complete the worst-case scenario was a scrubbed 'lock assembly.

Ambling noisily into the antechamber, Sam echoed her thought. 'No more parties till the 'lock's seen to, eh?'

Cheryl nodded as she released the seals on her starsuit's helmet. 'Could be messy if you wanted to step outside and puke, that's for sure.'

Cheryl disengaged her helmet and lowered it to the bench. 'Voice command: inner airlock door close, please.'

Sam removed his helmet and dumped it alongside Cheryl's. Condensation run-off from the starsuits was already collecting in the troughs in the flooring. It was always cold in the 'lock. Cold and wet.

'I dunno why you bother to say please. It's only a neural network.'

'Someday machines may have minds too. If the scurvy thing suddenly becomes spontaneously aware, I want it to remember I was nice to it.' She pitched her voice slightly higher for the neural net's benefit. 'Voice command: starsuit nine. Unseal please. Engage neural network linkage for systems check.'

Cheryl's spacesuit parted down the chest and back, splitting like a walnut shell along predetermined paths. Sam watched appreciatively as Cheryl stepped out from the suit. Her pleasantly rounded face lit up in a cheerful grin as the disembodied voice of starsuit nine's brain stated: 'Command acknowledged. Thank you for using this unit. Have a nice day.' The wall hatch opened to receive it like an advanced exercise in origami. As it walked back into the suit holding area for its usual systems check, Sam could see the ranks of other starsuits gleaming in the shadows, along with a rack of flimsy emergency spacesuits.

Cheryl swept back a matted wad of copper hair with an absent gesture. The necklace of diopals growing from the skin of her neck glinted in the bright, sterilizing light. 'There you are – see?'

'Programmed inanities installed at the whim of a matrix generator guilty of watching too many bad simularities.'

Sam dismissed the humanizing details of the machinery's software with a sweeping gesture. 'Voice command: starsuit seventeen. Unzip. Besides,' he continued, waiting for his suit to follow Cheryl's into the wall, 'neural networks might mimic human thought processes, but that doesn't mean they suddenly have to come alive to perform at optimum.'

Cheryl walked through into the ultrasound shower, and Sam became aware that he was still waiting for the suit to open. 'Voice command: starsuit seventeen. Unzip!'

He could hear Cheryl laugh as the suit replied: '*Please redefine command instruction. This unit is no longer programmed to receive colloquially-worded instructions.*'

Sam sighed with frustration. It had been a long shift; one way or another he was determined it wouldn't be prolonged by some recalcitrant hunk of space-junk. 'Voice command: starsuit seventeen – and before I take a can opener to you – unseal! Please,' he added, as a concession to Cheryl's theory.

'*Command acknowledged.*'

Above the faint buzz of the ultrasound shower, Cheryl howled with laughter.

Sam continued, trying desperately to hold his temper in check. 'Thank you. Now engage neural network linkage for systems check and software update.'

'*Command acknowledged.*'

The suit unfolded. Sam stepped out, naked and shivering.

'Told you it pays to be polite.' Shower over, Cheryl opened her locker and began to dress in her indoor clothes. Pulling on the smoothly-flowing material and fastening the ornate webbing, she added, 'You know, there's something odd – '

'About the starsuit?' Sam's eyes narrowed as he watched suit number seventeen retract into the wall.

'Yeah,' she mused thoughtfully. 'What did it say? "No longer programmed . . ." I thought all these suits were fitted with personality matrices capable of acting upon colloquial language instructions.'

Sam took Cheryl's place in the shower. 'So did I,' he said.

Cheryl continued, 'Voice command: starsuit seventeen. Detail: self-diagnostic check. Detail: run all-systems comparison algorithm. Parameter limits: from suit activation date to current date, inclusive. Purpose: collate information and report incidence of last programming update.'

The starsuit replied: '*Command acknowledged. Program running . . . Program complete. No parameter update recorded.*'

'So we were wrong.'

Sam poked his head out of the shower. 'Unless whatever has affected the instructions-input subroutine has also affected the self-diagnostics and other systems, in which case – '

'In which case we've got a big problem.'

Sam and Cheryl exchanged alarmed glances. Cheryl had definitely not understated the case. A software bug in an environment as hostile as Belial could mean severe danger for everyone on the base. The neural net controlled every aspect of their environment. It kept them all alive. If it crashed . . . Well, to say the shit would hit the fan would be a prize-winning understatement.

'Sam. Have you got time to get the suit unhooked before your shift on Moloch? I think I'd better report this to Piper straight away.'

'Sure. According to Tiw the Lift isn't due in for another half hour.' Sam left the shower and began talking to the wall as Cheryl left the antechamber. 'Voice command: starsuit seventeen. Unlink and prepare for excursion.'

The wall remained blank and smooth. There was no reply from the associated software.

Sam swore softly to himself. The starsuits, like everything of a mechanical nature on the base, were extremely expensive and impossible to replace from Earth. Something as fundamental as a suitbrain couldn't be whipped up from old bits of cardboard and tofu. Sam had more than a vague idea of who'd be for the high jump if this suit were found to be inoperable and the cause pinned on negligence in the Technical Section. He'd probably find himself floating home on the next pigeon-post message pod. Minus starsuit.

As Sam was trying to decide what to do next, he saw a tall shadow sweep across the wall in front of him.

'Hi Cheryl. Jealous of the machinery, huh? Bet you just couldn't bear to leave me alone down here, could you?'

There was no reply, just the faint whisper of the recycling vents and the buzz of the ultrasound. The shadow stood poised behind him, unmoving.

Sam turned, a devastating line poised for delivery. The joke never came. Instead his eyes bulged in shock and a yell of alarm was trapped in his throat.

He tried to run or yell out, but found he could no longer move.

In the complete and utter silence only achieved by very large, complex items of machinery, the shadow approached.

Only then, far too late to do himself any good, did Sam find the strength to scream.

But not for long.

Chapter Four

The man in the business suit stepped carefully across the dismembered body of a soldier and looked up dispassionately.

Behind him, the mist crawled across the churned ground like some huge, sluggish animal. Multi-legged scavengers, no bigger than a clenched fist, skittered along the tread-marks of heavy battle vehicles and into the craters left by sub-orbital laser bursts and tactical Z-bombs. The pale light of sunrise spilled over twisted bodies and broken weapons. In the violet sky, a wide swathe of debris, all that remained of the planet's moon, refracted the sunrise back in splintered rainbows. The heavier fragments were already beginning to re-enter the atmosphere in long shallow arcs of flame. The ground still shook violently in the grip of vast tectonic convulsions, but the man in the business suit did not flinch.

'No race or alliance has yet claimed responsibility for the massacre, which has left a billion settlers dead. Sifranos is the fifth planet to be devastated in the Arcturus sector since the beginning of the year. As usual, no clue remains to the identity of the attackers.'

A muted thudding seemed to swell behind his words like a slow heartbeat. As the sound grew louder the mist drew back, revealing more devastation, more death.

'Rumours that an unidentified alien fleet is massing around Epsilon Eridani are strongly denied by the President. "We have nothing to fear but fear itself," she said, during a speech at the Earth Central Complex in Damascus today. Meanwhile, the Earth Alliance of Corporations rejected a call for the planet to be put on a war footing.

"War is bad for business," said their Chairperson, Madrigal LaFayette. "And what's bad for business is bad for Earth." '

Behind the man the mist had retreated to form a circle, pushed back by some invisible force. A scarred metal object began to descend into the clearing. The red crescent on its side stood out like spilled blood.

'Meanwhile, on Sifranos, the long task of burying the dead\has only just begun.' The landscape behind the man faded, leaving him standing in a pastel-coloured room. 'That simularity was prepared earlier today from recordings supplied by the Interstellar Red Crescent,' he continued in the same level tones. 'And now a report on the opening of the Earth Embassy on Alpha Centauri Five – '

'News off,' Piper said as she walked over to the table where the Doctor and his friends were conversing quietly. The simularity in the centre of the refectory flickered and died. Nobody else in the crowded refectory seemed to notice; after all, they had seen it four or five times already. Piper thanked God that Federique Moshe-Rabaan wasn't around. She would have had a field day going on about energy being expended for no reason, even if the news and entertainment crystals sent out on the monthly robot supply-ships from Earth were the only link most of the crew had with home.

'You weren't watching, were you?' she asked as she sat down. Ace pointedly looked out of the window. Bernice was observing something on the far side of the refectory with cat-like intensity, and only the Doctor seemed to hear her words.

'History is always interesting,' he said with a soft burr in his voice. 'But never as interesting as good conversation.'

'History?' Piper couldn't help asking.

'Everything is history,' the Doctor replied, his eyes twinkling, 'if you look at it from the right perspective.'

'Excuse me,' Bernice said. 'I think I see a friend in need.' She uncoiled from her seat and walked off. Piper tried to make out who she was heading for, but all she could see was Christine LaFayette making rapidly for the door.

'From any perspective it's nothing but bad news,' Piper said, dragging her attention back to the Doctor. 'It's almost enough to make you want to stay here on Belial.'

'And do you?' the Doctor asked.

Piper looked at him. He was sitting bolt upright, arms folded and resting on his new umbrella, looking for all the world as if her answer was the most important thing in his life. With dawning amazement, she realized that he wasn't part of the Belial Base complement, and even as she did so she knew that it wasn't the first time she had remembered that. She tried to recall how he came to be there, but the memories were soft and fuzzy, and her mind didn't want to focus upon them. She couldn't seem to look away from his eyes. It was as if he and his friends had always been there. Had *always* been there.

Ace suddenly stood up. 'Got to go,' she said tautly. The Doctor looked away from Piper and watched Ace sadly as she walked towards the door.

Piper shook her head and frowned. She had been thinking about something, but she couldn't for the life of her remember what. She looked over at the Doctor, but he was still watching Ace as she picked her way between tables and barged past the people coming in. Had he asked her a question? Yes . . . About Earth, and whether she ever wanted to go back. She gazed around the refectory as she considered her answer. Most of the tables were full now, and the sounds of argument, conversation and clinking cutlery filled the air: B and C Shifts, just knocked off from work, looking for food, fun and frolics. *Her* crews. Her friends.

'What is there for me back on Earth?' she asked rhetorically. 'You can't breathe the air without a mask, you can't stand in the sunlight without a hat, you can't turn on a light without permission from the Energy Police.' She smiled bitterly. 'Funny, I didn't use to notice the half of it. I used to think life was okay for Ben and me. He had a good job with one of the corporations, and I used to write for a living. Then Ben . . . Well, Ben died – and I discovered that all those savings that I thought we had were gone, spent by Ben on keeping me wrapped up in my warm little cocoon. And I had to fend for myself.' Her voice was calm, almost dispassionate, but on the table her fingers were twining and untwining like a ball of worms.

'What happened to Ben?' the Doctor asked gently.

'He was an engineer for InterSpace Incorporated,' Piper replied. 'Six months out in one of their exploration ships, six months back on Earth. It was the only way we could manage to live in a room that small – him being away half the time. Ever hear of the *Hydrax*?'

'I think I may have done.'

'It was a scientific vessel out on an exploratory mission to Beta Two. It vanished, like some of them do. Crew of two hundred and forty-three. Including Ben.'

'I'm very sorry.'

She shook her head. 'Don't be. It was thirty years ago. I'm a different person now.'

'But the scars never heal, do they?'

She looked for tears, but found nothing. Nothing but emptiness. 'No,' she said. 'No, they don't.'

'What happened after that?'

'InterSpace refused to pay out on Ben's pension. They claimed that he might still be alive, somewhere. I couldn't afford to fight them, so I had to find myself a decent job. None of the corporations would touch me. No training, you see. There's damn-all use for a writer of kids' books in a world with a childbirth quota. So I retrained and took a position with the only people who were desperate enough to have me – Earth Central. The same goes for most of the people here. We're all rejects from the companies.'

'Speak for yourself,' a voice whined behind her. 'I relished the challenge. Company men do what they're told. I do what I want.'

Piper winced. 'You naturally gravitated towards the only employers who would put up with your arrogance,

59

Alex,' she snapped. 'Any company would pay you four times as much as Earth Government does, and give you more challenging work. Do you expect us to believe that you wouldn't be prepared to kowtow to the bosses for that?'

'Believe what you want,' Bannen sniffed. 'I didn't come here to debate motivations with you. I get enough of that from Christine. I came to find the Doctor.'

There was a sudden clatter as the Doctor's umbrella skidded sideways from beneath his folded arms. The Doctor didn't move for a moment – his arms suspended like a Cossack dancer's – then he bounded to his feet decisively. One moment his umbrella was clattering across the floor, the next it was clutched in his hands. Piper blinked. She hadn't seen him move.

'I've broken one already whilst I've been here,' he said apologetically, looking at her. 'I don't intend making the same mistake twice.' He turned to Bannen. 'What have you found?'

'C Shift have discovered some sort of control room in the deadspaces. Looks important. I've worked out most of the functions of the equipment, of course, but I would be interested in your opinion.'

The Doctor turned to Piper. 'Excuse me,' he said politely.

Piper stood up. 'It's all right,' she said. 'I'm supposed to be at a meeting with Miles in five minutes, and all my notes are in my room. You go on.'

The Doctor turned to Bannen and pointed his umbrella at the door. 'Lay on, MacDuff,' he said.

Two storeys high and hemispherical, buried deep in the centre of Belial Base, the Operations Room was the combined heart and brain of the Project. The members of Piper's team who clustered around the MultiCray Neural Net at its centre looked to Ace like worshippers at the feet of some bulky pagan god, deciphering its pronouncements and interpreting its moods; the flickering banks of equipment around the walls which monitored the state of the air, the water, the people and the Lift could have been taken for high-tech altars. The room made her uneasy. She detoured quickly around it, trying to avoid the eyes of the operators, until she found the ramp that was a short cut to the Pit and the deadspaces.

As she stepped out on to the circular landing that surrounded the Pit, she paused and listened. All around she could make out the constant background hum of the air purifiers, the babble of voices talking far off and the rhythmic pulse of machines. Nearer, there was nothing.

She relaxed slightly.

That'll make things easier, she thought.

She walked to the edge of the Pit and looked downwards. The circular chasm dropped away from her feet, dwindling dizzyingly to a point far below, and further still, to the far side of the moon and the Bridge terminal. Around its rim a white path corkscrewed downwards.

The Pit marked the boundary between what the Project Eden team had found when they arrived in the Lucifer system and what they had built since then. From what she'd managed to get out of people during conversations, Ace knew that this end of the hole through the middle of the planet had been discovered in the middle of a terrace of cracked and jumbled rocks. Miles and his team had built the Base on top of it, and had gradually plumbed its depths. It hadn't taken them long to find the other end, hanging above Belial's smaller sister Moloch, but the maze of tunnels and shafts, known generically as the deadspaces, that led off the Pit, were still being opened up. The Base team, chronically short of space, was already using the closest sections for living quarters, storage and laboratories.

Soon after she had arrived, Ace had made it a priority to explore the Base, learning all of its little nooks and crannies, mapping out short cuts, escape routes and bolt holes. Up until recently, her life had depended upon such information, and she didn't intend letting the habit slip. Every time she was in the refectory she surreptitiously studied the simularity of the Base, and every day she went for a long walk to test her knowledge. She knew precisely where she was going. And, more importantly, what she was doing.

Ace took another step. The toes of her combat boots hung over the void. She waited for a long moment, until her racing heart had steadied, then stepped back.

Yeah, she'd do.

She walked around the rim until she came to the beginning of the white path. It seemed to glitter slightly. She took a step forward, waiting for the bite as her body engaged with the path's gravity field. Her feet seemed to slide away from her but her body followed on, perfectly stable. She smiled involuntarily as childhood memories washed over her: walking down Horsenden Hill back in Perivale on an icy day; letting her feet slip along the frozen ridges of mud; holding her arms out to steady herself; falling over; her books flying as she screamed and giggled. The top of the Pit was a receding circle of light above her now. The path field kept her body steady and her stomach in place. Dark openings slipped past. As the fifth one headed towards her, she turned her body slightly. The field, responding to the movement, slowed her down. She stepped off, her body flipping through a right angle into the new passageway.

The corridor she was now in was triangular in cross section; the walls smooth to the eye but rough to the fingers, as if they had been etched by acid. Coloured striations ran along them. Power and neural network cables had been stapled along the ceiling by Piper's staff. The walls narrowed then widened out every few metres for no reason that anybody had been able to determine. Strange shapes protruded from the walls at random intervals. Theories abounded as to what they were – power boxes, monitors, artwork. Second Scientist Craig Richards was even running a sweepstake on it. The floor was steeply concave; engineers had laid metal grilles over the dip to make it easier to walk on.

Ace turned left at the first junction she came to, entering the living quarters of the Belial crew. Everybody had a suite of rooms down there, except for herself. Bernice had accepted a sleeping room in the main living quarters some weeks ago, and had transferred some of her things there. The Doctor seemed not to want to sleep anywhere. As for herself, she only felt comfortable sleeping in the TARDIS, despite its one careful owner.

She found the door she wanted. She checked the name plate to be sure.

Paula Engado – Psychology.

The door was locked but, with her natural talent for breaking and entering, Ace had it open within seconds.

'Mind if I come in?' Bernice said from the doorway.

Christine LaFayette didn't look up from her desk.

'I was just passing,' she continued, 'and I thought I'd drop in.'

'*Asseyez vous.*'

'I saw you leave the refectory just now.'

Christine wouldn't meet Bernice's gaze. 'I'd finished my meal.'

'You seemed to be in a rush.'

'I had some work to get back to.'

'You haven't even switched your terminal on.'

Christine looked up. Her eyes were red and puffy, and a badly-wiped tear glistened across her cheek. 'I'm . . .' She couldn't finish. The words seemed to catch on something in her throat. She shook her head.

Within a second Bernice was kneeling beside Christine, resting one hand on her knee and another on her shoulder. 'What happened?'

Christine turned a sob into a laugh. 'Hey,' she said, 'I'm the one who gets paid to comfort people and listen to their problems, remember?'

'Yes,' Bernice replied, 'but I'm a talented amateur. What happened?'

'With all my qualifications you'd have thought I could sort my own problems out.'

'It's like a universal law of nature: the best priests are

alcoholics, the best marriage counsellors are divorced, the best psychiatrists come from broken homes.'

Christine flinched.

'Sorry,' Bernice said. 'That was meant as a joke.'

Christine wiped a hand across her eyes. 'Did you see the news simularity from Earth?'

'Wasn't watching.'

'My mother . . . They mentioned her. Shook me up a bit.'

'Your mother?'

'She's Chairperson of the Earth Alliance of Corporations.'

Bernice looked blank.

'You know – they call it the Holding Company. It's like a board of directors for all the companies that trade off-Earth.'

'And your mother is Chairperson?'

'Yes.'

'Most people would be proud.'

'We don't get on. It just shook me up a bit, hearing her mentioned like that.'

'With a job like that I would have thought she'd get mentioned all the time.'

'It wasn't so much hearing her name, it was what she said. "War is bad for business." A lot of things were bad for business when I was younger. I wanted to study Arcturan literature, but that would have been "bad for business". I had to be a good little Chairperson's daughter and go into a respectable profession instead. The chiphead I wanted to live with was "bad for business", so I had to stop seeing him. And when it turned out that one of my mother's colleagues was "bad for business", he suffered a convenient heart attack just before he was going to reveal evidence of massive insider dealing within the Company. That's when I left the Company and joined Earth Central.'

'What about your father?'

'I never knew him. Mother made sure of that.' Christine hesitated. 'Do you know what? For a long time it was him I hated. Not her. Him. For not having the strength to come back.'

Bernice looked away, remembering how her own father had vanished during the Second Dalek War. 'Join the club,' she said.

'I've called it the Mushroom Farm,' Bannen said proudly.

The Doctor gazed around in the closest thing to awe that he was capable of. So complex, and yet precisely ordered; so large that clouds hid the roof and the far walls were lost in the distance. This room that Alex Bannen had led him to – first down the Pit, then along newly-discovered corridors carpeted with ancient dust – must have taken up quite a chunk of Belial's interior space; assuming that there was no dimensional transcendence at work, and the Doctor doubted that. Usually, some warping at the edges of one's vision indicated trans-dimensional engineering, and there was nothing of that sort here. Just peace and cathedral calm.

As far as the eye could see, the objects that Bannen referred to as 'mushrooms' sprouted from the floor, walls, ceiling; every surface able to support an outgrowth. Obviously artificial, they resembled nothing so much as masses of scrap metal which somebody had played a blowtorch over. Each was different from the rest, and they appeared at closely spaced, though apparently random, intervals. The rows retreated away, diminished by perspective, until they were lost in the haze of distance.

'There's obviously a pattern,' Bannen said, gazing around, 'but I'm buggered if I can find it.'

'It's based on a Fourier series,' said the Doctor absent-mindedly. He was listening for the slight, but unmistakable echo from Bannen's words. There it was, almost inaudible even to his sensitive ears, followed by another, and another. The Doctor estimated the size of the room as just a Drashig's eyestalk less than eight kilometres across – compensating for the non-homogeneous atmospheric density, of course – and irregularly septagonal in shape.

'Doctor,' Bannen said thoughtfully, 'is it my imagination, or is there something out there?'

The Doctor followed the line of Bannen's podgy pointing finger. Far, far out in the room, at the point where the Doctor estimated the centre to be, something massive and smooth joined the floor to the ceiling. The haze made it difficult to tell anything more. The Doctor squinted, fine-tuning the musculature of his eyes in an attempt to wring every last drop of information from the sight.

In the end, it was Bannen who identified it. 'Bloody hell,' he said. 'I think it's the Pit. All the times I've used it to get down to the Bridge terminal on the other side of Belial, and I never realized what it was going through.'

'Well, there you are,' the Doctor said as he walked further into the cavernous room. 'You should have taken the scenic route.'

On closer inspection, it could be seen that each mushroom was composed of a number of intertwining metal stalks which sprouted up together from holes in the floor and arched out overhead into a spiky umbrella. The surfaces consisted of a myriad tiny pieces of metal, each a different shape and shade of grey, forming a continuous mosaic. Bending closer, the Doctor could see tiny seams running between the jigsaw pieces.

'Tell me, Trau Bannen,' he said, 'how do you feel about the empirical method of scientific experimentation?'

'The what?'

'The "suck it and see" approach,' the Doctor said. Taking a step backwards, he reached out with his umbrella and pressed against a lozenge-shaped metal fragment half-way up the trunk of the nearest mushroom.

<PASSWORD?>

The letters hung in the air before her; three-dimensional yellow shapes floating a millimetre above grey shadows. Through them, Ace could make out the bright Tewa rug that, along with the simularity of a high cheekboned, rather sunburned woman, was the only concession towards ornamentation in Paula Engado's room.

On a whim, she poked her fingers through the letters. They rippled like reflections in a puddle, and curved to fit the contours of her fingers.

Be serious, she admonished herself. You've got work to do. She rested her hands on the smooth ebony of the desk, alongside the gently glowing section which marked the keyboard.

Password, she thought.

She drummed her fingertips on the desk. The contact lenses that enabled her to 'see' the simularity projection smarted, and she resisted the urge to rub her eyes. She'd been offered corneal grafts, like the rest of the Project Eden team, but had refused, hating the idea of somebody mucking around with her body. She'd had enough of that during the Dalek Wars.

Password.

Well, she could always try it the hard way. Ace had been trained to crack most types of security, and she had taken a lot of the icebreaking programs with her when she rejoined the Doctor. This security system was an antique compared to the cortical lattices on which she had been trained. It bore a closer resemblance to the DOS-based systems she'd used at school than to the more *outré* STROSS-based languages she had encountered in the past year or so. Easy meat for somebody as determined as herself. Still, if she didn't want to leave any traces of her presence, it could take her anything up to an hour to suss the password out. Anything could happen in an hour.

Perhaps there was a quicker way.

She glanced around the room, casting about for an idea. Most people chose something close to home, or so she'd been taught. It made sense; her own password on the rickety old Apple Mac back at school had been *Wicked!* She had kept the same password for the advanced cortical lattices which had run (would run?) the various ships she had served aboard – the *Saberhagen*, the *Corporate Raider* and the *Admiral Raistrick*. Passwords were usually chosen to be something that could be remembered easily. It was just a question of getting into the psychology of the person, and Ace had learned a lot about psychology in the last year or so, even if she still did prefer brute force to persuasion. Of course, it didn't help that she hadn't really known Paula that well. She'd just been a face in the corridor to her. Ace had been shocked at her death, yes, but she'd lost closer people than Paula and not cried about them. Surprisingly, the girl's death had hit Cheryl hard, and even Piper had looked haggard for a few days afterwards.

Ace found herself remembering another death, another body consumed in flames, back when she'd been another person. A more innocent person.

Yes, she could sympathize with Miles.

A sudden noise outside, like a sleeve brushing against the wall, snapped her attention back to the room.

She waited, every muscle tensed, every nerve screaming, but the noise was not repeated.

The sudden rush of adrenalin made her mind race. Facts and faces buzzed around like flies. Odd occurrences, unusual looks, conversations that suddenly changed tack when certain people walked into rooms. Shared laughter.

Like they said, it was a million-to-one shot, but it might just work.

<CHERYL> she typed.

There was a pause as the machine considered her answer.

<WELCOME TO THE BELIAL BASE NEURAL NET> it said.

Ace laughed aloud. This was easier than she'd expected.

She flexed her fingers and started to type. Minutes flowed by, unnoticed, as she worked. Now she was in the system, she could accomplish what she'd come here to do.

Ace caught a sudden movement out of the corner of one eye. She whirled, reaching for a gun she no longer carried. Her fingers clutched uselessly at her T-shirt as something heavy crashed into the side of her head.

Ace moaned with pain and fell to her knees. She was

aware of the sound of fingers tapping against the keyboard, shutting down the neural net she had been trying to access. Erasing its memory.

'No!'

She gathered her strength to stand, but before she could move another great weight smashed into the side of her head. And another.

'No . . .'

Her body slipped sideways. She tried to scream.

Blackness came first.

'What the hell . . . ?' Bannen shouted, lunging for the Doctor. But it was too late. There was a very small click.

And nothing happened.

'You little lunatic! Don't you realize the dangers?'

'But the rewards, Trau Bannen! The rewards!'

'Anything could have happened!'

'That's exactly what I'm interested in.' He grabbed hold of Bannen's lapel and dragged him closer to the mushroom. 'Look closely.' The Doctor placed a finger over one of the shards of metal and gently exerted pressure. The shard began to glow with a pale yellow light.

Bannen peered closer, momentarily forgetting his anger. 'Fascinating. If they're all the same, then this must be some kind of huge control room. Must be a heat sensor, since it didn't operate when your umbrella touched it.'

'Hmm,' the Doctor said mysteriously. He took Bannen's hand in his own and placed it against the same shard. The tiny fragment of metal glowed pastel blue.

'Interesting. But so what?'

'I'm not sure . . .' The Doctor touched the shard again. Its colours changed.

'Doctor, we're getting nowhere with this.'

The Doctor beamed and reached out again. The shard glowed pink. He scowled, keeping his finger pressed down, and the glow shifted through the spectrum to violet.

69

Bannen leaned closer. 'Does this mean what I think it means?' he said, and reached out with his forefinger.

'Miles Engado is Coordinator and you're not,' the Doctor whispered.

As Bannen's finger made contact, the switch turned red.

'What the hell do you – ' And then Bannen realized. 'Mood! The switches change their function depending on the mood of the person who touches them! Happiness, sadness, even,' he frowned at the Doctor, who stood there beaming with innocence, 'jealousy.' His eyes widened as he realized the full implications of what he was saying. 'We think in binary because that's the way our neurons fire. Off or on. Yes, of course, you see? On! Off! Plus! Minus! But not them. Not the builders of this! Perhaps the Angels, if it was the Angels who built all this, had brains wired up in different ways. Multiplexing! Parallel processing!' The frown came back like a sudden storm. 'But,' he snapped, 'that still doesn't give you the right to ignore proper scientific procedure!'

'It's perfectly safe,' the Doctor said peevishly.

'Says who?'

A wild smile crossed the Doctor's face. He jabbed out at random with his umbrella. 'You see?' he said brightly. 'As long as I don't actually touch any of the mushrooms with my bare skin – nothing.'

'Oh yeah?' Bannen said, gazing over the Doctor's shoulder. The Doctor turned to look.

As far as the eye could see, every mushroom in sight was lit up like a Christmas tree.

Ace was naked, gouging at a man's chest with a knife.

Blood gushed across her hands. The knife came free, bringing with it a tiny square of plastic embedded in a ragged lump of flesh. As bubbles frothed in the spreading stain of blood, the man tried to scream, but only succeeded in vomiting a crimson tide which poured in slow motion down his chin, his neck, her legs. His eyes bulged from his face, staring imploringly up at her: begging her to stop before it was too late. She tried to back away, but the floor was too slippery to get a grip. The knife slipped in slow motion from her nerveless fingers, tumbling slowly as it fell and jangling endlessly when it hit the floor. His mouth was working but his words never came.

His body spasmed once, then slumped to the floor.

'It wasn't like this!' she yelled, knowing it was a nightmare but unable to break the spell.

She shook her head violently and murmured softly in denial as a hand reached down to touch her face gently for a moment before moving away . . .

'What do you think?' Bannen whispered.

The Doctor stared across the cavernous room. Everywhere the eye could see, coloured lights twinkled. He removed his umbrella from the switch it was holding down. The lights went out. He rocked the switch another way, and a different galaxy of light was born. 'I always try not to think,' he said. 'I find intuition and guesswork so much more rewarding.'

'So much power,' Bannen said. 'The Lift goes up and down, the Pit path operates continuously, the lights go on and off, and we can't trace any generators, or accumulators, or anything! And meanwhile we have to fill in forms in triplicate if we want to run a shaver.'

The Doctor frowned. 'You can't trace a power source?'

'Nothing.'

'Then where do you get your own power from?'

'Cold fusion generators. Zyton seven fused with hymetusite using a parranium catalyst.'

'Isn't that terribly inefficient?'

'Tell me about it! We can't use solar panels because Belial's orbit about Lucifer means we get eclipsed too often, and we can't sink a geothermal shaft because the centre of Belial is cold.' He snorted. 'That's why we're here, although most of the rest of the team seem to be so wrapped up in trying to talk to the Angels that they've forgotten the fact. Earth Central sent a von Neumann probe past here, decades ago now. According to the reports it sent back, there's an element down in Lucifer's core that we've never come across before – one of the stable elements with very high masses that have been theorized since the twentieth century but have never actually been seen in practice. That's why we need to talk to the Angels. It's not some philanthropic crusade for communication, you know? It's about power. Power for Earth.'

'But even so – '

'Don't think we haven't tried to get something better in the mean time. Either Earth Central can't afford it or the Energy Police say it's irrelevant to our investigations.' He spat the phrase 'Energy Police' out as though it were a curse.

'Somebody has to remind you of the real world,' a voice snapped behind them. The Doctor turned to see a stocky figure dressed in the bright yellow *chador* of an Islamic woman, her head covered by a matching *hejab*.

'You must be Krau Moshe-Rabaan,' he said, removing his hat. 'We don't appear to have met. I'm the Doctor.'

The woman swept past him imperiously. Although she was shorter even than the Doctor, she gave the impression of towering over both men.

'Trau Bannen,' she said harshly, thrusting a clipboard at him. 'My records show that you've been using more than your allocation of energy. You'll have to cut back. We've only got a limited amount of zyton seven for the reactor, and Earth Central won't sanction the use of any more.'

Bannen snatched the clipboard from her, and watched disbelievingly as the glowing figures scrolled across a tiny screen. 'How can you possibly expect me to run a research programme on the miserly amount of energy you allocate to me?' he yelled. 'It's impossible. I shall take this up with the Base Administrator!'

'Take it up with who you like,' Rabaan spat, her *hejab* billowing. 'You know the rules. Any energy debt has to be recovered, if not from you then from somebody else. If you can persuade someone else to reassign their energy to you, fine.' She smiled. 'Although since you have the biggest allocation of anybody, that might be difficult. Otherwise, you're down to half allocation for the next two days.' She looked up at Bannen. Her eyes – the only visible part of her face – were burning. 'Don't you watch the news? IMC have tripled the price of zyton seven. The other companies can afford it, but Earth Central can't.'

The Doctor's left knee was beginning to ache. He recognized that ache. It meant that somebody, somewhere, needed his help. He had a shrewd suspicion who that somebody might be. He had to extricate himself from this scene as soon as he could. 'Pardon me for interrupting such a promising argument,' he said, 'but could you tell me how you collect the energy from the fusion chamber?'

Bannen, still seething, managed to spit through clenched teeth: 'The chamber is lined with photovoltaic cells. They absorb the energy and convert it to electricity.'

'Oh,' the Doctor said, turning away. 'I only ask because the zyton seven – hymetusite reaction gives ninety per cent of its energy of fusion up as neutrinos. If you lined the fusion chamber with neutrino detectors, of which there is a surplus sitting in your storerooms waiting for a rainy day, you could increase your power generation capability by a factor of ten.'

With that he was gone, leaving Bannen and Moshe-Rabaan staring after him, open-mouthed.

'Can I have a word?'

'So long as it's a quick one.' Piper slowed to a fast walk. 'I'm late for a meeting with Miles. Can it wait?'

Cheryl screwed her face up in uncertainty.

'I'm not sure. It's about the starsuits. Sam and I reckon there's something funny going on.'

Piper stopped dead. 'Funny peculiar or funny ha-ha?'

'Funny peculiar. One of the starsuit neural nets is acting up. We don't know yet whether it's a bug, a glitch or,' she grimaced, 'some kind of virus. Whatever it is, we need to check all the suits.'

Piper nodded. 'I'll organize a thorough software check straight away. Did you leave the suit hooked up?'

'No, Sam disconnected it.'

'Good. That means we may have isolated the problem before it spreads. Where's Sam now?'

'I guess he must have headed straight down to Moloch Base. He's doing a split shift – half up here with me, half down there. Do you want to talk to him?'

Piper thought for a moment, then shook her head. 'No, not yet. I'll wait till he gets back.' She smiled, and patted Cheryl's arm. 'Don't worry,' she added. 'I'll handle everything.'

'Thanks.' Cheryl headed back down the corridor as Piper opened the door to Miles Engado's office. Miles was sitting on the wrong side of his desk. Across from him, Adjudicator Bishop looked up.

'Ah, Krau O'Rourke,' Bishop said, looking across. 'Just the person I wanted to see.'

Ace awoke to find the Doctor leaning over her. He reached out to touch her temple, and his hand came away red.

'Oh Ace,' he sighed. 'I can't take you anywhere, can I?'

Chapter Five

Four days. That was the Tewa tradition. Four days of unease before Paula's spirit could rest.

Miles Engado dimmed the lights in his quarters to half strength before crossing to his desk and easing into his seat with a weary sigh. He rested his elbows upon the cool synthetic surface of the desk and cupped his chin in his upturned palms.

Paula.

Paula, Paula, Paula.

What were you thinking? How did you feel? Were you scared? In pain? Did you understand what was happening to you?

Did you think of me as you fell?

Did you still hate me?

Miles moved one hand to touch a heat sensitive area and the surface of the desk became transparent. Lights within the recessed space played softly across a circle of wood inlaid with stones and festooned with feathers. Miles slid aside a stack of admin schedules, peering into the desk and back into time.

At the beginning of all beginnings our ancestors came up out of the earth until they were living beneath the North Water. The world under North Water was as this one, but dark. Spirits, people and animals lived together; death was unknown.

Miles remembered the beginning of the Tewa story of origin as he had told it to Paula, as his father had told it to him when he was a child. Miles frowned. The words were the same, only this time they did not comfort him as they once had.

'A native American medicine wheel. Genuine, too; the workmanship's beautiful. Did you make it?'

'The wheel has been in my family for seven hundred years,' Miles replied automatically, then turned as he realized he was not alone.

The Doctor took off his hat and held it loosely in one hand. 'I'm sorry to intrude. I did knock, but I imagine you didn't hear me.'

'I was thinking of my – of the past.'

'I know. I've brought these for you.' The Doctor reached into his pockets and withdrew a number of articles. 'And Paula, of course.'

As Miles watched in growing surprise, the Doctor laid four different lengths of charcoal and an old leather tobacco pouch on the desk. 'Four days is too long to wait, Miles. Use the charcoal. Draw lines. Break her bowl and let her go.'

'You know of our traditions?' Miles said, amazed.

'I've travelled,' the Doctor said.

Miles's knuckles were white as he gripped the edge of the desk. 'And do you believe?' he whispered.

'Do you?' the Doctor replied, and to that Miles had no answer.

'We argued,' he said eventually, 'and she hid the bowl from me. Her spirit cannot be freed until it is found.'

'Then I will help you,' the Doctor said with authority. 'And in return you might help me.'

'If I can.'

'Release control of the security records to me. Those little prying eyes of yours wander all over the base, don't they? I was rather hoping to find out if one of them has spotted something that I might have missed.'

'I'm afraid that won't be possible. I have placed Adjudicator Bishop in charge of the investigation into Paula's death and he has chosen to retain control of the monitors, and their records, for himself.'

'I see.'

'Can you get the information you want from somewhere else?'

The Doctor frowned. 'Eventually. It would just have been quicker to use the monitors, that's all.' He drummed his fingers lightly upon the desk in a complex jazz rhythm, considering. 'Perhaps I'll have a word with the Adjudicator; see if he's amenable to a little friendly persuasion.'

'I have found him to be a reasonable man.'

The Doctor smiled to himself, remembering Bernice's run-in with the *reasonable* Trau Bishop. Then he wondered how Ace would deal with the Adjudicator when he chose to interview her in connection with Paula's death, and his smile widened even further.

'I am sure he is.' The Doctor replaced his hat upon his head with a deft movement. 'I have to go now. I'll watch out for Paula's bowl.'

The door whispered shut and the Doctor was gone.

Miles was left alone with a desk full of paperwork and prayers, and the prospect of four days of increasing spiritual tension and fear.

Ace fluffed her hair and massaged her scalp, trying hard to prevent the spread of the tension headache she could feel building behind her eyes. Not a hope. She stretched in the ultrasonic shower, trying to get used to the way the dirt and sweat on her body simply crumbled away, and wishing for the simple luxury of shampoo. All she really wanted to do was splash great double handfuls of icy water across her face and let the tension drain away with the moisture; to stand breathless and shivering in the aftermath of the cold, anticipating a hot towel and a tingling skin rub.

Again, not a hope.

The room to which Christine had showed her led off the Pit and was quite large, if sparsely appointed. She had a pneumatic chair and bed, a personal neural net inset in the desk with simularity contact lenses, and somebody had thoughtfully placed an entertainment cube on a freestanding base at the head of her bed. There was no lock on the door, no decorations upon the sloping walls, no windows, no taps and no water. It had no memories. She liked it.

Ace stepped dry from the shower and walked to her bed. As she moved, she was aware that the floor was neither warm nor cool, apparently adjusting itself to her body temperature. She ran her fingers through the hair at the nape of her neck. The odd-smelling brown paste the Doctor had smeared on the lump on her head had dissolved along with the rest of the dirt to leave the swelling reduced and much less painful. She wished the Doctor's questions had dissolved along with his medication. Instead they circled maddeningly in her mind, and she was unable to drive them away.

Am I really being fair to him? she wondered. She'd had plenty of time to think about it during the war, and had still come up with no solution.

She sat on the edge of the bed and listened to the wheeze of escaping air as the item of furniture accommodated itself to her weight. The sound reminded her of the pneumatic hiss made by her battle armour on her first day of combat. At first the noises had been intrusive and disturbing, but she had quickly become used to them, and soon they were like good friends. While the noises remained, the suit had been doing its job of keeping her alive. If they stopped – watch out. That was when you'd be wading hip deep in the remains of your friends and dodging selective energy pulses from squadrons of Bombardier Daleks.

Just now she'd felt as if she'd been dodging the selective questioning of her former friend in exactly the same way. *What were you doing in Paula's quarters? What were you looking for? What are you hiding from me, Ace?* He was beginning to sound like her old Sergeant Major. Or her mother.

There was a knock at the door, and Ace found herself again reaching for the gun she no longer carried.

'Who's there?'

'Benny. Can I come in?'

'Half a sec.' Ace grabbed her clothes and began to pull them on. 'Yeah, come on then.'

Bernice popped her head around the door. She waved a hip flask in Ace's direction. 'Want a drink?'

Ace considered. 'What the hell.' She accepted the flask and gulped down a mouthful of its contents. She gasped and her eyes popped.

Bernice grinned. 'Warming, ain't it?' she drawled.

Ace managed a nod.

Bernice moved to the chair and sat down. 'Heard you clocked out for a while. Thought I'd drop by with a little pick-me-up.'

'If the Doctor sent you to ask more stupid questions, tell him I'm not playing.'

'I haven't talked to the Doctor. I came here off my own bat.'

'There was an awkward silence.

'We need to talk, don't we?' Bernice said finally.

'Maybe.'

'Not "Maybe". Definitely.'

'Yeah, well . . . Maybe. Anyway, I'm knackered now and I really fancy a kip, okay?'

Bernice frowned. 'It was the war, wasn't it?'

Ace stared blankly at the wall, avoiding Bernice's gaze.

'Take a girl, any girl,' Bernice continued. 'Young, disillusioned, no dependants . . . Train her up, give her a smartsuit and a big gun . . . It figures. You were scared at first – who wouldn't be? But killing Daleks brought its own comfort, and after a while you realized you were going to be fine.'

Ace whirled to face Bernice, and the archaeologist recoiled from the raw ferocity in her eyes. 'Yeah? Well, so what?' she snarled. 'If anyone deserved to die it was those metal bastards. If you could've seen what they did. What they did to women like you or me. What they did to families, to *children*.'

'But you enjoyed killing them.'

'I got confused. Killing Daleks should've felt good. But it didn't. I drilled a hole through the motive units of a

Special Weapons Dalek once. It couldn't move. Couldn't kill me. Couldn't do anything. I'd used up my last charge on that hammerpulse and I wanted to see if I could steal the thing's energy banks for my own systems. You know what it did? It talked to me. It sat there helplessly while I stripped out its power systems and it begged me to kill it. God! Both sides are smashing seven kinds of hell out of each other and it's telling me it wants to die. I'd just watched it vaporize a Red Crescent ship full of children, and I could smell them burning there in the darkness, and God help me I pitied the thing. I just stood there, listening to it crying into the night, until its power ran down.'

Bernice's face softened with compassion and she made as if to move towards the younger woman.

Ace slid backwards along the bed, hands raised defensively. 'Don't touch me! I'm fine. I don't need comforting. I'm fine.'

Bernice stepped backwards. 'No problem.' She sat back down and Ace met her gaze squarely.

'I'd do anything not to be confused, Bernice. Anything.' Her voice hardened. 'So don't confuse me any more than I am already.'

'No, Doctor. I'm afraid I simply do not trust you.'

Adjudicator Bishop studied the agitated face of the irritating little man standing before him, and felt he was very close to the truth of the matter. If he pushed a little harder, he might find out something useful at last.

'I cannot and will not release control of the monitors to you. Furthermore, any information they may possess is now officially subpoenaed by the duly appointed representative of the Guild of Adjudicators. In case you're wondering, that's me.'

The Doctor twisted the handle of his umbrella in frustration. 'You have to help me. More lives could be at stake.'

Bishop looked thoughtful.

The Doctor stopped twisting the handle of his umbrella,

placing it instead foursquare upon the floor and leaning casually upon it. 'I wouldn't need to actually use the monitors. Just scan their records . . . Oh, say for the last twenty-four hours.'

Bishop pretended to consider.

'You've already said yourself,' the Doctor continued, 'that the gap created in the monitor coverage makes it difficult, if not impossible, to form a complete security record. What have you got to lose?'

'It's not a matter of what I would have to lose, Doctor. The procedure is very clear in circumstances like these. Rules are rules.'

'Poppydash and baldercock!' the Doctor snapped contemptuously. 'Rules were made to be broken.'

Bishop smiled coldly. 'I'm afraid I must disagree, Doctor. Rules are made for reasons. One life has already been lost. If you have any information concerning the safety of others, I might remind you that it is your moral and legal duty to tell me what that information is.'

The Doctor frowned in concentration. 'And if I do?'

'Well, since I am the sole representative of the Guild present on Eden, I imagine we could work something out.'

'And what about the rules?' the Doctor said in a cutting voice.

Bishop's smile dropped away. 'I believe, under the circumstances, that the "rules" could be interpreted in a mutually beneficial way.'

Alex Bannen stood in the centre of the Mushroom Farm with his eyes shut and his hands touching the roundly contoured, almost organic metal swellings. Every muscle in his body ached. He'd spent the last five hours along with Cheryl Russell and a team of sweating technicians installing neutrino shielding around Eden's reactor. Although he was exhausted, he knew that he had to come to the Mushroom Farm.

Bannen opened his eyes and glanced around the shadowy curves and glinting hollows of the vast chamber. Not for the first time, he tried to gain a sense of what the builders of this metallic phantasmagoria must have been like. What kind of things had been important to them? he wondered. Would it have been the precise application of technology so sophisticated it had to be housed deep within a lunar body, or just the glory of a sunset?

For a foolish moment Bannen tried himself to recall what an Earthly sunset had been like, and was glad when he failed. His only memory of the open sky came from his youth, when a forbidden excursion through a crawl-space in the shared hallway outside the family living unit had produced a single image of gunmetal clouds pierced by concrete towers, grey on grey, fading into the distance like the grainy picture on a cheap 2D television. A much younger Bannen had scared himself witless with this wild vision of *outside*, a far cry from the comfortingly well modulated environment within the building, and had immediately squeezed back inside, terrified that the tunnel would seal up before he could crawl back through it, leaving him exposed, naked beneath the polluted sky as a punishment for daring to let a whim take him beyond the prescribed living areas. He never told a soul about his trip, and never went outside again.

At least, not until he'd joined Project Eden.

Bannen shivered suddenly. He'd come here to get a handle on the Angels – or whichever species had built this place. That was what he needed to do. Not spend hours dwelling upon the shortfalls of his childhood.

He touched one of the silvery upswellings, rocking his finger this way and that across its smoothly chromed surface. Throughout the chamber, hundreds of yellow-green panels blinked warmly in response, their demands for attention unmistakable, their meaning still hopelessly unclear. He tried to recall an image of his wife, Sonia, and touched another mushroom; another swarm of indicators glowed, amber this time, equally mysterious. Unbidden, an image of MexTech rose in his mind, and a third sequence of lights burned. Bannen sighed with frustration. If only he dared take one of the things apart. For all he knew, there were a hundred redundant backup systems here which could be dismantled and studied without damage to the main systems. But there were so many controls, so many permutations of function, that it would take years for the number to be calculated, let alone understood.

Still, if he hadn't had the means, at least he'd had the time. Time to bring his own plans to fruition. Time whose use the Doctor had made more efficient by freeing energy Bannen could use. He had his theories about this control room. He'd spent years tracing cables, analysing rooms full of dusty equipment, puzzling over geometric patterns incised in walls. The Doctor was starting from scratch, but Bannen already had more pieces of the jigsaw to work with. He had a shrewd suspicion what the purpose of this room was.

Bannen walked slowly over to where an open-plan office-cum-workshop had been set up within the huge chamber, consisting of a set of filing cabinets, lab benches, portable analysis equipment and several desktop subsidiaries of Eden's neural net. He switched on a reading lamp over a desk and by its cosy light unlocked the bottom drawer of one of the filing cabinets. This was where he kept all documents too precious to be stored on neural net crystal. He withdrew a bulky file and took it to the desk. Five years of hopes and dreams were encapsulated within this file. Information that no one except him would ever see.

Information which would literally transform his life.

He'd been quiet as a child, too quiet. In later life, this had been reflected in a tendency towards over-loudness which alienated him from his few remaining friends even more than the shyness of youth. More than anything, Bannen was beginning to realize, he was a lonely man. A sad man. He tried to enjoy the company of others, but found it increasingly difficult to be patient with them. There had been few enough on Earth who shared his views. Here on Eden he could name only one.

If Bannen had his way there would soon be no more

arguments with Engado, Christine, Piper, Moshe-Rabaan . . . Anyone. He would dismiss his fear and loneliness with one flick of a switch, and become a new man. A whole man. Only the Doctor could interfere now. He had provided the extra energy Bannen needed, and he could probably devise a method of taking it away again.

It was just as well for the Doctor that he showed no signs of wanting to do so.

Bannen supposed he should really be grateful for this, but somehow it seemed like the least of his worries.

Beyond the circle of light cast by the reading lamp, out in the metallic cavern beyond, there was a tiny sound. A shadow moved, darkness within darkness. Quickly, he closed the file and slipped it by his feet under the desk.

Ace walked out of the darkness. 'How do you find your way around here?' she asked. 'This place is like the Carlsbad Caverns.'

'Hardly.'

Ace came round the desk, ran her fingers along the darkened neural net terminal, and perched herself on a three-legged lab stool. 'What do you mean?'

'An American subsidiary of a company called Panorama Chemicals filled the Carlsbad Caverns with plastic waste in twenty-one forty, three years after the repeal of the anti-pollution laws.'

'Earth was that desperate for energy?'

'It sure was.'

'What about tourism?'

Bannen frowned. 'What's "tourism"?'

Ace laughed, a cold sound which reflected back from the distant walls to counterpoint their conversation. 'You're not serious, right?'

There was a long pause. 'Ace, what are you doing here? I'm engaged in high-priority work. I don't want to be disturbed.'

'In the middle of the night, with the workstation switched off?'

'Physical observation.'

'What of – your knees?'

Bannen jerked his head upright, uncomfortably aware that the corner of his file was projecting from beneath the desk. 'I'm very tired.'

'Right.'

'So go away.'

Ace shrugged. 'Okay.' She didn't move.

'*Now*.'

'Though I'd much rather stay and chat. I'm interested, you see. Interested in all this. The others won't talk to me. They think I'm just a girl. Funny, it doesn't matter when we go to, there's always someone who reckons they're better. The high-and-mighties. The I've-no-time-for-yous. Sometimes I feel like a bit of an outcast, know what I mean?'

'No.'

Ace grinned. 'I believe you. Millions wouldn't.'

Bannen said nothing.

'What about this place, then? How come it's so big? What went on here?'

Bannen rubbed one hand tiredly across his eyes. 'Nothing I want to talk about.' He got up, switched off the reading light, and began the two-hundred-metre trek to the cavern entrance.

Ace took a last look around the hall, shrugged and followed. She'd learn nothing here.

Yet.

Cheryl Russell walked into the living area she shared with her husband Sam, disturbed to find him absent. Her extra shift at the reactor had just ended; as far as she knew, Sam should have finished his shift down on Moloch hours ago. Perhaps he'd logged in some extra time as well. Yep. That would be it.

She put down the food tray she had carried from the refectory, stripped off her dirty coveralls, stepped into the dryshower and programmed the cubicle for a sonic massage. Ten minutes later – scrubbed clean, and starving – she emerged from the unit, set the entertainment cube to play Glasst's *Requiem* and fell upon her meal with a vengeance.

Half-way through her fourth mouthful, something wet splashed on to her plate, and Cheryl realized she was crying. There was a ringing in her ears which drowned out the music, and her stomach rolled sickeningly with a combination of unsated hunger and loss.

She was thinking of Paula again.

There was a knock on the door.

Cheryl struggled to keep her mouthful of food down as she tipped the rest, plate and all, down the recycler chute. She pulled on a presentable face and answered the door.

'Hi!' Bernice Summerfield strolled into the room, digging into one of the deep pockets of her coveralls. 'I come bearing gifts.'

'That's a twentieth-century idiom, isn't it?'

'Nope. Its a twentieth-century gift, though. There you go.' Bernice handed Cheryl a lime-green bottle in a paper wrapper.

'Mineral water?' Cheryl's sadness was momentarily driven aside by incredulity. 'Real mineral water? Don't you know how much this stuff costs? Where the hell did you get it?'

'That would be telling.' Bernice tapped the side of her nose. 'And who'd be telling when they could be drinking?'

Cheryl set the bottle down beside the entertainment cube. 'Look, Benny. Thanks for the gift, but I couldn't possibly – '

Bernice took a seat. 'Of course you can. I'd join you, but I normally have something stronger in my water.' She glanced around the room. The suite was bigger than her own. The Russells had made it warm and cosy. There was a rug on the floor (who wove that? she wondered), and a couple of brave attempts at art hanging from the walls. There was a simularity of Cheryl and Sam beside a pottery bowl on a shelf beneath a variably reflective mirror. Low-key lighting filled the room with soft curves and pastel shadows. A piece of classical music was playing softly in a minor key.

Bernice asked: 'Sam not home yet?'

'Noticeable by his absence, right?'

'Sorry. Just being nosey.'

'Erase it. I'm not myself at the moment. Sam must be working a double shift on Moloch.'

'Right.' Bernice hesitated. 'Cheryl – if I'm out of order, say so – but you look as though you could use some company. Are you sure you don't want to open that bottle?'

Cheryl turned away without replying, and moved to the shelf containing the simularity of herself and Sam. The doll-sized figures within were locked in a kiss, the air around them heavy with a spray of coloured plastic. She touched a pressure pad on the base, and the tiny figures waved in her direction, the plastic drifting like motes of dust in a sunbeam. Party time. She touched the pad again and the display froze into a new configuration, one in which she and Sam were further apart.

'We had this taken on the journey out from Earth. We were married on the ship. Sam wasn't originally part of the Eden team, you know. He was one of the ship's officers. His captain married us and bought a place for him when one of the original technicians didn't make it out of coldsleep.'

'Sounds like this captain was a nice guy.'

'I think he was sorry to see Sam go, but he knew it was what we both wanted.'

Bernice smiled. 'Who says there aren't any happy endings any more, huh?'

Cheryl tried for a smile and didn't quite make it. 'I'm for bed, Benny. Catch you in the morning, all right?'

'Sure.'

Cheryl shut the door behind Bernice and wondered just how long it would be before she managed to close her eyes without wishing she'd never wake up again.

Piper O'Rourke closed the door quietly behind her as she entered Miles's quarters. With Bishop ensconced in the Coordinator's office up on the command level, she knew she'd find Miles here. He was asleep at his desk, head resting upon folded arms. At his elbow were four sticks of charcoal and a skin pouch full of some fibrous brown substance. She gently placed a slim file on one end of the desk and was about to leave when Miles stirred, alerted by some small sound she had made.

'Piper?'

'Miles, you're going to have a killer backache in the morning if you don't do your sleeping where it's supposed to be done.'

'Can't sleep.'

'You daft bugger, what do you think you were just doing?'

Miles sat up, wincing.

'See,' she continued. 'Told you.'

Miles smiled tiredly. His reaction surprised them both equally. 'You're right, as usual.'

'I certainly am. Now go to bed. I'll see you in the morning.'

'Thanks, Piper. You're a good friend.'

'Right.' Piper moved towards the door.

'Piper?' Was that a catch in his voice?

'Yeah?'

'You can stay with me if you'd like.'

Piper closed her eyes and sighed. 'Oh, Miles, your timing stinks. Tomorrow, okay? Things to do.'

'It's a date,' he mumbled sleepily.

Piper smiled sadly at him in the semi-darkness and then left the room.

Ace followed Bannen through the passages of the base to his suite. She was careful to make sure he didn't see or hear her. She wanted to make sure he was asleep before she got on with the next job she'd set herself.

Triangular decorations projected from the sloping walls every few hundred metres throughout the base. Ace knew Christine LaFayette had been studying a few pieces recently, hoping to pry loose a bit of information regarding the aliens. It was taking a long time and there were no real guarantees.

No real guarantees. That seemed to be the story of her life.

As Bannen closed the door to his quarters, she concealed herself behind one of the artforms a few metres from the entrance to his rooms. The lighting in the corridor was dim and reddish; Ace found plenty of shadows to wrap herself in. She'd give Bannen twenty minutes or so to fall asleep and then head back to the Mushroom Farm. There was stuff there she needed to check out.

She had been waiting for less than five minutes when Bannen cracked open the door to his suite and peered both ways along the passage. Satisfied that it was empty, the scientist left his suite and hurried away down the corridor.

Ace put her head in her hands and sighed with frustration. Didn't *anyone* sleep around here?

Bernice closed the door to her suite and stood in the middle of the room trying to work out why she was worried. The base was fascinating. The people were fascinating. The work was fascinating. So what was wrong?

She thought she had become used to the idea of not being a paid-up archaeologist any more. After all, the idea of travel had appealed to her long before the Doctor had turned up on Heaven. Time travel should've been an archaeologist's wet dream – but she was becoming increasingly obsessed by a dark thought; that ever since Ace had come back into the TARDIS things had changed. The Doctor had changed. Even she herself had changed, reluctant though she was to admit it, replacing her lost love of digging in the mud of some alien planet with . . . Well, with what? The clever ability to worm her way into other people's lives and fuel her suspicion with their pain?

No, dammit. No. Not her.

With characteristic suddenness, Bernice about-faced, left her room and strode back to the suite she had just left.

She owed someone an apology.

She banged on the door, and when there was no reply, pushed it open and entered.

The suite was empty. Cheryl was gone.

The Doctor closed the door to Miles Engado's office and walked slowly down the metal passage, reddish light from transparent windows lending his thoughtful expression vaguely demonic overtones. Bishop had been less than helpful. That hadn't mattered in the long run, of course. The Doctor had got the information he wanted and given away nothing of any real consequence in return, but he felt his relationship with the Adjudicator needed to improve if there was to be any chance of resolving the situation here. Unfortunately, Bishop was a man used to working within his own jurisdiction, and was comfortable with it. He didn't need to cooperate with anyone and knew it. What made matters worse was that he had the weight of interstellar law behind him. The only thing the Doctor had on his side was time.

The Doctor began to marshal his thoughts. Somebody – or possibly some*bodies* – connected with the Eden Project had become a killer. That much was certain. What was also certain was that Ace had changed. Changed beyond his projections. Her suggestion to come to the Lucifer system in this time period, though cleverly routed through Bernice and disguised as a field trip for the archaeologist, showed signs of a confidence which Ace had never displayed before. The Doctor frowned. Was Ace growing up just a little too fast for her own good? Or was he guilty of losing touch with the one species he professed to have such empathy with?

The Doctor felt it was time to clear the air between him and Ace. Previous attempts had failed. This time would be different. The identity of her mysterious assailant was still unknown – all Bishop had been able to turn up from the security monitors had been a number of corrupted files. Even his own ministrations had been unable to wring anything more informative from the simularities than a field of hissing static, and Ace had been hardly more forthcoming. Worse, Bishop had blamed the Doctor for the fault, citing his aerosol programmer as evidence. It had taken the Doctor thirty minutes of fast talking to convince the Adjudicator he was not to blame. Even then, Bishop had had the cheek to accuse him of –

The Doctor stopped. Something was wrong. There was a whisper of sound drifting down the corridor: anguish, horror, pain, fear.

A familiar cocktail.

The Doctor began to run. In seconds he burst in through the open door of Federique Moshe-Rabaan's personal suite.

Within a second, he had taken in everything – the folds of silk that hung from the ceiling and turned the room into a tent, the maze-like designs on the floor coverings, the cushions scattered around in place of chairs, the woman lying across her bed. Her *hejab* had been removed, and the Doctor could see blood and tears mixed upon her face. The same blood was streaked all across the front of her *chador* and soaked the ornate silken sheets which covered the bed.

Knowing he was already too late to help, the Doctor bent close to her face, struggling to pick up the words she was whispering over and over again.

'Allahu Akbar . . .'

God is great.

She stared up at the Doctor without seeing him. Her eyes were dark and ringed with heavy lashes; her complexion was a flawless olive colour. In human terms she was beautiful. He reached out to touch her temple, and her anguished moans ceased immediately. She blinked; when her eyes shut it was life that moved them, when they opened it was nothing more than a motor reflex.

There was a pen clutched in one hand, a crumpled piece of paper lying on the pillow beside her head. The Doctor stared at the writing on it for a long moment before sadly reaching back out to close her eyes.

Though her face was already cold, the blood running from her open wrists was still warm.

And there was a sound.

The Doctor looked more closely. Her bruised left hand was still moving.

There was no blood, as the vibroknife she had been clutching burrowed through her fist and dropped to the floor. Lacking a touch upon its pressure sensitive trigger, it immediately deactivated.

The Doctor made a quick circuit of the suite. It was empty, but that condition could change at any moment.

Quickly, he replaced the note exactly where it had been on the pillow and left the room. He left the door slightly ajar, exactly as he'd found it. The solution to all his problems, it seemed, had presented itself with almost classical timing.

He wasn't about to waste the opportunity.

Chapter Six

It was Christine LaFayette who, with characteristic tact
and subtlety, had forced a twenty-five-hour day on to the
Project Eden team. Claiming that the natural biological
rhythm of the human body went in cycles of that length,
she had produced an impressive array of studies and stat-
istics to prove it. Reluctantly at first, then with increasing
enthusiasm, her colleagues went along with her. They
found stress decreasing, tiredness evaporating, concentration increasing and job-satisfaction levels hitting the
roof.

It was Piper O'Rourke who, in her typically blunt
fashion, had tried to force through a hot shift system. It
made more sense, she had argued, to have one third of
the crew working whilst one third slept and one third
relaxed, rotating every eight hours and twenty minutes.
It was only when the crew threatened industrial action –
a recourse denied to company employees but still open
to those who worked for Earth Central – that she withdrew her plans. Despite occasional attempts to slide her
reforms through, the crews of both Bases worked, ate,
played and slept at the same times, with only a skeleton
crew of insomniacs and misanthropes working through
what had been arbitrarily designated 'night'.

So when Third Psychologist Shmuel Zehavi – who had
successfully managed to hide his sleepwalking habit from
all but one or two sympathetic colleagues – woke up to
find himself standing in a pool of partially congealed blood
and staring down at the body of Federique Moshe-
Rabaan, the majority of the Project Eden staff were
alone, asleep or both . . .

In her room, Cheryl Russell writhed in sweat-soaked sheets, dreaming of an androgynous lover whose face sometimes resembled Sam Russell and sometimes Paula Engado . . .

In the Mushroom Farm, Alex Bannen held a gentle conversation with an image from his past to keep the nightmares of Earth at bay . . .

In the corridor outside the Mushroom Farm, Ace listened to Bannen's voice, and to the quiet replies that followed his words, and wondered who was in there with him . . .

In the TARDIS, Bernice Summerfield wandered through vaulted white corridors and chambers, wondering why, no matter how far she walked in a straight line, she always ended up back in the console room again . . .

In the Coordinator's room, Miles tossed and turned uncomfortably in his sleep, disturbed by the distant drums of the Tewa ancestral dance; while his spirit, unable to cross the distance to the Earth Mother, watched enviously before unwillingly rejoining his restless body . . .

In her office, shrouded in shadows, Piper O'Rourke's thoughts wandered back over the years and light years of her life: the petty jealousies, the minor betrayals and the secrets buried so deep that even she had forgotten them, but which had returned to haunt her none the less . . .

Down at the Bridge terminal, First Technician Julie Ndema and Second Scientist Craig Richards, temporarily abandoning their duty schedule for a game of poker with Richards' lucky deck, were so completely absorbed in the turn of the cards that they had totally missed the subtle sting being worked by the artful Tiw Heimdall and Anuskia Smyslov . . .

In her room, Christine LaFayette slipped smoothly into

a familiar dream of a strong, cold, human-machine lover, the only lover she had ever lain beside . . .

In his ship, Adjudicator Bishop sneezed, and wondered for the thousandth time how much longer it would be before he slept . . .

In the centre of the dark and deserted refectory, the Doctor crooned a Venusian lullaby gently to himself, swaying from side to side and imagining an appreciative audience . . .

In her room, as Zehavi wondered what to do, Federique Moshe-Rabaan's body cooled, its muscles softening as it passed through the final stages of rigor mortis . . .

All over Belial, people slept, talked, wept, ate and otherwise lived their lives . . .

And in the labyrinths of the Belial Base neural network, tiny collections of charge multiplied and spread, sending out tentacles of insubstantial information; more than a mere ghost in the machine . . .

'I appreciate this,' Ace said.

Christine glanced over at her as they whirled round the spiral Pit path like kids on a helter-skelter. 'No problem. I thought you might want a change of scenery.'

Ace grinned. 'I've been wanting to take a gander at Moloch for ages.'

'Actually, I'm beginning to wonder if it's such a good idea.'

'Don't be a spoilsport,' Ace groaned. 'Not when I'm so close.'

'It's just that . . . Well, something's up.'

'Do what?'

'I saw Rabbi Zehavi rushing in to Miles' office just before I got to your room.'

'Zehavi . . . He's the little guy with the skullcap? The one who walks in his sleep?'

Christine smiled. 'You spotted that as well.'

'Couldn't miss it. He walked past me at about three o'clock this morning, like a zombie. Not a flicker. I could have been standing there stark naked with a banner above my head reading "Take me, take me," and he wouldn't have batted an eyelid.'

Christine blushed. 'What were you doing awake at three o'clock this morning?' she said.

Ace looked away. 'Couldn't sleep,' she said tersely. 'Why do you call him Rabbi?'

Christine looked at Ace strangely. 'Because he is,' she replied.

'What do you reckon's up with him, then? Crisis of faith?'

'I wish I knew. I really wish . . .'

Ace looked over as Christine trailed off. The Psychology Team Leader was sucking on her lower lip and looking pensive. She caught Ace's eye and looked sheepish. 'Sorry. It just worries me, all this intrigue. Paula's death, the Adjudicator snooping around, Sam and Cheryl acting up . . . I can't help wondering what's going to happen next.'

Something whizzed past them, heading upwards. It looked like one of the drone cameras, moving to its next scheduled snooping location. Ace followed it with her gaze. Far above her head, a circle of brightness was getting larger.

Larger?

She looked downwards, to where the path corkscrewed its way back to their drop-off point.

And up again, to the growing circle of light.

'Christine?'

'Hmm?'

'Is it my imagination, or have we got turned around?'

'What?'

'We started out at the top of the Pit going downwards. We now seem to be coming back to the top again.'

Christine began to laugh. 'I'm sorry, I should have warned you. You know that whoever the aliens were who built the Bridge, they bored the Pit straight through the centre of this moon? Well, there's some kind of Moebius discontinuity around the centre of gravity. Somehow the path gets twisted, although Bannen's topologists are having seven fits trying to work it out. Best guess is that it's knotted in the fourth dimension. Although you start out going downwards to the Bridge terminal, you end up coming at it upwards. If you see what I mean.'

'Clear as mud,' Ace murmured.

The rush of air past them abated as the Pit field started to slow them both down. Brightness spilled from above, turning the path into a ribbon of darkness above their heads and a ribbon of light beneath their feet. The path began to level out, and as they slowed to a crawl Ace gasped aloud at the beauty of the scene.

They had emerged on to the surface of Belial, inside a dome made of some transparent material. In front of them was a circular arena, where a small group of people stood talking. Great rippled sheets of rock marked the boundary of the dome. In the distance, a range of fretted mountains resembled a vast lace curtain drawn across the terrain. The horizon, so close that Ace was conscious of looking *downwards* at it, was made irregular by the bite-mark craters left by the debris of planetary and solar formation. And above them, dominating everything, was a sight that made Ace's stomach churn.

Moloch, the second of Lucifer's moons, hung directly overhead as if about to crash down upon their heads at any moment. Beyond it, the oppressive bulk of Lucifer itself covered more than three quarters of the visible sky like the outer ring of some vast bullseye.

Ace spent some minutes gazing in awe at the dark side of Lucifer. Eventually, the sight became too much, and she pulled her gaze back to study the second moon, Moloch.

A dusky grey orb scarred with fractures, it looked to Ace like a white marble she had once lost in the playground, only to find it weeks later, scuffed and cracked, in the corner of the bikesheds. And then a more menacing simile occurred to her. Moloch was an eye, veined with thread-like blood vessels and fogged by cataracts to a lacklustre shadow of its former self, but still staring balefully down upon her, despising her, judging her.

A faint tremor ran through her body. She thought it was tension, until the group in the centre of the dome started looking around.

'What was that?' Christine said.

'Dunno,' Ace replied. She couldn't see anything untoward, or rather, any more untoward than it should have been. The landscape was illuminated by a deep red light. Only at the far horizon did the ground return to its natural umber as stars peeped timorously out from behind Lucifer's disc.

Somebody left the group of people in the middle of the dome and began to move towards them. Ace tried to make out who it was, but a sparkle of blue between Belial and Moloch caught her eye. By the time she could refocus her eyes it had gone. A sudden yellow glitter closer to Moloch made her jump, but it vanished before she could shift her gaze. Again, down by the top of the dome, a long streak of scarlet seemed frozen against black space for a moment before disappearing.

'Am I seeing things, or what?'

'It's like an optical illusion, isn't it?' Christine said beside her.

'What is it?'

'It's the Bridge.'

'You're winding me up.'

Ace tried to stop looking *for* whatever was catching the light and tried looking at the whole scene instead. For a few moments the vision remained tantalizingly vague, with multicoloured glimmers appearing at random between Belial and Moloch. And then it was there, glittering in all its glory. Ace's brain, provided with enough clues, integrated all the information and filled in the gaps. An impossibly thin, impossibly straight line of light spanned the distance between Moloch and a blister on top of the dome, scintillating with all the colours of the rainbow. To Ace it looked like a strand of cobweb, spangled with dew and seen in sunrise. A cone of bracing threads seemed to rise from the dome to anchor it.

'Are you impressed?' Christine asked.

'Nah,' Ace said, 'I'm from Perivale.'

'Bifrost,' said the voice beside her. She looked round. A small man stood beside her, barely higher than her shoulder. His hair was blond, his face young but deeply lined.

'I said Perivale, dogbreath.'

He smiled, revealing a set of perfect golden teeth. 'Bifrost. The rainbow bridge of the Aesir. The trembling path.'

'I must admit,' Ace said, 'I was hoping for something more substantial than a trembling path.'

'Speaking metaphorically,' the gnomish man added. 'Norse mythology. Speaking realistically, single trisilicate molecular filament woven into a tube. Lift interacts with it using linear induction motors. We think. Impressive piece of engineering.'

'This is Tiw Heimdall,' Christine said from beside her. 'He's the caretaker of the Bridge terminal. One of Alex Bannen's staff.'

'Engineer by profession. Mythologist by inclination,' Heimdall added in his staccato fashion. 'Spend most of my time down here. Fascinated.'

'He even sleeps down here,' Christine said, shaking her head. 'I worry about him.' When Heimdall smiled and turned to her she rapidly added, 'Professionally speaking, of course.'

'Lift due any moment,' Heimdall said, cocking his head slightly. 'I can feel it coming.'

Ace followed the line of the Bridge up to where Moloch hung like a balloon on the end of a piece of cotton. She couldn't see any lift. 'How long does the journey take?' she asked.

'Varies,' Heimdall replied. 'Sometimes half an hour.

99

Sometimes two. No rhyme or reason. Sometimes stops half-way and comes back again.'

Ace frowned. 'I thought it just shuttled back and forth,' she said.

'No such luck,' Christine answered. 'It comes and goes when it wants to. The shift on Moloch tell us when it sets off from their terminal, and we just have to wait until it turns up at ours. If it does.'

'Sounds just like British Rail,' Ace muttered. 'You mean we could be waiting hours for it to trundle down the Bridge?'

'Not quite. Tiw here seems to have some sort of sixth sense when it's near.'

'I can hear wool growing on a sheep's back,' Heimdall said with a perfectly straight face. 'I can hear grass grow. The Lift – it comes now.'

'What's a sheep?' Christine asked.

'Extinct animal,' Heimdall replied. 'All died during Ozone Purge of twenty-one-oh-six.'

'If this lift's so unreliable, why not use Bishop's space-ship to get down to Moloch?' Ace asked. 'It's a neat little piece of kit. If Bishop won't pilot it for you, I will. I'm good with small ships like that.'

'We tried,' Christine said in a resigned tone. 'Piper worked out that it would save us hours each day if we could use the Adjudicator's ship as a shuttle, just whilst he was here. Miles asked him. "No problem," he said, "so long as you complete an *Increase in Crewing Levels of Spacefaring Vessels (Temporary) Form 3378b*." "Fine," said Miles, "where are the forms?" "Stored on the neural network in the ship," said the Adjudicator. "Can we come in and access one?" said Miles – '

'Don't tell me,' Ace interrupted. ' "Not without completing an *Increase in Crewing Levels of Spacefaring Vessels (Temporary) Form 3378b*." '

'How did you guess?'

'You've obviously never claimed Social Security,' Ace replied.

Heimdall looked up towards Moloch. 'It's here,' he said reverentially.

Ace followed his gaze. A translucent ring filled with glinting metallic highlights slid down the cord of the Bridge like a jellyfish sinking slowly into the depths of the sea. Beneath it the blister on top of the dome parted in welcome and sealed behind the device like some kind of airlock.

'Well,' she muttered, 'they say journeys end in lovers' meetings.'

Bernice was watching the Doctor arrange his collection of pins when they were summoned by Miles Engado. The diminutive Time Lord had them piled up in front of him on the refectory table and seemed to be sorting them by date, previous owner, length, material and sharpness. Around them the morning crowd ebbed and flowed as they collected freshly cooked food from Tanetoa, Project Eden's Samoan cook, or stasis-sealed items from one of the food dispensers. The smell of frying bacon and pimentos was making Bernice feel hungry, despite the remains of two breakfasts already stacked on the table before her.

'Do you think they'll notice if I go and get another breakfast?' she asked.

'No, but your metabolism would.'

'What's wrong with my body?' she asked defensively.

'Ah,' the Doctor replied. 'The answer to that particular question rests entirely upon a number of culturally dependent assumptions concerning the philosophy of aesthetics and its relationship to physiology.'

'Sorry?'

'Do you know, for instance, that the inhabitants of the planet Delphon regard the surgical removal of limbs to be highly sexually alluring?'

'Well,' said Bernice, 'that should raise a few eyebrows.' The Doctor wasn't listening.

'And that in the Axorc Sector it is considered to be the

101

height of good manners to serve yourself up for dinner on special occasions?'

'Does that mean you don't have to do the washing up?'

The Doctor was warming to his theme. 'And that the Rills of Galaxy Four have developed a political system in which the uglier they are the more power they are given?'

'Ah, the unacceptable face of politics.'

'And even your own culture fails to agree on what is and isn't attractive. Take the craze for duelling scars that ran through Imperial Germany some centuries ago.'

Bernice sighed. 'I guess it made them a cut above the rest.'

'Well, there you are.'

'I appreciate the sociology lesson, Doctor, but I'm still hungry.'

'You're always hungry.' He held up a filigree silver pin whose head was carved into the shape of a skull. 'Machiavelli or Medici?'

'Haven't a clue.'

'Medici, I think. You should take more exercise.'

'I went walking last night.'

'Or was it Lucretia Borgia? I know you went walking.'

'You've been spying on me!'

'The TARDIS was concerned.'

'What is she, my mother?'

'Only if you want her to be,' the Doctor replied enigmatically, and licked the end of the pin. 'Certainly not Borgia.'

'The Doctor to the Base Coordinator's office please. The Doctor to the Base Coordinator's office. Thank you.'

The disembodied voice echoing through the refectory was so bland that Bernice couldn't tell whether it was real or synthesized. Across the table, the Doctor sighed and swept the pins off the table and into a pocket.

'No peace for the wicked,' he said as he offered a gentlemanly arm to Bernice. 'Would madam care to accompany me?'

Adjudicator Bishop was sitting at Miles's desk when they

arrived. Miles was standing uncomfortably to one side. He looked tired and haggard, as if he hadn't slept very well.

'Doctor, come in,' Bishop said, beating Miles to the punch. Miles just stood there, his mouth half open.

Bishop frowned when Bernice followed the Doctor into the office.

'I don't recall inviting you, Krau Summerfield,' he said.

'You didn't,' she said coolly, and sat down.

The Doctor perched on a corner of the desk, positioning himself so that he could see Bernice and Miles but not Bishop.

'Well,' he said, smiling like a loon, 'no doubt you're wondering why I've called you all here.'

Whilst Bishop was searching for a rejoinder, Miles recovered the conversational initiative. 'There's been another death,' he said.

'I was expecting it,' the Doctor replied.

Bishop leant forward. 'What do you mean by that?'

'Deaths are like policemen: they always travel in pairs.'

'And there's never one around when you want one,' Bernice added. Bishop shot her a venomous glance.

'Who died?' she continued, unapologetically.

Miles sighed and passed a hand across his thinning hair.

'Moshe-Rabaan. She was the representative of the Energy Police on the base. She was also a *seyyed*, you know.'

'A what?' Bernice and Bishop chorused, and cast dark glances at one another.

'A descendant of the Prophet,' the Doctor said. 'Very important in the current Islam-dominated Earth Central hierarchy, I imagine.'

'Not a popular person here, by any means,' Miles continued. 'She put on airs. Oddly enough, we have few practising Muslims on the Project Eden team. She felt better than the rest of us.'

'Trau Bishop's not a very popular person,' Bernice said, nodding towards the Adjudicator, 'but that's not a good enough reason to bump *him* off.'

Before Bishop could interject, the Doctor spoke. 'I presume that Trau Engado is suggesting that Krau Moshe-Rabaan committed suicide.'

'Indeed,' Miles said. 'She left a note explaining everything. She killed my daughter . . . She admits that.' He paused for a moment, his face betraying the pain he still felt. 'She doesn't say why. She just says sorry.' He turned away and leant against the wall for support.

'Well,' Bernice drawled, slumping deeper in her chair, 'that's your job over with, Trau Bishop. Taking the murderer into custody shouldn't tax your skills too much, should it?'

'I don't think I – '

'Who found the body, Miles?' the Doctor interrupted softly.

Miles spoke without turning. 'Shmuel Zehavi. He came and told me a few hours ago. He sleepwalks, you see. Discovered her about five o'clock this morning. Funny thing is, he thinks nobody else knows about his somnambulism. He woke up in her room. Terrible shock for the man. All that blood. Terrible . . .'

He trailed off into silence.

The Doctor rubbed his chin thoughtfully.

'How was it done?' Bernice asked.

'Vibroknife,' Bishop snapped without looking at her. 'A very precise incision.'

'Would she have had that sort of medical knowledge?' Bernice pressed.

It was Miles who answered. 'We all would. Earth Central couldn't afford to send a qualified medic out here with us; the company rates are far too expensive. We all took hypnocourses in basic medicine and anatomy. Even the courses ate up a significant fraction of our budget, but the health and safety regulations demanded it.'

'I believe that to be irrelevant,' Bishop interjected. 'The knife made a very thorough job of her heart. Any ribs which got in the way would have been purely incidental.'

'I take it,' the Doctor said softly, not looking at anybody in particular, 'that your little security drones were elsewhere when it happened.'

A heavy silence followed his words, broken by a slight vibration that made the items on Miles's desk tremble.

'What was that?' the Doctor said, perking up.

'Something being dropped?' Bernice suggested.

'Hmmm . . .'

'I still can't quite believe it,' Miles sighed. 'I know Federique had problems fitting in, that's inevitable with the Energy Police, but this – '

'I only met her once,' Bernice mused, 'when she told me to turn the volume down on a simularity in my room to conserve power, but I didn't get any impression of weakness. Quite the reverse, in fact. She seemed to enjoy being able to tell people what to do. I think it was the way she walked, more than anything. She swaggered. People who swagger don't kill themselves. Other people, perhaps, but not themselves.'

'I have to rule this all as hearsay and speculation,' Bishop said, standing up. 'I have what amounts to a signed confession. Despite your doubts, I see no reason to delay my return to the Guild outstation on Earth.'

'You don't?' the Doctor said, gazing up at the ceiling. 'How interesting.'

'You wish to draw something to my attention, Doctor?'

'What could *I* know?'

'Then I shall prepare to – ' He broke off and sneezed suddenly. 'Leave,' he added, his eyes watering.

'Except . . .' The Doctor trailed off. Everybody in the room hung expectantly on his pause.

'What is it?' Bishop snapped finally.

'No, it's such a small matter. Forget I said anything.'

'Tell me.'

The Doctor pursed his lips and shook his head. 'I wouldn't want to bother you with such a minor point.'

'*Tell me!*'

'It's the hand,' the Doctor said, in a voice that had just a fraction too much self-effacement in it to be wholly convincing.

'What hand?'

'Krau Rabaan's hand.'

'Which one?' Bishop was getting increasingly angry.

'Her left one.'

'What was wrong with her left hand?'

'Nothing.'

'Then what are you babbling about?' Bishop shouted.

'She was holding the vibroknife in her left hand.'

'What of it?'

'Krau Rabaan was a Muslim, wasn't she?'

'I repeat: what of it?'

The Doctor whirled round. His face was set hard, his voice had taken on an accusatory tone. 'In the Muslim faith, the left hand is seen as unclean. Muslims will not use their left hand for cooking, for greeting people, for eating . . .'

'Yes?'

'Or for holding cutlery in.'

Bishop was silent. Bernice could almost see the wheels turning in his head.

'People do strange things in desperation,' he said finally. 'Even hold knives in the wrong hand.'

'But religion is the last thing to go,' the Doctor said. 'It's the final crutch. Krau Rabaan would not, could not go to Allah having profaned herself.'

Bishop swung round, his robes billowing. His hand beat out a rapid tattoo on Miles Engado's desk as he stared at the wall.

Eventually he turned back to the Doctor. 'It looks as if I may have to stay longer than I had planned,' he said. 'The possibility has to be acknowledged that Krau Rabaan was murdered and the murder made to look like suicide to divert suspicion from somebody else. I shall be informing Earth Central of my findings via message drone, Trau Engado. In the meantime, I shall want to talk again to Rabbi Zehavi, the man who found the body. That will be all, gentlemen.' He turned to where Bernice was slumped in the chair. 'And lady.'

As the Doctor passed Bernice, his hand snaked out and

grabbed her shoulder. She found herself hauled from the chair.

'Time to leave,' he murmured into her ear.

They had almost made it out of the door when Bishop said, 'Oh, Doctor?'

The Doctor stopped. Bernice looked across at his face. He knew something. She could read very little of the Doctor's true feelings, despite the time they had been together, but she could read that, at least. Unfortunately, so could Bishop.

'How did you know that Federique Moshe-Rabaan was holding the vibroknife in her left hand?'

The Doctor said nothing.

Bernice turned to look at Bishop. 'You told us,' she said calmly.

'No,' Bishop said. 'I did not.'

Bernice could see the Doctor's smile out of the corner of her eye. It gave her the strength to carry on. 'You did,' she said. 'And I don't see any of those little drones in here to prove otherwise.'

The Doctor dragged her out and slammed the door before Bishop could explode.

'I need to see Alex Bannen,' the Doctor said rapidly as he dragged Bernice along the corridor towards the Pit and the deadspaces. 'I'm worried about what he might do now that Rabaan is out of the way.'

'He's an intelligent man, isn't he?'

'More than I had given him credit for. And I made two serious mistakes because I underestimated him.'

Bernice positioned herself in the middle of the corridor and yanked on the Doctor's arm as he ran ahead. His feet flew out from underneath him and he dropped to the floor, his hat hanging in the air for a few seconds before falling to cover his face.

Bernice sat on his chest. 'I'm not letting you up until you tell me what's going on,' she shouted.

'Mmmph mrph hrrmph!' the Doctor said. Bernice removed his hat from his face and stood.

107

'Did you feel that tremor in Miles's office?' he rattled.

'Yes. I thought somebody had dropped something heavy.'

'I wish it was that simple. Bannen is meddling with the alien machinery. He has brains, but no patience. And I gave him some clues. That was my first mistake. I also made sure he had enough power to follow those clues up. That was my second mistake. I had hoped the influence of Moshe-Rabaan would hold him back from using that power, but now she's dead he has moved faster than I had anticipated.'

'But what's he doing?'

'He doesn't know, that's the problem,' the Doctor said, clambering to his feet. 'He's like a child in a motor car; he doesn't understand the difference between beeping the horn and starting the motor.'

'Oh great,' Bernice muttered. 'Sometimes I don't know which of you is worse.'

They ran off together towards the Pit.

There were three more tremors whilst they were on their way to the Mushroom Farm. The last was strong enough to make Bernice stumble and almost fall. By the time they arrived, alarms were going off all over Belial Base and the science personnel were running around chaotically.

Light blazed from the doorway, stabbing at her brain even through half-closed eyes. A deep drone made her head buzz and the ground vibrate beneath her feet.

Bannen was standing just inside the doorway, silhouetted against the light. The mushroom-shaped control consoles were blazing red and green. Arcs of light zapped from mushroom to mushroom. The concentration of ozone made Bernice's nose itch.

'Bannen,' the Doctor shouted, 'you must stop this madness! You don't know what you're doing!'

Bannen turned. His face was panic-stricken. 'I didn't think . . .' he screamed. 'I just . . . I thought I was just powering it all up! I didn't realize!'

'Turn it off, man!'

Bannen held out a file of blank paper. 'I can't!' His eyes filled with tears. 'Someone's stolen my notes!'

Something made Bernice turn around. Piper O'Rourke was standing in the doorway. The bright light had bleached her clothes, her skin, her hair, so that she was just a patch of brightness against the opening. 'The moons!' she screamed. 'Alex, the moons! You're moving them out of alignment. The Bridge is going to snap!'

Bernice turned back to the room.

'Oh Christ,' Bannen was crying. 'Oh my good Christ!'

The Doctor was looking at Piper. 'Ace was in the Lift?' he mouthed. Piper must have nodded, because the Doctor's face fell.

'Daddy?' said a voice behind Bannen. 'I'm scared.'

A small child stumbled out from behind the closest mushroom and held out its hand.

Bannen reached out to his son as madness engulfed them all.

PART THREE

MOLOCH

'And he dreamed, and behold a ladder set up on the earth, and the top of it reached to heaven: and behold the angels of God ascending and descending on it.'

Genesis, chapter 28, verse 12

Chapter Seven

Jesus Garcia de Soto y Delporto stared through the transparent Lift wall with a puzzled expression. His face clouded; first with alarm and then fear.

The stars were moving.

Even as he shouted for attention, Jesus had picked a target star and was tracking its apparent movement around the Lift. Within seconds, it was halfway between him and the place where the other five members of B Shift were grouped together, discussing procedure and checking through stacks of domestic stores for Moloch Base.

Jesus pushed himself off and floated rapidly around the Lift, bringing himself expertly to a stop less than a metre from the slight form of Christine LaFayette.

'Christine,' he said urgently, 'get everyone into their spacesuits.'

'What?'

'For God's sake, do it now! The Lift is spinning.'

'He's right, get moving!'

That was the newcomer. Ace? Was that her name? She seemed to have a sensible head on her shoulders. While the others stood and gawped, she had already pushed herself over to the storage lockers and was busy tossing the flimsy emergency spacesuits over. Jesus caught one and popped the seals.

'All right, move it!' Christine shouted. 'I don't know how strong the Bridge is, but it can't be designed to absorb this much stress.'

'How far have we turned?' Ace asked.

'Thirty degrees at a guess, but fast; my reference star

has already gone behind the filament engagement assembly.'

'The what?'

He pointed to the central area of the torus, where the otherwise transparent wall was a translucent pink. 'The area where the Bridge passes through the Lift.'

Over on one side, Lars Ulrich blinked his fashionably painted eyelids whilst he calculated moments of inertia and angular velocities on the wax tablet he always carried with him. 'Thirty degrees of rotation in – one minute, you say? Is angular velocity of . . .' The tall mathematician's thin face creased with surprise. 'Hell on ice, we should be flying through walls by now.'

'Suit up first. Talk later.' That was Ace again. She certainly didn't waste words. Even though she'd stopped to hand out the suits, she was still first into hers. 'Somebody check me.'

Jesus inspected her seals. 'Tight.'

Ace checked his in turn and then moved on to the other team members. 'Okay. Jesus, you'll do. Lars, fine. Christine, check your left elbow seal. Kosi, Yukio, you're both okay. Right everyone; latch your helmets back and don't switch to internal power until you have to. We're still spinning, but the integrity of the Lift seems to be intact for the moment. Jesus, how far round are we?'

'Coming up on one full revolution, Ace. No sign of slowing, either.'

'Right. You've got observation duty. Sing out every revolution. Yukio, alert Belial Base of our situation. Christine – how much do you know about the Bridge? Can you estimate how many turns it could take before it snaps?'

As Yukio Nakaguchi murmured in the background, Christine said, 'Ace, I'm sorry, I don't know. Tech studies aren't my speciality. I'm a psychologist.'

'Fine. Is there anyone here from Technical?'

Kosiana Kistasami nodded inside her suit. A fringe of hair plaited with tiny Belial clay beads bobbed gently in the reduced gravity, obscuring her dark skin and brooding eyes. 'The problem is, Ace, that nobody really knows. We've spent years examining the Bridge systems, but for all the good it's done us we might have been blowing bubbles. We do know the Bridge is made from an extruded monofilament of trisilicate which has been woven into a tube, but as to its strength – well, theoretically it shouldn't even exist. It should have collapsed under its own weight before it was even anchored.'

Ace frowned. 'So much for Technical.' She seemed to be lost in memories of her own for a moment.

'Second revolution starting now.'

The Lift shuddered.

'Helmets down.'

There were five clicks followed by the rising hum of internal systems powering up.

'Um . . . I think I may have a problem here,' Yukio said with a panicky laugh.

Jesus realized Yukio's problem straight away. Rebelling against the bland uniformity of the base, and to the amusement of many of his colleagues, Yukio had grown a bushy, spade-shaped beard in emulation of his cricketing hero, W. G. Grace. And he couldn't close his helmet over it.

Ace said without a pause, 'Christine, help Yukio get his helmet latched. Kosi, Lars, go round the Lift. Check the integrity. Take stress meters with you. Don't dawdle – but I want a thorough check.'

'Third revolution starting now,' Jesus chipped in as the technicians moved to obey Ace's instruction. He felt his heart thumping inside his chest. How could Ace stay so calm? As far as he knew, she had received no training for this type of situation. Nonetheless, she seemed to be coping with it the best of all of them.

Fria como aqua de nieve: as cold as ice-water.

'Any sign of slowing yet?'

'Sorry, no.' Jesus could hear faint noises through his spacesuit's external pickups. The structure of the Lift was creaking and the Bridge twanged like an overstretched wire.

'Ace! We have trouble now!' That was Lars, his accent thickening with the fear which now drove them all. Ace was already moving in his direction. Jesus blinked and recovered the target star. No – it was . . . Damn. Where the hell was it?

Lucifer's atmospheric corona was blotting out the stars again, and voices were babbling in his ears.

' – this is really embarrassing – '

' – just latch your helmet, Yukio. Everything'll be fine as long as you just – '

' – I'm getting a stress factor you wouldn't believe, here. The internal wall. The external wall. Everydamnwhere – '

' – you check again, is good idea. Perhaps the meters, they lose calibration – '

' – it's the damn *wall* we're losing – '

' – I want everyone in the centre of the chamber – '

' – fiddling with my helmet! I'm *sure* if I just – '

' – we're losing it, we're definitely – '

' – I *think* I've got it. I *think* I can – '

Jesus didn't have time to blink. The wall tore open, rips spreading around the torus as the air rushed outwards. Yukio gave a choking scream as the pressure within his suit forced his helmet back up over the latches. The scream didn't last long in the newly formed vacuum. Christine gave a yell of surprise as a spray of blood erupted from Yukio's eyes, ears and mouth. Crystallizing in the sudden deadly cold, it engulfed her helmet in a spray of pink ice. She staggered backwards, straight into the whipsawing edge of the monofilament shield, gasping with surprise and pain when the molecule-thin blade sliced through the toughened material of her spacesuit, neatly removing the arm she had automatically put out to protect herself. The arm drifted free, trailing ribbons of freezing blood and sinew.

The sudden vacuum pulled Jesus towards the ragged-edged hole and expelled him along with a mess of loose trash, a hailstorm of frozen blood and Christine's arm.

118

He was tumbling so fast that the stars became blurred circles of light around him.

A lump of frozen vapour and blood bumped momentarily against his visor before drifting off into the darkness. He recognized the spade-shaped mass of black hair projecting from the lump and began to scream.

'Jesus, shut up! I know you're drifting. You'll be okay. I need to think.'

'Christ, what about Yukio? And Christine . . . Her arm – '

'Forget about Yukio. And don't worry about Christine. Just get yourself under control and get back here now.'

Jesus took a deep breath. He felt like he was going to be sick. He chinned a switch and felt the autodoc press a needle pad against his neck. His stomach settled immediately. 'On my way.'

'Wicked. See you in a minute.'

Jesus chinned in the onboard systems. 'Spacesuit twelve: activate memory guidance. Return to source using minimum fuel trajectory.'

There was a momentary hesitation before the spacesuit confirmed his instruction. A gentle pressure in the small of his back told him that the thruster pack had fired. The stars began to slow from their wild dervish dance to a stately waltz. Then he was facing the Bridge.

'Ace, are you reading me?'

'Loud and clear. Turn your gain down a bit – or stop shouting.'

Jesus adjusted a control. 'I can see both ways along the Bridge.'

'What's the damage?'

'Difficult to tell. Both ends appear to be fixed, but it's vibrating like a violin string.'

'How bad?'

'Ace, I'm half a kilometre away. If I can see the movement, it's got to be bad, right?'

Ace swore.

'And that's not all,' he added. 'It looks from here like there are some frayed areas on the Bridge where fragments from the Lift sliced across it. They could rip at any time. The Bridge could unravel like an old pullover.'

Ace swore again. Jesus wondered where she'd learned words like that. 'Can you see the Lift?' she said eventually.

His gaze travelled along the length of the Bridge. The Lift was a small doughnut with the Bridge threading through the hole. A cloud of debris surrounded it. 'Looks okay. You're tilted slightly, and spinning, but you're still attached. How's everyone there? Is Christine – ?'

'No. The suit sealed off her arm. She lost a fair bit of blood, but the autodoc is medicating her now. If we're lucky, she'll make it.'

'Yukio wasn't lucky, was he?'

'Yukio was a bloody idiot.'

'Christ, what a mess. What do you think happened?'

'How the hell do I know? Now get a move on. We still don't know if it's over yet.'

'Right.' It would take several minutes at least to get back to the Bridge. With nothing to do in the meantime, Jesus tried to maintain a rational equilibrium by observing his surroundings. The observations might come in useful later. If there was a later.

Below the rotating Lift, the hot glare of Lucifer's atmosphere, backlit by the sun, formed a corona around the lower moon.

According to Tiw, the journey down to Moloch should have taken slightly less than two hours. During the course of that time, the light from Lucifer's atmosphere would have grown in strength until it blotted out the stars and enveloped both Bridge and Lift in a flaming glare. Then they would have entered the conical shadow cast by the moon, and the stars would have become visible again for a brief time before the Lift sank beneath the surface itself and came to a standstill, its massive kinetic energy somehow conducted away from the lower terminus and stored in a way that *hijo de la puta* Alex Bannen would have killed to learn.

120

A beep somewhere behind his head told Jesus that he was nearing the Bridge.

Twenty-five metres away, he disengaged the autoreturn sequence and navigated himself to a point level with the outside rim of the rotating Lift. The jagged hole through which he'd been propelled some minutes before now rushed past his face once every minute or so. The ragged edges of the hole glinted sharply, and Jesus knew that any failed attempt to enter the Lift would be likely to result in his being sliced to ribbons within a matter of seconds. He had neither the fuel nor the skill to match the rotational speed of the vehicle. Yet what other choices did he have?

He called Ace and explained the situation. 'I'm not a spaceman, Ace. Got any ideas?'

He could see a figure within the Lift detach itself from the group and glance quickly in his direction.

'Yeah. The Lift's wide, so the angular velocity is higher on the outside. Jet up over the top and attach your safety line to the Bridge, then abseil across the top of the Lift when you've matched spin. When you get to the hole, we'll grab you and haul you in.'

'Won't work, Ace. The Bridge is smooth, nothing to attach to. And it's too wide to loop the line around; I won't have enough slack left to lower myself to the hole.' Jesus sucked in a deep breath. 'There's only one thing for it. I'm just going to have to try a perpendicular approach and hope I can time my arrival to a point when the hole is passing in front of me.'

A new voice said, 'You could try an approach tangential to the curve of the Lift. That way it might be easier to match relative velocities for a few seconds. Thing is, if you miss . . .'

'I risk drifting off into space. Thanks Kosi. I'll stick with the perpendicular approach.'

Ace spoke again. 'All right. Give us a moment to clear a space for you and then pick your own time. We'll keep our fingers crossed.'

'Thanks.'

'See you in a minute.'

I hope so.

Jesus quickly gave the suit what he hoped were precise instructions, waiting until he was sure of the hole's period of rotation before whispering, 'Activate command sequence . . . Now.'

There was a familiar pressure on his back. The Lift began to speed towards him until he was only twenty metres away.

Fifteen.

The hole vanished around the arc of the vehicle.

Ten metres. Five.

The wall was rushing by in front of him now, glassy and smooth, offering no grip should he miss his intended target.

Four metres.

The hole was nowhere in – wait a minute! There it was!

Jesus grimaced. The hole was moving too slowly. He wasn't going to make it.

Three metres.

Two metres.

'Sorry Ace. I don't think I'm going to . . .'

There was a sudden bang as he crashed against the Lift, and a scraping sensation as he began to roll along the surface. Billowing sheets of material ballooned out to meet him: the edges of the hole, deceptively soft looking but with lethal edges. The Lift spun beneath him like a sickening carousel ride. The red glare from Lucifer seemed to engulf him, and the combined effects of yaw and pitch on his inner ear overcame the antinausea medication.

When he had finished vomiting, Jesus realized there was a firm pressure on his arms and legs. Ace, Kosi and Lars were holding him down.

'I reckon we can let him go now. How do you feel?' Ace asked.

'Embarrassed. And sticky.'

Lars and Kosi laughed. Ace did not.

Jesus sat up. The interior of the Lift, even in this

wrecked condition, had never looked so good. 'Thought I was a goner. How'd I get in here?'

Lars pointed down at Jesus's legs. He followed the mathematician's gesture and saw that his legs were completely tangled in a flapping web of cloth.

'Ace, she breaks open one of the store's canisters. It is full of bedsheets, yes? She makes net, reels you in like big fish.' He glanced sideways at Ace. 'That is right? You say fish, yes?'

Jesus shook his head in amazement. 'But what about the monofilament I saw? Surely it would have torn the sheets to pieces, synthetic or otherwise?'

'Naw. Kosi here showed us how to grab the edges of the hole with equipment clamps and fold them so the material wasn't dangerous. What you saw wasn't the monofilament, it was the sheets.'

Jesus smiled gratefully. 'You managed to organize all this in the few minutes I was out there? I'm impressed.'

'Minutes?' Ace laughed outright. 'You were out there over an hour, mate. We thought you'd got bored with our company.'

Jesus shook his head tiredly.

As the others began to discuss survival options, Jesus found his mind drifting. Adrenalin withdrawal made him introspective and sleepy. He turned over and tried to relax, but found himself looking downward through the metal grille which the Eden team had welded across the curved Lift surfaces as a floor, wondering what kind of anatomy would have been suited to use the original surface. It was crazy. There were no constants. Or rather, the only constant was . . . well, *change*. Jesus shook his head. The aliens, whoever they'd been, were dead and gone, a million years or more. They were history, and he doubted he would ever truly know them. The thought saddened him. They must have been such wonderful beings, and now even the legacy of their environment was being rewritten by the humans, changed with every curved floor covered by a flat grille, every piece of art ripped from the walls and studied out of context, every subtle nuance of space filled with metal and plastic, neural net cabinets, stores, machinery, even people.

Jesus felt a gentle sense of irony steal over him. They'd come here to learn, but it seemed all they would ever learn was how to alter that which they had no possibility of understanding into something so familiar there was no point in their understanding it.

A familiar voice came over the suit's comm-system. 'Feel cold. Arm hurts.'

Ace said, 'I know, Christine.' She switched channels and continued, 'Lars, could you administer another tranquillizer for me?'

'No problem.' The mathematician propelled himself towards the prone figure some yards away.

Ace turned her attention to Jesus. 'I've tried to communicate with Belial Base. I don't know whether they're receiving or not, but I'm getting nothing back. We're on our own. Both Kosi and Lars figure that we're a lot closer to Moloch than to Belial, but we're going to have to get there under our own steam. You're the environment specialist. I need an idea from you. One that'll save our lives. You up for it, or what?'

Jesus began to untangle his legs. His mind was whirling. Ace was right. They had to do something, but what? If they stayed where they were they were dead for certain. Before he could reply, Lars called for attention and he followed Ace and Kosi across to Christine's recumbent body. Lars was kneeling beside her, cradling the psychologist's truncated left arm in his suit gauntlets. He lifted up his hand. Tiny ruby globules were frozen to it.

Blood.

'Her suit integrity is breached, Ace. A slow leak, but the pressure, it drops. She could lose the rest of her arm.'

'I told her to check that seal.' Ace sounded furious.

'You also told her to help Yukio, if I recall.'

Ace nodded guiltily. 'Kosi, you're right. It's my fault. I should have checked her suit again. Damn!' She thought for a moment. 'See if you can patch it, Lars.' Ace turned to Jesus. 'Got anything for me yet?'

'I've got one idea, but you're not going to like it.'

Inside her helmet, Ace's head tilted curiously.

'We go down the inside of the Bridge,' he continued.

'You're right, I don't like it. How do we get in?'

'The Bridge is woven from a monofilament thread. All we have to do is force the weave apart.'

'And how do we get out when we reach Moloch?'

Jesus shrugged. 'I've no idea.'

Ace considered. 'It's got to be better than trying to abseil down the outside. Okay. We'll go for it. Let's see if we can widen the hole enough to get Christine through.'

It took thirty minutes for them to locate a frayed section of the Bridge; force its weave apart with clamps and keep the gap open with plastic crates. The Lift continued to oscillate as it rotated, swaying with the movement of the Bridge. Jesus stared around the chamber. Building up to the big one, he thought. He was developing a peculiar feeling in the pit of his stomach; a feeling beyond sickness, beyond shock. Ace would have known the feeling. It was called determination.

When the hole was big enough, Jesus stepped through and switched on his spacesuit lights. The interior space was about three metres across, a pastel yellow in colour, tubular and bulked out with strange-looking machinery which was attached to the crosshatched 'walls'. Jesus shone his light 'down' the shaft, thankful, for once, for the lack of gravity.

His light glinted on a surface that swayed and twisted sickeningly into the distance. It was like looking down the eye of a hurricane.

'How's it look?'

'Like something out of *The Wizard of Oz*.'

'What?'

'I said – '

There was a particularly violent jolt. More pieces of the machinery began to break away to join the expanding cloud of trash already in evidence inside the Bridge. A chunk of blood drifted in front of his visor. He batted it

125

away impatiently, not even pausing to consider how quickly he'd adjusted to Yukio's death.

'I said it's looking better every minute.'

'I hope you're right.'

Lars and Kosi carefully manoeuvred Christine through the gap.

Ace followed them in. 'Don't suppose you ever heard a story called *Jack and the Beanstalk*?'

'This would be soyabeans, yes?'

Ace sighed. 'Forget it.'

In complete silence, the interior of the Bridge began to rock again. He gripped the side of a curved triangular plate which was fitted to the wall, and began to manoeuvre himself further into the shaft. One corner came loose in his hands.

'Don't rush me. I think I can see electrical equipment in here, bigger than anything I've ever seen before. We're going to have to be careful.'

'We haven't got time to be careful.' Ace squeezed past Kosi and Lars. 'Give Christine to me and follow me down.' Ace took the psychologist from her two bearers and clamped her suit arms to the unconscious woman's shoulders. Then she took a quick sighting down the shaft and launched herself into space. Her lights dwindled rapidly in the distance.

'Ace, be careful!' he said.

Was there a measure of excitement in her reply? 'Careful or dead, at least it's my choice!'

Kosi and Lars exchanged brief looks and then launched themselves after the girl.

Jesus shrugged. It was one way of getting down, he supposed. He was about to push off when the Bridge rocked again; a much stronger oscillation this time. He thrust his helmet back through the gap one last time. The Lift was finally coming apart in curlicues of alien material and clouds of human-made debris. There would be a brief but spectacular meteor shower in Lucifer's upper atmosphere tonight, he thought, wondering if those on

Belial would watch and think of them, as he had thought of Paula Engado when she'd become a shooting star.

As the walls of the Bridge rippled, he pulled himself back inside. 'Instruction,' he said to the suitbrain, 'forward thrust full.'

The head-up display died.

'Instruction – ' he said again, but it was too late.

The walls closed on him like a vice.

Jesus screamed with pain and surprise. His limbs bent and snapped, his helmet cracked open and there was a stinging pain in his eyes. He tried to close them but the eyelids were frozen in place, unable to move.

They were still open when he died.

Chapter Eight

Alex Bannen was crying.

Piper had never seen him look so vulnerable. His cheeks glistened with tears and his hand hovered over the head of the thing he had called his son.

Behind him the Mushroom Farm was ablaze. Great arcs of energy flashed from cap to cap whilst thunderclaps pumped air through the forest of glittering stems. A haze of water vapour hung overhead and dripped from the underside of the mushrooms, making the ground slippery and treacherous to walk on. Piper had to fight to maintain her balance as the chamber shook.

The Doctor and Bernice were stumbling between the mushrooms of twisted metal, with the Doctor talking nineteen to the dozen and gesturing wildly with his still furled umbrella. Piper managed to catch Bernice's eye, but the archaeologist only shrugged helplessly. Piper turned to where Bannen was clutching the slender trunk of a tall mushroom to keep his balance. The wind whipped droplets of condensation into his face, where they mingled with his tears.

Bloody idiot, she thought savagely. What the hell did he think he was doing?

'Come on, Alex. Stop messing with things you don't understand. Leave that to the Doctor before you screw things up even . . .' Her voice trailed off as she noticed the boy watching her with grey, expressionless eyes. Bannen's son? Perhaps, but it hadn't taken her long to work out what the boy really was.

'It wasn't meant to be like this.' Bannen's face was slack.

'Yeah, well, that's as may be,' she said, unsure how to treat this new, defenceless Bannen. 'Come on, let's go.'

There was a slight cough beside them. Piper turned, and found the Doctor standing at her shoulder. She hadn't heard him approach. From the expression on Bannen's face, neither had he.

The Doctor began to speak, in a voice so quiet Piper wondered how she could hear his words above the storm. 'A great many years from now, in another universe, a man in a mirror told me to do nothing. "It is done," he said.'

Piper suddenly had the crazy idea that all the Doctor's masks had been stripped away, leaving him with no more armour than the truth. She shivered.

'It's very hard for me to do nothing,' he added softly. 'I – rebel against it. But there are times when nothing is simply the best thing to do.'

'What does he mean, Dad?'

Bannen didn't seem to hear the voice of his 'son'.

The Doctor glanced at the simularity. He crouched down so that his head was level with the boy's face, and smiled reassuringly. He seemed to have no trouble in accepting the presence of the child.

'My friend Bernice and I have been trying to work out how to stabilize the moons,' he said. 'This room is obviously the key element in an important system of controls. The controls were disturbed, and now we have to put them right.'

'Or your other friends will die.'

The Doctor nodded solemnly.

The boy turned to his 'father'. 'Dad. Dad!'

Bannen did not respond.

Piper scowled. 'It's useless. If Christine had used her eyes and spotted Bannen's instability she could've prevented all this. He's good for nothing but trouble now.' She looked at the Doctor, but he appeared not to be listening.

'Perhaps nothing is all we need from him, or from anyone,' he said at last, and smiled triumphantly.

'Do what?' Piper said.

'Feedback! The ability of a system to monitor its output and correct for mistakes. That's what I'm waiting for.'

'You think,' said a hesitant voice, 'that everything might be all right?'

The Doctor turned to where Alex Bannen was crouching and looking over at them.

'No,' he said sternly. 'Entropy demands that everything will *not* be all right, but sometimes we can rage against the dying of the light.'

A sudden, eerie flash illuminated the cavern. The pillar that marked where the Pit passed through the Farm had begun to glow. Bands of yellow light rose and fell across its surface; diaphanous spokes rotating about rose-hued hubs intermeshed with each other, beautiful reflections of a deeper order within.

A deep chime filled the chamber with rolling echoes.

' "It is done," ' the Doctor whispered.

Piper drew in a relieved breath as the wind fell.

The deep rumbling beneath their feet abruptly stopped, and the electrical discharges faded away. The blanket of fog above their heads began to disperse, sparkling the mushroom-shaped domes with soft diamonds of moisture.

In the upper part of the chamber, a rainbow glimmered.

From Bishop's ship, moored close to the Bridge, the scale of the disaster was apparent.

The Adjudicator had discarded his heavy black robes and ridiculous collar, and was slumped in his padded control seat wearing just boxer shorts, socks and electro-static sock-suspenders. His feet were resting comfortably on the ship's control panel. As he watched the events occurring between the two moons, he blew on a plastic beaker of fragrant Arcturan tea.

Ripples were travelling up and down the Bridge, but the anchors remained firm. The amplitude of the vibration even seemed to be reducing slightly, although the movement was still sickeningly massive. Staring for too long at the simularity made him feel dizzy.

He tried a sip of tea and winced as the hot liquid scalded his tongue.

Somewhere up there the Lift was disintegrating. Bishop was glad it was too small to see: it made suppressing the imagined screams of the people inside that much easier.

The ship's neural net interrupted his second sip of tea. 'You have a call, Trau Bishop.'

Muttering darkly beneath his breath, Bishop set down the beaker and dived for his robes. He wondered who was calling – Miles, perhaps, or that little clown the Doctor. They had already tried to get him to mount a rescue mission using his ship. He had explained that the amount of paperwork involved made it impracticable, but he was sure they hadn't believed him.

When the picture of the Bridge disintegrated to reveal the stern visage of Bronwen ap Bryn, Adjudicator in Extremis, he was shocked. The last he had heard she had returned to Ponten VI – the planet which had been ceded to the Guild of Adjudicators in perpetuity by a wary but appreciative Earth Central – but that was too far away for anything but the so-called pigeon post; recorded messages dumped into a hyperdrone and aimed at the recipient's projected location. If Bryn was calling 'live', she had to be nearby. Even so, the tachyon signal was so faint that the neural net was having problems extrapolating a recognizable picture. The face of the Adjudicator in Extremis seemed to be composed of flat green slabs. Fuzzy highlights delineated her features and her mouth lagged behind her words. Superimposed upon her face, flickering digits recorded the cost of the call. Typically, that part of the transmission seemed unaffected by the disruption.

Bryn's mouth worked silently. More than a second out of synch, a blast of static shot through the protesting audio system. Bishop winced.

'Your pardon, Extremis. I was not expecting a personal visit.'

'I'll not . . . sagree w . . . at. I was in . . . vicinity on . . . cial business and . . . Your repor . . . o far is . . . nconclusive.'

131

'There have been some – some additional problems.'

A flexing of the green planes making up Bryn's face could have been interpreted as a smile. Or a frown. With her, the two were practically interchangeable.

'Problems are your job, Adjudicator.'

Funny how the software let that one through unaffected.

'Flattered as I am by your confidence, Extremis, I'm afraid the situation is getting complicated.'

The green slab representing Bryn's left eyebrow slipped upwards questioningly. Or perhaps it was a system glitch. Bishop hesitated before going on. 'There has been another death – an apparent suicide – and indications of sabotage on a grand scale. Additionally, there are discrepancies in the Base personnel records, involving three extra people.'

'. . . tra *peop* . . .'

Bishop took a deep breath. 'I feel that the proceedings here may escalate seriously if a careful check is not kept on the situation. For this reason, I would like to request the presence of another Adjudicator.'

Bryn's mouth worked silently for a few seconds.

'. . . te out of . . . e questio . . . m afraid.'

'But why?'

'You a . . . ware of . . . e galact . . . ituation?'

'The planetary attacks? I thought they were isolated incidents.'

Perhaps through some fluke in the software, perhaps because of some local fluctuation in signal strength, the face of the Adjudicator in Extremis suddenly ballooned out to its full, impressive girth. Her voice regained its usual baritone boom. 'We have lost fifteen colony worlds in three weeks, Adjudicator. Azure, Qartopholos, Sifranos – ecologies devastated, entire populations wiped out – and we have absolutely no idea who's responsible! The Interstellar Taskforce is on continual stand-by alert. I am on a,' her pause was not due to a transmission fault, 'fact-finding tour of the outlying regions, and took the opportunity to contact you directly. All currently unassigned Adjudicators are working full-time following up leads, but frankly, the Guild does not look even remotely good. Besides,' her pudgy eyes suddenly narrowed and she ran a hand across her tattooed scalp, 'there are moves afoot which I am not at liberty to discuss. You may be receiving help soon from an unexpected source.'

'But Extremis, if you would only see the logic – '

'Adjudicator Bishop, I need hardly remind you that so far your case list borders upon the ludicrous: one accident, possibly murder; one suicide, possibly murder; one disaster, possibly mass murder. No evidence and a baseful of suspects. This is how careers end, Adjudicator: not with a bang, but with a whimper.'

'But – '

Bryn's face bulged and seethed in unlikely places as the signal began to corrupt again. Her eyes flickered sideways to read the digital cost display '. . . m afraid your budget . . . an no longer . . . ustain the price of . . . is transmission,' the Extremis said. '. . . uggest you . . . eep a tight watch on furth . . . penditure.' The picture flickered back into sync one more time before fading. 'I also recommend you wear your robes the right way round, Adjudicator; it's so much better for public relations.'

The transmission faded and he frowned, casting his mind back over the conversation.

How did she know that people had died on the Bridge? he wondered. All I did was mention sabotage.

As if he didn't have enough to worry about.

He sighed in frustration and reached for his tea.

It was cold.

It was cold in the crew room on Moloch Base.

Jesus Delporto's dying scream had followed Ace all the way to the lower moon, down the violently oscillating length of the Bridge, past bizarre machinery which seethed with naked power, and through the gap she had torched in the base of the column; it followed her as eager hands pulled her from the writhing Bridge, stripped away her suit and placed her with the others in the medical

133

unit; followed her into sleep, forced a path into her dreams, drove her screaming and unrested into wakefulness.

One more failure on her part; one more life lost; one more friend pulled away by the black tide. She tried to use Spacefleet hypno-techniques to block the remorse, but either they weren't that good or she hadn't learned them well enough.

Ace glared at her face in the mirror. She poked a finger into the luggage beneath her eyes, stretching the skin, trying to make it look young again. All her life she'd striven to be older, more mature, to experience more of what the universe had to offer. Now, here she was, with her life's dream in the palm of her hand, trying to turn back the clock. She shook her head as a short, unexpectedly bitter laugh bubbled up from her chest.

She stifled the sound as the crew room door opened and Kosi walked in. Her hand hesitated by Ace's shoulder. Ace was thankful the touch was not completed. She felt vulnerable enough already.

'Come back to the operations room, Ace. Get your mind off it, all right?'

'Yeah, right.' Ace followed Kosi from the room. 'Ta.'

The Ops Room on the lower moon was a twin to Belial's; a spacious, split-level hemisphere with a profusion of glimmering instrumentation, manned by serious-looking technicians, surrounding the towering bulk of a MultiCray Neural Net. Floor to ceiling simularity windows displayed the incredible landscape beyond the base, giving Ace the impression that the Operations Room was actually outdoors. Only the absence of wind marred the illusion.

She exchanged a few words with the shift supervisor, a dour Scot named Rachel McBride, and was told a message had been sent to Belial confirming their arrival and condition. Ace thanked the woman and then moved restlessly across to the windows, drawn by the view.

Whereas Belial Base had been built on the outer surface of a solid moon, Moloch Base was inside a hollow one; a miracle of planetary engineering which, after five years, still had Bannen and his team groping in the dark for answers to questions they didn't even know how to formulate. The ground of this bizarre world rose gradually in all directions, curving overhead until it was lost above the clouds. Vegetation ran riot. Duty teams maintained a neat lawn surrounding the base but, beyond the perimeter, a lush pink jungle rose in fantastic profusion towards the flat glare of a pale, artificial 'sun' whose energy was provided by the same mysterious means as powered the Bridge and the Lift. Translucent shapes undulated through the jungle, glimmering in the sunlight: the only life the Lucifer System had so far offered up for study. Ace felt her pulse racing at the sight. She grinned: all the shit in the world could not blow away the simple wonder of this pastoral scene.

'Horrible, isn't it?' Kosi had moved up beside her after checking in with the duty manager. 'All that space.'

Ace turned in surprise. 'You're not agoraphobic are you?'

'So what if I am?' Kosi replied a little defensively. 'All that open ground. No factories. No living towers. And those horrible white things floating up there, just waiting to fall down and smother us. Ugh!' Kosi shivered, seemingly unable to understand why Ace giggled softly.

'I can't understand you people,' Ace confided. 'All this space-cadet, sense-of-wonder stuff, and you're happier with four blank walls around you.'

'You forget,' said a voice behind her. 'We have been here for five years. Our sense of wonder has passed. Our sense of boredom has set in – with a vengeance.'

Lars Ulrich smiled as Ace turned, and continued, 'Christine will be fine. Minus an arm, but fine. There is no infection. Space, it may be cold, but it is clean, at least.'

It's not space you've got to worry about, Ace thought, it's the people in it. She said nothing, but instead left the two young people by the window and moved back to the duty manager's desk.

'I just wanted to say thanks for pulling us out of there.'

'No problem.' Rachel McBride smiled. 'Alex Bannen would've had a screaming fit if we'd left you to mess up his precious Bridge; God alone knows what Tiw would've done.'

'Given you a lecture on the sound of one hand clapping, I expect.'

'Aye – clapping against the side of my head, I've no doubt!' Both women laughed. McBride had a pretty laugh, Ace noticed. A laugh it felt good to join in with. 'Have they told you what goes on down here, then?'

Ace shook her head. 'Nope.'

McBride shrugged. 'There's the brass for you.' She called to a white-haired technician, 'Chas, do us a favour will you? Keep an eye on this lot and shout if anything weird pops up.' She turned back to Ace. 'Come on then. I'll give you the tour.'

'Oh,' she said, as she led the way from the room, 'I've been meaning to ask you. What happened to Sam Russell? He was supposed to be down here on the second part of a double shift. When he didn't turn up, I assumed he'd overslept, but when he didn't radio through to apologize . . .'

Kosi and Lars turned from the window to watch Ace and McBride leave the Operations Room.

'What do you reckon, then?'

'Ace? She's fine, I reckon.'

'That's not what I meant.'

'You ask odd question. Ace, she saves Christine's life. Would have saved Yukio and Jesus too if not for bad luck.'

'Yeah, I know. But she makes me uneasy. She always looks . . . I dunno, ready for a fight.'

Lars tapped his fingers reflexively against his wax tablet, a sure sign he was thinking carefully about what Kosi had said. 'I think you make big refinery out of small process. Ace, she's fine. Fine person.'

'Then how come when we pulled her from her suit I

found a folder full of Alex Bannen's notes stashed away inside the sleeve?'

The Atmospheric Vehicle Research Laboratory was a large, irregular enclosure filled with machinery of human design. In the centre of the room a large, asymmetric pod was suspended over an engineering pit. The pod was four metres in height, with a single hatch and an exoskeleton which supported various instrument modules and waldo limbs.

Ace touched the gleaming metal sides of the starpod. White alloy, highly polished, threw back the glare of multiple floodlights into her narrowed eyes.

'So this was what Paula was working on. An excursion module.'

McBride nodded. 'The girl was positive she could contact the Angels if only she could get deep enough into Lucifer's atmosphere. The ordinary starsuits are pretty handy bits of gear, especially compared with the emergency spacesuits you used in the Lift, but the pod was designed to go deeper still. Thousands of kilometres, in fact. God only knows why she didn't wait until it was ready, rather than rely on a starsuit.'

Ace ran a finger lightly across the saddle for the instrument packs. 'Thousands? Just how deep is the atmosphere, anyway?'

McBride shrugged. She walked across the semicircular pod bay towards the monitor station, sealed behind a transparent partition. 'Actually, it's difficult to say. Deep down the heat and pressure are so great that even hydrogen is a metallic liquid.'

Ace followed McBride into the monitor station. 'So it's hard to tell where the atmosphere ends and the planet itself begins.'

McBride nodded. 'Hence the size of the instrument array. There's an ocean of liquid zelanite alloy down there, you know, floating in the sky: big as a normal planet.' McBride shook her head. 'The damn thing's a bag of mysteries and no mistake.'

137

Ace skipped her fingers lightly across the tops of the consoles. She could see from the screen displays how the systems were designed to function. 'Nice system. Did Paula design it herself?'

'She specified the high-level design. Yukio wrote the software.'

'And now he's dead.' Ace frowned. 'Just like Paula.'

'You have a theory?'

'Naw, not really. It's just – well, it's just that if whatever killed Paula was a software virus rather than an accident, then someone would have had to infect the suitbrain. That would implicate one of the system engineers – someone like Yukio. The incident on the Bridge might have been a clumsy attempt by a third party to bump off the middle man.'

'Unless the same virus which attacked Paula's starsuit attacked Belial's neural net as well.'

'You're forgetting – the Bridge functions are not controlled by human technology. The original, alien system, whatever that might be, is still running them.'

McBride huffed softly in acquiescence. 'Ever thought about becoming an Adjudicator?'

Ace grinned. 'I'd look like the flying nun.' She studied the rest of the monitor station. The back wall was lined with storage cabinets. 'What's in there?' she asked.

'Paula's research files. Simularities, mainly. Oh, and her diary as well. Why, do you want to take a look?'

'Do I ever.' Ace opened the first cabinet, scanned the hundred or so labels quickly, selected the most recent crystal and fed it into a reader. She blinked her contact lenses into place and began to watch the file.

'I think you might want to check this out,' Chas said.

Kosi left her plastic beaker of tea steaming gently on the nearest flat surface while she and Lars headed for the centre of the room. The elderly Chas Varley was peering in some confusion at an arc of screens which pulsed with read-outs and rippling waveforms. 'What's up?' she asked.

'You tell me, lass.' Chas fine-tuned a few controls. 'I've never seen anything remotely like it.'

'Is software virus, maybe?' Lars asked.

'Yeah,' Kosi said, 'there seems to be a lot of it going around.'

Chas shook his head. 'No, look. It's a steady pattern. Not one of Lucifer's though.'

Kosi thought for a moment. 'Could it be the Angels, trying to talk to us at last?'

Before Chas could reply, Ace burst in from the main access corridor. McBride followed more slowly, wearing a worried frown.

'Oh, Rachel, I was just about to call you,' Chas said. 'The fifty-metre array is picking up an odd waveform. I've run a library comparison but none of the eigenvalues match with anything we've seen before. Do you recognize it?'

Before Rachel could reply, Ace walked quickly past them to the communications terminal. 'I have to talk to the Doctor,' she snapped angrily.

On Belial Base, Bernice and Cheryl walked back into the Operations Room, and into the middle of a furious argument.

At Miles's request, the two women had taken Alex Bannen and his son back to his quarters. He had curled up on to his bed at the first opportunity and fallen fast asleep. His son had just stood there, staring at them, until they left. They had returned to the Operations Room, where Bernice was surprised to hear Ace's voice – as far as anyone knew she was recovering with the rest of her party on Moloch – and even more surprised to hear it raised in anger and directed at – of all people – the Doctor.

'You didn't have to lie to me, Professor.'

'Ace, I don't understand – '

'Oh shut up! You make me sick. You understand everything. And you use everyone, for whatever little scheme

139

takes your fancy. Remember Jan, do you, back on Heaven? Remember what you did to him?'

'But that was different – '

'What about this, then, eh?' Ace tried to thrust a ghostly neural net crystal underneath the Doctor's nose and only succeeded in pushing it out of the image field. 'Don't try to deny it. I don't know why you didn't erase it after her death. Never had a chance, I suppose. But you didn't expect me to go rummaging around in Paula's diary, did you?'

'Ace, if you'd only let me explain! I thought we were friends – '

'Some friends you grow out of, *Doctor*.'

A sudden bang and a gabble of panicky voices distracted Ace's attention. She looked sideways. There were a few more garbled words, part of an argument, then a loud noise and a scream.

Something sprayed across Ace's face.

'What the hell – ' she said, disbelievingly.

She tried to blink the red mist from her eyes, failed, and toppled backwards out of the image field.

Static.

Bernice gaped.

The Operations Room was engulfed by sudden chaos. Miles was mumbling to himself. Technicians were frantically operating systems. Piper was yelling, 'I couldn't give a toss for the time-lag on the frequency search-and-lock processor, just re-establish the bloody link! Cheryl, help him will you. Or take over, I don't care which.' She turned to the shivering Administrator. 'Miles, your daughter's spirit is not walking the base, and none of us are going with her to the afterlife. Now for God's sake pull yourself together. We need you here.'

Miles blinked. 'Of course. Sorry.'

'I should think so too.'

Only the Doctor had not moved, through all this confusion.

Cheryl said, 'I have a transmission.'

'From Moloch?'

'No. From Adjudicator Bishop's spaceship.'

'Get rid of him.'

'Sorry; he's on priority override.'

Piper threw up her hands. 'Put him on then.'

A representation of the Adjudicator blinked into life on one side of the room. 'I've been monitoring the transmission from Moloch.'

'Ace is in trouble,' the Doctor said. 'I have to go down there.'

'We'll go together, Doctor. I think the case may be breaking at last.'

'I'm coming too,' a voice piped beside Bernice. It was Cheryl. 'Sam's down there.'

The Adjudicator's image hesitated momentarily, then nodded. 'Very well. Trau Engado, I will be requiring your presence as well. We leave immediately.'

Bernice sealed her starsuit helmet and stepped from the Adjudicator's spaceship on to Moloch's Bridge terminal. She found herself standing on top of a translucent bubble set in Moloch's ice-bound landscape, close to one side of a bowl-shaped depression some fifty metres across. High above them, the base of the Bridge passed through a cone of semi-transparent cables, which were anchored all around the edge of the depression, before continuing downwards to merge smoothly with the bubble itself. Following the thread of light upwards into the darkness, Bernice found that the curves and kinks which had been so obvious from the surface of Belial had straightened out a little more. The system was definitely coming back under proper control.

She began walking towards the depression, as four suited figures followed her from the ship, still arguing about the paperwork.

'Look at the Bridge,' she said over the commlink. 'It's self-repairing all right.'

'It had to be,' the Doctor replied. 'Such a complex system, left to run for millennia, without the simplest

141

form of housekeeping? No. The only answer was an active control system.'

'But where does the energy come from?' Miles obviously had a command override. He had been listening in.

'Isn't it obvious?' the Doctor said, not at all discomfited.

'If it were obvious, we wouldn't have been here for five years trying to find it, and Paula would still be . . . Would still be . . .'

'Look around you.'

'At what?' Bernice asked.

'At nothing. At everything.'

Shrugging, Bernice followed the Doctor's instructions. At first the glare from Lucifer – extending beyond Moloch's ice-locked horizon, and reflecting from Belial high above – turned the depths of space into a flat black backdrop that could just as well have been suspended a few feet in front of her eyes. She sighed, squinted, and still saw nothing. After a few moments, she realized that if she half closed the filters across the starsuit helmet she could cut out at least some of the light. Within a few seconds, her eyes had compensated, and she could see what the Doctor meant.

Space was alive with ghostly curtains of light. Pale violet in colour, they waved gently in some invisible wind. Stars glinted through their folds. Wherever she looked, there was faint colour and slow movement.

'It's beautiful,' Miles whispered.

'Commonplace,' Bernice said. 'Charged particles interacting with the magnetic field of Lucifer. You find aurorae around most planets.'

'Quite right,' the Doctor's voice crackled in her helmet. Bernice could see him raise a bulky suited arm and gesture grandly at the surroundings. 'But the Lucifer system is unusual in many respects. The parent star is a red giant nearing the end of its life, and as it runs the gamut of fusion reactions, exhausting one element after another, the spectrum of particles it emits becomes exotic. As the particles catch Lucifer's magnetic field, it is extended into

142

space like a fishing net caught by the tide. And drifting through that net are two little fishes named Belial and Moloch, feeding off the rich plankton of energy.'

There was a long moment of silence.

'Do you know what you're saying?' Miles said, awe-struck.

'Occasionally,' the Doctor replied.

Cheryl said slowly, 'Are you trying to tell us that something, either here or on Belial, is extracting the energy from the variations in magnetic potential that the moons are passing through?'

'Quite so.' Bernice could hear the smugness in the Doctor's voice.

'It's the Bridge. It's got to be.' Miles's voice was hushed, and Bernice saw his helmet tilt as he craned his neck upwards to look at the Bridge. 'But the power . . . Incredible! It's hardly feasible that they . . . And the storage problems!' From the way his voice grew alternately loud and quiet, Bernice could tell that he was shaking his head. 'Why didn't we realize?'

'Like the purloined letter,' said the Doctor smugly, 'it was too obvious to see.'

Bernice followed his gaze upwards as Cheryl began to speak. 'Yes,' she said softly. 'Yes, it would make sense. The Lift moves up and down the Bridge, reacting to the stimulus of local magnetic field strength, riding the isogonal contours and providing information to the feed-back mechanisms which direct its movement. That explains the apparent randomness of its motion. We were wrong. It's not a transport system at all; it's a whomping great accumulator!'

Miles's voice was bitter with self-reproach. 'All the power we could ever have wanted, and it's been right under my nose for years.'

'You couldn't use it on Earth, of course,' the Doctor said. 'There's a huge difference between the magnetic fields, for a start, and the radiation from Lucifer's sun is quite, quite different.'

'But it would have made all the difference to Project

143

Eden,' Cheryl muttered. 'Like your party trick with the neutrino collectors and the hymetusite: we couldn't have scaled it up enough to solve Earth's energy shortfall, but it could have supported us here whilst we searched for the long-term solution – the high-mass elements in Lucifer's core.'

Bernice had reached the apex of the terminal dome by now. She moved through the conical root-system of cables which formed the Bridge's anchor, down towards the centre of the depression, and waited for the others to catch up.

As she waited, she began to study the anchor cables around her. She looked upwards, trying to visualize how the Lift would be able to move past the point where they connected to the Bridge. Before she got very far with her thoughts, she realized the cables were moving, rising past her . . . No! They weren't moving, she realized in sudden alarm, it was her: she was sinking. She tried to take a step, but the suit wouldn't respond to her commands.

She looked down at her feet, and felt her blood run cold. They weren't there. She had sunk up to her ankles in the translucent bubble. Even as she watched, the gooey material oozed up to her knees. She tried to struggle, but she was held fast. Thick fingers of the viscous substance were reaching up from the surface towards her starsuit's hips.

'All aboard that's getting aboard,' the Doctor said with relish.

'This is supposed to happen?'

'This, unless I'm very much mistaken, is the airlock.'

'Well, that's original, to say the least.'

As the terminal surface moved past her helmet, she thought she could see a fine structure to it, a lattice of irregular cells which pulsed and churned while she watched. Then darkness enfolded her, and she found herself standing on a solid surface in a shadowed room, staring upwards at the underside of the dimple with a strange sense of having been reborn.

Over to one side, the stalk of the Bridge penetrated

144

the soft surface and, in a network of roots and capillaries, grew into the floor. There was a ragged hole in the side nearest her; she assumed this was where Ace and her companions had escaped from inside the hollow shaft. Watching in fascination, she saw that the material was gradually reforming.

The surface above her bulged out into a number of large teardrop shapes which hung above her for a moment, trembling slightly, before depositing the Doctor, Miles, Cheryl and Bishop beside her. She assumed that the Lift, under normal conditions, would have arrived in the terminal the same way.

The Doctor began to clamber out of his suit, peering around at his immediate surroundings. 'This is all quite fascinating,' he said, drawing his umbrella from his starsuit and using it to point at the terminal entrance. 'Moloch's Pit should be this way.' He set off at a brisk walk.

Bernice ran to catch up with him. 'How could you know where the Pit was if you've never been here before?' she asked curiously.

The Doctor didn't answer. Bringing up the rear, Bishop frowned thoughtfully. 'An interesting point, Krau Summerfield,' he said mildly, to himself.

Ten minutes later, they had passed through the kilometre-thick crust of the moon via Moloch's Pit, and were moving once more into the human-designed areas of the base.

At the door to the Operations Room, the Doctor paused briefly and sniffed. 'Hmm,' he said, as the door slid open and he led the way inside. 'Ionization. That's odd.' He took another sniff, wrinkling his nose with distaste. 'What do we know that produces a smell like that?'

Bernice grinned. 'Alex Bannen?'

The Doctor tut-tutted sternly; nobody smiled.

'Electrical activity.' Cheryl crossed the patchy carpet to the nearest window and began to study the landscape depicted on it.

The Doctor nodded thoughtfully. He made a swift circuit of the room, studying the read-outs of each station, pausing only once, to run his fingers across the MultiCray input terminal.

'What are you doing to the neural net, Doctor?' Bishop said sharply.

'Checking to see how much damage has been done to it,' the Doctor said with some irritation.

'Damage?'

The Doctor tapped the side of his nose. 'Electrical activity, remember?' He indicated a diagnostic panel, where several red lights had begun to blink in confirmation of his words. Information began scrolling across a virtual screen beside the Doctor's head.

Cheryl moved impatiently. 'I've had just about all I can take of this mucking about. If you want me, I'll be looking for Sam.'

She began to walk towards the door, but the Doctor stopped her with a look. 'According to the roster, your husband was due here but never turned up,' he said sternly.

'That's ridiculous!' Cheryl exclaimed in a voice that was far too loud. 'This is a bloody nightmare. Where are all the people?'

The Doctor had bent to examine something he had seen on the dappled carpet beside the communications terminal. He stood almost immediately, and only Bernice noticed that, by aiming a bony finger at the floor, he was covering the fact that he'd pocketed something.

She moved closer to see what he was pointing at.

The patterns on the floor weren't part of the design of the carpet.

They were patches of blood.

Chapter Nine

When the Doctor spoke, his voice was dark and foreboding. 'There's only one thing to do.'

Cheryl's voice was tense. 'We'll have to search for them.'

The Doctor nodded. 'Cheryl, I wonder if you would be so kind as to cast a professional eye over the experimental laboratories for me.'

Her voice was flat and harsh. 'Am I looking for anything in particular?'

The Doctor was vague. 'Oh, not really. Anything unusual will do. You could check on the medlab, too, if you wouldn't mind. Bernice, I'd like you to check the grounds for signs of activity. Trau Engado, I suggest you and Trau Bishop work back through the base, up the Pit and into the Bridge terminal. I understand Paula had a laboratory there; that'll need to be checked. I'll stay here and coordinate the search. We'll all meet back here in precisely – oh, a couple of hours.' He thought for a moment before adding dryly, 'So long as that's all right with you, Adjudicator?'

Bishop said evenly, 'I notice that this particular search pattern leaves you alone here, and free to – '

'Steal the silverware?' The Doctor raised an enquiring eyebrow.

Bishop said nothing.

The Doctor gestured towards the centre of the room. 'Someone has obviously interfered with the neural net. That means the security simulators are off-line. If you know anything about how to repair a MultiCray, you are more than welcome to stay and help me. Otherwise, you can stay and make tea. Arcturan, Lapsang Souchong or Earl Grey will be perfectly acceptable. Such a civilized drink.'

Bishop did not rise to the bait. 'Perhaps I should go with one of the ladies,' he said. 'After all, there may be danger.'

'That's quite all right,' Bernice said, frowning. 'When you've drunk the crew of a Grinch pirate skiff under the table, there's precious little you can't do. Besides, I think Miles has already made up his mind.'

While they had been talking, the Administrator had slipped quietly from the room. Bernice shivered. When they'd first arrived at the Base, she had quite liked the old Administrator, but since Paula's death he'd changed. There was something disturbing about the way he'd just – well, just left – without saying anything. What was he up to?

'Well,' the Doctor said briskly, 'what are we waiting for? We've all got plenty to do. Let's get on and do it.'

Miles Engado, impatient at his slow progress through the Pit, padded softly along the track which spiralled from the Bridge terminus, through Moloch's kilometre-thick shell, to the research centre. The sound of his footsteps was absorbed efficiently by the etched walls and curved pathway. That left a lot of silence to fill, and Miles filled it with fear and guilt.

And with confusion.

The fear and the guilt were his own, but the confusion – that was a different matter. It had originated from elsewhere, and infected him as surely as any virus. Less than two days since Paula's death, and already her spirit was demanding the companionship of others on its journey. How many would lose their lives to his daughter's marauding unrest, he wondered guiltily, and at whose door would the fault ultimately lie? Miles felt the confusion in his mind grow into a relentless horror. He was eighty-seven. A man still in his prime. A man of his century. How could he believe, really *believe*, that this primal stuff and nonsense, this superstition, could affect the day-to-day operation of the most important scientific expedition of its time? Miles groaned inwardly, knowing instinctively that the how and the why of a thing were almost irrelevant when placed against the fact. The fact was that he, the main proponent of the scientific method, was becoming increasingly frightened by a superstition society had considered dead before he was born. The fact was he felt like a child again, powerless against forces he could not understand – let alone control.

With an effort, Miles shook off the lethargy that had been creeping over him since Paula's death, blinding him to his duties and responsibilities.

He'd made his decision.

Now it was time to carry it out.

The Doctor checked to make sure the Operations Room was properly deserted before inputting a simple command into the MultiCray. Immediately, the blinking red lights on the diagnostic panel were replaced by steady green indicators. The system was back on line.

For a moment, the Doctor toyed lightly with the simularity crystal he had found while looking at the blood on the floor. He fed the crystal into a reader and watched with interest as the file scrolled up. He kept one eye on the entrances to the Operations Room. He knew Bishop was lurking around somewhere, but the Adjudicator presented no danger he couldn't anticipate.

Unlike Ace, apparently.

Oh well. It was a simple enough matter to –

'Yes, I would have started with the simularity records as well.'

Bishop.

The Doctor smoothly keyed in a new sequence of commands.

'Nice idea,' he muttered off-handedly. 'Shame about the software.'

'The files are corrupt?' Bishop asked.

'Completely.'

149

'Inconvenient, to say the least.'

'Undoubtedly.'

'Your recommendation?'

'Tricky.'

'But you do have one.'

'Possibly.'

Bishop clasped his hands together and steepled his fingers. When he spoke, his voice was completely without inflection. 'It may interest you to know that I, too, am developing a theory, Doctor. One in which your own involvement plays a significant part.'

The Doctor smiled engagingly. 'You know, I was rather afraid you were going to say something like that.' He turned and left the Operations Room.

Bernice lifted her face to the warming rays of an impossible sun, and wondered at the beauty and mystery of the universe.

Out on the fringes of the Vartaq Veil, looking for traces of her lost father, she had been part of a team excavating a Dyson sphere constructed around a white dwarf star. Built from the debris of planets, moons and comets, the sphere had originally been designed to completely enclose its star, collecting all the energy it gave out rather than letting the vast majority of it escape away into space. Like most engineering projects, it may have looked good on paper, but in practice it was another thing entirely. Tidal stress and gravitational asymmetries had pulled the sphere out of shape. Newtonian mechanics had done the rest. By the time Bernice and her colleagues had arrived, it had degenerated into a series of unconnected fragments which drifted apart over thousands of years, gradually leaking their atmospheres into the vacuum. The builders, overcome by the tragic outcome of their vast conception, had devolved into a shelled race who spent their nomadic existence migrating from one fragment of the sphere to another, living in the ruins of their once great cities and seeing the cosmos as a gigantic jigsaw puzzle being slowly assembled by God.

It was a funny old universe.

Bernice looked around. Beautiful though the interior of the lower moon was, there was also something disturbing about it. Perhaps it was the way the horizon curved upwards on all sides, like a bowl, or the way gravity worked when there shouldn't have been any. Perhaps it was the way the translucent 'grass' seemed to develop an immediate and lasting attachment to anything or anyone that walked across it. But she didn't think so.

Ordinarily she would have relished the variety which the creators of Moloch had offered up for her pleasure without a qualm or a second thought, but this time something was getting to her, making her nervous. Itchy . . .

Oh.

It was the Veil.

Moloch reminded her of the Vartaq Veil.

Not the precise pattern of plants and trees beyond the human enclave, nor the affectionate grass, nor even the strange and delightful animal life – if it was animal life – which peered from the undergrowth at the human installations with delicate curiosity. No.

It was the quiet.

And a sense of history gone terribly wrong.

She shivered, despite the heat.

A wafer thin translucent *something* undulated through the air towards her, chuckling gently to itself in a liquid voice. She put out a hand, and the thing wrapped itself around her arm, warm and dry and tingling – and Bernice was suddenly struck by a question so obvious it stunned her. If the builders of this artificial paradise had not been around for several millennia – as Alex Bannen seemed to think – how come the flora and fauna hadn't run riot and completely ruined the environment?

Bernice ran the fingers of her free hand through her thickly beaded dreadlocks as she tried to think. She was no naturalist, but it seemed to her that every living thing around her was controlled in some way, by some – force: prevented from over-breeding, over-growing. In some way patterned. She had a sudden feeling that if she could

151

only work out how the ecology of Moloch ticked, she would have a vital clue, if not to discovering Ace's whereabouts, then at least to getting a handle on the vanished aliens. With any luck, the rest of the puzzle – the missing personnel, the mystery of the Angels and, not least of all, the rapidly sliding situation on the Base itself – might follow on from that.

Bernice shook loose the amiable scrap of nothing and watched as it fluttered away, lost in moments in the gentle glow of Moloch's endless day.

She rubbed her arm. The skin tingled.

Cheryl palmed the access lock on the medlab door and the hatch rolled open. She moved cautiously into the room.

'Hello? Christine?'

There was a sudden movement behind a bank of filing cabinets.

Cheryl sucked in an alarmed breath. 'Sam?'

'I'm afraid not.'

The Doctor.

'Go away,' she snapped.

'I could do that,' he said, emerging from behind the cabinets. 'But I wouldn't be taking the problem with me, would I?'

'Who says I want you to!' Cheryl croaked out the words before lapsing into another long silence.

'Why don't you tell me about it? I guarantee it'll help.'

'You wouldn't understand. You're just a –'

'Just a man? Isn't that expression out of date yet?'

'I was going to say . . . Oh hell. I don't know what I was going to say.'

'That's good. Now we can start fresh, with no preconceptions.' The Doctor sat on one of the medlab's empty diagnostic beds, and drew his legs up into the lotus position.

'I'm not ready to talk yet. If you had any degree of sensitivity you'd be able to see that.' Angrily, Cheryl turned and left the room.

After a moment's thought, the Doctor followed her.

Miles re-entered the Bridge terminus. The floor of the chamber was obscured by a silver mist that had risen since their arrival. Tiny clouds swirled about his legs as he walked. On impulse, he reached out and passed his hand through the vapour. The silvery substance clung to his skin, looking like tiny beads of mercury, as slippery as graphite between his fingers. Miles flicked his hand absently. The stuff relinquished its grip upon him readily enough, drifting away to join the main mass of the stuff as it clustered around the end of the Bridge, where some kind of subtle activity seemed to be taking place.

Miles looked closer, his confusion momentarily overcome by curiosity. The hole through which the survivors of B Shift had left the Bridge was knitting back together like cloth, the weave forming as the bulk of the mist reduced. High above Miles's head, beyond the terminus bubble, the Bridge itself was trembling; it was becoming more difficult to see, as if something were being called into shape around the central shaft.

Miles blinked. Something *was* forming around the Bridge: a new Lift.

Miles felt suddenly weary.

It was time to carry out his decision.

He walked through the Bridge terminus to the Atmospheric Vehicle Research Laboratory: the room where Paula had spent most of her working time. The starpod, her creation, hung suspended in the engineering pit.

He looked around the room where she had spent much of the last few years. So stark. So cold. He crossed to the open storage cabinets and ran his fingers along the rows of simularity crystals; her files, her notes, her diary. Her life.

His fingers paused over one that was simply labelled 'Dad'. He pulled it out and looked at it blankly, then slipped it into his pocket.

Miles crossed decisively to the starpod, unsealed the

hatch and swung himself into the cabin, smiling as it snuggled shut behind him with a soft pneumatic wheeze.

He took one of the two pilot seats and began to strap himself in. Activated by his body heat, the onboard systems began to power up.

A representation of the Laboratory sprang into life around him, fed into his modified cornea by low power laser beams. Other sensors synched in with other senses. He could see in a three hundred and sixty degree sphere via the pod sensor modules, just as he could feel the ambient temperature, and even smell the lubricant that someone had carelessly leaked on to the floor. He moved his arm into a myo-feedback harness; a mechanical specimen grip unfolded and flexed in time with his movements.

He *was* the pod.

With a spoken command, he operated the control which would open the roof of the AVR Lab, allowing the pod access to free space.

Bishop pulled the crystal that the Doctor had left in the simularity reader free and turned it over and over in his hands. He reached beneath his robes and pulled free the personal reader he'd brought from his ship. Slipping the crystal into the device, Bishop watched as the file read up, observing the contents with great interest.

Evidence.

Suppressed evidence, no less.

He attached a judicial password to the file, saved it, pocketed both crystal and reader, and began to think hard about the information he'd discovered.

It could be the reason for everything.

Perhaps he was not as far short of solving this case as he had supposed.

Trying to avoid the undulants' over-affectionate advances, Bernice moved deeper into the jungle.

The 'trees' put her in mind of the Bridge: nests of translucent pink roots which burst from the powdery soil and curved upwards into single trunks which soared above her head and fanned out again into an inverted cone of branches. Put a beachball at both ends and the comparison would be perfect.

A faint breeze caressed the back of her neck. She turned, and gasped.

A wave of movement was sweeping across the forest. As it reached each tree in turn, the tree gracefully bent over, curving its trunk so that both roots and branches touched the ground. The branches burrowed into the soil; the roots relinquished their grip. The tree straightened, upside down, a perfect mirror image of itself.

'Wow,' she breathed.

When, after a few moments, no further miracles were forthcoming, she moved on.

As she walked, her mind was still puzzling over the mystery of Moloch's peculiar ecology. She was sure there was a pattern there somewhere, a pattern which included the missing personnel, the carefully planted flora, the tingling undulant, everyth–

Hang on a minute.

Undulants? Tingling undulants?

Bernice thought hard. The Doctor had mentioned ionization when they'd first entered the Operations Room; ionization caused by electrical activity. And the undulants displayed a conspicuous electric field whenever they moved; she'd felt it as static whenever they touched her. Bernice sucked in a deep breath, searching for a tell-tale smell – and there it was! The faintest hint of . . . Of –

Her thoughts suddenly interrupted, Bernice gave a cry of surprise and horror.

On the ground in front of her was a motionless human hand.

Bernice swallowed hard. The hand was connected to an arm, which vanished into the nearby undergrowth. Bernice hesitated. Skeletons in tombs and ancient embalmed bodies were one thing; this was entirely another.

She took her hip flask from her coveralls and emptied it in one long gulp. Alcohol doped with various smart

155

chemicals stung her throat. She looked down again. The hand was still there. The grass around it seemed to beckon her on.

Taking a deep breath, she forced apart the translucent boughs and peered through.

Jammed into the undergrowth were a number of dead bodies.

Ace's blood-soaked jacket lay on top of the pile.

Miles gazed out into space through the circular hatch in the roof of the chamber. From somewhere beyond the artificial horizon, the Bridge arced up and away into the darkness, the lower part of its immense length in shadow, the upper glinting with fiery reflections from Lucifer's atmospheric corona. Miles used his connection with the starpod to dim the chamber lights, and the stars sprang into sharp relief. He wondered where Sol was. He was an administrator, not an astronomer, and that question had always floored him. Was Sol even visible from here? He was damned if he knew.

Miles powered up the starpod's sensor arrays, enhancing his own senses and sending them arcing out into space in search of the planet of his birth. Paula would have a companion on her journey to the afterlife. He just wanted to say goodbye first. To take one last look at the electronic signature which marked out his birthplace from the countless other star systems he could see. To imagine for the last time the forests and oceans, green and alive, the way they'd always been in historical dramas. The way they'd always been for his people: the fishers, the hunters.

There was a shadow. Something vast and artificial. Something . . .

. . . slipped through the ether and smashed into his mind.

Miles screamed and fell into an unforgiving darkness filled with endless pain and memories.

Piper O'Rourke looked up from the shift supervisor's desk as a dishevelled and embarrassed Alex Bannen walked into the Belial Base Operations Room, followed by his son.

'Sleep well, Alex?'

'No.' The physicist was clutching a plastic beaker from which he drank greedily.

'That won't do you any good, you know.'

Alex's face assumed a shallow, humourless grin. 'It's tea.'

Piper raised one eyebrow in a surprised apology. 'Er – how's . . .' There was an awkward pause. 'I'm sorry, I don't know his name.'

Bannen set down the beaker. 'Mark. Come in here. I want you to meet a,' he hesitated, 'a colleague.'

There were hesitant footsteps. Piper got up from her seat. 'Hello, Mark. I'm Piper. We met before.'

The child's gaze was as piercing and intelligent as she remembered. 'You're the woman who hates my dad.'

Piper closed her eyes.

And opened them sharply at an insistent, warning buzz from her duty station.

'What's that?' Bannen's son moved to examine readouts.

Perceptive, she thought. But then, he would be.

'I owe you an apology, Alex.'

'Yeah. Me too.' He hesitated. 'Sorry.'

'Alex, what I need more than an apology is an explanation.'

He had the grace to look discomfited. 'I would have thought it was all round Belial by now.'

'We've had too much else to worry about.'

'He's not real, you know.'

'I know. There's no way you could have kept him hidden for this long, and Moshe-Rabaan would have noticed any excess oxygen usage, so he's a simularity, right?'

'Right.'

'Why?' Her voice softened. 'Why not apply for real children?'

'I did,' he said levelly. 'I had a son. He died.'

157

Silence.

'He died?'

Bannen rested his head in his hands. Mark just looked on dispassionately. 'Yeah. I was married. Her name was Sonia. She was good. A good person. She wanted a child, so we signed up for the eugenics lottery. We were both in the upper IQ bracket; we could've used channels, pulled strings, bypassed the system. But she wanted to do it properly. Be honest.' His shoulders gave a little heave. 'We got lucky.'

'So what happened?'

'Remember when America's economy collapsed, back in forty-six?' Bannen's voice was so quiet that Piper had to strain to hear it. 'I was teaching at MexTech at the time. I was on campus when the food riots hit full swing. Made it to the spaceport on a student bus. Last sub-orbital off the ground. I saw her in the crowd outside the ship as they sealed the lock.' Bannen tried to take his son's hand, but his fingers passed right through the simularity field. 'Saw them both.'

Piper felt something cold clench in her chest.

'What – what happened?'

He looked up with bleak, pain-scarred eyes. 'There were ten million people and no food,' he whispered. What do you think happened?'

Piper swallowed, her mouth suddenly dry.

Bannen said something in such a quiet voice she missed his words.

'Pardon?'

'I said, I could have gone back. For Sonia and Mark. I could have gone back for them.'

Piper found herself unable to meet the physicist's gaze.

'I could have gone back.'

Bishop was collecting the shattered fragments of an observation drone for later analysis when the klaxons began. The sound was a sharp, painful call to action. Swiftly, Bishop accessed the neural net and locked down the source of the alert.

The Atmospheric Vehicle Research chamber.

Bishop activated a commdesk and punched in the requisite code. A virtual screen lit up, immediately in front of his face. The picture it showed appeared normal; then Bishop realized the dome of the chamber was open to free space. Apparently there was some kind of unscheduled launch in progress, an experiment under preprogrammed control.

Bishop sighed.

So much to do already, and now this.

He left the Operations Room and was running up the Pit transport belt when Cheryl Russell swung in from a side corridor and very nearly cannoned into him. 'That's an experimental research warning,' she cried. 'What's going on?'

Bishop studied her face for a brief second. He noted the tear tracks for later consideration.

'Stop gathering wool,' she snapped. 'Someone's triggered the alarm. It could be an emergency!'

'The neural net identified the AVR chamber as the source of the alert.'

'Well, come on then!'

The main base entrance rolled shut behind Bernice, replacing the constant pinkish daylight of Moloch with the flat white glare of artificial light.

Catching sight of the back of Bishop's robes vanishing along the corridor leading to the Pit, Bernice began to follow automatically, but a firm pressure on her arm prevented her from continuing.

Her forward movement abruptly halted, Bernice threw the Doctor a cool glance. Apologetically, he removed his hand. He waved his umbrella in a distracted manner. 'Operations Room,' he said vaguely.

'Why?'

The Doctor's eyes suddenly focused. 'There's something I have to show you.'

The control room was exactly as she had left it. In a

beaker at one of the duty stations cold tea rippled in time with the siren.

Bernice perched on the edge of the shift supervisor's desk, watching as the Doctor strode quickly to the neural net cabinets and began to access a series of subsystems. He looked puzzled, then worried. He thumped the desk with an uncharacteristic display of temper. 'It's gone!' He quickly searched all his pockets. 'How could I have been so stupid?'

'It's Ace, isn't it?'

The Doctor sighed deeply, withdrawing his hands from his pockets.

'Well?'

He looked away. 'There are some things I need to know. I would ask her myself but –'

Bernice's eyes narrowed as she deliberately missed the point. 'But she doesn't trust you any more.'

'That's right.'

'So what do you want to know?'

'I've hurt her, Bernice. I keep hurting her. With the best of intentions, but still the pain exists. The mistrust. The feeling of betrayal.' The Doctor looked away from Bernice for a moment, and she could have sworn it was with genuine remorse. 'You're human. Tell me how I can make it up to her.'

'I'm sorry.' Bernice quickly unrolled the bundle she'd been carrying beneath her arm and thrust Ace's blood-soaked jacket into the Doctor's hands. 'I think it may be too late for words.'

Cheryl slapped home a series of circuit breakers mounted on a plinth beside the AVR chamber monitor station. Immediately, she felt the floor vibrate as the dome rumbled shut, sealing the chamber. Air pumped in as the warning sirens died away.

She waited impatiently as the pressure equalized inside the dome, finally punching an override and unsealing the lock early. She pounded into the frost-rimed chamber, breath freezing in front of her face, checking each possible place of concealment for a figure, dreading what she might find.

There was nothing.

She turned her attention to the starpod. If someone were still alive, that was where they'd be.

A moment behind her, Bishop entered the chamber, robes a-flap. He watched as she unsealed the lock on the starpod. Ice cracked away from the hatch at a pressure from inside.

Cheryl let out an involuntary gasp of surprise as a limp body fell clear of the vehicle to lie still upon the chamber floor in a slurry of melting ice.

Miles Engado.

Bishop carefully watched as first bitter disappointment and then professional concern chased startled horror from the woman's face.

Despite everything, had Cheryl expected to find her husband there?

Bernice and the Doctor entered the monitor room in time to help Cheryl stretch Miles out on the floor next to an open medkit, while Bishop probed intently into the racks of recording systems.

Bernice quickly moved the medkit to Cheryl's side. 'What happened to him?'

'I've no idea.' Cheryl passed a diagnostic wand across the Administrator's head and torso. 'According to this, he's in second-level unconsciousness. I found him hooked up to the interactive software in the starpod. Heaven alone knows what he was doing in there.' She prepared an injector pad.

'Thinking of Paula maybe.' The Doctor moved across to where Bishop was still methodically accessing the gallery records. 'Find anything interesting?'

Bishop kept his face carefully neutral. 'All systems are off line. Diagnostics report what can only be described as an – invasion. The software is corrupt and will need to be rebooted. All records of the last fifteen minutes have been erased.'

161

The Doctor leaned on his umbrella, his face assuming an expression of innocent concentration. 'Sounds familiar, doesn't it?' His voice hardened. 'Someone's covering up a trail.'

'I would have to agree.'

'The question is, who?' The Doctor allowed his eyes to fall to those of Miles Engado, as they moved spasmodically behind closed lids.

Remembering.

Bishop noted the direction of the Doctor's gaze, and his eyes narrowed as he regarded the Administrator's disturbed expression. He would know what had happened to the software, and why.

Bishop felt the slight weight of a simularity crystal in the pocket of his robe and allowed himself an inward smile. Despite all prevarication, the evidence was building. Soon a solution would be found.

And justice would be served.

'Adjudicator?'

Bishop looked at the Doctor.

'There's something you ought to know.'

Two hours later, Piper O'Rouke, Alex Bannen and a medical team were waiting as the Adjudicator's ship locked home against the Belial Bridge terminus.

Alex fidgeted impatiently as Miles was brought forth on a stretcher, ignoring the welfare of the Base Coordinator completely. There were more important things he needed to find out; things only the Doctor could tell him.

He moved forward importantly, pushing past Bernice and Cheryl as if they did not exist. 'Doctor – I must talk to you. Was there any record concerning the structure of the Bridge's interior?'

'No, Alex, we didn't find Ace or Christine. But thank you for asking,' Bernice muttered angrily.

Alex glared at Bernice. 'You're a scientist. You should understand that knowledge takes precedence over corpses. In my opinion, it may be the only way to prevent more deaths.'

With cold and deliberate fury, Bernice began to explain to the scientist exactly what she thought of his 'opinion'.

The Doctor interrupted her gently. 'I'm afraid Trau Bannen is right, Bernice.'

Bernice threw the Doctor a disgusted look. Bannen leaned attentively towards the Doctor and they began to speak in low voices. Bernice suddenly found she badly needed a drink, but her hip flask was empty. She began to make her way towards the entrance to the Pit.

The sound of someone's throat being cleared as a preliminary to speaking aloud caused her to stop.

'If I could have your attention, please.'

Bernice turned. Bishop had laid claim to an area of floor.

Cheryl and Piper, the Doctor, Alex, and the medical team all stopped talking.

Bishop continued, 'I would like to take this opportunity to inform you all that the judicial process requested by Miles Engado regarding the death of his daughter has now reached a conclusion. That conclusion is that Paula Engado was murdered.'

There was a hushed whisper of horror from the listening personnel. Bernice felt a sick feeling begin to develop in her stomach.

The feeling intensified as Bishop concluded his short speech in even, measured tones. 'I have in my possession a simularity file which clearly establishes the guilt of the murderer. It is now my duty to pass sentence.'

As Bernice watched, horrified, Bishop produced a large handgun from beneath his robes and aimed it squarely at the Doctor's head.

Chapter Ten

A security drone circled like a fat, lazy insect in front of the door to the Conference Room.

'It's all right,' Bernice said to it, raising her hands in surrender. 'I have permission. Signed, sealed and in triplicate. "Temporary Authorization, Prisoner, For The Visit Of", Guild of Adjudicators form one nine five three slash three.'

The drone orbited mindlessly.

'Come on, Bishop, I know you're watching me.'

The door remained shut.

Bernice reached into a pocket of her waistcoat and took out a grimy piece of paper: a bar receipt from some long-forgotten dive on a far away planet.

'I have in my hand,' she said ominously, 'a "Gratuitous Acts of Vandalism, Drones, To Be Performed On", Bernice Summerfield form zero zero zero.' She paused. 'Slash zero.'

She crossed her arms confidently. After a moment, the door slid open. Bernice grinned as she walked into the Conference Room. Applied psychology: there was no beating it.

The Doctor was hovering above the conference table in the classic lotus position. His hands rested, palms up, on his knees. Another drone orbited the room near the ceiling.

The sudden breeze introduced through the open door disturbed the orbit of the drone and sent the Doctor drifting slowly backwards. His eyes opened in alarm, but before he could say anything his concentration lapsed and he dropped like a stone, vanishing behind the far end of the table. There was a loud thud, and a torrent of abuse in an obscure Venusian dialect. The drone buzzed curiously across the room and vanished behind the table, making its own checks on the Doctor's health.

Bernice didn't know whether to laugh or cry, so she settled for sarcasm. 'Aren't Time Lords supposed to be above that sort of language?'

'It was a Venusian lullaby,' the Doctor said, clambering up from behind the table and cramming his hat back on to his head. The drone was orbiting his head like a dizziness star in an ancient cartoon. He glared at the offending object angrily. 'I find it useful to recite calming verse in moments of great stress.'

'Calming verse? *Klokeda partha mennin klatch*? You've got to be joking! It's one of the most bawdy rhymes in the known universe.'

' "Venusian is a language, as dead as dead can be",' the Doctor quoted with great dignity. 'If I say it's a lullaby, then it's a lullaby.'

'Oh yes? And who was it who decoded the Mk'kur'qa Inscriptions, then? Who worked out the structure of the language from first principles, then? Who is arguably the foremost galactic authority on the Venusian race?'

'Not you, surely?'

Bernice shrugged.

'Well, actually, no. But I met him once.'

The Doctor grinned, and so did she.

'I tell you,' she continued, 'the bit that I could never figure out was that *ablark, araan, aroon* refrain. What was that all about?'

'Ah,' the Doctor sighed, nodding wisely. 'It's to do with the number of limbs they had. More opportunities.' He rolled the word around in his mouth, savouring it.

'And *shunna teerenatch*?'

He shuddered. 'Don't ask.'

She gazed at the small, gaudily dressed figure; the clown, the madman, the genius.

'You know so much, don't you.'

'Too much,' he replied softly. 'Far too much.'

165

Her gaze hardened. 'Sometimes I hate you for it,' she said, more harshly, perhaps, than she had intended. 'I've spent years reconstructing, integrating, analysing and just plain digging through mud; cataloguing alien ruins square centimetre by square centimetre and sticking together the pieces of damaged artifacts to form implausible shapes. Then you come along, and you tell me not only who made it but what his name was, how many eggs he laid and the colour of his tentacles. Archaeology is my life, Doctor. And you've made archaeology worthless to me.'

The Doctor thought for a moment. 'Have I?'

'Yes! It's as if I've wasted my life searching for something that was never lost in the first place. What's the point?'

'Did you enjoy yourself?' he asked.

She smiled wistfully, remembering old friends, good times. 'Wouldn't have missed a second of it.'

'There you are then.' He looked away, and shrugged. 'I collect pins. Where's the point in that, if you'll forgive the pun? But I enjoy it. I'm fulfilled by it. Too many people spend too much time looking for a reason, and fail to take advantage of the simple pleasures that life offers.'

Bernice ran her fingers along the table top. No dust. This room had no secrets to hide. 'You know the worst thing about being here?'

The Doctor perched on the edge of the table, took his hat off and batted the buzzing drone away into a distant corner. Persistently, the device moved back towards them. The Doctor smiled at it, waited for it to approach – then whipped his hat through the air and down on to the table, neatly trapping the drone beneath it.

'I think so,' he said seriously, and for a moment his expression assumed the full weight of his nine-hundred-odd years. 'It's knowing, isn't it? Knowing what's ahead.'

'The curse of being a time travelling archaeologist.' Bernice looked away. 'How many years of peace have they got left?'

'Probably less than you think.' The Doctor glanced

sideways at his hat. It was sidling towards the edge of the table. He reached out with his umbrella and hooked the hat back. An indignant buzzing sound came from beneath it. 'The lights are going out all over the galaxy,' he said softly. 'They shall not see them lit again in their lifetimes.' He looked over at Bernice. 'Have you seen the news from the latest pigeon post?'

Bernice nodded. 'It's like seeing a snowball start to roll down a mountain. You know at the bottom it's going to be avalanche time. And the latest message pod was more than six months late, by all accounts.' She looked down at the diminutive Time Lord, her eyes full of quiet sympathy.

'I learned to live with it,' he said, in reply to her unspoken question. 'I deal with today's problems today. Tomorrow's problems I solve yesterday.'

'But what about the problems here – the sabotage, the murders?'

'Unrelated,' the Doctor said, once more reaching for his hat. He flipped it over, allowing the drone to escape. It immediately flew across the room, maintaining a wary distance. The Doctor reversed his hat, flipped it back along the length of his arm and perched it nonchalantly on his head. 'This is a purely human evil. And talking of which, what's been happening in the world at large since my incarceration in this impromptu dungeon?'

'Where do you want me to start?'

'Ace,' he said quietly. 'Start with Ace.'

Bernice sighed. 'Doctor, you have to understand. The conditions of the . . .' She swallowed. 'Piecing the bodies together is going to be a full-time job for some poor bastard. At the moment they've found . . . Kosi, and . . . Chas Varley's arm. They recognized it by his ring. But the rest are too badly burned or in too many pieces to identify without DNA tests, and that'll take time. Judging by the reconstruction work, there is considerable evidence of small arms fire: flamers, needlers and the like.' She paused. 'But there's also evidence that some of them just – exploded from inside.'

'And what's Trau Bishop doing about it?'

'He's locked away in Miles's office, scanning every simularity he can find with your face in it. I don't know what he's got on you, but it must be good. He's setting up a drumhead court-martial for tomorrow.'

'Followed, no doubt, by summary execution.' The Doctor cast a dark glance up at the innocently circling drone.

Bernice tried to read his expression, but it was untranslatable. But she had to know. 'Cheryl's nearly hysterical,' she offered, with carefully calculated innocence. 'There's no sign of Sam anywhere.'

The Doctor wasn't going for the bait.

'Rumour Control has it,' she added, 'that he's either an undiscovered victim or your accomplice. Craig Richards is running a sweepstake on it.'

'What are the odds on me?'

'Favourite for a short trial and a quick death,' Bernice said, and immediately wished she hadn't.

'There's something else, isn't there?'

She sighed. 'I could be imagining it, but . . . Well, people seem to be turning against us. Nobody's saying anything, not to my face anyway, but there's something about the way they move, and the way conversations change tack when I walk into rooms. It's very subtle, but there's an undercurrent of distrust that wasn't there yesterday.'

He gazed up at her with eyes much, much older than his face.

'It's you, isn't it?' she said, with sudden realization. 'Wherever we land, people accept us. I've always wondered why, just like I've always wondered how we can always understand what everyone says, no matter what language they're speaking. And now you're out of the way, whatever spell you've put on them is fading.'

He just smiled sadly.

'And do you do the same to Ace and me? Do you blind *us* to your faults?'

'*Et tu*?' he quoted softly.

'You said something, didn't you?'

'About what, Bernice?'

'About what I told you. Cheryl and Paula.'

The Doctor adjusted the brim of his hat to shadow his eyes. 'Of course not,' he said, but she didn't believe him.

Rabbi Shmuel Zehavi was leaving Miles Engado's quarters as Piper arrived.

'How is he?' she asked.

The wiry psychologist shook his head, almost dislodging his embroidered skullcap in the process. '*Oy!*' he exclaimed. 'That *meshuggener*! He's already broken three appointments to see me. "Pressure of work," he says, as if that's an adequate excuse. I've tried to tell him that the last thing Project Eden needs is an Administrator who's as crazy as a dakkabug, but will he listen to me?' Before Piper could enquire further about Miles's odd behaviour, Zehavi moved rapidly away down the corridor, muttering angrily to himself.

More worried now than she liked to admit, Piper extended her search for the Base Administrator to the refectory. The Bridge disaster, along with the subsequent events on Moloch, had thrown Piper's carefully calculated schedules into complete disarray. Members of all three shifts were milling about the circular room: repeating rumours, distorting facts and generally hyping themselves up.

Piper spotted Alex Bannen and his son sitting in the centre of the refectory. The table before them was loaded down with jellies and ice cream.

Unbelievable, she thought. For years he keeps the kid hidden away like the greatest secret in the galaxy, and now he's showing him off for everybody to see.

And then she saw Miles.

He was sitting alone, off to one side, watching a historical simularity, shipped in on the last supply drone, that was playing in the centre of the room. She walked over and joined him at the table.

'Miles?'

169

He didn't react.

'Miles! I've been worried.'

His gaze flickered over her, then back to the simularity.

'You know the Doctor was arrested for Paula's murder while you were unconscious?' she said, trying to provoke a reaction.

'That charlatan?' His lip curled slightly. 'He deserves to die.'

Piper looked away for a moment. 'I must know what happened to you down there on Moloch. Cheryl's been saying some odd things. Bishop's not saying anything, and as for Bernice and the Doctor – '

'The Doctor again. Always the Doctor. I've been suspicious of him since he first arrived.'

Piper frowned, trying to remember exactly how the Doctor and his friends *had* arrived on the base. She pulled her thoughts back to the present with an effort as Miles stood.

'No wait – don't go!'

Wearily, Miles sat down again.

'Tell me about it, Miles. I have to know.'

There was a long pause. 'I was in the pod. Paula's starpod. It was all powered-up and ready to go. I . . . I just wanted to look at the Earth. Well – Sol, anyway. If the instruments could pick it up from here. I was looking for it. I saw something. A waveform . . . Then there was just pain. Endless pain. And,' he hesitated.

Piper nodded eagerly. 'Yes?'

'And – I woke up here, in the medlab. Zehavi wanted to analyse my brain, but I'm fine. I keep telling him that. I'm fine.'

'I know,' she said.

'I wish everyone would just leave me alone!' His voice softened. 'Except you, Piper. You care. And . . .' He stood again. 'There's something I need to show you.'

Some kind of historical simularity was coming to an end as Bernice entered the crowded refectory, passing Miles Engado and Piper O'Rourke as she did so. She watched,

170

fascinated, as the beautiful computer expert destroyed the hideous alien invaders and claimed the handsome young museum curator as her own. As the end credits rolled and the title came up, she realized that it was a dramatized retelling of the Martian invasion of Earth *circa* 2090. She would never have guessed it from the wildly anachronistic costumes.

She smiled, remembering. She had made her reputation excavating the abandoned Ice Warrior citadels on Mars. That was many years ago in her own personal time-scale, many years in the future of the era she was in. It was also the first time she had been back to Earth since being drafted into Spacefleet, escaping, and running for the stars in a clapped-out old trading ship owned by a clapped-out old trader.

Climbing painfully up monolithic shafts of blue crystal. Making love with Tim in the vaulted egg chambers. Finding discarded shells stacked up with piles of Ice Marshal helmets, their glistening wetware implants still intact. The temptation to don one, to experience Martian life firsthand, almost overpowering . . .

She shook herself, and walked on. Her visit to the Doctor seemed to have stirred up old memories, like sediment at the bottom of a pond.

Cheryl Russell was seated on the far side of the refectory, watching the simularity. Although the credits had finished, and the picture had been replaced by a robotic continuity announcer, Cheryl's expression had not changed.

'Fancy a drink?' Bernice stopped by Cheryl's table and held out her refilled flask.

'Thanks,' Cheryl said, and to Bernice's amazement, drained the entire flask without stopping for breath.

'Cheryl, there's something I ought to tell you.'

'I've lost them both,' Cheryl said, without intonation.

'I tried to talk to you the night before last, but – '

'First Paula and then Sam.' It was as if she wasn't listening.

'Look, I think I owe – '

'You told someone, didn't you?'

'Oh Cheryl, I didn't mean to.' Bernice hung her head. God, she thought, how did it ever come to this?

'Sam found out that I was seeing Paula. He never said anything, but I knew that he knew, because he was nicer to me than he had ever been before. Then Paula died, and Sam disappeared, and I can't find him on Belial, and I can't find him on Moloch, and part of me is frightened that he might be dead, and part of me is frightened that he's not.'

She lowered her gaze to the plate of food she had ordered a while ago. She toyed with it with her fork, pushing it slowly around the plate, swirling it into patterns.

Without raising her eyes, Cheryl whispered, 'You were the only one . . .'

In the background, a news simularity presenter was wittering on. Bernice tried to focus her mind on the report, which featured outbreaks of a mystery virus that had wiped out millions in the *barrios* of Brazilia, Los Angeles and Tycho City. She had almost succeeded, when Cheryl looked up from her food. Bernice found herself unable to look away, inexorably drawn to the guilt and sadness she saw in Cheryl's face, and which she blamed herself for.

'The only one who knew we were sleeping together,' Cheryl continued, 'and – '

'Cheryl, I'm sorry! I didn't mean to walk in on you. I – '

'I keep wondering why I did it,' Cheryl said, as if Bernice hadn't spoken. 'It's not as if I don't love Sam, because I do. I love him like nothing else in my life, but Paula and I had been together when we were all planning Project Eden, before I even met Sam, and I loved her too, and somehow I just couldn't stop seeing her . . .'

The news broadcast had moved on to other matters now; the loss of contact between Earth Central and a Space Fleet flotilla which had been on its way to intercept a supposed alien fleet near Epsilon Eridani. Bernice remembered her conversation with the Doctor, and shivered. History ought to stay where it belongs, she thought: in the past.

'Cheryl,' she said carefully, 'when I walked in on you and Paula Engado, I was – surprised. I wanted to talk to someone about it. But I swear, I only mentioned it to one person, and he's the most trustworthy person I've ever met. He wouldn't have told anybody. Not Sam, or anyone.'

'Who was that?' Cheryl asked, uninterestedly.

'The Doctor,' Bernice said.

Cheryl looked at her for the first time. 'I should have guessed,' she said bitterly. 'You're in it together, aren't you? I don't know how you all managed to worm your way into our confidence, but someone's already taken care of one of your friends, and the other will be lucky if he lives until his trial.'

'What? Cheryl, what do you – '

But Cheryl did not reply. She stalked off, leaving Bernice shaken and alone.

As Miles opened the door to his office, Piper could see Adjudicator Bishop sitting at Miles's desk. A simularity of the Doctor sat above Miles's desk, strobing slowly in extreme close-up. Bishop's hand flicked the surface of the desk, blanking the picture. 'Can I help you?'

'I was hoping to be able to use my office,' Miles said slowly.

'That won't be possible. I'll be needing it for the rest of the day,' Bishop said. 'Guild of Adjudicators business. Perhaps another office?'

'Use mine,' Piper said, pulling Miles away before he said something she might regret.

Miles was silent as he followed Piper to the Technical Support area. He walked so slowly that Piper had to stop every few seconds and wait for him to catch up. When they arrived, he hesitated on the threshold, waiting for her to lead the way.

'Tea?' she said.

'Synthetic, or the real stuff?'

'Need you ask?' She placed scoops of tea essence into a couple of beakers and added water from the reconstituter. She could see him out of the corner of her eye, removing a crystal from his pocket and placing it in her desk reader. By the time she turned around, Paula Engado was frozen in space like a china figurine. A wave of guilt washed over her and receded, leaving her feeling slightly sick.

'Like a ghost,' Piper said.

'Pardon?'

'Paula. She haunts this Base like a ghost.'

Miles winced, and Piper suddenly realized what she had said.

'I didn't mean . . . Not literally, Miles! For heaven's sake, it was a metaphor.'

'Of course.' He paused, and passed a shaky hand across his face. Piper watched as he typed instructions into the desk.

```
<LOAD FILE G225/A/22/2/2154>
<SETUP>
<SET LINGUISTIC ANALYSIS = ON>
<SET SYNTAX = FULL>
<SET CONTEXT = FULL>
<SET POINT-OF-VIEW = PAULA ENGADO>
<SET STYLE = 15>
<RUN 58932.12>
```

'It was with her diary, down in the AVR lab on Moloch,' Miles said, a slight catch in his voice.

He hit <RETURN> and the tiny figure in the simularity began to move.

Paula ran a hand through her hair, and took a deep breath. Her heart was pounding, and she felt sick. Okay, she thought, here goes . . .

'Dad,' she said, 'if you're watching this, then I'm dead.'

The palms of her hands were sweating, and she wiped them against the legs of her tunic.

'I need to be alone for a while, and there's nowhere

here on Belial or Moloch where that can be true for any length of time. Whatever I do, I seem to hurt someone. I've had a talk with . . .' She hesitated, wondering whether to name the person, but decided on the spur of the moment against it. Dad would only blame them for what she was doing. 'Well, with a friend. And I think I can see things a bit more clearly now. I'm going down into Lucifer's atmosphere in a starsuit. I know it's risky – a lot more risky than if I waited for Yukio to finish programming the starpod – but I just need to get away for a while, by myself, and think. If I'm lucky then I'll be back with some decent results before anyone knows that I'm gone. If I'm really lucky then I'll come back with a tame, talkative Angel for you. If my luck has run out . . . Well, I'm going to leave this simularity in the starpod for you. I know you'll find it.'

She slipped one hand into a pocket, and scratched her nose with the other. So far, so good, she thought.

'There's something I need to say to you, Dad, and I'll never have the courage to do it face to face. When . . .' The words seemed to catch in her throat. Every time she thought about her mother, the tears were there. It was like the pain from an old wound, so familiar that she never noticed it until she deliberately picked at the scar. 'When Mum finally . . . When she . . . You just locked yourself up tight and never talked about her again.' The tears were coming; she could feel them. 'And I wanted so hard for you to love me. I worked my guts out getting my Doctorate, so that I could be a member of Project Eden and be with you. But it was like you never noticed me.' Warmth on her cheek, and the muscles at the corners of her mouth were clenching, dragging her lower lip downwards. 'You never noticed me. Dad, I'm sorry. I know you and Piper are – are more than friends, but please Dad, don't – don't marry her. It wouldn't be fair. It wouldn't be fair to Mum. And it wouldn't be fair to Piper, because I know how much you still love Mum, even though you never say so.'

It was no good. She was losing it. She had to cut it

short now and just leave, otherwise she wouldn't have the courage to do it.

'Goodbye, Dad,' she sobbed. 'If I'm lucky, you'll never have to watch this. I love you, remember that. I love you . . .'

She stabbed at the recorder controls, though her eyes were blurred with tears and she couldn't even see them.

<STOP>

<END>

Miles fumbled for the right controls, and eventually stopped the simularity. His eyes glittered with unshed tears. 'Piper, I'm sorry,' he choked, and reached out for her.

'Thanks, Miles. You really know how to inspire confidence in a woman.' She turned and walked away.

'No, wait! You don't understand. That's what Paula thought, not what I – '

It was too late. He was talking to a closed door.

Bernice knocked at Miles Engado's door. There was no answer, but then, she wasn't expecting any. She had seen the Adjudicator leave a few minutes before.

The door wasn't locked, and the simularity crystal was still in the desk reader. Whatever evidence Bishop had on the Doctor, she had to check it out. And then . . . Well, all archaeologists were thieves, of a sort.

She pressed <RUN>, glad now that she kept forgetting to take her simularity contact lenses out. Two heads appeared in mid-air: the Doctor's and Paula Engado's. Judging by the settings, the scene was being told from Paula's point of view. As the conversation replayed, Bernice felt herself go cold.

'Did Cheryl really say that?' Paula's voice was shrill, disbelieving. 'She loves me, but she can't leave Sam?'

'That's what she told me.' The Doctor's voice was harsh.

'It's all so stupid!' Paula said, on the verge of tears.

'It doesn't matter what *you* think,' the Doctor sneered. 'It's Cheryl's feelings that count.'

A sudden hatred of Sam Russell welled up within Paula. 'I know how Sam is going to feel,' she hissed.

'Don't be stupid.'

'You're right,' she sighed. 'It's Cheryl's decision. I can't argue with that.'

'And are you still going down in the starsuit?'

Paula gazed into the Doctor's bleak eyes. What is there left here for me? she thought. I might as well end the pain now.

He nodded, as if he could read her thoughts, and moved to leave.

'I might not be coming back,' she said.

He nodded, and left.

'Damning, isn't it,' said a voice from the doorway as the scene cut off.

Bernice looked up. Bishop was watching her.

'Superficially,' she admitted.

'It's Paula's own simularity diary. It was still recording when the Doctor walked into the lab on Moloch. It looks to me as if the Doctor manipulated Paula Engado's feelings with a faked message from her adulterous lover Cheryl Russell to the effect that Cheryl wouldn't leave her husband, Sam. The Doctor suggested a method of suicide. Paula, distraught, took his advice. Some time later, Krau Ace discovered the crystal and accused the Doctor of manipulating Paula's suicide. The Doctor arranged for Ace, and all potential witnesses on Moloch, to die. Am I missing any salient events?'

'The death of the Energy Policeman, Moshe-Rabaan, and the disappearance of Sam Russell?' Bernice replied snappily.

'Oh, Krau Rabaan controlled the security drones. Perhaps the Doctor suspected she too might have evidence against him, and killed her. Sam . . . Well, a cuckolded husband – I'm sure I can fit him in somewhere.'

'A trifle thin.'

'It's all I need.'

Bernice thought quickly, trying to remember her history. Like lag-ships and vargol generators, simularities had died out pretty quickly in historical terms. The fad hadn't lasted to her time, but she still remembered articles in the learned techno-archaeology journals.

'These simularities, they can be set to interpret body language and voice inflection, can't they?'

'That's their main function,' he said, inclining his head. 'The neural net records all details of a scene – body posture, words, tone of voice, movement – and when the scene is replayed it enhances certain features to make the record less ambiguous.'

'Enhances?' Bernice was on to something.

Bishop didn't seem discomfited. 'Yes. For instance, if somebody shows evidence of being tense whilst being questioned, that can be emphasized in order to make their behaviour clearer.'

'But any characteristic can be enhanced.'

'In theory, yes.'

Somewhere at the back of her mind, it occurred to Bernice that Bishop was giving her an awful lot of rope.

'May I try an experiment?' she asked.

Bishop gestured to the table. 'But I do have copies of the simularity,' he warned.

Bernice tried to recall the initial lessons that Cheryl had given her, soon after the TARDIS had landed on Belial. Her fingers danced over the keyboard, uncertain at first, then more sure.

'Let's try it from a different perspective,' she said, and pressed <RUN> again.

'Did Cheryl really say that she loves me?' Paula asked ecstatically.

The Doctor nodded.

'But she can't leave Sam,' she said, hoping that the Doctor would contradict her. It was all too good to be true.

'That's what she told me.' He smiled conspiratorially.

'It's all so stupid,' Paula said, and giggled.

'It doesn't matter what *you* think,' the Doctor chided gently. 'It's Cheryl's feelings that count.'

'I know how Sam is going to feel,' she said wistfully.

'Don't,' said the Doctor, and shook his head. Paula searched his eyes for an answer. '*Be* stupid!' he encouraged, and smiled.

'You're right.' She smiled back. 'It's Cheryl's decision. I can't argue with that.'

'And are you still going down in the starsuit?'

She remembered the smoothness of Cheryl's skin, the fullness of her lips. 'I might not be,' she said.

He got up, startling her. There was something about his presence that made her feel calm and peaceful.

'Coming back?' she asked, as he raised his hat.

He nodded, and left.

'You see,' Bernice said triumphantly. 'Same words, different meanings. The Doctor could be innocent!'

'I know,' Bishop said. 'I've run fifteen variations of that conversation, and every one has come up with different motivations for the Doctor. Either the software is playing up, or your friend is the most complex character I have ever had the pleasure of arresting.'

'In that case – '

The floor shook with a distant explosion. Klaxons began to wail.

'Bloody hell! What was that?'

'The Conference Room.' Bishop's voice was so calm Bernice wanted to scream.

'Oh Christ. The Doctor!'

Bernice left the office at a dead run. By the time she reached the Conference Room, the air was filled with the smell of burning, more even than the atmosphere recyclers could deal with. The corridor was filled with people, some wielding fire extinguishers, others rushing medkits through the smoke. Bernice pushed her way through the confused mass of people, looking for Miles or Piper. Neither was in plain sight. The Russian botanist Anushkia

Smyslov seemed to be in charge, directing people to clear twisted metal beams from the corridor and check the Base's integrity with air-pressure sensors.

'Doctor Smyslov, what's happened? Have you seen the Doctor? He was in the Conference Room.'

The big Russian shook her head with a marked lack of sympathy. 'Sensors have confirmed the Conference Room is open to space. Unless your friend can breathe vacuum, he's dead.' She pushed past Bernice. 'Now if you'll excuse me, I do have a job to do.'

Chapter Eleven

Miles Engado faced west along the bay and watched the sun sinking past the village into a golden haze of spray. Soon it would be time for the ceremony to begin: for him to walk into the darkened woods and connect his mind to that of the Whale. To pray for the great creature's cooperation in tomorrow's activity.

The season of the hunt had come again to the people of the North Water.

He walked along the beach, past rows of low cedar huts, his bare feet kicking at the surf which swept in from the north, enjoying the cool water and the tickling sensation of sand being swept between his toes and around his ankles. Other men of the village were beaching their canoes even as he watched, pulling ashore the dead seals which would ultimately become floats to slow the Whale in the hunt. Children combed the shoreline for strong shells which the women would sharpen and affix to spears twice the height of a man. The spears would serve to fish and hunt with, as well as defend the village against competing tribes.

Miles offered up a silent prayer as he walked. He was lucky to have been born in this particular tribe. The ocean provided a bountiful supply of fresh food and, together with the forests inland, provided all the raw materials necessary to reap the harvest, as well as jealously guard it.

Miles thought back to his first season as a hunter. He remembered the heat of the sun on his back, and the way the cold water cleaved at the touch of the canoe, as it was propelled forward in search of prey by the hunters.

He remembered squinting eagerly to catch sight of the basking seals, content and sleepy in the afternoon sunshine, and pointing with excitement when he did. The other men in the canoe had laughed at his impatience and berated him for pointing. Everyone knew that to point at the seals was taboo. Miles had hung his head in shame. He'd had no wish to wake the seals and drive them away. His friend Okawi had signalled to the other canoes by gently shaking his thumb in the direction of the sleeping animals. Paddles had dipped silently into the water; the canoes sped closer, but the seals had awoken suddenly, and swum away.

Just three seals had been killed that day, when more than twenty were needed; and only one cleanly, by a single spear-thrust from Okawi. Later, Miles had carved the dead seals' faces on the two killing clubs to honour the animals' sacrifice. He had never shown impatience or eagerness again.

Miles smiled. He had been little more than a boy then. Now he was a man, Chief of his village. It was his responsibility to convince the Whale to cooperate in the hunt, so the people of the village might be fed and clothed for another season. He watched as the women of the village – his new wife, Beruna, among them – rushed down to the waterline in their reed skirts. There they would gut the seals and render their oil, which they would later store in the stomachs and bladders of sea lions.

Moving closer, Miles watched as strips of blubber were placed along with heated stones into canoes filled with water. The oil floated to the surface and was skimmed away to be used later as a food dip.

He moved slowly along the beach. Preparations for the hunt seemed to be going well. Okawi had prepared the hunting canoes and was now praying over their steep sides.

Beruna glared as he walked past to join Okawi, her hands full of seal blubber, a bone knife beside her on the sand. He knew she was angry with him for allowing their daughter to join the hunt, traditionally something only a select few men were allowed the honour of, but she would see his way soon enough. Paula had proved to him she was as able a fisherwoman as any of the men. And he was Chief, after all. Perhaps it was time for tradition to change just a little. He smiled back at Beruna, trying to silently communicate how proud he was, of both her and Paula, but her eyes fell angrily to her work.

Miles looked up. The topmost edge of the sun was about to dip beyond the North Water. The sky was cloudless and glowing. Tomorrow the hunt would begin. Even now Miles could feel the great Whale approaching, assured of its destiny, its place in the scheme of life.

It was time to pray.

Leaving Okawi and Beruna, Miles turned away from the village and padded silently across the beach to the tree line.

Beyond the first line of trees the forest was shrouded in darkness. Only the topmost branches were still gilded by daylight, the illuminated areas shrinking as the sun dropped below the misty horizon. Miles stepped across the threshold and into a different world. The thunder of the surf became a muted whisper, driven into silence by the rustling of branches and the innumerable calls of night animals, bats and insects. His feet, still speckled with sand, moved confidently through the undergrowth. He made no sound: he was one with the land.

Above him, the trees became black silhouettes against a midnight blue sky. Stars shone thinly. Miles walked on into the night, to a special place, a secret place, that only he knew. His praying pool. There he slipped soundlessly into the cold black water and remained submerged, except for his face, floating easily as the night deepened.

As he swam he dreamed the Whale calm, asking the great creature politely for its cooperation in garnering that which his village needed. He remembered the words of his grandfather, so many years ago:

'The Whale always gives our people something. The Whale always helps someone who needs him. When you are in the forest, take water at every creek. Blow it and

183

start praying while spraying mist from your mouth. In this way will you grow closer to the Whale. In this way will it do what you ask of it.'

In his mind the Whale drifted closer through the piebald darkness, and sang:

I have come to see how your house is. Is it prepared for large crowds?

At the touch of these words, Miles felt calmness leave him. He knew doubt. 'Large crowds?' His grandfather had never mentioned these words. No Whale in previous seasons had sung these words. 'Is your house prepared for large crowds?'

Disturbed, Miles swam slowly to the edge of the pool and climbed out of the water. He stood shivering in the cold air, no longer one with the land, his eyes dim and sightless, his ears blocked to the night sounds, and tried to think.

His house?

Miles moved back through the forest, back towards the beach. Fires loomed in the night, driving back the darkness. He moved to his hut. Beruna. She was wise. She would know what his vision meant. He stooped to enter the hut – and paused.

There were sounds coming from inside. His wife. And another.

Another!

Angrily, Miles stepped into the hut. Beruna stood to face him, blocking his view into the hut.

'You should not be here. You should be praying to the Whale. Without prayers, the Whale will not cooperate in the hunt and the village will starve for lack of food and oil to trade.'

'I!' Miles felt a fury boil up within him. '*I* should not be here? What, then, of this other, skulking in the shadows like a crab?' Miles moved to pull his wife aside. Before he could touch her, the concealed figure rose.

'I am no crab, Miles Engado,' said Okawi. 'As you are no Chief, any longer. Any man who allows his daughter to hunt with warriors does not deserve to lead the tribe.'

184

'We will see this tested tomorrow, in the hunt.' Miles turned and left the hut.

The pursuit began as the sun rose across the bay. Strong, silent paddling brought three canoes close to the great Whale. The canoes were loaded with sealskin floats. Miles stood at one prow, Okawi at another. Cedar harpoons were clutched in their hands, anchored to the floats by long coils of rope made from cedar bark. The water was choppy. Hatred showed in Miles's face. Jealousy glittered in Okawi's eyes. The hunters paddling each canoe were terrified. This was not the way a hunt should be. Each remembered all too clearly Okawi's parting words before they had pushed each canoe clear of the beach:

'Beruna will not lie still in her hut for you this day, and so the Whale will thrash about. She will not face inland, and so the Whale will not swim ashore. Today she is mine. Today you will catch no Whale, and I will be Chief.'

And of course – there was Paula, gripping her harpoon in the third canoe.

Miles had remained silent as they had paddled out into the water, though his heart was full of anger and grief. At first sight of the Whale, he had gripped the harpoon tightly, perhaps wishing it was Okawi's neck. Fear was in him. Fear, and betrayal. Yet the Whale must be caught or else the village would know hardship and death.

Ahead, the Whale breached the surface and blew. A fountain of stinking saltwater erupted into the air. Great flukes slapped the ocean with a sound like thunder. Spray drenched the canoes. Miles signalled, and the hunters drove on.

As if sensing their approach, the Whale turned and headed away from shore. Okawi stood in his canoe and yelled triumphantly. 'I am right, Miles Engado! I am right!'

Miles called to the hunters to increase their speed. The canoes shot forward, Paula's drawing level with the Whale's head. Miles watched as she levelled her harpoon and drew back her arm. With a triumphant yell, she hurled the harpoon. It sank into the Whale's glistening skin just behind its head. The animal thrashed with the sudden pain, and sounded with a great gout of water tinged with blood. Once again its flukes slapped the water, and this time the effect was disastrous. A huge wave swamped the canoes, overturning them and tipping the hunters into the foaming water. Miles found himself in the water, tangled in coils of rope, battered by sealskin floats.

Paula was floating nearby, blood trickling from a rope burn across her shoulders. Unable to free himself from the tangle of ropes and floats, Miles swam laboriously across to his daughter. Just as he reached her, the Whale surged upwards again and Miles was caught by the wave. He could only watch helplessly as Paula was hurled head-first into the canoe floating nearby. There was a sickening crunch, and he lost sight of her in the swell.

He tried to yell instructions, but water smashed into his face, filling his mouth and nose, suffocating and blinding him.

Then the rope tightened around his body, and he felt something pulling him beneath the surface.

The Whale.

He was caught on the harpoon rope.

Water rushed past his face, growing swiftly darker and colder as he was pulled down. He tugged uselessly at the ropes, but could not free himself. His knife was gone, swept away in the confusion. His chest burned savagely as the ropes bit into his skin. There was a sudden sharp pain in his ears. He opened his mouth to scream his anger and pain, and the water rushed in, eager to silence him. His limbs became heavier, until the effort needed to move them was simply too much. It grew cold and dark as a winter night, and there was no Beruna to hold him, and no daughter to comfort him, only the rope's cruel embrace, and the Whale's anger.

His last sensation was of pressure waves rippling against his body.

The Whale was . . .

. . . screaming as he lurched from his bed, his hands

groping for his throat, his chest heaving convulsively as he fought for air. He fell to the floor, tangled in a single sheet, thrashing in panic. The Whale! Okawi! His wife was . . . She was . . .

Miles became quite still.

His ancestral village and its myths were three hundred years in the past, and the clear, blue waters of the bay were a sludge of industrial effluent through which thrashed the occasional blinded seabird. His unfaithful wife was nine years dead. Only Paula was left to him now.

His face fell and he began to sob as he came fully awake and remembered that even that was no longer true.

Bernice scrambled madly through the twisted wreckage as Anushkia Smyslov lost herself in the chaos, shouting orders. Tears were driven from her eyes by the smoke. She pushed past Julie Ndobe, grabbing a medkit from the woman's hands, and running further into the smoke, only to fetch up hard against a metal barrier.

'No!' Uselessly, she hammered on the pressure door. 'Somebody help me get the door open!'

A hand fell on her shoulder. Bernice spun, grabbing for the body at the end of the arm, not caring who it was. 'You've got to help me! We can get him out. He has a respiratory bypass system, we can – '

'Bernice, it's too late.' Teal Green grabbed her shoulders and shook her hard. 'He's gone. Gone.'

Bernice gazed stupidly at the engineer. 'Bullshit! He's *alive!*'

'No.'

'Christ. Oh, Christ.' Bernice pulled away from Teal. 'I've got to get this sorted out.'

'Where are you going?'

'Bishop had the whole place monitored. I'm going to find out how this happened – and who's responsible.'

Bernice rushed off into the smoke. Teal moved worriedly after her.

Piper O'Rourke stepped out of the murk behind them,

wearing a concerned expression. She turned on her heel and vanished into the murk.

Bishop tried to block the sound of the explosion from his ears, but couldn't. He tried to imagine what the inside of the Conference Room would look like now, and found he all too easily could.

He sighed, and reached for his tea.

It had all been so simple until now.

As a child he had lain in bed long into the night, plotting his escape from an alcoholic father and a mother who managed not to see the bruises and the tears. He studied in every spare moment he could find, not because he wanted to but because, in the absence of parents who would pay, he needed to win a scholarship even to get to school. He got it. And he fought every moment of his time at school to keep it. With no family money or family privilege to protect him, he was easy meat, so he learned how to protect himself. He learned how to talk his way out of trouble and, when that didn't work, how to cripple an opponent in the shortest possible time. He went from school to college, and he graduated top of his class. A still, small voice inside him murmured 'this is all too easy', but offers flooded in from the combines, the multi-nationals, the companies who had profited from the rape of the Earth, and who were now taking their ecological molestation into space. He had got himself noticed. But something inside him, some long-ago echo of a boy beaten into insensibility if he cried, said, no, money isn't everything, satisfaction isn't everything, what about justice?

It was a small man in long, black robes who turned Bishop's life around. He had engaged Bishop in conversation on the travel belts one day, displaying an uncanny knowledge not only of Bishop's life, but also of his innermost thoughts. Bishop had known what was happening: the Guild of Adjudicators was famed and feared in equal measure amongst the Earth colonies. Unconstrained by authority, independent of financial influence, they dispensed their own uncompromising brand of justice across the galaxy. Their indirect recruiting methods were legendary.

Bishop didn't take much persuading.

After five years intensive training on the secluded world of Ponten VI – a curious mixture of legal precedent and target practice – Bishop was allowed out in the field as squire to a more experienced Adjudicator. He found that he enjoyed the work. More than that, he was good at it. He moved up through the system rapidly enough to make his mark without looking flashy. Perhaps, on every promotion, a little voice inside his head muttered, 'Who are you kidding? You can't possibly do this job,' but his cases were always brought to a conclusion in the minimum time and, more importantly, with the minimum expense. He was dedicated. His social life didn't suffer, because he didn't have a social life. Sometimes, in the long reaches of the night, the philosophical difference between what was right and what was just bothered him, but a cup of tea and a good night's sleep usually solved that problem.

He never thought about his family.

Eventually, more as a matter of course than as a reward, he was made an Adjudicator; judge, jury and executioner, all rolled into one. He deserved it, there was no doubt about that, but still something inside him whispered, 'You're heading for a fall.'

From the messy consequences of the Kroagnon affair to the vraxoin raids off Azure, from the Macra case to the Vega debacle, Bishop's record was immaculate. Not one failure, not one incorrect prosecution, not a hint of doubt anywhere.

Until now.

Bishop listened to the rolling echoes of the explosion which had destroyed the Conference Room die away deep within the base. He reached for his tea.

'I made a fresh pot,' said a soft voice at his elbow.

'You, Doctor, might very well have destroyed my career.'

The Doctor grinned. 'That'd be a clever trick for someone who's just been blown up.' Calmly, he took a sip of

189

tea. 'Nice. But it would taste so much better from a Wedgwood pot.'

Bishop sighed impatiently.

The Doctor set down his beaker. 'Well, Adjudicator. Are you ready for the moment of truth?'

Bishop nodded. 'Neural net,' he said quietly. 'Access simularity file one. Location: Conference Room exterior. Let's see who the murderer really is.'

The lights went out; all power to the neural net was severed.

Teal Green was coughing up a lungful of smoke when the Base was plunged into darkness. Immediately, a string of curses echoed down the corridor and there was the sound of someone falling over. Teal felt his way carefully forward. His foot thumped against something soft in the darkness.

'Be careful! That's me you're kicking!'

'Bernice?'

'You were expecting the Isley Brothers?'

'Who?'

'Grief, help me up will you? And what's going on?'

'Power failure.'

'How can that happen?'

'It can't. All systems are independently monitored by the neural net.'

'Well, I hate to disagree with you, but – '

'Yeah, right. Point taken. Come on.'

'Where to?'

'The backup systems should have kicked in by now. We must be looking at a general systems failure. If we don't get life support up and running soon, we'll all suffocate.'

'Wonderful,' Bernice said dryly. 'What do we do first?'

'Finding a torch would be a good trick.' Teal groped around the corridor wall. 'There ought to be a – ah! Here we go.'

A door opened. From within the room came the sound of a man sobbing.

'Miles?'

'Paula? I'll be with you soon. I promise.'

Before they could move, someone pushed past them and shambled off down the corridor.

The Doctor pulled a small torch from his pocket and clicked it on. The beam was more than adequate to illuminate the non-operational neural net systems. He tapped a key experimentally, but there was no response. 'Someone has a positively dramatic sense of timing.'

Bishop drained his beaker of tea. 'Power failure.'

'Yes, but what caused it?'

'More sabotage?'

'Not unless the saboteur planned to take his own life as well.'

'Or unless – '

'The saboteur had already worked out an escape route.'

'There is another possibility.'

The Doctor nodded. 'Whoever, or whatever, invaded Moloch Base is now attempting a similar takeover here.' He led the way to the office door. 'Come along, Adjudicator. I rather think your services will shortly be needed in the main airlock. And your gun.'

Alex Bannen swung the beam of his torch wildly around the Operations Room. 'Piper? Are you here? What the hell is going on? The power's out all over the base, the temperature is dropping, the air's running out and Mark's gone. He's just – switched off.'

Piper rose from the MultiCray inputting terminal. 'I'm doing my best to restore emergency power. Until the backup generators come on line, I can't get enough ergs to run a full check on the main systems.'

Bannen sighed. 'For God's sake. Ask a scientist to do a scientist's job – not an overblown plumber's mate.'

He pushed Piper aside and unclipped a service hatch in the main neural net cabinet. Piper glared angrily at his bulky silhouette. If she didn't do something now, he was going to screw everything up.

The Doctor rushed down the corridor, his small feet making virtually no sound on the metal grillework. Puffing hard, Bishop followed close behind. Either the corridors were empty of people, or the Doctor had managed to follow a less well-travelled route from Miles's office to the main airlock, several levels below. With no power to drive the klaxons or the air recyclers, the Base was eerily silent. Only distant clangs and echo-distorted snatches of conversation drifting along the cross-corridors testified to the tremendous effort being put into restarting the systems.

The Doctor slid to a halt at the inner door to the main airlock. He tapped quickly at the opening mechanism.

The door remained shut.

'Odd. The door's been locked with a command level override.'

Bishop frowned in the darkness. 'Only Miles Engado has that clearance.'

The Doctor cleared his throat. 'Ahem. Well, actually . . .' He tapped out another rapid series of digits and the lock disengaged. The Doctor grabbed the manual locking wheel and began to spin it rapidly. Hydraulic pressure built up slowly until the door wheezed open.

Umbrella held high, the Doctor led the way into the chamber. There were clanking noises coming from further within. He shone his torch around the chamber. 'Miles? Miles Engado? We know you're in here . . .'

There was a hollow clunk, and the rising whine of power. Ten metres away, lights bloomed in the darkness.

Bishop drew his gun. 'Miles Engado, I am arresting you for the – '

'Miles, no!' The Doctor rushed forward, but was too late to prevent Miles latching down his helmet and powering up the starsuit. Warning lights flashed on the suit's shoulders as it lumbered slowly to the airlock outer door. One servo-driven arm reached out to grip the door's locking wheel.

'Get out!' the Doctor called, running back towards the inner door. After a moment's hesitation, Bishop followed.

The locking wheel turned. The door began to open. 'All the failsafes are power driven – if we don't get out the whole section will depressurize!'

Air began to whistle out of the airlock. Together, the Doctor and Bishop scrambled through the inner door against the mounting pressure of air. The Doctor swung himself round the door and gripped the locking wheel. The door slid shut as the wheel spun. The air-scream ceased.

Bishop holstered his gun.

A light bobbed up and down further along the corridor, accompanied by the sound of running footsteps. Bernice and Teal halted breathlessly beside the Doctor and Bishop.

'Doctor! My God, you are alive!' Bernice said, stunned.

The Doctor found a second to doff his hat.

'It's Miles, we have to stop him,' she said.

'He is responsible for the sabotage on the Base and he has implicated himself by trying to escape,' Bishop said harshly.

'No, you don't understand.' Teal waved a piece of paper under Bishop's nose. 'We found this in his quarters. It's a suicide note. He's not trying to escape; he's trying to kill himself.'

'Then who's responsible for all this?'

There was a groan from the darkness, and Alex Bannen stumbled into the splash of light made by the torches. He raised one hand to the back of his head; his fingers came away stained with blood. 'Piper. It's bloody Piper. She brained me when I tried to reboot the neural net.'

He fell to the floor with a groan, blood pooling around his head.

Chapter Twelve

Kreig was counting her ears again.

'Thirty-eight,' Ardamal prompted from the far side of the squalid, duralinium-lined bunkroom. 'You had thirty-eight yesterday morning, and thirty-eight last night. 'Less there's someone woke up today hard of hearing, there's thirty-eight there now.'

Kreig looked up, an ear held delicately in her hand like some alien flower.

'You trying to make a point?' she snarled.

'Just wondering.'

'Wondering what?'

'Why you keep counting.'

'Case some dumb-ass tries to steal one.'

'Yeah, stupid of me,' Ardamal muttered, as Kreig wrapped the ear in soft plastic, placed it gently back in its box, and picked another out.

Dommer had been following the exchange from his bunk, where he was obsessively stripping and reassembling his flamer. 'How many d'you get in that last action?' he asked. His throat had been badly scarred by praxis gas during a bankruptcy action three years ago, and his words came out sounding like fingernails scratching glass.

'Come on, Dommer,' Ardamal said. 'You know her rules. One every time. Like a keepsake. For luck.'

Dommer laughed. 'Yeah,' he said. 'Beats hell out'a crappy tourist gifts.' His fingers idly stroked the oiled metal of his exposed weapon.

Kreig wasn't listening. Her deeply lined face was creased into a smile as she gazed at the tiny ear in her hand.

'Asset-stripping InterSpace Incorporated, back in Tokyo in fifty-six,' she whispered. Her face was radiant. 'Tiny kid, daughter of the Chairman. We Zed-bombed the barriers and went in with shielded skimmers. Corporate lawyers went in under our covering fire to deliver the paperwork.'

She turned the ear until Ardamal could see the crust of blood beneath it.

'They wanted the Chairman's retinal print for the waiver forms,' she continued. 'Didn't say nothing about wanting the rest of him, though. And I got his kid.'

'I remember Tokyo,' said Dommer, and laughed. 'Had a good time, and Jeez, the bonuses! Those shares're still paying off better'n the regular paycheck.'

'I thought you was on the InterSpace payroll back then?' Ardamal growled.

'Yeah, but I got head-hunted. IMC bought out my contract. I've spent thirty years as a Company Shock Trooper, and IMC's the best thing that ever happened to me. I mean, take this last action. Nobody firing back, and we still get a percentage of the profits. Just a turkey shoot, that's all it was.'

His voice was beginning to grate on Ardamal.

'Had myself a nice piece of Scottish ass, though,' Dommer reminisced with a gap-toothed smile. 'Wildcat, that one.' He ran a hand over the parallel scratches down his cheek. 'Had to give her a good talking to.' He fondled the scorched barrel of the flamer. 'A *good* talking to.'

'No cover,' Ardamal said, just to shut Dommer up. 'Be thankful nobody was firing back. The way the ground just curled up at the edges until you lost sight of it, we couldn't have crept up on a hunk of soya.'

'Yeah.' Dommer had reassembled his flamer now, and was checking the calibration on the sights by centring the laser marker on Kreig's temple. 'That was kinda – '

The alert sirens screamed. Three sets of boots hit the floor.

'*All crew to stations*,' the tannoy rasped. '*Escaped prisoner. Repeat; escaped prisoner. Amber alert. Repeat;*

amber alert. Troops one to seventeen adopt search pattern spiral delta. This is not an exercise. Repeat; this is not an exercise.'

Ardamal just beat Kreig out of the door, while Dommer was still fumbling with his flamer. The last thing Ardamal heard as he raced down the corridor was the tinkle of metal parts hitting the floor.

As he leaped for the null-grav shaft, he caught sight of the prisoner thrashing through the air two storeys above. Her pony-tail was weaving like a snake, and she was still dressed in blood-stained black armour and shiny leggings; the same kit that she had been wearing when Ardamal and his section had dragged her, kicking and screaming, into the IMC executive transporter. This time she had a gun.

Ardamal twisted lithely, presenting the smallest possible surface area to the woman whilst simultaneously lining up his needler on her left breast. 'Body shots are best,' he heard the long-ago voice of Sergeant Cribb saying, back at the IMC training camp, as he demonstrated various weapons and aiming techniques on a row of terrified ElleryCorp prisoners. 'If you miss the heart, you might still put a hole through something vital. If you miss the head, you've missed them completely.'

Kreig swam to one side, hugging the walls, boosting her speed with handholds and seams, trying to overtake the woman and pin her between exits. Textbook stuff.

The woman was drifting upwards now; trying to read exit signs whilst still watching for pursuit. Klaxons echoed up and down the shaft. The peculiar properties of air under null-grav conditions added an extra resonance to the noise.

Kreig passed the woman without a sound, without a breeze, climbing like a rocket to Exit 347, where she hung, waiting for the woman and Ardamal to catch up.

Ardamal manoeuvred himself to a position below and slightly behind the woman, hidden by her legs. As his needler's laser marker passed across her back, he pressed the compensation stud. Micro-gyros kicked in, stabilizing the bright dot on the base of her spine. Somewhere in the back of his mind was the knowledge that Legion wanted the woman kept alive, but the sight of Kreig's ears had given Ardamal a thirst, and he needed to slake it. The needler felt like it was locked in space. He took up the trigger pressure.

Body shots are best.

'Ard' old buddy, where's the . . . Shit!'

Dommer had come flailing into the shaft below Ardamal. He caught sight of the woman at the same time she heard him. Her eyes widened. Dommer swung his flamer up to cover her as she twisted her handgun around. She hadn't trained in null-grav, that much was obvious. Her body spun in the opposite direction to her gun as she fired, conserving angular momentum and throwing her aim completely off. Energy flashed past Ardamal in a long arc of fire, blistering the side of the shaft, missing his face by less than half a metre.

Dommer, chanting some kind of battle hymn, fired.

His incompletely assembled weapon exploded, smothering his head, arms and shoulders in a mass of flames. Screaming, he cartwheeled into the side of the shaft and rebounded, leaving a smear of grease and soot. The smell of roasting flesh drifted up the shaft.

Ardamal ignored the distraction and took careful aim again.

The prisoner was trying to stabilize her spin, and failing. There was no fear in her eyes: only hatred, and the knowledge that she could never, ever die.

He pulled the trigger.

The space where she had been was obliterated in a flash of hard radiation. When the blaze cleared, there was nothing.

For hours the planet had grown no larger in Miles Engado's faceplate; seeming instead to retreat as he fell towards it. Lucifer was indifferent to him. It tolerated his advance, but would make no concessions. He berated it, screaming out his rage and his fear until his voice was a croak, and small droplets of sweat and spittle hung about his face. It made no difference. Lucifer did not hear him. Or, if it did, it paid him no heed.

Drained by his ranting and lulled by the way he could float in the starsuit, just touching the padded interior, he drifted into and out of sleep like a man wandering through the rooms of an empty house. His dreams were short and violent, punctuated by images of a vast, barnacle-encrusted shape which drifted disdainfully away as he swam towards it.

When he finally surfaced, his mouth stale and his eyes hot and gritty, Lucifer's atmosphere had already enfolded him like a shroud. He twisted his head to look upwards, but Moloch was just a faint disc half hidden by the clouds: a burnished coin beneath polluted water.

He floundered in panic as, for a brief moment, he could not remember why he was there. He knew that he had written a note explaining everything, but the note was back on Belial and he had forgotten its contents. Had he said that he was going to his death in Lucifer's inferno? Had he written about the great hunt, the rites of the warriors? It was all so far away now. There was only him, and the clouds, and the hidden face of Lucifer.

He was not falling. Rather: thin muslin sheets of brown and red were being pulled past his eyes, patterned like the blankets woven by the women, patterned like the rug that hung on the wall in his daughter's room. Shadows drifted past him like fronds, dappled with refracted sunlight, tied with thin streams of bubbles as he sank slowly into the welcoming depths of the ocean, under the incurious eye of the great Whale . . .

When he awoke again, it was with a pounding headache. The starsuit was hotter now; the heat of re-entry and the energy of Lucifer's interior triumphing over the best human life support technology. His sweat had floated from him whilst he slept, and whilst he fell, overwhelming the humidity regulators, pooling in the extremities of the starsuit and soaking into the padding. The atmosphere had closed in: now it was as if a clumsy child had finger-painted amorphous swirls and blobs in dull colours over his faceplate.

His thoughts were clearer now. Perhaps the heat had given his mind the boost it needed to throw off the dream world that had gradually surrounded him since Paula's fall into the maw of the Beast. He remembered the note. He remembered writing of Paula's death, of how he could not live without knowing the truth, and how, if he gave himself into the hands of the great Whale, he knew that he would be reunited with her in death.

He remembered wanting to write a farewell to Piper. He wondered if he had.

Miles shook his head wearily. Project Eden had eaten five years of his life, and spat them back at him, empty of meaning. There had been no contact with the Angels; there would be no power source for Earth. He had failed his race as he had failed his family.

The indicators were beginning to flicker hesitantly, reminding him of his foolishness. He was a stupid old man who deserved to die. Like his wife. Like his daughter.

He prepared to give himself over to whatever fate Lucifer had in store for him.

And that was why, when Paula's face swam out of the murky clouds and peered incuriously at him, Miles Engado screamed.

The room was warm and inviting, like a gentleman's club, or the lounge bar in her local back in Perivale. It engendered immediate feelings of friendship, of belonging. For the first time since Heaven, Ace thought of Julian, and of the times they had sat in worn green leather armchairs, the hum of traffic from the A40 outside making waves in their glasses, knowing that the barman thought they were underage but also knowing that Ace intimidated him so much that he wouldn't say anything. This room was like that: oak panelled, plushly carpeted, lined with portraits, slightly musty. The chandeliers floating near the ceiling were a touch ornate for her taste, but she liked the huge wooden table stacked up with what looked like real fruit.

199

After so long eating recycled meals on Belial, her salivary glands sprang into life with sharp little pangs of anticipation.

It was entirely inappropriate, but she couldn't help herself. Moloch seemed so long ago.

And there was something else in the room with her.

She turned slowly, ready for action.

Whatever it was, it vanished as she turned.

She caught sight of a movement out of the corner of her eye, whirled, but was too late to see anything. She was alone.

Bugger this for a game of soldiers, she thought, and opened her mouth to speak.

'I must apologize for my staff. Their actions can be – precipitate.'

The voice surprised her. Or was it voices? Bass, tenor, alto and soprano; the words seemed to glide up and down the scale from moment to moment with no consistency. Their direction seemed to change as well. It was almost as if she was surrounded by a choir, with each person allocated one word, but so well rehearsed that the sentences flowed seamlessly along.

'Precipitate!' Ace snarled. 'Your "staff" killed my friends. I don't care what fancy words you use, I call it murder!' She waved her weapon menacingly. Whatever vanishing act had saved her from the goon with the gun, it had left her armed. Foolish, very foolish.

There was a laugh from behind her. Ace snapped around, priming the weapon as she moved. The laugh curled around her, beginning as a soft chuckle, evolving through a deep guffaw, and ending as a childlike giggle, once more behind her. Her lips thinned. Her finger slipped inside the weapon's trigger guard. 'I'm warning you. Stop taking the piss.'

'The Terrestrial sense of humour,' said the voice. 'There's nothing quite like it anywhere else in the cosmos.'

Ace frowned. She'd intended to appear threatening, not amusing.

'Yes, I'm afraid they're ruined,' the voice continued, as if engaged in a different conversation. 'Perhaps you would like to slip into something more comfortable.'

Ace frowned. What was going on here? The conversation was hopping all over the place like a dakkabug on a griddle.

'Albert, the master of witty repartee, says "Piss off",' she retorted, finally finding a use for the punchline of the worst joke she'd ever been told.

A whiff of burned material caught her attention. She glanced down, trying to trace the source of the smell, and suddenly noticed that her leggings were scorched and her polycarbide armour was blistered and smoking, its structural integrity ruined.

'Oh sod,' she said. 'I'd just worn them in, as well.'

'Ah, no, your friends are not dead,' the voice said. For a moment, it was a child's voice, just behind her shoulder, but then it was old, and quavery, and a million miles away. 'No, merely anaesthetized. I have them under medical supervision.'

Ace frowned. She remembered . . .

. . . *A spray of warmth across her face . . . A flash of light . . . Shadowy figures emerging from a doorway with weapons raised . . . Hands grabbing her and pulling her down . . . Rachel and Chas sprawled in undignified positions on the floor . . . Lars screaming and falling . . . A hypogun . . . A coldness spreading across her shoulders and racing through her limbs . . . The long fall into darkness . . .*

She supposed it was possible that they weren't all dead. She suddenly found it much easier to breathe. There had been too much death already in her life. She wanted to believe that her friends were still alive.

But – it didn't quite make sense. The weight hovered over her shoulders, ready to settle. Her finger tightened on the trigger. 'Why am *I* awake and pissed off, then?' she started to ask, but the voice interrupted her before the 'awake' was complete.

'Your constitution is strong, for a human,' it said. 'You

fought off the effects of the anaesthetic faster than my medical orderly thought possible.'

It made a strange sort of sense. She remembered waking up in a long room filled with covered beds; knocking a uniformed man to the ground; taking his gun and running.

She felt disoriented: like Alice in Wonderland, everything seemed to be arse-about-face.

'All around you,' said the voice suddenly.

'Where are you?' Ace snapped, and stopped, taken aback.

'No, I can't,' the voice continued.

'Can you read my . . . ?' She bit off the sentence, waiting for the voice to continue.

Not a sound.

She opened her mouth experimentally.

Nothing.

'If you can't – ' she said quickly, and stopped.

Nothing.

' – read my mind, then how could you answer my questions before I had a chance to ask them?' she gabbled, and took a deep breath.

'How embarrassing,' the voice said. 'I appear to be slightly out of synchronization. My apologies.'

A fleshy black shape swelled up from nothing in front of her. Thin tendrils spilled from it and trailed to the floor. Beside her another, squatter, shape appeared, its tendrils quivering restlessly. Above her head, a pancake-shaped mass of blue flesh slowly spun. Something moved down by her feet. She took a quick step backwards. The thing stayed where it was: a small, grey, pear shape made of some doughy material.

Ace raised her stolen gun, unsure which of the things to aim at. Her fingers gripped thin air.

The gun had vanished from her hand.

'Allow me to introduce myself,' the voice said. The grey ovoid pulsed in time with the words. 'My name is Legion, and I am acting captain of the Interstellar Mining Corporation vessel *Insider Trading*.'

Tendrils from the two black shapes reached out to entwine with each other, pulling their cores closer together until, as Ace watched in amazement, they melded together into a single muscular column of flesh crowned with thorns.

'Bloody hell,' she said. 'Why didn't you say so earlier? I've been trying to find you for ages.'

They fell together, father and daughter, through the poisonous atmosphere of Lucifer. Father and daughter – and something else.

'You're alive.' Miles whispered. He felt sick with joy. His tears floated from his eyes and star-splashed perfectly against his faceplate, one by one. 'You're alive!'

Paula was not the daughter he remembered. She had undergone a sea-change into something rich and strange down in the depths of Lucifer. The great Whale had turned its terrible gaze upon her, transfiguring her once-smooth skin into sheets of light which hid deeper firefly gleams, like the Northern Lights back on Earth.

And yet he recognized her.

'Dad?' He heard her voice in his head. 'Dad, you shouldn't have come – '

'I had to. The Angels saved you. They *care*. They want to help us.'

'They didn't save me.' The pain in her voice cut him deeply. 'I was dying, and so was one of them . . . There was a connection . . . Somehow, we drew strength from each other, enough to stave off death for a little while longer. We joined, but the joining can't last. Our time has come. We've been waiting for you. We had to tell you . . .'

His throat was tight, and his mouth was twisted out of shape by grief. 'Tell me what?'

'To leave. Get everybody out of Belial and Moloch now, before it's too late.'

'And walk away from the best chance we've had in years to complete the mission?' He felt a wave of exasperation rise within him. 'Don't you understand? The Project will finally be able to work! You can translate for us, human to Angel, Angel to human. You'll be the saviour of the Earth.'

'You haven't been listening to us. We can't save anyone. We're dying. We can feel the pull of the core, dragging us down, forcing the last change upon us – '

'There must be a way you can help us communicate with them. If there's just one thing you can tell me, one clue to how they think – '

'You were the same when Mum died,' she wailed. 'She wanted to tell you so many things, but you were too busy talking to listen. She needed to know that you loved her; so you told her all about the new drugs she could get from the Arcturans, or the huge advances in radiation treatment since rho mesons had been discovered. She didn't *want* any more pain, she wanted to be held. *You never told her that you loved her.*'

'Do you blame me? After what she did?' His voice was quiet and bitter. Her silence was answer enough. He closed his eyes for a minute. When he opened them, he had an audience.

Paula was floating in the centre of a circle of Angels.

They hung before him; swirling, shifting, changing, somehow moving whilst staying perfectly still; their bodies evolving like glowing patterns in a three-dimensional kaleidoscope.

'They want you to go,' Paula said without words. Her voice bubbled and changed like her body. '*We* want you to go.'

'You don't understand,' he cried. 'My whole life has led me to this point. To here. You can't tell me it's for nothing. Nobody can. I won't hear that! Paula. I love you. I want – need – answers!'

'I don't have any for you, Dad. I'm sorry.'

The uniform fitted Ace perfectly. It wasn't as sophisticated as the one she had worn whilst attached to IMC during the Dalek Wars, three hundred years in the future, but it brought back memories of belonging, of finally being accepted on her own terms by a group of her peers.

She looked over at the pile of burned clothing she had shed like a snake's skin, and shuddered.

It was a mistake to go back, she thought. I've outgrown the Doctor now. He needs me more than I need him. My future lies elsewhere.

Legion was seated at the head of the table, and to either side of her, and floated up near the ceiling. One of the black, tendrilled parts of its body was picking apart an orange and ingesting it, segment by segment. The grey ovoid, some distance away, expanded and contracted in a movement which reminded Ace of nothing so much as chewing, although there was no way that she could see whereby the fruit could have been transmitted from one part of Legion to another.

'This is probably a stupid question,' Ace said from her position at the foot of the table, reaching out for another piece of fruit, 'but are all these bits you, or what?'

'I see you have noticed a certain peculiarity about my appearance.'

'No shit?' she said, straightfaced.

Ace could sense a sudden chilliness in Legion's manner. The various parts of its body strained towards each other and collected into a hairy spherical fragment balanced on three pipe-cleaner legs at the head of the table.

'I will not tolerate disrespect!'

'Sorry, Captain,' she snapped automatically. She sat up a little straighter and resolved to regard her host with more of an open mind. Legion was obviously intelligent, and deserved to be treated as such.

'Very well,' Legion continued. 'I am not human, as you are.' It paused, obviously expecting some kind of shocked reaction.

Ace nodded, saying nothing.

'Whereas the lives of humans, and other linear races in the cosmos, are constrained to four dimensions, we are privileged to move through seven.'

205

'There aren't seven dimensions,' Ace exclaimed, and then added, 'are there?'

'The space-time continuum has eleven dimensions,' Legion replied, 'although four of them are inaccessible.'

'So, what's it like then, living in seven dimensions?'

She took another bite of fruit. Legion did not reply.

'Legion?'

'Indescribable.'

'Nice one!'

'But imagine, if you are able, watching small creatures floating on the surface of a pond. Imagine that these creatures cannot look up or down, but only across the water itself. They are not aware of the air, or the depths. Their world is flat.'

As it talked, Legion's voice changed. The various elements combined until it seemed to Ace that a choir was whispering to her.

'You reach down from your exalted position, beyond their understanding, and put your – the things on the ends of your forelimbs . . .'

'Fingers.'

'. . . fingers into the water. What do these creatures see?'

After a few seconds, Ace realized that this was not a rhetorical question. 'Er . . . My fingers?'

'No, because your fingers exist in three dimensions, and they can only perceive two. They see . . .' It paused. 'How many – fingers – do you possess?'

Ace held up a hand.

'And is that normal for your species?' Legion asked.

'You don't pay much attention to your staff, do you?'

'I have more important considerations.'

'Yes. Five fingers on each hand, if you include the thumbs.'

'Thumbs?'

'Never mind.'

'Then these creatures see five discs suddenly appear in the water. As far as they are concerned, these discs are five separate entities. Why should they associate them with each other? But if you plunge your hand deeper into the water, up to the – the hinge section . . .'

'The wrist.'

'Up to the wrist, then the creatures who inhabit the surface of the water will see the five discs suddenly merge into one large ellipse. Do you understand?'

Ace had actually understood some time ago, but if there was one lesson that she would take away gladly from her time with the Doctor, it was that it was better to have people underestimate your abilities than over-estimate them.

'I think so,' she said cautiously.

'And if you pick one of these creatures up and place it a little distance away on the surface of the water, all its fellows will see is that it vanished, and reappeared elsewhere. Neither they, nor it, can see the air through which it moved. Do you understand?'

'Uh-huh.'

'What you see of me,' and the hairy, three-legged blob standing at the front of the table stretched like hot toffee and broke apart into fifteen warty blue spheres which bounced, very slowly, between the floor and the ceiling, 'is merely a three-dimensional cross-section of a seven-dimensional shape. As my body moves in and out of your perception, you see different aspects of it. Your three-dimensional brain is not capable of appreciating the – *beauty* of my true body.'

Ace was fascinated. 'So all I can see are your fingers, your toes and your naughty bits?'

The spheres coalesced into a black and vaguely hairy shape that threatened to develop three thin and multi-jointed legs. Ace was beginning to get the message.

'I apologize, Captain,' she said formally. Best to get on its good side. 'And so when our conversation was out of sync before – '

'What you call time is a dimension, like any other,' Legion said casually. 'I tend to drift around in it, if I am not concentrating. Sometimes I answer questions that you will ask in a while, sometimes I respond to queries from moments ago.

'Well wicked!' Ace said. 'But what are you doing working for IMC? You could wipe the floor with them.'

'My race has no interest in power,' Legion replied haughtily. 'A mere three dimensions is nothing. I may as well offer you complete control over the direction east.'

'But why bother working for a scurvy Earth company, then?'

'You ask a lot of questions.'

'You're not wrong.'

'I am under contract. Our respective worlds have only recently met. We have certain technologies that humanity lacks, but we in turn lack – protection. IMC have offered us weapons in return for specialist help. I am that specialist.'

'But what do you need the protection from?'

A shudder seemed to run through the various sections of Legion's disconnected bulk. 'There are dark forces in the universe before whom we are powerless. I can say no more.'

Ace thought for a moment. 'Okay then, what is IMC doing in the Lucifer system?'

'Ah,' said Legion, 'you humans and your obsession with business affairs. We have come across other species like you – the Cimliss, the Usurians, the Okk. Always worrying about the indefinable moment. To put it simply: your Earth Government has declared bankruptcy. Its affairs, its goods and its chattels have been put in the hands of the receivers.'

Ace pushed aside a feeling of dread. 'And who are these receivers?' she asked.

'Something called the Earth Alliance of Corporations; a collection of the most powerful companies and conglomerates which trade off-Earth. You may know it better as the Holding Company.'

'And IMC?' She already knew the answer.

'We get the mineral rights,' Legion said, almost happily, 'of all subcontracted colonies. Like Eden.'

208

The medlab on the IMCV *Insider Trading* was large, high-tech and as soulless as a plaster saint. Legion led Ace into it with a certain swagger, if a green balloon trailing pink strands could be said to swagger. A medical orderly bustled towards them. He gestured towards the first of a long row of recuperation pods, where Christine LaFayette's face was visible through a clear plastic window. She looked to Ace like a frozen corpse.

'Trauma and some tissue damage,' he said, snapping to attention as Ace peered into the pod. Ace absent-mindedly returned a sketchy salute.

Old habits die hard, she thought.

'Cost?' Captain Legion asked in a host of voices.

'With immediate treatment, plus physiotherapy, psychotherapy and prosthetics, the estimate is thirty thousand adjusted ergs, Captain.'

'Charge it to my account,' Legion said.

Ace moved to the next pod, anxious to find her friends from Moloch. She recognized the face of one of her attackers beneath a layer of blue gel. His face was burned right down to the bone in places, and one eye had curdled into a white lump.

'Faulty weapon discharge, Ma'am,' the orderly explained. He had obviously mistaken Ace for one of the regular crew, and she did not bother to correct him. 'Third-degree burns over most of the face and neck. Seventy per cent flesh reduction on hands and arms. Left radius and ulna suffered heat recrystallization and associated brittleness.'

'Cost?' Legion asked from behind them.

'The reconstructive surgery is fairly basic. If standard EB Corporation ocular replacements are used instead of cloned organs the estimate is only nineteen thousand adjusted ergs.'

There was a pause.

'Too much,' Legion said. 'Terminate treatment.'

Ace stepped towards the next pod.

'No time for that,' Legion barked, and its tone made Ace automatically stop and stand to attention. Part of her was appalled at the ease with which she had slotted straight back into the military lifestyle; part of her welcomed the safety of knowing exactly where she fitted in and what she was supposed to do.

'You can visit them later,' Legion said. 'For now, attend me.' It moved towards the door, aspect changing moment by moment.

Ace followed, casting a last glance back over her shoulder into the medlab.

When it was clear that IMC's newest recruit would not turn back, a grossly fat woman stepped from a side room. 'For an alien, Legion certainly knows which buttons to push.'

The orderly shrugged as he went about his task of switching off Company Shock Trooper (Third Class) Jason Curtis Dommer's life support machine. 'Have you heard the scuttlebut about her? Apparently, she typed a message into the Belial Base neural net, right where the viruses that Legion's agent planted there would find it and transmit it back here.'

'A message?' the woman asked, jowls quivering.

'Just Legion's name, and the words: "We must meet".'

'Very cryptic.'

'Yeah. Trouble is, Legion's agent spotted it, thought she'd been rumbled, knocked the girl senseless and deleted the message.'

'So she knew Legion was here?'

The orderly glanced up, his face underlit by the row of tell-tales along Dommer's pod. 'Yeah, but the word is that she didn't realize IMC sent a whole fleet. She thought Legion was working alone. When Dommer and the others burst in, she freaked. Lucky she's still alive.'

He flicked a last switch, and Jason Dommer slid unknowingly from life into death.

'Aren't we all?' Bronwen ap Bryn said, as she stroked her tattooed scalp thoughtfully and turned to leave the sick-bay.

Chapter Thirteen

Piper O'Rourke used her hand to shield the beam of her torch as she crept along the darkened corridors of Belial Base towards the main airlock. The cold light silhouetted the bones of her hand like an X-ray. Part of her wanted to stop and stare, entranced by the sight: the rest of her screamed silently in the darkness. She was losing it. *She was losing it.*

She stopped and rested her forehead against the cold metal walls of the corridor. Keep it together, Piper, and you might still get out of this alive. She lifted a hand to her face and wiped away a greasy sheen of sweat. Although it was cold and the air was running out, she was burning up.

Burning up.

Paula.

Oh, Christ.

Sucking in a lungful of cold air, Piper moved once more down the corridor. She only had to make it to the airlock, seal the inner door behind her and wait . . .

Wait as Paula had waited, as Earth was waiting . . .

For IMC to help.

Piper stopped, suddenly, twenty metres short of the airlock. Sounds echoed out of the darkness towards her.

Voices.

'You don't understand . . . He's trying to kill himself!'

'Then who's responsible for all this?'

' . . . Bloody Piper. She brained me when I tried to reboot the neural net!'

More voices, speaking in hurried whispers.

Bannen, whom she'd left in the Operations Room, sup-

211

posedly wracked with grief over the abrupt crash of the simularity of his son. Damn his thick skull: she should have splashed his brains across the wall. Bishop. Teal. Bernice.

The Doctor.

But that was impossible! She'd *killed* him.

Piper groaned inwardly.

They knew. They'd tricked her, and they knew. She'd even given them the evidence herself.

Fool!

Piper ran a hand through her hair. Her torch flickered across the wall and she switched it off, holding her breath in case someone had noticed the distant gleam of light.

Nothing. The pitch of the voices did not change. They didn't know she was there. There might still be a chance of escape.

As silently as she could, Piper backed away from the airlock, into the darkness.

And a light silhouetted her against the wall.

Her body suddenly became numb. An icy sensation rushed through her limbs. Her heart faltered, then resumed its steady rhythm. She gasped, clutched her chest and sank to the metal grillework which served as the floor of the corridor. Her head spun and her left arm tingled painfully with pins and needles. She blinked. The light was shining in her eyes, swooping towards her.

Something simultaneously velvet and diamond insinuated itself into her body, slipping easily between the molecules of her skin and coalescing within her. Piper screamed. The sensation moved around inside her, filling her up, shuffling, searching, passing through to leave her sick and trembling and curiously empty.

The light faded, driven aside by the darkness of the Base. She heard footsteps: people running towards her, attracted by her scream. She struggled to her feet, her only thought to avoid discovery, and staggered off into the darkness.

Bernice ran forward into the darkness, her torch beam

bobbing in front of her. A babble of conversation filled her ears.

'What was it? Did you see it?'

'See what? I heard a noise, like a whisper – '

'There was something – a light, shadows – '

'How can you see shadows? It's dark!'

'What the hell – there's someone there!'

'Hey! Hey you!'

Teal's hand found her arm. 'Don't. Bernice, don't go any further.'

'But I have to see – '

'No.' The Doctor's voice rang out like a ship's bell in the darkness. 'You don't have to see anything. Come back here, now. All of you.'

The running footsteps faltered, slowed, began to return along the corridor.

The Doctor shone his torch on to Bernice as she returned from the darkness. Her face was flushed with excitement. 'Did you see it? What was it?'

Beside her, Teal's voice trembled in the darkness. 'There was nothing to see. I only heard . . .' He faltered. 'I only heard . . .'

The Doctor spoke firmly. 'Get everyone together. Anushkia, Julie, Craig . . . Get them all and meet me in the Operations Room. Bernice, Bishop: carry Alex will you. And mind you go carefully with his head. We'll need him to get the neural network back on line.' Without another word, the Doctor strode into the darkness.

Bernice stared distastefully at the physicist, recumbent on the floor. 'Come on then, Sleeping Beauty.'

Christine LaFayette blinked a layer of viscous blue gel from her eyes and sat up, coughing. '*Ciel!*'

She coughed again, and spat a wad of blue gel to one side. Her throat stung with the effort. She tried to massage her neck but her left arm would not move. She peered down at it, noting that a white smock, like a hospital gown, clothed her from throat to ankles. Projecting beyond the sleeve, the flesh of her hand was pallid and sweaty. It hung uselessly at her side. She rolled up the sleeve to her elbow, the fingers of her right hand brushing her left forearm as she did so. She felt nothing. She pinched herself, but might as well have been pinching the padded plastic of the bed on which she sat for all the sensation she felt. She rolled her sleeve up further. Above her elbow, the flesh displayed a normal skin tone. A razor-sharp line divided the quick from the newly grown. She pinched herself on her left biceps and yelped with pain.

As the pain subsided, she looked around. She was sitting on a diagnostic bed in what was obviously a medlab of some kind. But where? There was no equipment this sophisticated anywhere on Eden. Straining, she tried to gather her thoughts. The last thing she remembered was . . .

Yukio's face erupting before her, stumbling backwards, a pressure on her elbow. My arm! Is that my arm? Why is it floating in front of –

And then the pain, and the darkness.

And then here. Wherever here was.

Feeling her stomach churn with the painful memories, she leaned sideways and was violently sick. Something metallic slithered from beneath her bed and vacuumed the debris away, before slipping back under the bed and deactivating with a click. Medical droid.

Not on the Base, then. Not anywhere on the Base.

Painfully, Christine swung her legs to one side until she was in a sitting position. Her muscles were a little stiff, but, although she flinched in anticipation, there was no pain.

She glanced down again at her left arm. Prosthetic? Cloned? Easier to believe that it was hers, and there was something wrong with it. Damn the memories of seeing it floating away in front of her. Nerve damage, say, or muscle wastage. Something. Anything.

She ran her right hand lightly over the rest of her body. Everything seemed fine. She took a deep breath. Time to leave then, and find some answers.

Peering around for a locker where she might find some clothes, she stood.

A medical alarm sounded.

Bernice helped Bishop lay Alex Bannen on the floor beside one of the main Operations Room workstations. There was a loud clattering and muted conversation as Anushkia Smyslov, Shmuel Zehavi and a morose Cheryl Russell followed them into the room and placed their torches so that the beams played over the domed ceiling, throwing a dim reflected light, like candlelight, back into the room. Bernice stood. 'Anyone here got med training?'

Anushkia pushed forward into the circle of torchlight. 'Yes. I'll take charge here. You and Teal go and find Craig Richards and Tiw Heimdall.'

'I'll find the Doctor,' Cheryl said dully, as she picked up a torch. 'Craig's probably checking the power linkages. God alone knows where we'll find Tiw.'

Bernice nodded. 'Let's do it.'

Bishop stepped forward as the women left the room.

Anushkia looked up from beside Alex Bannen's prone body. 'And where are you going?'

'Orders to the contrary notwithstanding, Krau Smyslov,' Bishop produced his ubiquitous thin smile, 'to apprehend the villain of the piece.'

The Doctor ran soundlessly through the darkness. He had no torch, but darkness did not impede his progress. In the back of his mind he knew the air in the Base was getting staler as the crisis progressed, but he couldn't afford to worry about that now. More urgent was the need to find out why Piper had felt it necessary to shut down the neural net like this. Only then could he decide if it was safe to reboot the system.

His foot touched a black rubberized cylinder, and he stopped his headlong dash instantly. He bent to examine the device. A torch. Piper's?

Pocketing it, he moved on.

Behind him, unnoticed, faint beams of light shimmered

softly, and without apparent source, across the corridor walls.

'Atten-*shun*.'

Six pairs of polycarbide-armoured boots slapped the IMC executive transporter bay deckplates at the Staff Sergeant's command. Six high-power weapons chunked as they were slung across six heavily muscled male and female shoulders.

Silence hung in the air.

'Squad Number One: prepare for executive transporter embarkation. You know the drill, now let's move! Point!'

Sharon Kreig and Jay Ardamal double-timed it up the footramp and into the waiting executive transporter. By twos the rest of their squad followed, stowing their gear as the Staff Sergeant followed them in.

A coiling black ribbon writhed into being and floated in mid-air next to the Sergeant's head. 'You have the paperwork?'

'Affirmative, Legion.'

'Good.' The black ribbon gathered itself into a knot, turned inside out and was gone.

The osmotic field opened and the executive transporter lifted gracefully into space.

Craig Richards finished his torchlit check of the power control systems and slammed the access hatch shut with an angry growl. Ergs were there aplenty: they just weren't being channelled anywhere. That meant the control circuits were down, and that meant a whole new set of checks was going to have to be made. What really cheesed him off, though, was the fact that the food reconstituters were down as well. He could really have done with a steaming hot beaker of –

He paused, his thought uncompleted. From deeper within the Power Bay came a sound. He frowned. The sub-standard systems Earth Central had seen fit to install in the Base made some weird noises at the best of times, but this . . . This was unlike anything he'd ever heard

216

before. Craig scratched his head. 'Hello? Anushkia? Who's there? Zehavi, are you sleepwalking again? Come on, stop playing silly buggers, you're putting the wind right up me.'

The sound came nearer, resolving into a kind of low whispering. Flickering beams of dim light came with it, caressing the machinery which shielded their source from direct view. The light moved like smoke, or heavy gas – not in straight lines, but floating ribbons . . . Or tentacles.

Craig reached into his pocket and caressed his lucky deck of cards, then felt around with his other hand and picked up a flat toolcase made of heavy-duty plastic. It wasn't much of a weapon but –

'Craig! Craig Richards! Are you in here?' The voice came from outside.

Slipping the toolcase into his overalls, Craig backed away from the strange phenomenon.

'Damn right I am. And I'm coming out now.'

Without taking his eyes off the stacks of machinery which shielded the glimmer from direct sight, Craig walked quickly backwards until he felt the entrance hatch to the Power Bay thump into his shoulder. He jumped as a voice beside him said, 'Leave this lot, will you? The Doctor wants everyone back in Operations, pronto.'

Craig turned to face Bernice and Teal. 'I can handle that,' he whispered fervently as he pushed past them and rushed off up the corridor.

Bernice glanced at Teal. 'What do you suppose is biting *his* arse?'

The engineer shrugged. 'Your guess is as good as mine.' He gazed into the Power Bay. Apart from the light from Craig's torch, still propped where he had left it against the main power conduits, the chamber was dark and empty.

Christine stared in fascination at the being that had appeared in the medlab before her.

'You have the paperwork?'

'Paperwork?'

'My name is Legion.'

217

'What paperwork? Who – what – are you?'

There was a pause.

'I am the captain of Interstellar Mining Corporation vessel *Insider Trading*.'

'IMC!'

'Good.' There was another pause. The black construct before her split, spun into a thin loop, fleshed into a globe, flipped inside out to reveal a hovering pink mass, which detached itself from the main bulk and drifted some distance away. The black elements passed through one another and recombined.

Christine stood. She said firmly, 'Well, thank you, Captain, for being so informative. May I have my clothes back now?'

'Of course. I would not want to return you to your female progenitor in what, from my briefings on human culture, I perceive to be an indecorous condition.'

Christine's face hardened. 'My mother!'

'Is responsible for IMC's presence here. Yes.'

It wasn't Piper O'Rourke but Tiw Heimdall that Bishop found on his excursion through the Base. The little man was standing in the middle of the Bridge terminus, head cocked to one side as if he could hear something, fists clenched at his sides.

Bishop stopped a few steps into the chamber. Tiw didn't move.

'Trau Heimdall.'

Tiw's head turned slowly. He smiled thinly at Bishop. Something glittered with a golden sheen between his lips. 'Something comes, Adjudicator. My teeth – they tingle.'

Despite himself, Bishop shivered when he heard the flat intonation of Tiw Heimdall's voice. He moved carefully into the chamber, glancing around at the curved walls, and the curtains of rock beyond. He drew his gun, letting it guide his eyes around the rest of the chamber.

'I can smell it.'

'What, Trau Heimdall?'

'Something . . . Something . . .'

Satisfied the chamber was empty apart from himself and Tiw, Bishop holstered his gun. 'Trau Heimdall, we must leave here immed . . .' His voice died away. 'Who said that?'

'I said nothing.'

Bishop drew his gun. 'Can you hear anything?'

'Smell something, I can. Like grass growing in the meadows, like thunderclouds gathering in the sky in the days before the weather control – '

'Come on. We're leaving.'

'I think I will stay.'

'No!'

Bishop turned to face Tiw Heimdall. There was a dim light behind him, writhing slowly in the air. Bishop levelled his gun, but Tiw prevented him from getting a clear view of the target.

'Trau Heimdall. Move aside!'

Tiw slowly turned to face the phenomenon. 'Be not scared.'

'Move aside!'

'I will not.'

Scowling, Bishop leapt forward and grabbed Tiw around the waist with one hand. Without holstering his gun, or taking his eyes off the glimmering phenomenon, Bishop dragged the little man from the chamber and threw him bodily into the Pit. The light grew closer. Without even pausing to catch his breath, an ever more difficult prospect in the thinning atmosphere, Bishop dived in after him.

Christine stared down at the executive transporter bay from an observation gallery thirty metres above the floor. Below her, technicians were preparing a long-range executive transporter for launch. Across the far side of the bay, a shimmering window of electric blue in the wall looked like an upended lake.

'What is that?' she asked.

Beside her hovered Legion, in a multiplicity of bodies,

all of which somehow gave the impression of looking directly at her.

'An osmotic field,' it replied, basso and treble in harmony. 'It keeps the air in and the vacuum out. I'm told that humans prefer it that way.'

'And IMC market it? I'm impressed. Technology has moved on since we left Earth.'

'IMC want to market it,' Legion corrected. 'My people lease the rights to IMC for a substantial sum. One of the many dimensional technologies that IMC court us for.'

Christine's gaze travelled downwards to where the slab-sided long-range executive transporter was being refitted and refuelled.

'There's no way I'm going anywhere in that shuttle. If my mother wants me off the Project, she can damn well go through channels and see how far it gets her.'

'But, Krau LaFayette, your female progenitor has gone through channels. With Earth in receivership, control of Project Eden transfers to the Earth Alliance of Corporations. Being head of the Board of Directors, as well as a major stockholder in said company, your female progenitor has complete control over mission profile – and personnel.'

'I don't believe it. We've been out here too long and risked too much for Earth Central to give up on us now.'

'Earth Central no longer exists. My brief is to reorganize the Project along more efficient and profitable lines. Prompt action is required to salvage what might otherwise turn into a most embarrassing financial debacle.'

'Action? What action? And what about the people?'

There was a momentary pause.

'In light of the current financial situation, all employment contracts have been terminated.'

'What about the Project? You can't ship us all home now!'

'You are correct. Sufficient funding for transport of non-essential personnel does not exist.'

Christine gaped. 'What do you – '

'Please excuse me. There are things I must attend to.'

A uniformed officer walked along the gallery towards them. His face was pocked with scars from one of the many auto-immune diseases that were still rife on Earth.

'Staff Officer Atrimonides will make sure every comfort is provided for your journey home.'

Legion wrapped itself into five separate knots and shrank to nothing.

Piper O'Rourke sank to the floor, her chest heaving, unable to draw breath. The air. The air was going. That was it, then. It had all been for nothing; the fear, the guilt, the deaths . . . All for nothing. She slipped sideways and felt a familiar coaming beneath her hand. The airlock! She had come full circle.

Dragging herself to her feet, Piper stumbled across the threshold of the chamber. All she had to do now was –

'Piper O'Rourke. I know you're in there.'

The Doctor.

'You can stop running now. I'm nine hundred and forty-three, and that's far too old to be chasing around like a S'ss'arian gyeet.'

'What!' Despite herself, Piper yelped with surprise. 'You're never – ' She stopped, abruptly aware that the Doctor was trying to gain her confidence.

The Doctor's face appeared from the darkness, smiling. 'Do you mind if I sit down? Ahh. That's better.' He shook his head. 'Why did you do it, Piper?'

Piper fought to get her breathing under control. She looked into the Doctor's eyes, noticing that they glowed faintly, as if gathering and enhancing the available light.

'Why should I tell you anything? Bishop's going to kill me anyway.'

'I'm not here to judge you, Piper. But can you tell me a reason why everyone else on the Base must die to protect your secret?'

'No. Nobody should have died. Nobody!'

She took a deep breath and began to speak.

Christine watched as flight technicians finished preparing the executive transporter for launch. Atrimonides gestured with his gun, indicating that she should precede him from the gallery.

'What if I don't want to go?'

'As it happens, Ma'am, you do have a choice. You can either walk, or we can freeze you where you stand and ship you back in a refrigerator.'

'Charming.'

'Efficient.'

Christine glared at the man. She opened the pressure door and moved into the executive transporter bay control room, a semicircular chamber filled with operations and monitoring equipment.

Christine looked around. IMC employees – risk analysts and financial assessors like clones in their sharp plastic business suits and laced necklines – moved busily from one station to another, checking systems as the time for launch approached. One balanced a beaker of steaming coffee on a nearby terminal before moving on bearing a full tray.

Christine acted without thinking.

Scooping the cup from the workstation with her good hand, she whirled around and flung its contents into Atrimonides' face. He screamed and clawed at his eyes. Christine made a grab for his gun as it spun away, but only succeeded in pushing it into a console, where its trigger caught on the corner. A searing beam of high-energy protons blistered the air. Something on the other side of the room exploded, and kept on exploding.

Christine didn't wait to see what damage she'd caused. She headed for the door at a dead run, her new arm thumping uselessly against various items of furniture.

Teal saw torch beams bobbing towards him from a side corridor and grabbed Bernice's arm. Seconds later, Bishop and Tiw Heimdall came into view.

'Picks me up! Like a piece of luggage, he picks me up and throws me, he does, *throws me* down the Pit!' Teal

and Bernice exchanged grins. 'Teal, you tell him. I'm
important, me. I should not be thrown around like luggage!'

'Okay, Bishop. What have you been doing with Tiw?'

The Adjudicator did not smile. 'I saw it again. We both
did. The light. *He* wanted to stay.'

Teal's smile faded. 'Are you sure?'

Bishop crossed his arms. 'As an Adjudicator, I am a
trained, completely impartial, observer.'

'Yes, and I'm a Martian Queen,' Bernice snorted.
'We'd better get back to the Operations Room.' Spinning
on her heel, she led the way back along the corridor.

Christine ran.

Somewhere behind her, Atrimonides was screaming in
pain above a babble of voices.

' – this mess cleared – '

' – wait a minute, can you smell – '

' – Earth Mother preserve us! We've got a fire – '

' – an extinguisher! Somebody get – '

' – no good, I can't hold them – '

' – what? How many systems? Bloody – '

Christine slapped her palm against the lockplate of the
door. Behind her, Atrimonides lurched clear of a rising
pall of smoke. She dashed clear of the control room and
on to the second half of the observation gallery, thirty
metres above the main executive transporter bay. Sirens
blared across the chamber. Technicians dropped their
tools and ran for the interior of the ship.

The control room door slammed shut behind Atrimonides as he ran on to the gallery and hurled himself at
Christine. His face was blistered from the hot coffee and
one eye was closed. The other glared malevolently.
Christine turned to run, but there was a muffled thud in
the control room. The observation windows blew out in
a shower of glass. The shock rocked the gallery and sent
her sprawling back into Atrimonides.

There was another concussion. Atrimonides snarled.
Christine fought for her balance as he grasped her with

hooked fingers. The guard rail twisted beneath her hands, and they fell backwards into empty space.

Cheryl moved towards the airlock. She stood at the door, the Doctor's name poised on her lips, but just before she called out, something made her hesitate. There were soft voices coming from inside. The Doctor . . . and Piper! She crept closer, straining to hear what was being said.

' – and the Project had been going for so long, you see. So long, with no results. The situation on Earth was desperate, we all knew that. We had to succeed.'

The Doctor's voice said, 'And so you infected the star-suits with a software virus.'

'That's right.' Was that a note of desperation in Piper's voice? 'Earth needed results and we couldn't get them. IMC could, but there was no legal way to transfer infor-mation – so they gave me a virus and I implanted it into the starsuits. The virus travelled into the neural net during a regular systems update and began to transmit infor-mation to IMC. To facilitate their takeover.'

The Doctor sighed. 'But the virus was cheap. Cheap and nasty, like everything about IMC. It caused system malfunctions. Suit malfunctions.'

Cheryl felt a cold fist clench around her heart.

'Like the one that killed Paula.'

'Yes. But I – '

'You bitch! It was you all the time. You killed her!' Cheryl ran into the airlock chamber and grabbed Piper by the throat, jerking the woman harshly to her feet.

The Doctor stood as well. 'Cheryl, please, I hardly think this is the right moment for – '

'Shut up!' Her eyes narrowed and she drew back her fist. 'I'm going to kill her!'

She slammed her clenched fist into Piper's face.

Time seemed to slow down as Christine fell into the executive transporter bay. She could see a row of tiny faces gaping from the balcony before being engulfed by a huge sheet of flame. The smell of Atrimonides' burning face and hair was thick in her nostrils. She gagged. And then the floor of the bay was rushing up towards them.

Atrimonides was grabbing wildly at her, desperately flailing his hands and feet, and Cheryl realized he was trying to use her as a reaction mass to slow his own fall. Unaware that she was screaming, Christine reached towards his face with her one good arm and hooked her fingers into the burns which crusted his cheek. He screamed and jerked. Christine whirled out of control.

There was another explosion. Christine felt her stomach lurch as the executive transporter bay gravity generator fluctuated, flinging her and Atrimonides into a spiralling loop, then failed completely, leaving her weightless. Foam began to spread through the air as the fire-fighting systems reacted automatically to the emergency. Half blinded by the foam, Christine scrambled for something to grab on to to break her fall.

Bernice, Bishop and Tiw Heimdall entered the Operations Room. Julie Ndobe, Shmuel Zehavi and Teal Green were talking in low voices. Craig Richards was standing alone, some distance away. Anushkia Smyslov had bandaged Alex Bannen's head, and the physicist was propped in a sitting position against a workstation.

He looked up eagerly as Bernice walked over to him. 'How are you feeling?'

'Well enough to reboot this pile of rust.'

Anushkia said, 'I've told you, Alex. Not until the Doctor says. We still don't know why Piper crashed the system. Until we do, it would be foolhardy to even consider – '

She stopped.

'Did anyone hear – '

There was an explosion of light.

Someone was yelling, but Christine couldn't make out the words. The executive transporter bay was a chaos of foam and whirling shapes which might or might not have been armed troopers. A fist lashed out at her from the

225

whiteness. Christine gasped. Her lungs burned as she inhaled foam; she vomited.

Small-arms fire scorched a web of gaps through the foam.

'Who's the idiot still firing? Huang? If that executive transporter goes up, I'll personally eat your kidneys, *capishe*? Now get her!'

Atrimonides.

Something huge and black loomed out of the mist of foam. Christine slammed shoulders first into one of the slab-like metal sides of a long-range executive transporter. She gasped. Her head banged against the surface. Momentum carried her down the hull into the deadspace between the executive transporter and the bay wall.

She shook her head to clear it. The foam was not so dense down here, and the recyclers were beginning to suck away what little there was.

'Get her!' Atrimonides swung into sight followed by a group of troopers. Strings of bloody vomit drooled from his mouth, a legacy of prolonged foam inhalation.

But as the gauntleted hands of the first trooper made a grab for her hair, Christine felt an empty sensation in the pit of her stomach.

The executive transporter seemed to be pressing against her back.

It was moving!

Face twisted with rage, Cheryl drew back her fist and threw another punch. Blood burst from Piper's nose. She fell back against one of the emergency spacesuit lockers, and the unpowered door flipped open at the touch of her body.

Cheryl stepped forward to deliver another blow – just in time to catch the dead body of her husband as it fell from the locker.

The slab side of the executive transporter loomed like a cliff out of the white fog, getting larger by the second as the shock wave from the explosions which had set it adrift

226

in the first place propelled it nearer and nearer the executive transporter bay wall. The troopers were scattering away from Christine, thrashing through the foam, well aware that although the executive transporter had no weight, it still had mass, and hence momentum. A lot of momentum. Enough to squash Christine, and anyone else in the vicinity, against the wall like bugs.

She glanced quickly from side to side. There was a lot of transporter, and she was half way along it: too far in either direction to make it to safety. She glanced up; no chance there, either: a loading gantry projected from the wall above her head. It was already buckling as the executive transporter moved remorselessly nearer. She scanned its side, looking for something – anything – that might help her survive the impact. All she could see before a whirling storm of foam obscured everything were attitude control thrusters, IMC logos and refuelling ports.

Cheryl clutched hopelessly at Sam Russell's body and burst into tears. She nestled his mottled face in the curve of her shoulder, stroked his cold hair, felt the awful grating of the bones in his neck.

Her eyes were cold when she lifted them to Piper's face.

'The suit malfunctioned!' Piper cried. 'I didn't know! I found him here on the floor with his neck broken. I didn't kill him!'

Cheryl let Sam's body slump gracelessly to the floor and moved towards Piper, hands outstretched.

The executive transporter was six metres away.

One group of troopers had tangled together in their panic, still in the executive transporter's path. Fights were breaking out as the knot of flailing bodies rotated gently in mid-air.

Five metres.

Christine could now make out charred patches of hull and the seams where metal plates had been hyperglued together.

Four metres.

Klaxons hooted. Sparks from the balcony drifted through the foam, becoming soggy bits of black carbon which mixed with it, looking like dirty snow. Voices screamed.

Three metres.

Two indistinct figures had broken away from the struggling mass and were desperately flailing towards Christine and the safe area at the other end of the executive transporter.

'ACCESS HATCH', she read embossed into a transparent panel, and, in smaller letters underneath, 'IN EMERGENCY, ENTER CODE 398.' A small keypad sat smugly beneath the panel.

Two metres. One.

The troopers were screaming.

She flipped the panel up and keyed in the code, banging her elbow against the wall as the executive transporter pressed close.

The word 'ERROR' scrolled up in glowing virtual letters on the metal panel beside the keypad.

Bernice's torch flickered and died. People scrambled away from the centre of the Operations Room in panic. A nimbus of light had collected there, spinning gently. A low whispering sound echoed around the room.

'What the hell – ' she said.

Thin air gathered itself around the light, thickening. A shape was forming there, something . . . Something . . .

Someone screamed. Bernice felt something, some force, move through her, penetrating her skin as though it were ether. A yell of surprise was wrenched out of her. The sensation passed, leaving her nauseous and curiously empty . . .

In the centre of the room, the light gathered into a curling ribbon and solidified, erupted into a rippling curtain of sparkles.

'Is that . . . *Paula?*' someone said.

There was a smell, like summer, like –

A final flash of light and the phenomenon was gone. In its place stood Miles Engado.

Christine had to bend her arm down by her side to get her fingers to connect with the keys. Because of her awkward position, she was forced to use the prosthetic arm (the fake one, she kept thinking), and the fingers were dull and leaden. The sudden pressure of cold metal against her nose forced her to turn her head sideways until she couldn't see the keys any more. She prayed, and fumbled the code in.

A hand clutched at her shoulder, then moved to circle her neck with killing force. A burned face loomed out of the greyness. Atrimonides. Sweat stood out on his brow, fury was bright in his one good eye. The fingers tightened their grip. Unable to bring her hands up to defend herself, Christine began to choke.

'Christ. Sam. Sam! Oh, Christ. Piper, you bitch.'

Cheryl threw another punch. She laughed hysterically as Piper grunted with pain and fell to the deck. Cheryl knelt beside the sobbing woman, drew back her fist and prepared to follow up her blow with another.

The Doctor casually took her wrist in his hand and held her motionless, without the slightest effort. 'That'll be quite enough of that, thank you very much.'

'You don't understand. She killed Paula. I loved her and I loved Sam and that bitch killed them both!'

Piper was cowering abjectly against the far wall, her face streaming with tears. The Doctor turned furiously to Cheryl, and was about to speak when there was a grating clunk from the outer airlock door.

He paused, his words unspoken. Cheryl wiped tears of her own from her face. All three looked at the door.

There was a moment's silence.

With a tremendous crash, the centre of the door exploded inwards. Seven figures in military uniforms strode through the clouds of smoke and across the rubble into the chamber.

A short figure in a sergeant's uniform and full battle helmet stepped forward, gun raised. The figure kicked aside Sam Russell's dead body without a second glance, like so much extra trash. 'Project Eden is now in receivership. All employment contracts are terminated. I have a warrant granting all property and chattels, in full, in situ, to IMC.'

The Doctor's eyes widened at the sound of the voice, and at the face revealed as the sergeant raised her helmet.

'Full cooperation is advised,' Ace said tersely, and fired a blast from her weapon into the wall beside the Doctor's head to illustrate her point.

With Atrimonides' fingers biting painfully into her neck, the hatch slid away to reveal blackness. The executive transporter moved past Christine on all sides. With a desperate cry she fell forward, into the carpeted interior of the executive transporter's emergency airlock. The grasping hand at her neck convulsed once, agonizingly, and then relaxed.

The executive transporter boomed like a giant bell as it impacted against the bay wall. Christine didn't hear the scream.

No longer attached to his body, Atrimonides' hand drifted free of the hatch coaming.

Something red and pulpy squeezed out of the centimetre-wide gap between the executive transporter and the bay wall, forming shivering globules which clung to the wall's hexagonal bracing struts.

As the emergency airlock hatch slid shut, Christine curled up into a floating ball and was violently sick.

PART FOUR

DEMOGORGON

Corporations have neither bodies to be
punished nor souls to be condemned, they
therefore do as they like.

Edward, First Baron Thurlow

Chapter Fourteen

As Bernice entered the refectory she almost bumped into the Doctor. He was standing just inside the doorway, supporting Piper O'Rourke, who was looking old, tired and bruised. Beside them both, Cheryl Russell was sucking her bloodied knuckles.

Over the Time Lord's shoulder, Bernice saw that the refectory was full. The entire Project Eden team – or what was left of it – was milling around: cowed, shocked and submissive. IMC troopers stood along the periphery of the room with raised weapons. The simularity in the centre of the refectory was even displaying the company logo: the letters IMC in brushed duralinium, curved around a spiral galaxy. It looked to Bernice like a hand crushing a butterfly.

'Move it!' A muscular Company goon in macho combat gear slapped her rump. She turned and was about to deck him when she realized that his needler was aimed at her stomach.

'I said move it!' He grinned. His teeth were even and white, and Bernice wanted to ram them down his throat. His chest tag read 'ARDAMAL'. Bernice stared him down: memorizing his face and making sure that he knew it. His smile grew wider. She stalked off before she said something that he might regret, stepping accidentally on one of the deactivated security drones now littering the Base, and cracking its delicate shell.

Clang. The massive airtight door to the refectory swung shut. Silence fell. People glanced fearfully around at the impassive troops, waiting for the executions to start. The baleful light from the windows cast trembling shadows towards the IMC logo. Somewhere in the background, the food dispenser drifted aimlessly, offering tasty delicacies to uninterested people.

Bernice beckoned the Doctor over. 'What do you think they're going to do with us?' she hissed.

'If they wanted to kill us, they'd have done it already.'

'Oh yes?'

'Look at it from their point of view. Why waste the energy?'

'We have to do something,' she urged.

'I'm open to suggestions.'

'I thought you were supposed to be the one who always had all the answers.'

He smiled bashfully. 'A convincing bluff, I'm afraid.'

'Certainly took me in.' Bernice glanced around. 'Oh hell,' she continued, 'I'm going to make a break for it. Can you cause some kind of distraction, Doctor?'

'Distraction is my middle name.'

'Yes, one of them,' Bernice muttered as the Doctor bounded into the centre of the room.

'Well,' he announced, 'no doubt you're all wondering why I called you here.' All heads turned to watch him as he reached into his pocket and took out three multi-coloured balls. 'You'll like this.' He began to juggle, making it look as if he was just on the verge of dropping the balls each time he caught them. 'There is nothing up my sleeves but my arms, there is nothing down my trousers but a ferret.'

People started laughing: nervously at first, and then with real amusement. A wave of relaxation swept across the room. Even the troopers seemed to be fascinated as they crowded closer for a better look. Perhaps their orders didn't cover lunatic Time Lord jugglers.

Bernice took advantage of the show to slide sideways, until she was standing behind Miles, Teal Green and a psychologist named Filo Julee. A few yards away, the food dispenser's sensor light was on as it scanned the crowd for likely clients. She looked it over. It was just about large enough . . .

236

'Hey,' she whispered. The food dispenser ignored her. 'Hey, over here! Don't you recognize a customer when you see one?'

The machine wafted away from her and attempted to interest a pale Miles Engado in a tofu bar.

The Doctor had four balls in the air now, although nobody could see where the extra one had come from. He was milking the audience for all he could get: throwing the balls out in every direction and catching them in a windmill of arms. He was mugging terribly, his rubber features running the gamut of exaggerated emotions from wide-eyed amazement to crumpled despair.

'Oh, for . . .' She tried to catch up with the machine, but she didn't want to attract any undue attention from the IMC troopers, and the thing seemed determined to ignore her.

Christ, she thought savagely, a person could starve to death whilst that thing forces sticky buns on dieters and ham rolls on vegetarians!

Finally, she grabbed hold of the dispenser's cooling fin whilst it was waving a krill doughnut around in a vain attempt to attract custom, pulled it close and, in a casual and unremarkable manner, moved her hand down to the dispenser's access plate and ran her fingers around the seam until she felt a magnetic bolt buzzing beneath her fingers.

The Doctor was standing on one hand now, and juggling five different balls whilst singing a medley of songs by Abba. Under cover of the racket he was making, and the laughter of his audience, Bernice quickly removed the first four bolts. The fifth one decided, for some mysterious mechanical reason that only small but vital components are privy to, that it was going to play up. Bent over at an ungainly angle, trying to wrench the thing free, Bernice was acutely conscious of the picture that she must be making. The small of her back began to feel warm as she imagined a small bead of laser light centred there, cueing a flamer, or a needler, or a screamer, or anything nasty and permanent.

There! The bolt came away with a tacky wrenching sensation. Somebody had probably spilled something on it. Bernice straightened from her crouch with the five bolts buzzing like bees in her hand, pulled the access plate open and furtively tried to check the space inside the dispenser. Most of the food seemed already to have been disseminated, and a safety cut-out had switched off the stasis field when she opened the hatch. Bernice dumped the remaining food on the floor with a few sweeps of her hand and kicked it under the rubber skirts of the machine. She glanced around with an innocent expression on her face, but all eyes were on the Doctor's antics. She pulled the shelves out and climbed swiftly inside the food dispenser, jerking the leads from the stasis-field generator and pulling the plate shut after her.

There was something sticky beneath her fingers. Chocolate? Machine oil? Whatever it was, it was just the icing on a whole mountain of complaints. She was forced to crouch in the bowels of the machine with her knees up around her ears, her elbows jammed against the interior dispensing machinery and her back wedged so tightly against the shelf supports that she was going to come out with her spine looking like a piece of corrugated duralinium. And the machine did have bowels – she could smell them: a dark, rancid odour comprising the spilled residue of a hundred types of food. She wanted to be sick, but that would be a bad idea. A very bad idea.

Paper-thin knives of light penetrated through air vents in the dispenser's casing and drew hot lines across Bernice's face. Motes of dust sparkled and died as they drifted in and out of the beams. Bernice wanted to sneeze.

By screwing her eyes up against the glare, she could just about make out what was going on in the refectory.

The Doctor was standing on his head and juggling the balls by knocking them with the soles of his feet whilst gargling 'The Star-Spangled Banner'. One of the troopers was passing his helmet around his colleagues, who were putting money into it. A collection? Bernice didn't know where the Doctor got his talent from, but if he ever got tired of fighting ultimate evil, he could make a healthy profit as an intergalactic busker.

Suddenly the balls were gone. The Doctor stood frozen with his legs waving wildly and a baffled expression on his face. The laughter swelled, and was supplemented by applause, which died away slowly as the crowd gradually realized that this was not part of the act. The Doctor clambered petulantly to his feet, with the thunderous expression of a child whose toys have been impounded.

Bernice watched, amazed, as a spiral of pink flesh rotated in the air behind the Doctor. Six more joined it, slowly screwing out of nothing, until they suddenly stretched together into a tangled web of pulsating tendrils. Four of the Doctor's five balls appeared in the midst of the fleshy curtain.

Silence.

'Allow me to introduce myself,' said a multitude of voices. 'My name is Legion, and I am your new Managing Director. Earth Central has ceased to exist. The Earth Alliance of Corporations now rules your planet.'

'Didn't your mother ever tell you it was polite to knock?' the Doctor exclaimed, turning. 'Assuming you had a mother, of course.' He reached up, plucked his balls from Legion's body and stashed them inside his capacious pockets. He frowned, and looked around. 'One missing. Ah!' He stood on the tips of his toes and stretched a hand above his head. Bernice squinted through the air vents, trying to get a better look.

Hang on a tick, she thought. That can't be right.

The Doctor's hand appeared to have vanished from the wrist up. His arm waggled, as if he were groping for something, and then his hand appeared as softly and suddenly as it had vanished: holding the fifth ball.

'You have knowledge of higher dimensions, I see,' Legion boomed.

'A smattering,' the Doctor said, carefully dusting off his ball. 'Trau Bishop?'

'Doctor?' Bishop detached himself from the watching crowd.

'Arrest this being.'

'On what grounds?'

'Sabotage and murder.'

'You can prove these allegations?' Bishop asked levelly.

'Of course.'

'Forgive me,' Legion interrupted, sincerity oozing from each of its voices, 'but I have only just arrived in this solar system. I was light years away at the time these alleged crimes took place. IMC records will prove it.'

'But the responsibility is yours,' the Doctor trumpeted. 'You gave the orders. You provided the virus which caused the software to crash in Paula Engado's starsuit, resulting in her death in the atmosphere of Lucifer. That same software caused a rogue malfunction in another starsuit, killing Sam Russell. Your agent on Belial also murdered Federique Moshe-Rabaan in an attempt to divert Adjudicator Bishop's suspicions: an attempt which would have succeeded had it not been for my,' and he preened himself, 'abilities at detection. That same agent blew up the room I had been in because I was getting too close. Fortunately, Trau Bishop and I had set that room up as a trap, knowing that your agent wouldn't be able to resist the bait. But they pulled the plug on the Belial neural net before we could use the security drones to trace their actions, risking the lives of everybody. Another crime to add to the register. And it was, of course, your troops who invaded Moloch Base, killing all the people who were there. Apart from one . . .'

'This is pure fabrication,' Legion protested as the Doctor looked across at one of the troopers, the one in the mirrored visor who had followed him in. The trooper stepped forward, raising the visor to reveal Ace's face.

The food dispenser seemed to sway around Bernice's body. Pins and needles tingled in her fingers and toes, creeping along her limbs until she felt as if she were disconnected from the world. Ace! She was alive! And with IMC? Something in the back of her mind was saying: shock, Bernice, you're in shock, snap out of it, woman, but she tuned it out and just stared at Ace until the world came back into focus around her and she heard Bishop saying calmly:

'So, this is the agent IMC planted on Belial.'

'No,' the Doctor sighed. 'Ace is just confused. Legion's agent is someone else.'

'Who?' Bishop asked calmly.

'I . . . I can't say.' The Doctor's gaze momentarily flickered across the room, but too fast for Bernice to tell who he was looking at.

'Really? You surprise me. Or rather, you don't. A transparent attempt to protect your former friend.'

'Permission to speak, Legion,' Ace said.

'Permission granted, Staff Sergeant.'

'The Doctor is lying.'

A murmur ran around the unwilling audience.

'How so?' Bishop asked.

'All of the people from Moloch are still alive.'

'You have seen them?'

'Yes. Well, no . . . but I've seen their med pallets. There was some shooting – some people were injured – but the people from Moloch, they're okay, I think . . .'

To Bernice, Ace seemed to be losing the thread, getting confused but, never the less, she could see the relief in people's faces. They hadn't wanted to believe that Kosi, Lars, Rachel and the rest were dead. It was far easier to think that a terrible mistake had been made.

'It's not true,' the Doctor protested. 'We found the bodies.'

'The bodies were of IMC troops,' Legion said; softly, loudly, and in tones ranging from baritone to treble. 'I sent them in to retrieve Christine LaFayette, the female offspring of the woman who now . . . manages . . . your Earth. As Staff Sergeant Ace said, the people on Moloch became violent. The only deaths were of IMC staff.'

Bernice almost wished she was out there in the refectory so that she could confront Legion. The alien was lying. Genetic tests had matched up the body parts on Moloch with everyone who had been there, apart from Ace and Christine. Damn Miles for wanting the information suppressed until the crisis was over and the shock could be minimized. Now, whatever they said, it was too late. Good news was always more palatable than bad. Teal, Craig, Tiw – they wanted to believe. Faith was a powerful drug.

The Doctor knew it too. Bernice could tell as she glanced over at him. He seemed to have shrunk inside his clothes. Legion had outmanoeuvred him. Getting Ace on his side had helped: the Doctor had an attachment to the woman that went deeper than either of them would admit. It made Bernice jealous, but she would never let that dictate her behaviour. Ace had a prior claim on the Doctor's affections. No matter what he and Bernice had been through, she knew in her heart of hearts that his guilt over what he had done to Ace on Heaven – and before – was a weakness: a button which would always work to throw him off balance when pressed.

Everybody's attention was on the centre of the room, where the IMC logo had been replaced with a densely written virtual document.

'Study it closely,' Legion was saying. 'You will find your terms of redundancy are fair. You will each receive one month's salary and a reasonable amortization of your pension contributions. As of this moment, Project Eden is no more.'

Tiw Heimdall stepped forward, his golden teeth glittering.

Before he could say anything, Legion answered his question in a prim falsetto. 'IMC cannot be held responsible for the fact that your Earth Central contracts failed to guarantee your return journeys.'

'And what about the return to Earth?' Tiw asked, trailing off into a mumble as he realized that Legion had anticipated him.

'However,' Legion rumbled on, 'despite the fact that IMC is a mining company, not a people-mover, we may be able to provide some berths.'

'For a price,' the Doctor said, scowling.

'For a reasonable price,' Legion agreed. 'Now for the documentation. Where is Coordinator Engado?'

'Here . . .' Miles staggered forward, with the support of Teal Green and Craig Richards. He waved them off, and pulled himself upright to face Legion. His knees looked to Bernice as if they were on the verge of buckling.

'I believe you'll find everything in order,' Legion said. For a moment, the voice echoed inside the dispenser casing, as if somebody were leaning close behind Bernice and whispering in her ear. She jumped, thinking she had been discovered. The feeling only lasted a second, but from the way Tanetoa, Belial's Samoan cook, flinched, some thirty feet away, Bernice guessed that Legion's voice was doing a little travelling. Not that his body was terribly stable. The pink lacy curtain had been slowly turning green and rolling up into a thin worm, studded with tiny thorns, that hung in mid-air. Little silver spheres at either end seemed to scan the crowd hungrily.

Miles's eyes were dull. His body sagged. A computer crystal had appeared in his hand, and he looked at it in mild bemusement, as if it were a fish, or a coloured party hat.

'Please scan the document and affix your personal ident code,' Legion was saying brusquely, his voice faint. Across the far side of the room, Shmuel Zehavi jumped as if goosed.

Something large and black stepped in front of the air vents. All Bernice could see was a large utility belt with a screamer pistol in a holster and a row of charge packs. A huge hand loomed in her field of vision. Was that the sound of keys being tapped? Shit! Some IMC trooper obviously couldn't wait for lunch. Bernice looked around desperately. She didn't even know what they had ordered. She scrabbled around on the floor of the dispenser, frantically trying to find something edible, anything that she had overlooked when she had cleared a space for herself; but it was useless.

'Come on. Come on . . .' the trooper growled.

A robotic dispenser arm was whirring nervously and

jabbing into Bernice's neck as it tried to locate an item that wasn't there from a shelf that had been removed. Bernice took a few moments break from her search to reach up and snap it off. It flexed once or twice in her hand, then died. She went back to her frantic exploration of the machine's interior.

There! In the corner. Some kind of cylindrical container. Bernice grabbed it and shoved it through the dispensing slot.

'What the zark! I didn't order this,' the trooper grumbled, shoving the container back into the slot. It split, drenching Bernice with some sticky fruit drink. With a sinking sensation in her stomach, she heard the trooper's fingers pound the keys again. She fumbled around her feet again, but there was nothing but crumbs and scraps of wrapper.

'Oh shit,' she said, surreptitiously pushing the access hatch open a crack and thrusting her fingers through, hoping nobody would notice.

'What's wrong with this thing?' the trooper snarled.

Trickles of sweat dripped from her hair and down her temples, leaving an itchy heat behind them. Her coveralls were damp, and stuck to her body as she writhed, trying to find something – anything – outside the machine. Her fingers clutched vainly at empty air. It was useless.

Her fingers suddenly brushed against a plastic wrapper. Yes! It was one of the items she had shoved beneath the machine's rubber skirt to make room. She quickly pulled it in and shoved it through the slot, hoping it was the right thing. Or even close.

'What is the *problem* with this machine?'

Oh hell, Bernice sighed. What was happening out there? Was the trooper's behaviour attracting attention? She twisted herself and tried to see through the buckled plate again. Nobody in her line of sight was looking her way, but that didn't mean anything.

'Hey, popcorn!' the trooper in front of Bernice's food dispenser said, surprised. 'I didn't know this thing had popcorn.'

The heavy utility belt vanished from Bernice's field of view, revealing the refectory again. A wave of relief swept over her, making her nauseous and dizzy.

'You can't go down to Lucifer,' Miles said from somewhere in the refectory. Bernice twisted to see him. She hadn't been keeping track of the conversation, but he seemed to have pulled himself together over the past few minutes.

'I'm sorry?' Legion said.

'You can't go down to Lucifer.' Miles's voice was firmer.

'Trau Engado, IMC can do anything it likes.'

'No. You don't understand. You cannot go down. You will be prevented.'

'By whom?'

'By my daughter,' Miles announced.

A sound like an electric drill ran round the room. It was Legion's laugh.

'Your female offspring? As I understand it, Trau Engado, she is dead.'

'No,' Miles said obstinately. 'I've seen her. I've talked with her. She's alive.'

Bernice could see Legion's body splitting into a firework display of multi-coloured fronds, and slowly drawing together into a hairy black ovoid supported by three pipe-cleaner legs. The hairs on the ovoid waved gently in a non-existent breeze.

'I grow tired of the reasonable approach,' Legion said. 'The Earth Alliance of Corporations has bought out Earth Central. There are no limits any more. No rules. No regulations. Nothing about environmental impact, customer care, or good business practices. IMC have been given a free . . .'

There was a pause. Bernice heard Ace murmur something beneath her breath.

'. . . hand,' Legion continued, 'to exploit all planets colonized, occupied or claimed by Earth for their mineral wealth. This Project Eden of yours: five years and nothing to show for it. I personally do not have time for delays in this operation, and my approach has been ratified at the highest levels. You, Coordinator Engado, are a hopeless incompetent. I shall not be requiring your services any longer. Is there somebody called Bannen here?'

Alex Bannen's footsteps echoed hesitantly through the refectory. 'Yes, sir?'

'I am informed that you will be amenable to cooperation.'

Bannen's voice positively glowed with anticipation. 'Oh yes,' he said. 'Oh yes indeed!'

Outside, Adjudicator Bishop cleared his throat. Events seemed to have overtaken him. To Bernice, he sounded suspiciously like a man whose job had evaporated, leaving him high and dry.

'I still have to find my murderer,' he announced.

'Well that's easy,' Bannen said nastily. 'Arrest Piper O'Rourke.'

There was a silence in the refectory.

'That is an as-yet unproven accusation,' Bishop said slowly, 'albeit with some corroborative substance to it. I shall require time to develop a case, to amass evidence – '

'No time,' Legion said brusquely. 'IMC is the law here, and the law is death.'

'Wait,' Bishop and the Doctor chimed together. Bernice watched as the Doctor took a step forward and opened his mouth. Bishop grabbed his collar, hoisted him back and stepped in front of him.

'I am still an Adjudicator of the Guild of Adjudicators,' he announced, his voice ringing out around the refectory. 'And I will have justice done this day!' To emphasize his point, a massive gun suddenly appeared in his hand. The troopers, reacting late, made Bishop the focus of their aim.

'Wrong on three counts,' said a gruff voice from the door. Bernice threw her weight against the side of the food dispenser, trying to swivel it discreetly around.

The refectory door was open again, and standing in it, filling it, was the most grotesquely fat woman that Bernice had ever seen. Her scalp gleamed as if freshly oiled, and pornographic tattoos seemed to writhe across it with a life of their own. Her robes were long and black; the points of her collar rose high above her head. She stepped forward in a manner that was so delicate it was repulsive.

'The Adjudicators are finished,' she growled. 'IMC has ruled the Guild to be an illegal organization. And there is no justice.'

Bishop seemed to shrink within his robes.

'Staff Sergeant Ace,' Legion said. Its voice seemed to hover over them all. 'In accordance with IMC regulations, and at the behest of Trau Bannen, Coordinator Designate of Project Eden, take Krau O'Rourke away to somewhere private and have her made redundant. With prejudice.'

For a long moment, nobody moved. Finally Ace stepped forward. She gestured at Piper with her flamer. 'Come on,' she snapped. 'Let's go.'

Silence reigned after they had left.

Nobody but Bernice caught sight of the devastated expression on the Doctor's face.

'You will all be segregated for the duration of the operation,' Legion announced to the assembled Project Eden team. 'To ensure a smooth transition of responsibility.'

Bernice had seen enough. She tilted her body sideways. The dispenser hummed as the null-grav units tried to compensate, and the machine juddered to one side.

Slowly, and with much complaining, the food dispenser wandered towards the door.

Piper slid from the Pit and into the transparent dome of the Belial Bridge terminal. Moloch hung overhead like a small but angry demon. Behind Moloch, the vast sphere of Lucifer cast a malignant crimson glare.

'Move,' Ace snapped behind her.

Piper stepped into the dome. Ace moved to cover her.

'Ace,' Piper said, 'I've talked to the Doctor. He said – '

'Shut up!'

'What are you doing, Ace? Don't you know what sort of a creature Legion is?'

'Well, you should know.'

'Well, there's nothing more to say, is there?' Piper took a deep but shaky breath. 'Are you going to get on with it, or what?'

'Or what,' Ace said, and fired.

Chapter Fifteen

While the IMC troopers escorted small groups of the Project Eden team to various rooms all over Belial Base, Alex Bannen prattled excitedly to five swirling nodes of flesh which hung unsupported in the air beside him.

'We don't actually need that much technology, it's just that the production facilities on the base are so out of date. There are a few micro-components, some control circuitry – but mostly we just need that dwarf-star alloy derivative IMC marketed last year. With that and a bit of thought we could design a starpod that could penetrate the atmosphere and the zelanite ocean and go all the way to the core.' Bannen drew a breath. 'What do you say, Legion? Cooperation could bring us both a fortune in marketable designs and accomplish the mission to find new stable heavy elements for Earth.'

Legion's voice trumpeted from each fleshy node in turn. 'The suggestion merits attention. Prepare your list.'

'And I'll need some of the Project Eden technicians released to help me. I can't do it all alone, and your people haven't had the five years of experience we have.'

'Piper O'Rourke provided us with a list of potential rebels amongst the staff,' Legion chorused. 'You may have access to anybody not on the list. In the meantime – ' a multi-jointed limb extended towards an IMC technician manning one of the neural net stations ' – if you would be so kind . . .'

'Of course, Legion.' The technician operated controls. There was a delicate glimmer of light in the centre of the room. A small figure formed out of the centre of the glow.

'Dad!'

'Mark! You remember me! I was afraid the systems crash would have . . .' The physicist stumbled to a halt, choked with emotion. 'I was just so scared you might have . . . might have . . .'

Mark grinned. 'Come off it, Dad.'

Legion spoke again. 'All memory systems were recovered intact. I return your simulated male offspring to you, Trau Bannen, in anticipation of a fruitful working relationship.'

Bannen gazed in turn at each of the hovering shapes. 'I don't know what to . . . Thank you. Thank you!'

Bannen took his son to one side and began to talk in a low, earnest voice. As he did so, Ace, who had been waiting for an opportunity to speak, stepped forward.

'Piper O'Rourke is dead, Legion. What are your orders?'

Legion answered in chorus, 'Corporate assessors are preparing to re-initialize Project Eden. Assessment and assimilation should take no more than three hours. I will travel to Moloch to oversee the second stage of the operation.'

Ace glanced across to where the physicist was fawning over his son. She lowered her voice. 'You'll be supplying Alex Bannen with the equipment he needs, then?'

'Naturally not.' Somehow Legion managed to convey surprise that Ace could ever have been in doubt of its intentions. 'IMC operations take precedence here. Redundant personnel are a fiscal burden on IMC operations. Alex Bannen must believe that we need him, otherwise he might become a problem. That means we must at least pretend to go along with his ludicrously primitive plan.'

'Understood. I'll supervise the takeover personally.'

'That will not be necessary. Executive staff have been fully briefed to assume control of the base; non-redundant personnel will assist as required. Take the executive transporter and join me in the flagship in one hour.'

As she hesitated, Legion's body extruded rose-hued

filaments which formed complex symbols in the air. 'The message you delivered gives you certain powers,' it whispered. 'But remember, you still work for me.'

Legion vanished like the fabled Cheshire Cat – a piece at a time. Ace let herself relax slightly when she was sure that her line officer had gone. She wished the sick feeling in her stomach had gone with it.

Miles Engado sat on the floor in his office, his knees drawn up to his chin, his back pressed firmly into the ribbed panels which formed one corner of the room. His gaze was blank and uncomprehending, despite all attempts to get him to speak.

'Oh, this is ridiculous!' Teal Green stormed as he paced impatiently along one short wall of the Administrator's office. 'He's been out into space and been brought back by an Angel. He's talked to them for chrissakes! He may have the key to getting us out of here and kicking IMC the hell back into space, and what does he do? Formulate a plan? Tell us what happened? Oh no!' Teal rushed towards Miles and thrust his face aggressively into the Administrator's. 'First of all he signs away the rest of our lives with a casual ident, and then he just sits in the corner as if he were a bloody corpse himself.' Miles showed absolutely no reaction to Teal's aggression. His face was placid, the pupils fixed. Teal turned away in disgust. 'I had a stuffed toy once that spoke more than him.'

'Violence isn't the way, Teal,' Julie Ndobe said quietly.

'It's IMC's way, Julie.'

'Miles is sick.'

'Unless we do something, he'll be worse than sick, he'll be dead, and the rest of us along with him! How the hell does that grab you?'

Julie threw up her hands. 'What do you want me to say? Ever since they locked us in here you've done nothing but mouth off. So why don't you shut up while those of us that can, try to think of a way out of this?'

Teal was about to respond angrily when a third voice

251

interjected, 'Ladies and gentlemen: all the time we're fighting amongst ourselves, we're not fighting IMC.'

The Doctor looked up from his place at Miles's desk. 'Not that I expect the simple truth of that statement to ameliorate your argument in the slightest.'

Teal rounded angrily on the Doctor. 'Do you think we're too stupid to recognize a sensible course of action when we hear it?'

'What I think doesn't matter. What do you think, Trau Green?'

Uncharacteristically, Teal was silent.

Julie said softly, 'What, then?'

The Doctor reached out to press a switch on Miles's desk. The interior lights came up as the office lights dimmed.

Julie and Teal both moved closer. Julie reached out to touch the glass shielding the disc of polished wood, the pieces of stone, scraps of cloth, feathers. 'It's beautiful.'

'It's a Tewa medicine wheel. And, incidentally, the key to the whole situation.'

Teal frowned. 'I don't see how – '

There was a sound beyond the office door. The Doctor placed one hand on his lips in a 'shushing' gesture as he flipped the switch to alter the room lighting back to normal.

The door opened and a figure was pushed inside.

'Cheryl! You okay?' Teal asked.

Cheryl just looked at Teal with no life in her eyes. A uniformed figure filled the doorway behind her. 'Ndobe, Coordinator Bannen wants you in the Operations Room.'

'Go and stick your pointy head up a – '

The Doctor shook his head almost imperceptibly. Julie subsided.

'Okay. Fine. I'm coming. Catch you later, guys.'

The door locked behind her.

Cheryl stood in the middle of the room until Teal guided her to a seat.

'Cheryl?' the Doctor said softly. 'Cheryl? What's happening out there?' When she didn't respond, he knelt down in front of her and, taking her head between his hands, stared deep into her eyes.

'Anushkia and Filo Julee are being forced to help as well,' she said finally. 'They didn't need me; support services are no longer required, the neural net has been disinfected and most systems are up and running again.' She shook her head, and for the first time some life appeared in her expression. 'Even the corridor twelve toilet is working for the first time in five years. They're taking over.' She frowned at the Doctor. 'But what are we going to do about it?'

The Doctor grinned as Teal answered for him: 'I think the Doctor may have that angle covered.'

'I might have guessed.'

The Doctor doffed his hat politely. 'Bernice should be along any time now to get us out of here. In the meantime, I think a little dialogue with The Man Who Knows would be in order.' He crossed to where Miles was scrunched into a corner, staring blankly into thin air, and crouched beside him.

'Miles? Listen to me, Miles.' He began to speak in a language which had been dead on Earth for more than two centuries.

The null-grav units on the food machine packed in halfway down the main corridor. Bernice had a moment to direct the machine into a side-tunnel before it crashed to the floor and she cracked her head painfully against the interior casing. She kicked her way clear of the device, rubbing life back into her bruised shoulders and knees. 'Time to diet,' she muttered to herself ruefully, peering around and trying to orient herself in the dim, night-lit corridor. As she did so, there was a series of heavy clicks and the lights came back on. Great. That was all she needed.

Footsteps echoed loudly from the direction of the main corridor. Military footsteps. Quickly, Bernice looked around for somewhere to hide. She'd be no good to the

Doctor if she were recaptured almost straight away. Besides, it would be embarrassing.

Running silently to a nearby doorway, Bernice thumbed the lock and slipped into the darkened room beyond. She held the door open a centimetre as the footsteps approached, and peered through the gap.

It was Ace.

Bernice pulled distractedly at her dreadlocks, trying to be angry at the girl, trying to feel betrayed. But her own childhood was still too close for the effort to be effective.

She looked around. She was standing in some kind of cable run: wires of all thicknesses and colours passed through collars in the ceiling, crept down the walls and exited the room through collars bolted into the floor. There was, needless to say, no other way out.

Oh well. Only one thing for it.

She inched the door open a little more and peered in both directions. Apart from Ace and the wrecked food machine, the passage was empty.

'Ace,' she hissed. 'Ace, it's me, Benny.'

Ace stopped in her tracks. She turned quickly, flattening against the corridor wall in automatic anticipation of hostile fire. Bernice opened the door fully and stepped into the corridor.

Ace was looking at her with wide eyes.

Bernice swallowed. 'It's okay, there's no one else here. We can talk now.'

Ace's arm was a blur of motion. Bernice instinctively jerked backwards. When she refocused on Ace, there was a gun clutched in the girl's fist. The barrel was pointing straight between Bernice's eyes.

Oops.

'On the other hand, maybe I'll just shut up.'

Ace's cold expression was answer enough.

Getting into an unfamiliar starsuit one-handed hadn't been easy, but Christine had persevered with the same determination which had brought her to Eden in the first place. Now she was inside and sealed tight, the hollow,

254

ringing thump and the vibrations of the executive transporter grapples were much reduced. Also reduced were the cries of disgust from technicians as some new crushed atrocity was found glued to the outer hull or smeared across the wall of the executive transporter bay. She had been lucky: more lucky than she had deserved. The troopers who had been outside the executive transporter with her had been so thoroughly pulped that it was impossible to tell the bodies apart, and that meant there was a fair chance her body would be assumed to be one of them. Thankfully, nobody had considered that she might have managed to get inside the transporter.

With a great effort of will, Christine put all thoughts of her narrow escape from her mind. A new objective had presented itself, and she intended to carry it out thoroughly. Fate had placed her in a position to find out what the hell was going on. If there was one thing Christine had learned over the years spent at her mother's side, it was never to waste an opportunity, whatever the consequences.

'Starsuit . . . uh . . . starsuit ten. Engage linkage for mainframe hookup and systems update.'

'Mainframe link engaged. Specify whether auto or manual update required.'

'Manual.'

'List systems to be updated or other command.'

'Other command. Interface primary data structure. Locate . . .' Christine hesitated. What exactly was she looking for? 'Locate files containing references to the following keywords: Lucifer; Eden; Angel or Angels; Christine LaFayette.'

'One file located. Access restricted. Security clearance required. Please state security clearance and authorization.'

Christine swore.

She thought for a long time. 'IMC zero zero one.'

'Clearance not recognized. Please restate security clearance and authorization.'

She thought again. 'Security clearance – by authorization of Madrigal LaFayette.'

255

'*Clearance not recognized. Please restate security clearance and authorization.*'

Christine swore. That should have been it! Her mother was responsible for the mission, so it was logical that – hang on. Christine half smiled. 'Johann LaFayette,' she said.

'*Code clearance valid. File Lucifer: High Level Briefing is now open. Menu as follows: Overview, Special Orders, Methodology.*'

Christine shook her head sadly. 'Oh Dad,' she whispered, 'she uses all of us in the end. Even you.'

'Access Overview,' she continued after a few moments.

'*Sub-file open.*'

A virtual screen opened in front of her eyes, obscuring the head-up displays. The screen showed a living colour portrait of her mother. Christine flinched involuntarily at the stern expression, the iron-grey hair, before remembering that, life-like as it was, the file was just a simulation, a recording.

She whispered, 'Activate.'

Her mother began to speak. 'Plans for the exploitation of planet Lucifer. Copy two of two. Classification Most Secret: Eyes only. Overview. Overview begins.

'Hello, Legion. As you are no doubt aware, the current status of Project Eden is somewhat less than ideal. With the political situation being what it is, I have . . . persuaded . . . the Board of Directors of the Holding Company to accede to my wish to return control of the Project to a commercial body; one which will be able to carry out the mission objectives without complications and without delays. I am pleased that your company picked up first refusal on the contract; IMC has a reputation for getting the job done at minimum cost, and we all know how important that is in today's marketplace.'

The image of Madrigal LaFayette smiled thinly. 'The Board has approved your plan to remove the planetary atmosphere to facilitate exploitation of the core. For details, see the file labelled "Methodology". Preliminary checks confirm our suspicions that the planetary core material is of a previously unknown, stable, high-atomic-weight element, and hence of incalculable commercial value. The placement of an IMC agent on Eden is approved, as is your suggestion to terminate employment of current staff. Nominal contractual obligations will have to be honoured, but these should not provide any of the staff with enough credit to book passage with IMC back to Earth.'

Christine tried to quell the sick feeling welling up in her stomach. Her mother, her own mother, responsible for the deaths of her friends. The thought was appalling.

'Your assessment of the indigenous life forms, named Angels, as being non-intelligent and therefore unimportant is also confirmed. And of course,' she added, 'there will be a bonus, as discussed, when Psychologist Christine LaFayette is returned, unharmed, to my office. I invested too many adjusted ergs circumventing the Eugenics Lottery to have the result waste herself on a guilt trip for planet Earth. Oh, and one more thing. I am aware of the particular . . . problems . . . that your planet is facing at the moment. I trust you not to let it affect your judgement. Good day, Legion. Overview terminates.'

The screen darkened.

So that was how her mother saw her. A 'result'. She laughed with a mixture of loathing and contempt. Not a child, not a woman, not even a human being, but simply a result. An investment. A showpiece of her mother's corporate power.

'Fuck you, mother,' she whispered softly. 'Fuck you to hell and back.'

She began to cry.

But she still accessed the file entitled 'METHODOLOGY'.

The Doctor stood up, extended a hand to Miles, and helped the Administrator to his feet. Miles stood, trembling, his face pale and sweaty.

Teal exchanged looks with Cheryl. 'I didn't think we were going to see him up and around again.'

Cheryl brought a finger to her lips. 'Shh!'

Miles was talking softly. 'Yonder in the north, there is singing on the lake. Cloud maidens dance on the shore. There we take our being.'

Teal frowned. 'I don't understand. What's he talking about?'

Cheryl hissed, 'It's part of the Tewa story of origin. The legend of how the tribe began. Paula told it to me once. Now shut up, it might be important.'

'Yonder in the north, cloud beings rise. They ascend unto cloud blossoms. There we take our being.'

The Doctor stared raptly at Miles, his eyes wide, drinking in the imagery. There were answers here, he was sure of it. Connections. His lips moved almost silently. 'Come on, Miles. Tell me the rest. Tell me it all.'

'Yonder in the north, rain stands over the land. Yonder in the north stands forth at twilight the arc of a rainbow. There we have our being.'

Ace forced Bernice at gun-point through the jury-rigged remains of the Base's main airlock. Only hours before, the IMC troops had hyperglued a temporary 'lock on the outside of the Base to hold air as they blasted their way inside. Bernice had admired the pragmatism, if not the intent. Forget about picking locks; just blow the damn thing open.

Ace caught her glance, as she directed her through the new 'lock. 'It's quicker. Also there's the shock value. Always useful when you need immediate compliance. Here. Put this spacesuit on.'

Bernice shuddered as she obeyed the girl's instruction. 'Of course, the psychological angle. I don't know why I didn't see it myself.'

'You're being sarcastic again, Bernice. Why do you hate me so much?'

'It's not you I hate, it's what you've become.'

Ace was silent for the few minutes it took them to walk across the broken surface of Belial to the parked IMC executive transporter. They climbed in through the airlock after Ace deactivated the security lasers. The hold behind them was already full of passengers: high-spirited troopers and a disdainful Alex Bannen.

Dumping her suit as soon as she could, Bernice was forced to wait as Ace racked hers neatly before leading the way up to the control cabin.

'Take a seat,' Ace said.

Bernice settled into the co-pilot's couch as Ace prepared the executive transporter for take-off.

'What's Bannen doing here?' Bernice asked.

'He is Coordinator, now. I'm supposed to take him to Moloch Base after I've dropped you off on the *Insider Trading*. He could take the new Lift, of course, but the fat idiot just wants to throw his weight around.'

'So, we're going to the IMC flagship. Want to tell me why?'

Ace was silent.

'Ace, I asked you a question.'

'Don't push it, Bernice. I told you before not to confuse me. I have enough to deal with every time the Doctor opens his mouth.'

Savagely, she shoved her thumb down on the *initiate sequence* switch and the executive transporter's engines thundered briefly, lifting the craft clear of the moon.

'But you wouldn't be confused if you weren't travelling with the Doctor any more, would you?' Bernice said quietly.

Ace set the executive transporter on auto-control and swivelled in her chair to stare at Bernice. 'I wouldn't bank on it,' she whispered.

Bernice gazed through the executive transporter's viewscreen as the immense bulk of Lucifer slipped gradually higher above Belial's bleak horizon. Several hundred kilometres away, she knew, the IMC ships were assuming orbit, deploying for the best position. She strained her eyes, but the scarlet glare of Lucifer obscured any tiny glints of reflected sunlight from the fleet.

She looked sideways once more at Ace. 'Do you trust

IMC any more than you trust the Doctor? Do you trust Legion?'

'Legion is my line officer. I trust it completely.' She turned back to the controls. 'I trust it with my life.'

Bernice shuddered at the change in Ace's voice. 'And everyone else's lives? Do you trust Legion with them as well?'

Ace did not reply.

Miles Engado slumped once again to the floor, his wave of verbosity apparently expended with the end of the Tewa story of origin.

The Doctor regarded him sadly, aware that the best thing he could do was simply to leave the man alone. At least he'd managed to convey the gist of his conversation with Paula, or rather, with the thing she had become.

'What now?' Cheryl whispered.

The door opened with a soft click.

'Aha! That'll be Bernice, and not before time, either.' The Doctor turned to the door with a smile, which faded when he found that it wasn't Bernice who was standing there, but Bishop. The smile came back full force when he saw the two troopers who were lying, either unconscious or dead, outside the room.

Teal and Cheryl gazed in surprise at the newcomer.

Bishop sighed. 'I do hope you aren't planning to spend the next few minutes of this escape engaged in a similar lack of motion,' he said calmly.

The Doctor blinked. 'I'm glad you have decided which side you're on, Trau Bishop. Cheryl, you and Teal get up to Operations. I need to find out what's going on there. Try not to get caught. Meet Trau Bishop and myself in the Mushroom Farm as soon as you have any useful information.'

'Sure. What about Miles?' Cheryl said.

'I think it'll be best if we leave him here.'

'If you say so. Come on, Teal.'

After checking the passage was clear, Cheryl led Teal from the office, stepping over the guards on the way.

'Trau Bishop?'

'It's a long story. I'll tell you on the way.'

In another moment, the room was empty. A few minutes passed with only Miles Engado's shallow breathing to break the silence. Then, with no appreciable change of expression, the Base Administrator clambered stiffly to his feet and moved to his desk. Sliding aside a glass door, Miles removed the ancient medicine wheel from the desk and, clutching the device to his chest, walked slowly from the office.

Chapter Sixteen

The troopers in the back of the executive transporter were jabbering away like schoolkids on an outing. They didn't seem to mind that it was cramped, and dirty, and smelled of old sweat. Alex Bannen, Base Coordinator *pro tem*, had squeezed himself into a corner and was trying, haughtily and without much success, to ignore their sarcastic jibes.

Ace, sitting up front beside Bernice, could feel hard fingers of tension digging into the muscles of her neck. Jerks and morons: she was surrounded by them.

Jeez, how had she got herself into this?

As she guided the executive transporter towards one of the myriad spiracle airlocks which lined the gothic bulk of the *Insider Trading*, she remembered her careers master, long ago, asking her what she wanted to be when she left school.

I want to be a racing driver.

If only you could go back and talk to yourself, she thought; sit yourself down in a nice snug bar somewhere, and tell yourself about the rocks ahead, draw a map of life's rosy path as it winds through the swamps and the man-traps, dole out some advice and then get absolutely rat-arsed with yourself. Look kid; grab hold of Dave at Ange's party and snog his brains out. He wants you to, and if you don't do it, you'll regret it. Don't go off to Margate with Julian when he asks, 'cos when you come back, your dad'll be in hospital with a stroke, and he'll never wake up, and you'll wish you'd been with him for those last precious moments after all those years apart. If you see a pair of cheetah-spot leggings in a shop in

Salisbury, don't buy them, because you'll look like a right pranny wearing them and nobody will dare tell you.

If you find yourself serving in a bar on Iceworld, stay there.

If you see a large blue box, don't go in it.

Never wear a uniform.

Never fall in love.

I want to be a racing driver.

'I need to ask you some questions,' Bishop panted as he raced to keep up with the Doctor through the aeons-old, alien-built corridors that led from the Pit into the heart of Belial. He couldn't understand how the Doctor's legs could be so short and yet cover the ground so quickly.

'Ask away, Adjudicator Bishop. Ask away.'

The Doctor turned a corner into another of the dead-space corridors. Bishop followed, and was aghast to see the Doctor already fifty yards away.

'Federique Moshe-Rabaan!' he yelled, pounding past the dark openings of offshoot corridors.

'Lovely lady. What about her?' a voice floated back.

'You did find her body first, didn't you?'

The Doctor had turned off again, far ahead. Bishop's footsteps clanged on metal grillework, slowing to a halt as he came to the turning, stopping as he found a junction of five dark openings, any one of which the Doctor could have vanished into.

'You found her and you didn't tell me,' he whispered. 'You left it for Shmuel Zehavi. You didn't tell me.'

'I had my reasons.' The words echoed faintly from the left-hand corridor. Bishop took a deep breath and set off in pursuit.

'You kept information from me,' Bishop shouted. 'That's a crime!' He checked himself, and muttered, 'Well, it *was* a crime.'

The Doctor almost smiled. 'For me, concealing information is a crime. For IMC, obtaining information is a crime. The law moves in mysterious ways, doesn't it, Adjudicator?'

There was a dog-leg turn ahead where the corridor narrowed down and turned back on itself. Bishop slowed, and squeezed through the constriction.

'I wanted you to suspect me and lock me up, so that the real killer would feel more secure and come out into the open,' the Doctor said. His voice was loud and clear, albeit slightly muffled by the neutron cannon which was pressing his face against the wall.

'They're all out of breath,' Ardamal said in mock-sympathy.

'Let's make it permanent,' growled Kreig, as her cannon swung to cover Bishop. 'I could do with some new ears.'

Methodology.

Christine stood glaring at the starsuit's virtual screen for a long time after the simularity faded.

Methodology.

A simple word for an appalling crime. A meaningless word; a mask behind which you could hide anything which you didn't want the shareholders to find out about, or didn't want to think about too hard yourself. A label attached to a hidden horror.

A movement outside the executive transporter attracted her attention. She watched as another shuttle penetrated the osmotic field of the bay, slowed to a halt and descended into an open space. Technicians ran forward with magnetic grapples. The troopers who had been scraping the remains of their friends from the back of Christine's executive transporter moved out to form an honour guard.

Displacement activity, she thought. Typically Freudian. I've got a conflict of desires, because I know I have to act on what I've learned, but I don't want to have to think about it, so instead I concentrate on trivialities like looking out of the window. Come on, Christine! Pull yourself together and get back to the matter in hand.

She called back the simularity and watched, sickened, as the mottled crimson bulk of Lucifer rotated sedately before her. Belial and Moloch swung past, linked by the rainbow filament of the Bridge, distorted by false perspective so that Belial loomed larger than its sibling, and scooted faster across the simularity's field of vision. A slight disturbance in Lucifer's atmosphere was the only sign that something was wrong: a whirlpool centred on a speck of light where, moments before, there had been nothing. And then Lucifer's atmosphere seemed to stretch towards the blazing point. Another spiral of gas, a storm in a teacup, drifted into sight higher up around the planet's horizon. And another, lower down but traversing the face of the planet towards the pole, dragging the atmosphere with it. With a motion of her finger, Christine pulled down an information box containing a skeletal representation of the main picture with the animation accelerated for effect. Eight points danced around Lucifer; their orbits criss-crossing its surface in a complex web. Equations scrolled past; orbital element sets, thermal convectivities, gravitational gradients, Doppler-distorted spectra. It was like trying to fathom Venusian, but the simularity made a good Rosetta stone.

The points were black holes: quantum collapsars orbiting Lucifer, sucking away its atmosphere in a scream of hard gamma-rays. Tamed, and under control. So that was her mother's plan: strip the planet of its atmosphere and clear the way for concentrated robotic mining of the core. Screw the planet, screw the Angels, keep your eyes fixed firmly on the profit margin.

And that, no doubt, was what IMC needed Legion for. Humanity didn't have the technology to control black holes – even the atom-sized ones that had been formed by density fluctuations during the Big Bang. They were leasing the technology from Legion's race.

She had to stop it before it started.

Christine stood up and headed for the airlock.

Bishop slipped a hand inside his robes and wrapped his fingers around the butt of his judicial weapon. He could certainly take out one of the troopers, but he estimated a forty per cent chance that the Doctor's head would end up sizzling on the wall before he could disable the other.

'Wait!'

The troopers looked up as a massive bulk glided from the shadows.

'IMC policy is that there should be no unnecessary deaths,' Bronwen ap Bryn rumbled.

'Seconded,' the Doctor said around the muzzle of the neutron cannon.

'Ah, well, that all depends . . .' Kreig shifted from one foot to another.

'. . . on your definition of unnecessary,' Ardamal finished, removing his cannon from the Doctor's mouth and wiping saliva from it. The Doctor massaged his gums resentfully.

'Get on with your rounds,' Bryn snapped, gesturing the troopers away. Bishop noticed with some satisfaction the distaste with which they squeezed past her. Interesting: they obeyed orders, but they didn't seem to like it. He filed that one away for later use.

'The company I'm forced to mix with . . .' Bryn said apologetically.

'I'm surprised to find you so reluctant to aid and abet murder,' Bishop said, stepping forward to confront her, 'considering how you must have stood by and accepted the slaughter on Moloch.'

'There was no slaughter on Moloch. You heard Legion.'

'On the basis that the Project Eden team were issued with no weaponry,' Bishop said, falling into his Adjudicatorial manner, 'how do you explain the wounds, if not by organized IMC butchery?'

'Don't come the high and mighty with me,' Bryn snapped. 'Your record isn't exactly lily-white. How many murders have you committed in your time?'

'None,' Bishop said, affronted.

'You killed fifteen people on Callisto.'

'Drug dealers.'

'And another thirty-eight in Macedonia.'

266

'Revolutionaries.'

'And the entire population of Frinelli Minor?'

'Energy-wasters and dysfunctionals.'

'Correct me if I'm wrong,' Bryn simpered, 'but you currently hold the Guild of Adjudicators record for most deaths incurred in the course of duty.'

'Judicial executions,' Bishop snapped.

'Murders by another name,' Bryn chided. 'The Guild of Adjudicators, IMC, what's the difference? They both decide what is right and what is wrong. They both kill in line with that decision. Who is to say that one is any better than the other?'

'There are laws – '

'Laws are made by humans. When Earth Central made the laws, the Guild enforced them. Now the Earth Alliance of Corporations makes the laws, and they have their own enforcers. The Guild has no rationale any more, no justification. The future is with the EAC.'

'You may have sold out,' Bishop spat bitterly, 'but I still believe in truth, and justice, and right.'

'You don't understand, do you?' Bryn's deep voice was smothered in malicious pity. 'There's nothing left to sell out *from*. And the EAC decide what is true, what's just, and what's right.'

'It's the golden rule, isn't it?' the Doctor said from the sidelines.

'You understand,' Bryn said. 'I'm so glad.' She turned and waddled daintily back into the shadows. 'I remember you as a young squire, Bishop,' she said as she retreated. 'You were good. Too good to waste your life clinging to outdated ideals. When you've changed your mind, let me know.'

Her footsteps echoed loudly through the corridor for a few moments, and then there was silence.

'She let us go,' the Doctor said, surprised.

'I was her squire, for a while,' Bishop said. 'Long ago, when I was young, and she was honest. Perhaps she thought she owed me something.'

'Perhaps she suspects she's made the wrong decision, and wants to make some kind of amends.'

'Either way, she should keep personal sentiment out of justice.' Bishop took his hand from the butt of his weapon, where it had been all the way through the conversation. 'Oh, and what is the "golden rule"?'

The Doctor smiled. 'Whoever has the gold, makes the rules,' he said, and walked off.

The side of the executive transporter had been cleaned by the time Christine stepped out of the airlock. She was wearing a spacesuit whose name tag read 'SHIPARELLI', she had the helmet screwed on, and she had the polarization set on full. It was like she was stumbling around in the dark. There were enough technicians and pilots around dressed the same that she didn't look conspicuous, but that didn't stop her feeling like she had a big glowing holosign above her head saying *Escaped Prisoner! Please Apprehend!*

The bustle around the newly arrived executive transporter was attracting a lot of attention, and Christine managed to get to the side of the bay without being noticed. She didn't actually know where she was going: it was like some autopilot had kicked in, some part of her subconscious which kept her putting one foot in front of another whilst the rest of her mind sorted out the difficult things – like reason, and direction.

The airlock in the new executive transporter had opened now, and two suited figures were emerging.

She had to find the Doctor. If anybody could fight IMC, he could. That meant stealing an executive transporter. Damn! She was heading in the wrong direction. She should have stayed back in the –

'Hey, you! Stop right there!'

There were upwards of thirty people in the bay. There was a good chance she was safe. She took two more paces.

'One more step, Christine, and I burn your spine out!'

It was over. Somehow, the thought bought its own measure of relief. No more decisions. She turned.

Ace's face was set into an implacable mask. The barrel of her gun was a long, dark tunnel with death at the end of it.

'Hi!' Bernice said brightly. 'Glad you could join us.'

There were signs in the heavens.

Miles Engado stared out from the Lift into the depths of space. Messages had been spelled out across the cosmos – in stars, galaxies and nebulae – just for his eyes. They whispered to him of the importance of his life, of the vital part he played in creation. The Great Whale had arranged them for him. Only for him.

The medicine wheel was a painful weight in his arms, but he did not want to loosen his grip. It reminded him of what was important. It connected him with the only thing he had left: the past.

He had to see Paula again. He had to make the long journey down into the depths and confront the Whale on its own ground, to apologize to it, to ask it for his daughter back again and, if necessary, to sink into its maw in her place.

As the Lift inched closer to Moloch, he sank to his knees. He was tired, more tired than he had ever been. The stars broadcast their messages to him, but he could not understand. Their voices were a babble in his head: their words flowed together like the barking of the seals as they bobbed on the spume-tipped sea, like the endless beating of the waves. Rush and retreat. Rush . . . and retreat.

The coldness of metal on his cheek jerked him awake. Somehow, he had slid down to the grille floor which separated the main body of the Lift from the curved underside and provided a flat surface for the Lift's human occupants to walk on. He lay there, the metalwork making a waffle-iron impression on his cheek, his mind moving back and forth over the walk from his office to the Pit, the slide down to the Bridge terminal and the wait for the Lift to arrive. For the first time, he marvelled at the lack of any troopers on his journey. It was as if he were alone on Belial. It was as if he were being protected.

The focus of his gaze moved from the grille, to the darkness beneath the grille, to the curved metal of the Lift walls and the supporting spars.

And to the eye that watched him from the shadows.

'Miles,' said a muffled voice, 'I'm so sorry . . .'

'I'm sorry,' Bernice said, 'but we did ask for an ocean view.'

The room was panelled in what appeared to be oak. Heavy glass chandeliers hung suspended from null-grav units, and computer-generated portraits of previous IMC Chairpersons adorned the walls. The massive slab of mahogany that passed for a table was laden with fruit and wine.

Bernice strode in as if she owned the place. 'No, this just won't do. Please take our baggage to another room.'

Christine followed her in.

Ace, gun in hand, stood in the doorway. 'You think you're so smart,' she snapped. 'Have I ever told you just how tired I get of your wisecracks?'

'I don't suppose there's any chance of you telling us what's going on?' Christine asked in a weary voice.

'What's the point in asking?' Bernice said levelly, staring at Ace. 'She's not operating on logic. Legion's played around with her mind.'

'That's a lie,' Ace snapped.

'What other reason could you have for abandoning your friends?'

'Deeper loyalties – ' Ace stopped abruptly, as if she had reconsidered her words.

'What deeper loyalties? The Doctor did everything for you!'

'The Doctor did everything *to* me. He relates to his companions the way a pusher relates to his pitbull terrier. We're useful to him, or are you too stupid to realize that?'

'And you prefer blindly following IMC's orders?'

'We all follow orders,' Ace said, and met Bernice's gaze fully for the first time since they had left Belial. 'But at least my boss says he's my boss, and doesn't pretend to be my friend.'

Bernice looked liked she was going to explode. 'But don't you – '

'No, Bernice.' Christine stepped forward and rested her good hand on the archaeologist's shoulder. 'Ace has made her choice. You can't change it.'

'Remember that,' Ace snarled, and slammed the door. There was silence in the room for a few moments, broken only by the heavy clink of a magnetic lock.

'She was lying,' Christine said to herself, with some surprise. 'She doesn't want it to be this way at all.'

Bernice crossed to the table and picked up a bottle of wine. 'I thought as much,' she agreed, triggering the in-built cooling unit. 'She was tense in all the wrong places. She wants us to do something, but I don't know what.'

'There's obviously a history between you two and the Doctor. Care to tell me a little about it?'

'Why not?' Bernice took a swig of the wine. 'After all, there's precious little else to do.' She perched herself on the edge of the table and adopted her lecturing stance. 'It's just your basic, everyday story of a boy, a girl and a fungus . . .'

'Oh Miles, what's happened to you?'

Miles Engado stared out into space as if he hadn't heard. The glare reflected from Moloch's approaching icy surface emphasized the deep creases and folds of his face. As she climbed up into the main body of the Lift, Piper O'Rourke was appalled. This man wasn't the smooth-faced Administrator who had so impressed her at the interviews for Project Eden. Miles seemed to have aged ten years in as many hours.

'Miles?'

No response. She flung the hatch in the grille flooring shut with all her strength, hoping that the sudden noise would shock Miles out of his lethargy, but he didn't even flinch.

'Miles, I can understand your anger, but – '

'I'm not angry,' he said, with no emotion in his voice.

'But Paula – '

'Paula is still alive.'

'You said that back in the refectory. I wasn't sure if – '

'You should have faith. All things come to those with faith. All things . . .'

There was something seductively convincing about his flat delivery.

'Is it possible?' she murmured to herself. 'Could the Angels have rescued Paula?'

'No,' he answered, still with no inflection in his voice. 'It was an accident. That's what she told me. She collided with an Angel. Somehow their . . . souls . . . fused. She's one of them now.'

It was that calm correction that finally persuaded Piper that Miles hadn't slipped over the edge into insanity after all. She felt a strange kind of elation well up within her, but reality deflated it. 'What about the Project?' She tried to see the expression in his eyes, but it was like staring into a dry well for a glimmer of light on water. 'I betrayed you all.'

'It was written.'

'Don't you want to know why?'

Miles said nothing, but she needed to tell him. It didn't matter whether or not he wanted to know.

'It was Ben. My husband . . .'

No reaction from Miles. She was obscurely disappointed.

'IMC contacted me six years ago, just after I'd been accepted on to Project Eden. They told me they'd found some trace of the *Hydrax*, the InterSpace ship he vanished on: some wreckage drifting across the trade lanes, or a rumour of a sighting by some newly contacted alien race, or something. They kept stringing me along for months during the training sessions on Earth, holding out false hope, making me feel guilty about the effort they were putting into finding him. They asked for a few little fav-ours – a complete crew list for the Project, the name of the vessel we were to ship out on – small things, and I felt glad I could do something to repay them. I didn't tell anyone, of course – I wasn't stupid, I knew that what I was doing was wrong – but all the time I was thinking of Ben, and what it would be like when he came back.'

She sighed deeply, and looked away from Miles out to the harshly glittering stars. A point of light was paralleling their course, moving down towards Moloch. An IMC executive transporter? Probably. Did it matter? Probably not.

'They lied to me, of course, but by the time I realized, it was too late. I was in too deep. They threatened to expose me if I didn't do as I was told.'

She was looking past the stars now, to a young face, framed by black hair, which smiled at her over a gulf of years.

'And there was always a little voice in the back of my mind that said, "Perhaps, just perhaps, he *is* still alive out there." Justification? Yeah, but I had to believe in something, or I would have gone mad.'

She took a deep breath and pulled herself back to the here-and-now. 'I should have guessed that Legion would want me out of the way as soon as IMC came out in the open. I didn't know he'd suborned Ace, though. She was a nice kid. I wonder what he offered her.'

She frowned as she remembered Ace's dispassionate face in the Bridge terminus on Belial, sighting along the barrel of her gun. She shivered as she recalled saying, 'Are you going to get on with it, or what?' and Ace replying 'Or what,' then closing her eyes, deliberately aiming wide, firing, and walking away without looking back. Piper didn't know what Ace's motives had been. She wasn't even sure that Ace knew herself. All she knew was that she owed Ace her life.

She glanced over at Miles, trying to gauge his reaction. 'And that's my story. Miles? *Miles*?'

His face could have been carved out of stone.

'Please Miles, say something. Anything.'

'I'll need your help.' It was as if he had heard nothing she had said.

'To do what?'

He turned to look at her, and the fanatical light in his eyes made her take a sudden step back.

'I'm going back to Paula,' he said. 'And this time I'm going to bring her back. Your virus is still in the starpod software, and I need you to debug it.'

The medlab was locked, but with the sophisticated devices that Ace had managed to retain from the future, that was not a problem. She moved quietly through the shadowed room, amazed at how easy it was to remember the covert reconnaissance drill she had been taught.

The recuperation pods looked like tombs in the ghostly half-light of the sterilizing radiation. The first one – the one that had nurtured Christine LaFayette's injured body before she had made her escape attempt – was empty. The second one was empty too, but Ace held out no hopes for the wellbeing of Shock Trooper (Third Class) Jason Curtis Dommer.

The third pod was empty too.

And the fourth.

Ace quickly checked the remainder of the line. None of the recuperation pods was occupied, either by her friends from Moloch or by anyone else. Judging by the status read-outs, they had been empty for quite some time.

For a moment, she looked around indecisively, and then she left, as quietly as she had arrived.

She had a passenger waiting.

As the executive transporter rose from Moloch's icy surface and set course for Belial, Alex Bannen gave it no more than a cursory glance. He was too concerned with navigating across the treacherous landscape. Ace had used some cock-and-bull story about incompatibility of airlocks to justify dropping him in an ill-fitting spacesuit a hundred yards from the translucent blister of the Bridge terminus. She hated him. They all hated him, but he would have his revenge.

High above him, the tordoidal shape of the Lift was gliding down the gilded ray of the Bridge. As Bannen plunged into the soft skin of the terminus, he wondered briefly whether he should have waited for it, rather than submit himself to the indignities of the executive transporter. The uncertainty lasted only for a moment, until he remembered the rush of self-respect that he had felt when he ordered Ace to take him to Legion. No, he had authority now. He didn't need to rely on the vagaries of an alien technology that was several millennia past its sell-by date.

Warming power fantasies filled his mind as he quitted the Bridge terminus, found his way to the head of the Pit and was swirled down the shining path towards Moloch's interior. It was only as he stepped from the Pit and made his way through the deserted Moloch Base that the stench of burning organic matter pulled him from his dreams.

Moloch was ablaze.

As Bannen walked out of Moloch Base and entered the clearing in the forest, he saw IMC troopers standing around its periphery with flamers. The diaphanous trees were burning, their tendrils flailing the air wildly, trailing sparks behind them and wailing thinly, like a jungle of leaky balloons. Greasy columns of smoke rose slowly up into the air, curved into widening spirals by the anomalous air currents of Moloch's interior.

Bannen watched, amazed and oddly aroused, as the flames spread through the forest, moving upwards around the interior until it seemed as if he were standing at the centre of the lowest circle of hell. The troopers moved in deeper, long flames licking from their weapons. Robotic construction units were busy erecting an IMC office complex on the razed ground.

'You want to tell me that arrangements have been made for your excursion to Lucifer's zelanite ocean,' said a multiplicity of voices behind him, 'but that you need certain items from IMC which have not been forthcoming.'

'How do you know?' Bannen stuttered as he turned. Legion was looking almost normal: four thin, multi-jointed legs supporting a thorny husk of a body with one magnificent, black and violet eye.

'I know.'

A flock of translucent creatures burst from the branches of the trees and made a break for the centre of Moloch. There was a flurry of activity amongst the troopers as they exchanged bets, then the things began to explode in showers of sparks as they were fired upon. As the last one burst like a firework, money exchanged hands amid much laughter.

'When will the dwarf-star alloy derivative be ready?' Bannen asked hesitantly. He wasn't sure quite how far he could push Legion. Still, the alien had obviously realized Bannen's leadership potential, and needed him to keep the rest of the Project Eden team in line.

'Time . . .' Legion sighed. 'You humans think it is so important. You and your pathetic power fantasies. Bishop and his obsession with an ideal. Ace and her mysterious mission from the future, thinking that she can stay aloof from our mission here. If you could see the universe from my perspective, you would realize how meaningless it all is. Leave me, Bannen.'

'But, Legion – '

The IMC leader's body leaned towards Bannen until the huge eye was level with his face. The eye split into a thousand silver globules that chased each other round Legion's body.

'*Leave me,*' it chorused.

As Bannen scuttled back towards the Pit, and the interminable wait for the Lift back to Belial, a small seed of paranoia sprouted in his mind. Was Legion really committed to helping him investigate Lucifer, or was it just stringing him along, excluding him from something bigger?

Righteous indignation filled him. He had debated about

whether to tell Legion what he knew of the true purpose of the Mushroom Farm controls, but the alien could whistle for it now.

Chuckling, Bannen walked past the entrance to the Atmospheric Vehicle Research Laboratory without seeing Miles Engado and Piper O'Rourke sink back into the shadows.

In their plush, oak-lined cell on the *Insider Trading*, Bernice and Christine were just putting the final touches to their escape attempt. Christine had pulled down the floating light-fittings with her one good arm, and Bernice had taken out some of her aggression on the heavy mahogany table by smashing its legs off.

'Okay, bring those things over here,' Bernice said.

Christine moved carefully across the room. Holding the null-grav units down under the tablecloth, she passed them to Bernice. With deft movements, the archaeologist retrieved them and strapped them securely beneath the table with napkins. The table wobbled: rising into the air in fits and starts as each unit was fitted. Eventually, the table was hovering unsteadily in the centre of the room.

Bernice gestured to it. 'All aboard the *Skylark*,' she chanted, and climbed on. The table rocked alarmingly.

Christine extended a wary hand. 'Are you sure this thing's safe?'

'I very much doubt it.'

'How reassuring.'

Bernice grabbed the hand and pulled. Christine clambered on to the table and slid across it on her knees. They stared at each other for a moment or two.

'Well, what now?' Christine said.

'Let's rock and roll.' Bernice reached under the table and tilted one of the null-grav units away from the door. The graviton field interacted with the far wall and the table began to move, slowly at first, but gathering speed quickly until it was hurtling towards the door, too fast for Christine to do anything but hang on and pray.

The door exploded outwards in a shower of splinters;

by the time they hit the floor, Bernice, Christine and the table were half-way down the corridor.

Chapter Seventeen

Having examined the files on Alex Bannen's unmanned workstations near the door to the Mushroom Farm, the Doctor and Bishop moved deeper into the forest of glimmering silver pillars.

The Doctor said quietly, 'Somewhere in here are the last pieces of the puzzle of Lucifer.' He poked into the shadows with his umbrella, skipping backwards with an embarrassed smile when a hundred columns began to glow in shifting colours. 'We have to solve the puzzle if we're to protect it.'

'From IMC?'

'From anyone who wants to exploit it.'

Bishop frowned. 'Why should you want to protect it?'

'How much do you know of Amerindian history, Trau Bishop?'

'I fail to see what relevance the science of social anthropology has at this juncture.'

The Doctor shook his head sadly. 'Put it like this: you do still believe in the concept of justice for the innocent, I presume?'

'Would I be here if I didn't?'

'A moot point.' The Doctor dismissed the counter-question out of hand. 'But I'll take it as a "yes".'

'And?'

'And . . . that's all.' The Doctor strode off into the forest of glimmering stalks. Bishop suppressed an angry glare as he hurried after him.

Behind them both came a third set of footsteps. Quiet, military footsteps.

It seemed to Teal Green that he and Cheryl Russell had wasted all their time since escaping from Miles's office ducking and weaving. IMC troopers were everywhere: guarding the rooms where the remnants of the Project Eden team were being held, escorting IMC scientists and economic analysts around the Base, and lounging around watching pornographic simularities in the refectory. The two of them had scuttled from closet to ventilation duct, from generating room to kitchen, always one step ahead of capture, always one step away from finding an unguarded way of getting to the Mushroom Farm and the Doctor. No time to think; just enough time to react.

Teal slumped to the ground as the bulkhead behind him swung shut. 'Where to now, boss?'

Cheryl, crouching on the grilled flooring like a cornered animal, just snarled.

'Fine,' he said with a panicky nonchalance. 'Just asking.'

There was a soft hiss.

The wall beside his head blistered and ran.

'Down!' Cheryl shoved Teal away and fell in the opposite direction as another bolt sped between them, smashing into the wall with a hiss of vaporizing metal.

She began to crawl along the corridor as a trooper moved towards her. She wasn't sure, but she thought she recognized him from the corporate takeover. Three metres away, Teal had clambered to his feet and was beginning to run.

Immediately, the trooper swung the barrel of his gun to cover the power technician. 'Nobody move!'

'Give me a break,' Teal muttered as he ducked into a side corridor and vanished from sight.

Cursing, Cheryl was left alone facing the trooper.

He moved closer.

He was smiling.

'Allow me to introduce myself,' he said, the smile widening. Cheryl began to get to her feet.

'Not so fast! Stay on your knees. That's better. Now then, as I was saying, Jay Ardamal . . . at your *service*.'

Cheryl gazed upwards into the barrel of Ardamal's gun. She looked beyond it to his smile and his even white teeth and the blank desire in his eyes.

She shuddered. 'All right, you've got me; I surrender. I want to see Legion. Take me to him – it – now.'

'Oh, I'll take you to see Legion all right. But first, I think a little *interrogation* is in – '

Teal Green burst out of the side corridor holding a solid plastic casing prised from a length of the cable conduit. Screaming wildly, he swung the cover in a short, vicious arc, which connected with the side of Ardamal's helmet. The IMC man dropped without a sound.

Cheryl scrambled to her feet. 'Thanks, Teal. You can stop screaming now.'

'Oh. Er . . . right.' Teal gazed stupidly at the plastic conduit cover, and the large dent it had sustained. 'I don't reckon that's going to go back on the pipe without a bit of – '

'Stop babbling, Teal.' Cheryl bent to retrieve Ardamal's gun. 'Let's get going and find the Doctor, before another one of these goons finds *us*.'

'Yeah. Right.' With shaky steps, Teal followed Cheryl down the corridor.

Leaning casually on his umbrella, the Doctor gazed down into the vast depression in the floor of the Mushroom Farm. With its metres-high layer of control units, the landscape looked like nothing so much as a small valley, complete with undergrowth and trees, sculpted entirely from glinting chrome.

'Obviously this is some kind of nexus, a meeting point . . .' the Doctor mused. 'But of what? A control point? A fuse box? Maybe . . .'

He shaded his eyes from the myriad reflections and looked further into the valley. About half a kilometre away was the slim, vertical column of the Pit. At that distance, it resembled the trunk of a huge tree, climbing ever upwards and vanishing into the high bank of silver clouds that shielded the rock ceiling. Its surface rippled with intermittent tentacles of pale yellow flame which coloured the surrounding landscape a deep bronze.

'It's like Jack's beanstalk, isn't it? Only a different colour.'

Drawing his gun, Bishop turned in surprise.

The Doctor did not move. 'Hello, Ace.'

Ace hovered nervously. 'Hi.' She paused.

The Doctor remained facing into the valley. 'It's out there,' he said. 'The secret thread that binds together Lucifer and the Angels. If only I could touch it, run my hands over it, unknot it.'

Bishop lowered his gun, but did not holster it. 'Trau Bannen had the answer, judging by the files on his work-stations.'

'If only the irritating man hadn't insisted on deleting the most important information and keeping it with him on paper all the time so that nobody else could read it, and then having the criminal negligence to lose that hard copy.' Now the Doctor turned to look directly at Ace. 'You wouldn't happen to know anything about that, would you, Ace?'

Silently, she held out a plastic folder stuffed full of paper. 'Thought you might need these, Professor.'

'Indeed.' The Doctor's voice was hard. Bishop's eyes narrowed, and he tightened his grip on his gun, although he wasn't entirely sure why.

'Yeah. Got a problem with that, have you?'

The Doctor took the folder and flipped casually through the pages of closely written notes. 'The man could have done with a few calligraphy lessons.' He closed the file and looked up at Ace. 'Problem? Why should I have a problem?'

Ace's grin slipped a little. 'I don't know. 'Cos I was working for IMC, perhaps? 'Cos I thought I was better off with someone who couldn't move backwards and forwards in time quite as much as you can?'

The Doctor frowned. 'Why should I think that? Our relationship's been fine until now, hasn't it?'

'Yeah. So like I said, got a problem?'

The Doctor smiled. 'No, Ace. No problem. Not now. I'm just very glad you're alive.'

Ace laughed. '*You're* glad!' She sat down, cross-legged, and stared out across the valley. She brushed a hand across her face, continuing the gesture to take in the surrounding landscape. 'So what's this all about, then?'

'I'm not really sure yet. Some of these notes are encrypted. Who did he think he was, Leonardo da Vinci? I'll need a code word to work out some of the more important passages.' He thought for a moment. 'I don't suppose Trau Bannen will volunteer the information, but – '

Ace interrupted, 'I bet it'll be on file somewhere at his workstation. I bet it's something really easy like his logging-on codeword, or his son's name. Do you want me to go and suss it out?'

The Doctor beamed. 'I'd be very grateful.'

'Colour me gone.' Ace jumped to her feet and ran off into the landscape behind them.

As soon as she was gone, the Doctor sat heavily on the ground. His smile vanished, to be replaced with a look as black as thunder.

Bishop holstered his gun. 'What's the matter?'

'Everything.'

'I don't understand. Krau Ace seems to be back on our side again – '

'Is she?' The Doctor drew his knees up to his chest and hugged them. 'Or is she still on Legion's side? Or on her own side? How many sides are there? How long is a piece of string? How many beans make five?' His face reflected an increasing panic. 'Sometimes I think that I am a Doctor of no brain at all.'

He sighed theatrically. 'In almost a millennium,' he said glumly, 'I don't think I've ever had a companion who has been this much trouble.'

Piper O'Rourke gripped the arms of her acceleration couch as the starpod sank through the bloody glare of Lucifer's atmospheric corona. Her knuckles were white, her jaw clenched in fear. The virtual interaction module she wore showed her the outside view as a great ocean of boiling cloud through which she fell at faster and ever faster speeds. She blinked sweat out of her eyes. Had this view of hell been the last thing Paula had seen before being crushed to pulp? Perhaps it was ironic that she, Piper, should now feel the same fear as the girl whose death she had been responsible for.

'I have come to see how your house is,' Miles Engado's soft voice intruded into the roiling cloudscape. 'Is it prepared for large crowds?'

With an effort, Piper unclenched one fist from the arm of the couch and paused the simularity software. Muscles trembling, she slotted the device back into its receptacle. She blinked as her eyes momentarily lost focus, before the starpod interior swam back into view.

The interior space was curved and dimly lit, bulked out with navigational equipment. Additional equipment was fastened to the curving walls. Across from her, in the copilot's couch, Miles's face was lit from one side by blinking coloured lights from the main instrument spread. His face was as blank as it had been back in the Lift.

A wave of guilt crashed into Piper's mind. Another life destroyed. The life of a man whose love she did not deserve. Guilt and regret welled inside her until she wanted to scream. Her shoulders began to heave and her eyes filled with tears. Shaking, she buried her face in her hands, too ashamed to face the man she loved for any longer. After a moment, Miles reached out and hesitantly touched the side of her face, wiping away the tears.

Without thinking, she slipped the catch on her safety harness; then she was in his arms, and she couldn't tell whose tears were the hottest, and he was whispering her name over and over again: a litany against the darkness.

'Teal! This way!' Cheryl dodged sideways down an access corridor.

Seconds behind her, Teal gasped as molten metal from a near miss splattered across his arm.

The sound of running feet followed. Ardamal turned

284

the corner behind them, new gun primed. Both walls of the passageway blistered. No warnings this time, then. It was fight or flight. Flight or death.

'Cheryl, the gun. Use the . . . bloody gun!'

Ardamal's gun! She'd forgotten she still held it. It must be the shock –

'*Cheryl!*'

She skidded to a halt, spun, dropped to one knee and sprayed hard radiation back down the corridor. Teal ran past her as the trooper dived for the side of the corridor. Without waiting to see the results of her action, Cheryl turned and began to run again. Thirty metres away, the wide double doors which opened on to the Mushroom Farm beckoned invitingly. The doors began to open as Teal hammered on the outside lock. Cheryl increased her speed with an effort.

'Come on, Cheryl! You're nearly there!'

Another energy pulse sizzled past her head and blew chunks from the wall, but Teal was through the portal, head down and running for the lock controls.

She dived in through the doors as they began to close. Panting, she scrambled across the glimmering chrome floor.

Teal moved away from the doors, bent double, sucking in great lungfuls of air. He straightened with a sigh. 'Christ on a stick, that was – '

An energy pulse flashed between the closing doors, skimmed the top of Cheryl's head and punched a hole the size of a fist in Teal's chest.

He gazed down stupidly at the smoking wound. There was no blood: the perfectly circular wound had cauterized instantly.

Cheryl didn't scream until he actually fell, as the doors clanged shut and the smell of burnt flesh and melted clothing seeped into the air.

'He shouldn't have hit me.'

Cheryl whirled with a gasp.

Ardamal stood in front of the doors, a field dressing

on his head, a new gun clenched in his hands, the same blank desire in his eyes.

Cheryl scrambled for her gun. Ardamal seemed to move in slow motion. Casually, he shot the weapon from her hands.

'Naughty, naughty. Can't have a loaded gun in untrained hands now, can we? No telling what might happen.' His expression did not change as he stepped forward and pressed the barrel of his own weapon against Cheryl's cheek. She winced as the heat blistered her skin.

'Look at me. I like to know I'm being listened to when I speak.'

Shaking, Cheryl gazed upwards into his face. He was smiling.

She closed her eyes.

The Doctor looked up as the sound of gunfire crackled through the Mushroom Farm. In moments, he was racing back through the forest of glittering stems towards the entrance. Bishop was hard on his heels, gun drawn, his face set and grim.

Ten minutes of hard running brought them within sight of Alex Bannen's workstations, and the entrance beyond. Ace was standing over the smoking body of Teal Green; Cheryl Russell struggled madly in the grip of an IMC trooper. Even as he watched, the man struck her heavily across the face and she fell.

'That's enough, trooper,' Ace said.

The man glared with undisguised hatred at Ace.

'I should have . . .' he snapped, and stopped.

'Fried me in the null-grav shaft?' Ace completed the sentence for him. 'Perhaps you should. Meanwhile, let's see that gun holstered.'

The trooper snapped to attention, putting his gun away as ordered. There was murder in his eyes, and the Doctor couldn't tell if it was for Ace or Cheryl. 'Consider yourself on report, trooper.'

'Yes, Ma'am.'

'Now open those doors.'

'Right away, Staff Sergeant.'

In another moment, the doors glided apart. Accompanied by another trooper, Bronwen ap Bryn stepped delicately into the Mushroom Farm and peered down dispassionately at Teal Green's body, her oiled skull gleaming softly in the glimmering light from the control stems, the tattoos emblazoned there seeming to writhe seductively.

The Doctor pushed forward. 'I demand to know the meaning of this atrocity!'

Ignoring the Doctor completely, Bryn directed her remark to the space behind him. 'Adjudicator Bishop; you see the consequences of acting without authority. Perhaps now you will accede to the reality of the situation, and put yourself once and for all under my jurisdiction.'

The starpod floated in a sea of Angels.

From within, both Miles and Piper gazed in awe at the signals interpreted by their headsets.

Beyond the thin shell of the pod, the atmosphere of Lucifer changed smoothly from a churning cloudscape to something which almost defied belief. An ocean of liquid-metal zelanite alloy surged and crashed against islands of cloud. The liquid was viscous, a dull silver, and oily in texture. Where it slapped against the shore, pink and ochre clouds peeled away in vaporous streaks. Dull pseudopodia splashed upwards in slow motion, reflecting the colours of the cloudy bluffs. The surface of the ocean was not flat, nor did it even follow the curve of the planet, as gravity dictated that it should have. Instead, great whorls like moon-sized fingerprints spun within the liquid, endlessly moving, shifting, evolving. Some parts of the surface were kilometres higher than others, and at different angles, and all were constantly shifting, as if, in some obscure way, the ocean were alive.

And there were Angels, more than she could count, glimmering, shifting, merging, evolving.

'Sweet Jesus . . .' she whispered in awe. 'They're dancing.'

'Yonder in the north, there is singing on the lake. Cloud maidens dance upon the shore. There we take our being.'

'What?' Piper snapped her head around at the sound of Miles's voice, but the reality projected by the simularity software and interpreted by her retinal implants prevented her from seeing him. All that happened was that she widened her view of the ocean and the Angels.

And of one particular Angel.

'Miles. *Miles*.'

The Angel wore human eyes.

'Paula!'

'Hello, Dad. Piper. Glad you could make it. You're just in time.'

'What for? What's happening – some sort of cultural activity?' Miles asked.

'Don't you know? I suppose not. You never were that good at just listening, were you, Dad?'

Paula spun closer to the starpod, as if to emphasize her words.

'It's my funeral.'

Somewhere, a Tannoy system was booming out an intruder warning. The sound was much diminished in the small storeroom located just off the main executive transporter bay in which Bernice and Christine were changing into their new clothes.

'How do I look?' Bernice smoothed the front panel of the stolen business suit, fastened the collar laces and gave the IMC logo on her breast a final polish.

Christine smeared a little more graphite lubricant across the front of her coveralls. 'The corporate image suits you.'

'Thanks. I think.'

'You realize there's no way this is going to work?'

'Rubbish.' Bernice tied up her dreadlocks with a piece of wire and firmly pulled down the IMC executive cap on top. 'My pretending to be an executive courier is our best ticket off this barge. Where's your clipboard?'

Christine looked around the storeroom.

'Come on, come on. No one will ever believe you're a whitecoat without your clipboard.'

'Ha-ha.' Christine found an LCD clipboard and a light pen, and scooped them up. As a bonus, there was a toolkit stowed in one corner. Christine attached a couple of the more interesting devices to her workbelt. 'Okay. Ready?'

'Let's do it.' Taking a deep breath, Bernice eased the door open a crack, peered through, then opened the door fully and walked briskly into the executive transporter bay.

The ocean heaved and another uncountable horde of Angels was disgorged. Piper sighed. 'So beautiful . . .'

The Angels whirled upwards, approaching to within a kilometre of the starpod. The original Angels had moved higher, away from the pod, already vanishing into the storm-racked cloudscape above. Piper's hands danced across the console, and the starpod's brain began recording and analysing the events for a future that neither of them might ever live to see.

'Yonder in the north, cloud beings rise,' Miles intoned. 'They ascend unto cloud blossoms. There we take our being.'

The Angel that was Paula Engado appeared to turn, without turning. 'I have to go, Dad.'

'Yes, but you don't know why I've come here.'

'It doesn't matter.'

'What do you mean?'

Paula began to drift slowly away, drawn by the new configuration of Angels. In desperation, Miles reached out for her. The starpod's external manipulators swung through a short arc, intersected with Paula's body, passed through it with no resistance.

Paula's voice held a smile, if her eyes did not. 'Careful, Dad. You might hurt me.'

'Paula, wait! There's something important I have to tell you. All of you.'

'It doesn't matter, Dad. Nothing matters any more. It's nearly time.'

Paula began to move faster. Her eyes began to lose their shape. Gradually, the colour bled away into the amorphous glowing mass of Paula's body.

'Oh, God . . . Oh, God . . .' Miles said.

'Miles . . .'

There was a long silence. The Angels rose to meet Paula and she merged with them a final time. The conglomerate creature formed a spinning ring from which tentacular shapes erupted and whirled in orbits of their own. Within the mass, Paula began to undergo her final change. There was a burst of glittering fragments.

Paula appeared to shrink.

She fell clear of the ring of Angels.

And kept falling.

'NO!'

Miles's voice was a roar. His hands blurred across the navigation console and the starpod lurched into motion.

Piper screamed, 'What are you doing?'

'I can't let her go again, Piper. Not again. I can't!'

Frantically, Piper fastened her safety harness, and tried to take control of the pod from Miles. 'Miles! Unlock my board! You'll kill us both!'

Miles did not reply. The starpod gathered speed. Far below, Paula hit the ocean with a soundless splash. Dull silver liquid cascaded upwards, and shockwaves rippled outwards for kilometres.

'I'm going to get her, Piper. The Whale won't have her this time!'

'Whale? What are you – '

There was a tremendous crash as the starpod drove through the ring of Angels and impacted with the ocean of zelanite. The cabin lights blinked and went out, then came on again at reduced power. The console flickered with a rash of warning lights. Miles clamped his jaw and sent the pod spinning into silver-tinged darkness.

Alex Bannen watched as Adjudicator Bryn led two troopers, Bishop and the Doctor from the Mushroom Farm. Ace brought up the rear with her gun trained on the Doctor's back.

He waited until the party was out of sight, then sidled towards the doors.

'You're back early, Dad. You told me you'd be gone for hours.'

He turned swiftly. 'Mark. You made me jump. There's something I have to do in here.'

'Can I come with you?'

'No.' He reached out for his son, smiling sadly when his fingers passed through the boy's. 'It's something I have to do on my own, I'm afraid.'

Bernice strapped herself into the executive transporter pilot's couch and began the warm-up procedure, as she remembered seeing Ace do only a couple of hours before. Behind her, Christine spared a glance for the executive transporter pilot, out cold on the floor.

She dropped the short, heavy tool she was holding beside the body. 'Speaking purely as a psychologist, I am beginning to understand the attraction of physical violence.'

Bernice laughed aloud as Christine strapped herself into the copilot's couch.

The executive transporter began to move.

Legion corkscrewed out of nothing on to the bridge of the *Insider Trading* as the proximity warning klaxon sounded.

In chorus, it whispered, 'Executive transporter three is no longer important. Its destruction is already assured. Begin Phase Two.'

A technician, used to Legion's habit of answering questions before they were asked, said, 'Executive transporter three is leaving the docking bay without authorization. What are your orders?' and then began to operate controls.

Surrounding Lucifer at the points of a cube, eight IMC

heavy-duty tugs began to position their cargoes for release.

The technician spoke again. 'Orbital trajectories are firm. All systems are reading positive.'

'Release.'

Three million kilometres away, the first tug switched off its containment field. The tug vanished, squeezed out of existence in a microsecond by the most powerful force in the universe. Moments later, the planetary envelope began to whirl in patterns that were not determined by purely meteorological phenomena.

On the bridge of the *Insider Trading*, Legion whispered a quiet prayer of exultation to its own private god.

'Profit margins are in the black . . .'

The rape of Lucifer had begun.

PART FIVE

LUCIFER RISING

Let justice be done, though the world perish.

Emperor Ferdinand I

Chapter Eighteen

Lucifer was a vision of hell filling the upper quadrant of the executive transporter's viewscreen. The atmospheric ring was beginning to distort in three places, bulging towards the centre of the planet. Light from the sun, seen for so long in eclipse, was wrapping around the planet like a shawl, twisting into impossible lines and curves, refracting into rainbows which vanished into the minuscule black holes.

From the executive transporter's viewpoint beneath Lucifer, protective globes of energy encircled the ships of the IMC fleet, their immense size reduced to insignificance by the bulk of the planet they orbited.

Bernice shivered. It had taken only eight such ships to unleash enough power to utterly destroy the magnificent planet – and there were over a hundred in the fleet. Terraformers, factories, mining structures, laboratories, crew ships . . . the list was endless. They hovered patiently beneath the planet, having released their death blow; all they had to do now was wait for their mighty opponent to weaken, as inevitably it must, before moving in for the kill. Stripped of its atmosphere, Lucifer would give up all its secrets to its vanquishers..

Bernice found to her surprise that she was beginning to feel sick, and shut off the viewer.

Christine glanced sideways at her. 'Stop anthropomorphizing. You'll be crying in a minute.'

'It's not right.' Bernice's voice was a lot harder than she had intended. 'You want to find out about a planet, you take a trowel and ten years of your life and you ask it politely. What they're doing is impatient, irreverent, destructive – '

'And, unfortunately, very, very lucrative.'

'That should have been my line,' Bernice said dryly.

'You're right, it should have. Call it a psychologist's prerogative.'

'It's a psychologist's prerogative.'

The transporter shuddered violently.

'What the hell was that?' Bernice asked.

Before Christine could say or do anything, the transporter kicked again. This time a scattering of indicators on the flight controls turned red and a siren began to buzz insistently.

'I think that was the reason Legion didn't worry about our escape.' Christine switched the monitor back on. Dead ahead, close by the planetary horizon, the stars appeared to bend in a ring enclosing an area of darkness.

Bernice peered closer, and was able to discern shreds of vapour spiralling from Lucifer and vanishing into the darkness. 'Oh shit,' she whispered.

The Belial Base Operations Room was bathed in angry red light. You didn't need the direct view of Lucifer afforded by the refectory observation windows to know there was something terribly wrong with the planet: the Operations Room simularity was quite sufficient. Cheryl rubbed her hands against the sides of her tunic, aware that her palms were wet and her skin crawling. There was something obscene about the remorseless ease with which the invisible pinpoints were . . . *eating away* at the planet's atmosphere. Small circles of utter blackness were creeping slowly across the darkened face of the giant, and Cheryl knew that less than a million kilometres away the great cloudscapes were rolling into immensely thin, immensely hot discs and spiralling into the gravity wells of the black holes, dropping past the event horizons and being crushed out of this universe altogether. Cheryl was sure this was happening to the Angels as well. She tried to imagine the sensation of being stretched and squeezed until the very molecules of her body ripped apart, but her mind could not encompass the thought. She wondered what the Doctor was thinking as he stood gazing up at the simularity. His face was a blank mask, but, she noticed, his hands were clenched into fists at his side. Ranged around the Operations Room, Ace, Bishop, Ardamal and Kreig were similarly transfixed. Even the other Adjudicator, Bronwen ap Bryn, was silent, her polished scalp shining with reflected light as if on fire.

There was a subtle and complex movement to her left. Something pink and rope-like twisted into being about two metres above the floor. The rope coiled and merged with itself before hovering in the air, pulsing gently.

When it spoke, Legion's voice whispered around the room like a moth. 'An impressive display of technology, wouldn't you say, Doctor?'

The Doctor turned to face Legion, his face a black thundercloud of rage and contempt. 'I would say that your action today is an atrocity unparalleled in my long and bitter experience.' Though his voice was quiet as a whisper, the force in it drove through the room like a forest fire. Cheryl felt her face redden, and suddenly realized what it meant to have this funny little man angry with you.

Legion shivered slightly, its body rippling unsteadily. Was it laughing? Actually laughing at the Doctor? Cheryl shuddered.

Legion spoke again. 'I wonder if you truly understand the relative values of matters of importance,' it mused. 'My action today may be an atrocity in your eyes, but it will mean a new lease of life for the planet Earth and, hopefully, the saving of my own planet.'

'What do you mean by that?' the Doctor asked.

Legion's voice – or, Cheryl corrected herself, *voices* – were hushed and sad as it said: 'Over a recent span of time, there have been a number of unprovoked attacks on various of the planets close to Earth – colonies and independent worlds. Vast black fleets appear out of hyperspace, there is a brief but titanic conflict, and then the fleets disappear, leaving a razed world in their wake. There are reports of such a fleet near Epsilon Eridani – my home. I am . . . concerned.'

'And that,' the Doctor's voice dripped with sarcasm, 'is enough justification for the appalling slaughter of humans and Angels in which you are engaged?'

Legion pulled a cluster of eye-analogues into the moment to study the Doctor. 'Of course,' it choroused. 'My consultancy contract with IMC ends when this job is complete. It is thus in the best interests of myself and my planet to finish the job as rapidly as possible. And my virus detected no signs in the Eden neural net that the Angels were of a high order of intelligence.'

'Then who built the Mushroom Farm and the Bridge?'

'Irrelevant. The Angels are animals. Unimportant to me, unimportant to Earth.'

The Doctor scowled. 'I suspect that you are wrong, Legion. Very wrong. On both counts.'

The starpod slammed into a cloudbank only slightly less dense than the zelanite ocean they'd just fallen through. Only moments before, Paula – what was left of Paula – had fallen this self-same route, but she had been falling freely, whereas the pod was under power. If the atmospheric pressure didn't crush them first, Piper thought they now stood a good chance of catching up with her. Though what Miles would do when that happened was anybody's guess.

The pod shook as Miles drove it closer to the thing that had been his daughter. Piper gripped the arms of her pilot's couch tightly and clamped her jaw shut. She was beyond trying to remonstrate with Miles now, unable to compete with the sound of Lucifer which filled her ears. The atmosphere cheeped and buzzed with electrical activity. A great thunderclap like a slowed-down bell rolled through the clouds and parted them. The sound began to affect her mood as well as her conscious thoughts. She felt bitterness and rage, then a sudden overwhelming joy, before the sound receded, leaving her trembling and sick. She closed her eyes, but the darkness only called to mind an image of Miles, his face a bleak mask, hunched over the controls with fervent intensity as the pod drove deeper into the atmosphere.

New sounds interjected themselves into the wall of white noise building up around her. Metal stress. Sirens. An odd whining noise.

The pod began to shake wildly. Piper felt her muscles protest even though every safety strap was tightened to its limit. The whining noise increased. She wondered how long it would be before atmospheric pressure caused the pod to implode. She wondered if she'd even notice the moment of her own death, or care.

Then her thoughts faltered as the whining noise grew to piercing levels. She became aware of a new light-source strengthening in the cabin. She gazed in amazement at Miles's tribal medicine wheel.

It was glowing with power.

'Doctor? Hey, Doctor. It's Dad!'

The simulated child had entered the Operations Room, unnoticed by anyone except Cheryl, during the Doctor's conversation with Legion. Now he stood beside the Time Lord and gazed up hopefully, stopping short of actually tugging on the Doctor's coat-tails. First Ardamal and then Kreig whirled, their guns levelled at the sudden noise. The Doctor glared at them for a moment. They lowered their weapons. Bishop and Bronwen ap Bryn watched this interplay with silent interest. Ace was looking increasingly uneasy.

The Doctor looked down at the child. 'What about Trau Bannen, Mark?'

'Well . . . I didn't really want to say, because he told me it was secret, but I'm scared.'

Cheryl began to get a cold feeling in her stomach.

'What was secret, Mark?' the Doctor asked with sudden urgency. 'Was it something to do with the Mushroom Farm?'

Mark nodded solemnly. 'He's locked himself in. He won't tell me why. Have I done something wrong?'

The Doctor smiled. 'I very much doubt it.'

Legion moved closer. 'What does the physicist Bannen hope to gain from this action?'

The Doctor looked up sharply. 'Don't you know?'

'Sergeant!'

Ace snapped to attention, grasping Legion's intent immediately. 'Kreig. Ardamal. Let's check it out.'

The doors had no sooner closed behind the three troopers and Bannen's simulated son than the Base Tannoy crackled to life.

'This is Alex Bannen here. I have something important to say, so you'd all better listen really carefully.'

'Executive transporter three. Calculate escape vector and initiate maximum thrust,' Bernice said.

Bernice and Christine were pushed back into their acceleration couches as the executive transporter's engines began to fire at full power, straining to keep them free of the black hole's gravitational well. Bernice swallowed hard as the thrust, conflicting with the pull of the collapsar and the executive transporter's own internal artificial gravity field, churned her stomach into knots.

Her sick feeling increased as an alarm buzzed and the computer spoke. *'Reserve power source at minimum. Fuel exhaustion imminent.'*

'*Reserve* power? Who said anything about reserve power?' Bernice punched the arm of her couch in frustration. 'What's the matter with these IMC cretins? Don't they have maintenance contracts?'

The computer made an enquiring noise; she attempted to think up more specific commands.

From her pilot's couch, Christine strained to speak. 'Don't take this the wrong way, Bernice, but . . . I really don't think there's . . . anything more you can do.'

Bernice grimaced. 'I'm . . . crushed.'

'Ah . . . sarcasm . . . . a typical . . . defence reaction.'

'To tell you the . . . truth . . . I'm scared . . . shitless.'

Bernice squeezed out a half-hearted laugh. 'I've . . . never done this . . . before.'

The rumble and comforting pressure of the engines stopped.

'Reserve power is now exhausted. Systems will shut down as per standard maintenance schedule.'

The lights went out.

Powerless, the executive transporter began to spiral closer in towards the black hole.

Bernice's laugh turned into an agonized scream as she felt the pull of the black hole's immense, uncontestable gravity.

Ace led Kreig and Ardamal along the main access corridor to the Mushroom Farm at a dead run, Alex Bannen's words still pounding in her ears.

'I am accessing the original operating centre of the Lucifer system. There will be power for Earth. Power beyond your ability to imagine. There will be room to live. Air to breathe. There will be grass again, and trees. And fish . . . and . . . and cats . . . and . . . '

Ace unslung her weapon, and ran towards the double doors which opened on to the Mushroom Farm. They were locked shut from the inside.

'. . . there will be . . . peace.'

'Burn the door down!'

'All I ask is that I be remembered as . . . saviour of the Earth.'

Three beams of energy lashed out at the door.

The creaks and groans of the executive transporter's overstressed plates suddenly ceased. Bernice took an experimental breath, expecting nothing but vacuum. She could breathe. More than that, she hurt. Slowly, she opened her eyes.

'What happened?' came Christine's muzzy voice from the copilot's seat. 'Did we pass through the black hole and out into some anti-matter universe the other side?'

'Don't be absurd,' Bernice said, overawed by the sight

303

outside the executive transporter's viewscreen. 'It's *much* stranger than that.'

Bannen's last words echoed and re-echoed in Cheryl's mind. What was the idiot playing at now? If he could have done what he claimed, why hadn't he done it already? Her attention was drawn to the Doctor, standing quite still with a look of tremendous concentration on his normally quizzical face. 'He has no idea what he's doing,' the Doctor whispered. 'No idea.'

Legion unravelled towards the Time Lord. 'If physicist Bannen can do what he says, perhaps we should let him. My brief is to provide a power source for Earth. Why should I squander IMC resources and money if I can fulfil my part of the contract without it?'

The Doctor turned to Legion with a snarl. 'I take it that question was rhetorical? Legion, tell me, is it true IMC troopers have been burning the forests of Moloch?'

'To facilitate exploration and analysis of the interior structure of the moon. Excess vegetation is of no importance.'

The Doctor thumped the heel of his hand against his forehead. 'You narrow-minded fool! That vegetation was the negative feedback control for the entire Lucifer system. The trees, the grasses, even the undulants, they were all a vital part of the mechanism, just like the Bridge and the Lift. And you've destroyed them!'

Amazingly, the pod began to slow. The tremendous battering it was receiving began to abate. With an effort, Piper tore her eyes away from the glowing nimbus of energy surrounding the medicine wheel and restarted the real-time simularity. Lucifer leapt into sharp relief around her.

Stretched out before the hull of the starpod were its mechanical arms. Cradled in them was a tiny glowing bundle – all that was left of Paula. Piper was reminded of a mother holding her newborn infant, except, of course, that Paula's life was ending, not beginning.

New tears began to course down dry tracks on her cheeks as Miles's voice whispered in her ears, 'Paula . . .'

Did the object seem to glow a little brighter for a moment, as Miles brought it nearer the pod? Did the heat on her arms and face from the medicine wheel grow just a fraction hotter?

'Dad . . .'

Piper strained forward to catch the words, which drifted past as if they were no more than a part of the cloudscape through which the pod was moving.

'We can't keep . . . meeting like this . . .'

Miles began to shake. Piper got the impression the glowing bundle on the pod's arms was smiling, and then Paula died.

Again.

Piper reached out for Miles. Quietly, he took her hand. She took off his eyepiece and saw that his eyes were bloodshot from crying. He was shivering.

'Cold . . .'

'I know, I know.'

Quickly, Piper reached across Miles and unlocked the second pilot's board. She set the pod computer to pick a course upwards through the churning atmosphere, then returned her attention to Miles.

He was staring blankly at the glowing medicine wheel. 'Why?'

'I think *how* would be a much better question to answer.' Piper reached out for his hand a second time. 'But we can worry about that later.'

Miles was silent for a moment. Then, 'We have to bury her Piper, break her bowl . . .'

'We will, Miles. We will.'

'Her soul must be released.'

Almost without realizing what he was doing, Miles reached for a control. The manipulating arms released their hold of his daughter's body and it began to fall away from the starpod for the last time. Piper placed her hand on his shoulder. She suddenly became aware that the cabin was growing darker. She glanced towards the medicine wheel. The powerful glow was fading. She cast her eyes frantically over the starpod's control console. The podbrain was still faithfully recording the scene, breaking it down into numbers and graphs and presenting the information to an, until now, uninterested audience.

'Miles,' she whispered excitedly, 'I think I know why – '

Before Piper could finish her thought, the pod began to shake again, gently at first, then with increasing violence. Leaving Miles for a moment, she returned to the simularity. What she saw made her throat tighten in an involuntary gasp.

For hundreds of kilometres in every direction, the roiling cloudscape was being ripped into plasma and sucked upwards into an area of blazing radiation containing a tiny, dark, heart.

She checked instruments, and a cold knot of fear began to grow in her stomach.

The starpod was being swallowed along with the clouds.

Piper turned her attention back to the scene outside. The starpod began to shudder as the gravitational fluxlines converged. The thermometer climbed as the molecules that scoured the starpod's skin raised the temperature. Beads of sweat sprang from Piper's forehead and floated like tiny moons around the interior of the pod.

And then . . .

The plume of dying matter spiralling into the black hole seemed to suddenly unfold. The collapsar blossomed like a flower, vomiting out the gases that it had swallowed in a spray of fundamental particles, which buffeted and spun the starpod, leaving behind it . . .

. . . leaving behind it . . .

. . . an impossibility. Piper tried to find any words, any concepts to express what she was seeing, but the closest she could come was a rip the size of the universe through which she could see things which her mind rejected as inconceivable this side of madness. It was a singularity; the heart of a black hole; the point where all

306

the laws of physics are suspended, all bets are off, and both space and time cease to exist.

And, arrayed around it in concentric circles, were the Angels. All apart from one of them were singing. One of them was heading straight for the starpod.

Ace re-entered the Operations Room. 'We have been unable to gain access to the Mushroom Farm. I've left Troopers Ardamal and Kreig down there, still trying.'

Legion began to shiver. Cheryl was now certain this was a sign of agitation. Something was going terribly wrong, she was sure of it. Why else would the IMC Captain spend so much of its time here?

The Doctor spoke up. 'Trau Bannen must be stopped. He is meddling with things he does not fully understand.'

'I do not agree,' Legion said, its multiplicity of voices drawing together to form a chorus. 'We must observe the results of the physicist Bannen's actions and correlate them with the existing objective.'

'Correlating anything will be impossible if he is allowed to proceed. Everyone here will be dead!' the Doctor said furiously.

'How do you know this?'

The Doctor studied Legion carefully. 'By keeping my eyes open and my mouth shut.'

'You know nothing! You are unimportant!' A rope-like tentacle lashed out towards Bryn. 'All non-essential personnel are to be moved out of the Base confines immediately. Further interference will only create inefficiency in executing contractual obligations.'

'You can't do that! We have no means of survival on the surface. When the air in our starsuits runs out, we'll suffocate,' Cheryl said.

'Bryn; expedite my command immediately.'

Bryn lifted her gun.

Bishop slammed a clenched fist into Bryn's meaty forearm, twisting the gun from her grasp with a practised motion. He stared at her in contempt. 'This isn't justice. This isn't a contractual obligation. This is murder, plain

307

and simple.' He turned to Legion and began to speak again. 'IMC Officer Legion, I arrest you on charges of – '

With a speed Cheryl would have thought impossible from a woman her size, Bryn pulled a tiny pistol from beneath her robes. The gun was almost swallowed up in her huge hand. In a second, the muzzle was resting against the back of Bishop's head.

The Doctor, who had begun to move towards Bishop, froze. 'I don't think that's a very good idea,' he said softly.

Bryn ignored him completely. 'I see you made your decision, then, *Adjudicator*,' she rumbled to the back of Bishop's head. 'A shame. I could have used you on my side.'

She squeezed the trigger.

Ace shot first.

As Bronwen ap Bryn's massive body crashed to the floor, Legion sent a tentacle lashing towards the girl. 'Sergeant, place yourself on report and under arrest. Return to the *Insider Trading* immediately.'

Ace's face was twisted with indecision.

'No . . .' she said finally. 'I'm sick and tired of being told what to do. What you're doing here is wrong. I went along with it because I had a job to do, but I can't blindly follow orders any longer.'

Legion began to gather itself quietly into thin air.

Bishop gestured with Bryn's gun. 'If gambling were not against Earth Central's edicts,' he said casually to the IMC Officer, 'I would have to say I bet I can squeeze off at least one shot before you can do your vanishing act.'

Legion appeared to consider Bishop's words.

'Now I don't know how much damage destroying this part of you would cause,' the Adjudicator continued, 'but since you haven't already vanished, I imagine it would be rather more than an extradimensional flesh wound.'

Legion began to shrink and expand, apparently in some agitation. Bishop smiled, thinly.

Cheryl switched her attention back to the Doctor and Ace. The Doctor was frowning; you could almost see the thoughts whirling through his brain. Eventually, his expression cleared.

'Oh, Ace. I think I see it all. It's IMC, isn't it? IMC from the twenty-sixth century, three hundred years in the future. They've sent you back on an intelligence mission. That would explain why you stole Bannen's notes, why you were trying to tie into the neural net . . .' The Doctor lifted one hand to his brow. An expression of immense tiredness seemed to settle on his face. 'Is that it, Ace? Have you used me to affect the outcome of future events? Events like the Dalek Wars?'

Ace smiled contemptuously. 'It's a horrible feeling, isn't it? Knowing you've been used.'

In the background, Legion's body was swelling from the size of a baseball to that of a small donkey.

The Doctor wrung his hands in frustration. 'Ace . . . Ace . . . I can't believe this is you talking. Not after all we've been through. All I've taught you.'

'All you've *taught* me? Like how easy it is to be manipulated, you mean – used. Just as,' Ace gestured with her sidearm, 'as I'd use this gun?'

'Like a good little soldier, blindly obeying orders that mean the death of her friends.'

Ace took a step forward and levelled the gun. 'It was you that manoeuvred me into Spacefleet, remember?' She smiled bitterly. 'Well, IMC paid a lot of good money into Spacefleet. All of the big corporations did – after all, they didn't want the Daleks to win, any more than the rest of us did. I served on an IMC-funded ship called the *Corporate Strategy* for a while. They already had records of you and some pathetic companion of yours, and they knew that you were probably a time traveller. So they asked me to go on a mission for them. They didn't order me, they didn't even try and manipulate me. They asked me. And they told me that in the time of the Third Dalek War, the location of this star system is of paramount strategic value, and neither the Daleks nor the Alliance can come anywhere near it. There's some kind of total exclusion zone around it – a force field or something. It started up just after the collapse of Project Eden. IMC wanted to know why, and whether there's any way round it. So they said, if you ever came back for me, I should go with you, and try and persuade you to take me to Lucifer at about this time, and then try to get the information back to them.'

Legion's size changes, although slower now, had become even more extreme. Bishop raised his weapon in warning.

'Trouble is, a lot of IMC records got lost in four hundred years, so the only info they could give me was that IMC had an agent in place on Belial, and they gave me a message for someone called Legion. I assumed that Legion was the agent. And that was my first mistake . . .'

At the smallest extreme of his fluctuating size, Legion vanished.

A hideous scream shattered the air. Cheryl wrenched her eyes away from Ace and the Doctor in time to see Bishop lose his grip on Bryn's gun and fall to his knees, clutching in agony at his stomach and chest. She ran towards the Adjudicator. Something in the room was wrong. Something was . . . Legion was missing! Somehow it had managed to –

Cheryl gagged as Legion emerged from Bishop's body in a flood of multicoloured flesh, blood and torn shreds of clothing. Bishop gave a strangled shriek as his heart, lungs and other internal organs were forced through his ribcage, shattering it. Legion swelled into a baggy, green-hued pancake, flanked by two grey pears, shrugging off bloodied shards of Bishop's body as it did so. Christine staggered backwards, and was sick.

'Staff Sergeant,' Legion's many voices boomed, 'you are hereby reinstated as a line officer. Your orders are to facilitate the takeover of Project Eden by terminating the contracts of all non-essential personnel.'

The Doctor leapt forward. 'Ace, no! You can't do it! It's lives we're talking about. Human lives.'

Ace looked from Legion to the Doctor and back again.

She swung her gun to cover the Doctor, then looked hesitantly back at Legion, her face a mask of indecision.

'Kill!' Legion's body stretched and altered as it pulled itself further into the moment, blossoming into a shaggy, many-eyed mass supported on three spindly limbs.

'Not for you, Legion,' Ace said quietly, and threw the gun to the Doctor. 'And not for you either, Professor. I make my own choices from now on.'

The Doctor stared at the gun. 'I have often felt myself to be at a disadvantage when confronting evil,' he said to himself, 'given that I would rather have somebody other than me pull the trigger. I condemned untold billions to death by not destroying the Daleks at the moment of their birth, and I could have saved billions more by shooting down Davros like a mad dog when I had the chance.'

He sighed, and looked up at Ace. 'I have come to recognize that manipulating others into doing my dirty work is almost as evil as the acts of those I choose to fight. I have been so careful not to stain my hands that I have stained my soul instead.'

He glanced over at where the Adjudicator's shredded body lay amongst his bloodstained robes, then up at Legion, and both Cheryl and Ace took a step away from the ferocity they saw in his eyes.

'Welcome to hell, Legion,' he said, and suddenly the gun was pointed at the dark bulk of the IMC Captain. Legion's body split and shimmered as it tried to pull itself out of the area, but the Doctor was too fast. The gun jerked in his hand, and a small grey node which had been blossoming above Legion's body exploded with a wet splat. Pink droplets showered the floor. Legion's scream spanned four octaves. Its body seemed to be sucked from the room in a shimmering montage of three-dimensional shapes. Flailing tentacles wrapped around banks of equipment and chairs, which were ripped from their anchors and pulled into nothingness as Legion's body shrank. Within moments, it had evaporated away to a spidery core of gristle and webby flesh. A last, despairing scream seemed to linger beyond the moment, pitch-shifting downwards as it echoed into silence. Legion was gone.

'Yay, Doctor!' Cheryl shouted, exultant. 'Way to go!'

A brilliant flash of light interrupted her words. When it cleared, there were four people sprawled on the floor. Hovering above the bodies was a shimmering drapery of light which Cheryl could not focus on.

'Are you . . . ?' she began.

'*Our temples are sacred*,' the Angel said. '*You cannot pray here.*'

It vanished.

Chapter Nineteen

The massive doors to the Mushroom Farm, already damaged during their earlier battering, finally shattered beneath Kreig and Ardamal's determined assault. As the troopers strode in, Bannen's pseudo-son ran ahead to find his father.

'Bannen? Professor Alex Bannen? We're under orders to . . . to . . . Jeez!' Ardamal's voice trailed off into silence as he took in the scene. The mushrooms were blazing white silhouettes linked by curved flux lines of energy, and the glowing column of the Pit had become translucent to the point where he could see the spiral of the Pit Path through its gently strobing walls.

Kreig muttered something to herself.

'What was that?'

'I said, "Screw Legion". If he wants to oversee Bannen's operation, he can damn well – ' Kreig choked. 'Damn well – '

As Ardamal watched incredulously, Kreig's voice ran in a liquid stream from her mouth and splashed across her chest armour before hitting the floor in a shower of glowing syllables. Her face creased in horror as she lifted her eyes to his. Behind her, the glow from the Pit intensified, spreading throughout the chamber like ripples on the surface of a pond. As the waves began to pulse through his body, Ardamal felt himself begin to *change*.

He tried to scream, but reality wouldn't let him.

In the Operations Room, the Doctor watched as Ace and Cheryl helped Piper, Miles, Bernice, and Christine to their feet. His voice rang out over the rising hubbub. 'Quiet!'

Everybody stopped and looked at him expectantly.

'Now,' he continued, 'nice as it is to have you all back again, especially you, Krau O'Rourke, and much as I would enjoy a cosy chat over a cup of tea about all of our respective adventures, I'm afraid we just haven't got the time. So if you would be so kind, a quick update from all of you is what I need. Bernice?'

The archaeologist seemed disconcerted by the Doctor's peremptory demand. 'Er . . . something happened to the black holes: it looked to me as if they turned inside out. Then an Angel brought us back.'

'Thank you. Christine?'

The psychologist waved a tired hand at Bernice. 'Like she said.'

'Miles?'

He held out the medicine wheel from his office. It glowed with a soft and calming light. 'My daughter's legacy,' he whispered.

'Paula's final gift, ' Piper added softly. 'I had the starpod record her,' she glanced towards Miles, then reached out to touch his shoulder, 'her final moments. I'm no scientist, but I've spent enough time arguing with Alex Bannen to be able to interpret the read-outs. She changed, Doctor! As she died, the constituent elements of her body actually altered into something, well, something that the podbrain couldn't identify. And I think she deliberately changed Miles's medicine wheel into the same substance.'

'The high-mass elements that we've been searching for!' Cheryl said, stunned.

'We thought they were in the planet's core all the time,' Piper confirmed, 'and in a sense, we were right. We thought the Angels could help us find the elements. It didn't occur to us that the Angels *were* the elements. I don't know how they manage it – I don't even know if it's voluntary or involuntary – but they can modify their body structures. When they die, they become heavier –

much heavier. And they sink down into the core of Lucifer. And before you ask, I don't know why they do that eith–'

Ace slapped her forehead. 'It's like in RE at school. When the Angels die, they fall into the core of Lucifer. It's their Heaven! The rest of the universe is their Hell.'

Christine shook her head. 'Ace, listen to yourself. You're assigning a human belief system, and an outmoded one at that, to an alien species. There's no way it could make sense. The Angels won't even talk to us.'

'Suppose they're scared of us?'

Christine stared at her.

'If this is hell, then we're the demons. That's why they never communicated!'

'And,' the Doctor said breathlessly, 'that would explain the business with the black holes, too.'

'I'm lost,' Bernice announced.

'But the singularities – '

'Don't bother.' She sat down and pulled her hip flask from her pocket. 'Procedural switch-off. I'm not listening.'

He turned to Ace, who watched him patiently.

'At the core of every black hole there is something called a singularity, where the entire mass of the collapsar is concentrated into a single point, and the laws of space and time fail. Strip away the mass, strip away the event horizon, and you're left with a gap in reality through which anything can come. *Anything*.'

'So what do the Angels want with singularities?'

The Doctor's face darkened. 'I'm not sure yet. It connects up with the Mushroom Farm somehow, but I don't – '

A far-off rumble abruptly punctuated his sentence.

He sighed heavily, and announced: 'Trau Engado, Krau Russell, Krau O'Rourke, Krau LaFayette, this is where we say goodbye.'

Everybody tried to speak at once, but the Doctor quelled them with a glance. 'There isn't much time left. Alex Bannen has finally discovered the true function of the

315

Mushroom Farm. He thinks he can turn himself into the saviour of the Earth, but a little knowledge is a dangerous thing. I have to stop him. *You* have to collect the rest of the Project Eden team and leave, because, from what Ace has told us about the future of this star system, if you don't get out now, you never will.'

'How – ' Piper started to ask, but the Doctor beat her to it.

'By using Adjudicator Bishop's ship.' He looked down at where Bishop's body lay scattered, and smiled sadly. 'Under the circumstances, I think you can dispense with the paperwork.'

'But there'll be IMC troopers everywhere!' Cheryl interjected.

The Doctor opened his mouth to reply, but Ace beat him to it.

'I know the way that IMC operate,' she said. 'Now that Legion is dead, they'll be leaderless. They'll act to minimize their losses, and pull out immediately. Any IMC troopers you see will either be running round like headless chickens or withdrawing faster than you can say "boiled asparagus".'

The Doctor stepped forward and took Miles's hand. 'I would hesitate to say it's been fun, but it's certainly been interesting. Goodbye.'

'Doctor, I – '

The Doctor shook his head, smiled, and glanced at Cheryl. She stepped over and embraced him. He clutched at his hat to stop it falling off. Finally, ruffled, he broke free and looked over at Piper.

'Thank you,' she said, 'for trying to protect me.'

'Perhaps you could do me a favour in return?'

'Anything.'

The Doctor delved into his capacious pockets and removed a small twist of paper. Handing it to her, he whispered something in her ear. She frowned, and nodded.

'If that's what you want,' she said, puzzled.

'It's what I want,' he confirmed, and, raising his hat

to Christine, left. Ace shrugged, looked around at the company, and followed him. Bernice briefly embraced Cheryl and smiled at Christine, Piper and Miles.

'No time,' she sighed. 'Story of our lives.'

On the bridge of every ship in the IMC fleet, chaos ruled. Without Legion's tight control, and with the black holes turned inside out, panic had spread like wildfire. Heads of department held interminable meetings; scientists and engineers came to blows over whose fault it was; accountants tried to work out exactly how much eight quantum black holes were worth to Legion's race.

And at the same moment, on the bridge of every ship in the fleet, a kaleidoscopic mass of energy appeared from nowhere, spoke the words, *'Our temples are sacred; you cannot pray here,'* and vanished.

As, shortly afterwards, did the fleet.

Technically, Kreig beat Ardamal out of the Mushroom Farm doorway, but it would have taken a photo-finish to tell the difference. Her skin was purple and spiny: his hands faced the wrong way on his arms and he stumbled as he ran, as if his legs were jointed differently from the way they used to be. He reeled into her as he ran and was disgusted and horrified to find he was unable to separate himself. He began to thrash about in panic.

Kreig screamed, and struggled against him.

Both troopers' minds disintegrated into madness as their bodies began to respond to each other's neural stimuli as well as their own.

As Julie Ndema sneaked into the airlock chamber, her lungs suddenly started metabolizing fluorine instead of oxygen. Choking wetly, she fell to the metal grille floor, passed out, and died. She was hundreds of light years from home, and about twice that far from the nearest planet with a fluorine atmosphere.

Satvindha Mudan, a chemist, locked by IMC in Piper's

317

office along with two other Project Eden staff, suddenly went blind, deaf and dumb. Screaming, he thrashed around the office. If his brain had changed as much as his sensory organs, he would have been able to process the raw flood of radar data from the bony dome that now comprised most of his face; unfortunately, the changes that had flooded through his body were major, but not comprehensive. He smashed his head against the wall, cracked the radar-transparent dome, and died of shock and loss of blood.

His two colleagues noticed neither his change nor his death. They had their own problems.

Craig Richards, sprinting frantically down the Pit, felt a burning sensation running through his body. He slowed, and watched, horrified, as his fingers began to melt and the flesh up to his elbows fell away from the bone. For a long moment, he was staring at the bloodied and pitted bones of his forearms, and then his newly acidic lymphatic fluid ate through to his heart, and he died.

Within moments, all that was left of him was his lucky deck of cards, sliding down the frictionless surface.

Monsters lurched and slithered through the Base, crying out in voices that Ace recognized with horror. Twisted corpses littered the floor in pools of unrecognizable bodily liquids. It was a vision of hell.

A few feet from the wrecked doors of the Mushroom Farm, two bodies lay entwined with the remnants of two IMC uniforms. One looked like a large crab, with a mottled grey shell and eleven corkscrew legs; the other was a mucus-covered atrocity with multiple eyes and a fluted snout. They looked like they had been fighting, and the arthropod had one of the long-nosed creature's ears in its mouth. The Doctor just stepped over them, but Bernice crouched down and rooted amongst the shreds of cloth, emerging with a metal name tag. She held it out to Ace.

ARDAMAL, it read.

Bernice stood up with an unreadable expression on her face, and followed the Doctor into the Mushroom Farm.

'It's just one damn thing after another,' Ace muttered, and stepped over the troopers' bodies.

Whatever wave of reality-altering energy had splashed out from the alien control room had passed by, leaving curved flux-lines of energy which spiralled back to the hub of the Pit like the backwash of water rushing down a beach to the sea. Through the now transparent wall of the Pit, Ace could see that the spiral of the Pit Path was rotating in time with the flux-lines.

'Doctor? Doctor!' Mark Bannen rushed through the forest of glowing metal mushrooms to them and grabbed hold of the Doctor's coat-tails.

'Mark! Where's your father?'

'Over here,' Bannen said as he emerged from behind one of the mushrooms. His skin was tanned, his hair was perfectly coiffured and he had lost a lot of weight. He looked to Ace a bit like Harrison Ford would have done had he been cast as the lead in *The Alex Bannen Story*. 'I've been waiting for you.'

'I wondered how we managed to get here unscathed,' the Doctor said. 'Trau Bannen, you have to stop what you're doing.'

'I let my family down once before, Doctor. I can't do it again.'

'Let the dead rest, Alex.'

'Easy for you to say.' The physicist leaned heavily against the nearest mushroom. Light from the stem seemed to soak into the flesh of his arm, creeping upwards. Bannen brought his hand in front of his face, watching with a deep fascination as the light spread in gentle ripples towards his shoulder.

'Easy for you to *do*,' the Doctor whispered. 'Just switch it off.'

Bannen shook his head. A sprinkle of light flew from his neck like droplets of sweat. He smiled beatifically. 'Why should I want to? As soon as I realized what the

319

Mushroom Farm was for, what it could do, why then my choice was clear.'

'And what *can* it do?' Bernice asked.

'The Doctor knows,' Bannen said.

The Doctor scowled. 'No time to explain.'

'Nonsense. If I'm about to change the human race, people should at least know how.'

'And have the choice not to be changed?'

'People don't know what's good for them, Doctor.'

'And you do?' Ace asked.

'Yes. Yes, I do. And, now that I have access to the morphic fields, I can implement a change for the better.'

'I hate to act the dumb brunette,' Bernice said, 'but morphic fields?'

'An interesting, but obscure offshoot of biology,' the Doctor said, grasping hold of his lapels and leaning forward in his best lecture-room manner as if nothing else were happening around him, 'first put forward on Earth by a scientist named Sheldrake in the twentieth century. The theory states that all living beings have a field associated with them which defines their entire biology, just as an electric field defines an electron. Humans are the way they are because there's a morphic field for humans, just as there's a morphic field for Alpha Centurians and Arcturans and, Rassilon help us, Daleks, and just as there *was* one for sparrows and for sheep. Morphic fields are reinforced by every successive generation, so that human babies look the way they do because the human morphic field influences the development of the embryo in the womb.'

He looked over at an astounded Bernice, and smiled briefly, like a flash of summer lightning.

'And that is why there are so many humanoid races in the universe. The Gallifreyans evolved first, and thus created a morphic field for humanoids. That made it more probable that the next race to evolve would be humanoid, and that made it much more likely that the next race would be humanoid. The majority of the non-humanoid races developed in environments where two legs, two arms and a head would have been a positive handicap.'

'Twentieth-century science foolishly discarded the theory,' Bannen interrupted. 'The race who built this installation,' and he gestured at the Mushroom Farm around him, 'obviously didn't. I don't know where they originally came from, but my researches prove that this whole place is a machine for altering morphic fields, just like an electromagnet can alter magnetic fields.'

'And the Angels are what they turned themselves into,' Ace said flatly. 'Big zarking deal.'

'Don't judge them too harshly,' Bannen said, and frowned. 'We don't know their motives. There may be advantages to living the way they do now that we cannot even begin to guess at. They may be happy.'

His eyes suddenly blazed.

'And if the Angels could use the system to rewrite their own morphic fields, then I can use it to do the same. Don't you understand? I can rewrite the morphic fields of everybody on Earth so that they can live longer, don't catch diseases, don't get poisoned by pollution and don't need as much energy to live! I can re-create the animals that we made extinct! We can have whales again, and cats, and the dodo if we want! We can have everything! We can have *anything!*'

Ace jerked her thumb at the door. 'And what about Doctor Bannen's House of Horrors out there?'

Bannen flinched. 'I'm still learning how to use the equipment. You can't expect me to understand every function straight away. I can control the local fields,' and he looked down proudly at his slim, young body, 'and I can even safeguard individuals from harm, such as your-selves, but I'm still practising with the extended functions. Don't worry, I'll get it right before attempting anything major!'

'And that brings us to the sixty-million adjusted erg question,' the Doctor snapped, stalking up to Bannen and staring up into his eyes. 'Why exactly *did* you safeguard our forms? Why do you want us here?'

321

'I . . .' Bannen looked away. Droplets of glowing sweat trickled down the sides of his face like fiery scratches. 'I need your help. I can't operate it by myself. As you suspected, Doctor, the machine's functions are switched by emotions, and –'

'And you can't do it!' Bernice breathed. 'When was the last time you felt happiness, or contentment, or anything apart from guilt and jealousy? It's a built-in safeguard! You can only access the power of the machine if you are emotionally stable. And you're not!'

The Doctor shook his head in frustration. 'Even if you weren't eaten up by guilt and jealousy, Bannen, or even if I were misguided enough to want to help you, it would be no good. IMC burnt the interior of Moloch. The forests and the undulant creatures were the fine-tuning, all this,' he gestured around him, 'is a powerful but uncontrollable engine.'

Bannen's smile faltered. 'That's a load of crap! The interior of Moloch was just an artificially created habitat for the aliens to live in whilst they were building this equipment.'

'Not so. Moloch is the mechanism. The Bridge is the power system. Belial – the Mushroom Farm – is the control point; the keyboard which gives access to the computer. Alex, how much of the forest has been destroyed? Which systems will work now? Can you tell?'

'I –'

'With the forests gone, whatever you attempt here will not work. It cannot.'

The glow had spread across Bannen's neck and into his chest. His face suffused with a terrible anger. 'You're wrong! You have to be wrong!'

The Doctor shook his head sadly. 'I wish I could agree.'

Bannen let out a soft moan of anguish. 'But I can make it work. I know I can.'

'End it now, Alex. Before it all gets out of control. Morphic fields don't follow the normal laws of space and time. You could be sending out ripples of change that will affect the universe. Billions of races could end up unable to breathe their own atmospheres, or eat anything that grows on their planets' surfaces. Chaos could stalk the universe. You don't understand the changes you might make!'

Tiny gold sparks fell like moisture from his hands as Bannen held them out beseechingly to the Doctor. 'I can't. The system has control now. It's taking all my energy to keep us stable in here.'

Mark had been looking from the Doctor to the physicist in growing fear. Now he released his hold on the Doctor and ran to embrace his father. For the first time, Bannen lifted his son into the air and held him tight.

The Doctor frowned. 'Reality is changing as the morphic fields of local space are being rewritten.' He took Mark's tiny, human, hand and looked at it with mingled awe and horror. 'It's beginning,' he whispered. 'Where – and how – will it end?'

Chapter Twenty

Piper O'Rourke grabbed Miles Engado's hand to drag him faster through the heart of Belial Base towards the airlock chamber. Behind them, Christine and Cheryl led a ragtag bunch of stray personnel they'd collected on the way. Questions were flung back and forth in panicky voices. Off in the distance were screams and the sound of small-arms fire as the IMC staff attempted to fulfil their orders to withdraw, and found their attempts subverted from within. Piper ignored it all as she drove forward, intent on reaching the dubious safety of the Adjudicator's ship before the waves of energy rippling outwards from the Mushroom Farm altered them forever.

There was a terrible cry from behind. Despite her resolve, Piper looked back. Beyond Cheryl and Christine, glowing waves of light lapped at the walls and the floor. Tanetoa blurred as she watched, his bones stretching, his skin tearing, eyes and mouths breaking through all over his body. Piper wasn't sure whether it was him or her who was screaming as she turned and pushed her body to even faster flight.

Bannen did not answer the Doctor's question, but sank instead to the floor and embraced his son. Tears flooded from his eyes.

Ace stepped forward. 'Let me have my gun back, Doctor. There's more than one way to switch off a computer.'

The Doctor turned away from the poignant display. 'But how many safe ways are there? The Mushroom Farm is controlled by emotional feedback. Between Bannen's emotional instability and the partial destruction of Moloch, who knows what the Lucifer System is capable of?'

Bernice was appalled. 'Can't the Angels stop it? After all, they built the damn thing.'

'The Angels don't know that IMC have destroyed Moloch's forest. They think that the feedback mechanism will cut in, like it did the last time that Bannen fiddled with the controls.'

He sighed theatrically. 'They're leaving it up to the last Angel.'

'What do you mean?' Bernice asked. 'It looked to me like the Angels were all tied up with their black holes.'

'The mathematics of morphic fields are too complex for any machine,' the Time Lord answered, 'no matter how sophisticated. It requires an imagination capable of leaping through mathematical flights of fancy without requiring rigorous proofs all the time. It requires a living mind.'

Bernice was horrified. 'You mean . . ?'

'The forest, the undulants – they were an Angel. Or had been. It had been transformed into the necessary form to work as part of the mechanism.'

Ace frowned. 'How did it change itself into the forest if the machine wouldn't work without it already being the forest?'

'An interesting bootstrap question,' the Doctor answered, scowling, 'which I shall consider at a slightly less fraught moment. Besides, I might be wrong. Ace tells us that an exclusion zone will form around the Lucifer planetary system in the short-term future. Perhaps the Angels don't care what's happening in the universe at large, in Hell, as it were, so long as they can preserve the integrity of their local area of space. They've got the singularities. That's all they want.'

'Like I asked before,' Ace said, 'why do the Angels want the singularities?'

The Doctor sighed. 'Is this important, Ace?'

'It might be.'

'The Angels can rewrite space and time the way they

325

want – but . . .' His voice trailed off as he realized what he was saying. 'But singularities are beyond their grasp. Space and time don't exist inside singularities. They worship them. They think that's where their God lives.'

He stared past Ace, overawed by the thought, and shuddered. 'I don't know whether they took advantage of IMC's presence, or whether they somehow arranged for Legion's race to be brought in as subcontractors to IMC, but either way it's a scary thought.'

There was a moment's silence filled by the crackling of energy around the Mushroom Farm and Bannen's racking sobs.

'Still doesn't explain what we're going to do about it though, does it?' Ace stared at the Doctor. 'Well?'

The Doctor took a deep breath. 'There is a way. But you have to trust me.'

He gazed at each woman in turn. 'Especially you, Ace.'

A deep rumble shook the Mushroom Farm. Arcs of energy blazed in a complex web around the kneeling form of Bannen and his son. He seemed larger than she remembered him, more muscular.

'Bannen!' the Doctor shouted above the harsh noise of the Angels' machinery. 'Bannen! You have to help us! The machinery is linked with your brain now.'

Bannen looked up. His face was a glowing mask. 'I can't operate the machine. You told me that.'

'No human can.' The Doctor indicated his companions. 'But we can, between us.'

'And what about the feedback control mechanism that IMC destroyed?'

The Doctor's face was harsh. 'That, I'm afraid, is up to you.'

Bannen stared into the Doctor's eyes for a long moment, and then nodded. 'It's all my fault, isn't it?' He looked at Mark, then reached out and ruffled the boy's hair. 'I could have gone back,' he whispered. 'Perhaps this time, I can.'

He pulled his son to him, and nodded again. 'Let's go.'

The Doctor took Bernice's hand, and looked over

gravely at Ace. Ace turned away. Bernice obviously trusted the Time Lord, as Ace herself once had. How hard was it going to be to recover that trust? What might happen if she didn't . . . or couldn't?

Abruptly, she turned back. 'What the hell. Family's where, when you come back, they've got to take you in. Like it or not, you're my only family.'

She reached out and took his hand.

Cheryl saw the main airlock up ahead as she felt Sonny Lopez's three-fingered claw slip from her hand. The scream came as she knew it would. She didn't even look back. Couldn't. Mustn't. If she did . . .

Ahead, Piper slapped her fist against the emergency controls, punching the doors when they were slow to open, driving them apart by force of will. Cheryl was practically crying by the time the airlock slammed shut behind them, imprisoning them in the blessed cool darkness of the starsuit chamber.

'Suits on, everyone. And be snappy! We don't know how long we've . . .'

Cheryl looked up as Piper faltered. The doors were glowing. Light was seeping through in fizzing runnels.

The new reality had reached them.

Ace flinched. The Doctor's grip was firm, and warm. Hot, in fact. She tried to pull her hand back, but his grip was too tight and she couldn't let go.

Glancing across at Bernice's face, she saw the same seeds of panic that she herself was feeling. The heat in her hand was painful now. She looked down, and felt cold waves of horror lapping across her mind. Her flesh had flowed into the Doctor's; their hands had vanished into each other to form a knobbly knot where their wrists joined.

'*Trust me.*'

Miles clutched his glowing medicine wheel as the new reality began to weave around them. Light interacted with light. There were screams. His mind turned briefly inside out. As if from a great distance, he was aware of hands clutching at his body, moving him, pushing him into a starsuit.

'No good . . .'

'Shut . . . up . . . and . . . *run*.'

The Doctor's other hand had run together with Bernice's, and Ace could see their flesh rippling as it drew them together. Rather than pulling away, Ace reached out on impulse to the older woman. Bernice extended her hand hesitantly and touched Ace's fingertips. Their skin flowed like treacle. It was as if Ace had dipped her fingers into a perfectly still pool and watched herself and her reflection merge, except that instead of the coolness of water there was the heat of . . . Of what?

The Doctor was joined to her up to the elbow now. Even their clothes seemed to be running together in a bizarre melding of corduroy and battle armour, tweed and lycra.

Bernice tried to say something but, as her face blurred and ran into the Doctor's, it was his voice that said, 'Are we having fun yet?'

The last thing Ace saw as a separate individual were the Doctor's impossibly blue eyes growing larger and larger, as if to swallow her. Then darkness wrapped its comforting arms around her, and she was borne away by a torrent of faces, words, feelings, betrayals, loves, lovers, pains and pleasures. Like a child in the world's largest sweetshop, she was overwhelmed by the magnitude of choices. Everything was possible. Everything was there, if she could only find it . . .

Bishop's ship was homely for one: cramped for nine.

Nine people. That was all they had left from an original team of twenty-eight. Miles Engado, Cheryl Russell, Piper O'Rourke, Christine LaFayette, a systems analyst named Sulio N'Farr, Filo Julee, Tiw Heimdall, Shmuel

Zehavi, a scheduler called Brandon Courdry. Survivors, all.

Piper sat with Miles in the pilot's cabin, whilst their friends laughed and cried and slapped each other on the back, or simply lay still in the small cargo bay, too exhausted, both emotionally and physically, to move.

On Miles's lap lay the softly pulsing medicine wheel. Had it been the power of the wheel that held the forces from the Mushroom Farm at bay, or had it been blind luck? Whatever, Earth would be pleased to have a sample of the precious high-mass elements, if that was indeed what the wheel was now composed of. And if there was anything of the old order left on Earth.

Unable to even think any more through sheer exhaustion, Piper glanced at the real-time simularity which overlaid the blank forward bulkhead, displaying a receding Lucifer. Belial and Moloch were too small to see. She was glad that the view was a simularity rather than a real porthole or viewscreen: it meant that she couldn't see her reflection. She felt every one of her eighty-odd years: she was sure she must look them as well.

'I wish I knew what was going on back there,' she said.
Miles put his hand over hers. 'Just be glad we got out.'
'You'll never know how glad.'

She leant forward to kiss him. Unnoticed, Lucifer's red glare shifted through orange, yellow, green, blue and violet, before the planet, its moons, and every trace of human and alien habitation, vanished from the universe.

In their place, a black void took shape, a warning to all not to disturb the Angels at their worship, a shell to shut out the demons.

The smell of boiled cabbage and disinfectant trickled down stained walls, lurked behind cheerful posters of cartoon bunnies with toothbrushes, collected in unvacuumed corners, and pooled in the worn holes, the cigarette burns and the high-heel imprints in the threadbare linoleum. Acedoctorbernice's footsteps echoed through the ward like the tapping of a blind man's cane. Faces turned to watch from the sanctuary of their beds: scarred, scared, bandaged and burned.

The curtains around the last bed in the line rippled ponderously as Acedoctorbernice approached. Behind it, lungs laboured to suck in air. A machine beeped with the same maddening regularity as a fly beating against a window.

Acedoctorbernice didn't want to draw back the curtain, but somehow it drew back anyway. Her father lay there, projecting from the starched sheets like a pressed flower in an envelope. She barely recognized him, his half-forgotten features made more unfamiliar by illness and pain. His dull brown eyes stared vacantly at the punchboard ceiling and the flickering fluorescent light. The fingers of his right hand had dug into the sheets as if trying to find a last handhold on life.

'Hi. Remember me?'

Jan stepped out of the bright sunlight which spilled from the window on the other side of the bed.

Acedoctorbernice's mouth was suddenly dry, and the buzzing of the fluorescent light seemed to suddenly intrude far too much upon reality.

'Yeah, I remember.'

He was wearing an old army greatcoat slung over a baggy T-shirt and a tight pair of psychedelic knee-length shorts. His hair was matted on top and plaited down the back. Someone with patience and no imagination had tied little ribbons into it. Acedoctorbernice had forgotten about the dirt ingrained into his face, and the slackness of his smile.

'Memory plays funny tricks, you know? Like, did we love each other once? Did we fly to the moon together? Did I put flowers in your hair?'

'Yeah we . . . we did that.'

Acedoctorbernice was edgy, and guilty about the edginess. This was *Jan* for God's sake! Her lover! The man she had been willing to leave the Doctor for, and who the Doctor had cold-bloodedly led to his death for what he fondly supposed to be the greater good.

330

'Then why the sad face?'

'It was a lot of years ago.'

On the bed between them, her father went on grasping one moment after another, the rasp of his breath and the beep of his heart filling the silence between their words.

'Love is forever. Or did you forget?'

'Then maybe I didn't love you.' She wanted to slap her hand over her mouth, but the truth had escaped and hung between them, vibrating gently like a struck bell.

Jan's face seemed to sag. 'You said you did.'

'I was wrong.' There was strength in the truth: she felt it, drew power from it.

'But we shared time, space, our bodies – '

'I was *young*.'

His shoulders were rounded, his lower lip swollen and childish. She felt pity for him, mixed with something dangerously close to contempt. Why hadn't she seen how pretentious he had been?

'We shared so much.'

'Yeah, like you shared me with Máire? Like you would have shared me with any other woman who took your fancy?'

'You were the special one, Ace.'

'Lying bastard! I was only special because I fell for your crude charm.'

'You must have felt something for me.'

Acedoctorbernice glanced down at where her father held on precariously to his life, and was unsurprised to see that he was wearing a brown corduroy jacket and a pullover covered in tiny question marks. She brushed his fine brown hair out of his eyes, and marvelled at the tiny wrinkles that surrounded them.

'You, you, you. It was always about you, wasn't it, Jan? I don't love you. I never loved you. I only went with you because *he* disapproved.'

Acedoctorbernice turned on her heel and left, only looking back when the dirty linoleum became softer and rose up beneath her feet, but all he could see was the tiny blue flowers which carpeted the slopes of Mount

331

Cadon, their long stamens waving gently in the breeze as they searched the air for unwary lizards, flicking back in momentary alarm as Doctorberniceace climbed past them, returning to their search within moments as their small vegetable memories forgot that anything had disturbed them. Down at the base of the mountain, where its slope blended gradually with the arid plains of southern Gallifrey, the Prydonian Academy erupted in ebony splendour. High above, higher even than the violet clouds and the hovering flocks of air diamonds, the peak of the mountain was abruptly cut off by the pearly orange sheen of the transduction barrier.

The Hermit was sitting, as always, in the shade of a bush.

The small, intense boy who sat beside him looked up casually at Doctorberniceace's approach.

'You're early,' the Hermit said with a sunny smile.

'I . . . I skipped temporal protocol.'

'As you can see, I am busy. Come back later.'

'I was hoping you would tell me – '

'Tell you what?' the boy beside him cut in. 'About the vampire swarms and the legions of the Sphinx? He's told me all that!'

'Do I know you?' Doctorberniceace asked carefully in third-level High Gallifreyan, using the intonation specifically reserved for dismissive politeness.

'Not with this face,' the boy said, in a voice like oiled silk. 'Not yet.'

Doctorberniceace turned impulsively to the Hermit, his cheeks flushing with childish anger. 'I thought I was the only one you told stories to!' he yelled. 'I thought I was the special one!'

'You're all special to me,' the Hermit replied. 'All of you young renegades who come and sit at my feet and listen to me talk.'

Doctorberniceace stamped petulantly. 'I don't understand.'

'One day. One day, when you will have forgotten we ever talked here, high above the constraining walls of the

332

Citadel, when you have met the others who have shared my stories, then you will understand.'

'But I'm better than the rest. I deserve the stories. They don't.'

The Hermit's face hardened. 'Your path will always be difficult,' he said, 'for as long as you think that the universe knows who you are. Laugh at yourself, and practise humility.'

The boy at the Hermit's side looked away and scowled.

Doctorberniceace met the Hermit's calm, ironic gaze, and somewhere deep inside him, a door seemed to open. He turned and walked away down the hillside. Memories of future events filled his mind: one by one he examined them, and was shamed by his arrogance. Hot tears filled his eyes, refracting the landscape and making it appear fragmented and harsh. He wiped a hand angrily across his eyes; the blurriness vanished, but, through the canopy of the archaeology jetter she could see that the landscape remained essentially the same. Berniceacedoctor looked around. Outside – beyond the equipment dump containing her excavating gear – the terrain of the Vartaq Veil Dyson sphere rolled endlessly on, rising gradually in the far distance, the details lost in the atmospheric haze and the dim light of an old, weak sun.

Far to her right, one of the many fault lines between the different fragments of the sphere ran in a zig-zag for thousands of kilometres. Berniceacedoctor followed it with her eyes as it curved along, and up, and across, and back down again, until it joined up with itself – a snake eating its own tail.

She slid back the jetter's canopy, stepped out into the rich sunlight and walked towards the edge of the fault line, wary of loose soil where air leakage had eroded the ground away from the skin of the world. Although the Dyson sphere's gravity was enough to maintain a breathable atmospheric envelope, much of that atmosphere had leaked away through the cracks between the plates and ended up as puddles of ice on the cold exterior surface.

The little that was left was breathable – just – but weak and cold.

One of the Vart was standing nearby, spindly legs supporting its patterned carapace as it stared silently into the abyss. It hissed, but whether in greeting, whim or warning her translator could not tell.

Berniceacedoctor felt a tiny bud of anguish unfold in her stomach. The ship which had been sent to take her to the new dig on the Draconian-discovered planet of Heaven was leaving in a few hours. This was her last chance. She had been seeking this particular creature since her team had discovered an intact but deserted Spacefleet Dalekbuster, stripped of all insignia and identification, sitting on a hill some thirty thousand kilometres from their base camp. She hadn't been surprised. She'd been following the trail of her father's lost ship for years: moving from dig to dig, planet to planet, looking for the subtle traces of his passage. And now, just hours before she was due to leave, she had managed to locate a Vart who had seen the ship land.

'Vart?'

The Vart rotated its carapace to watch her as she walked up to it.

'I am told that you have memories of seeing others, like me, many . . . er, many . . .' God, how do you say 'years' to an alien whose world is wrapped completely around its sun? 'A long time ago.'

The Vart shifted its head so that it was facing forward, elevated its front sets of legs and began to edge slowly into the crack between the vast plates of rock.

'Please,' she cried. 'Please! It's taken me months to find you.'

The Vart halted, and looked back at her, grinding its mandibles slowly.

'I'm looking for my father,' she blurted. 'He – he went away, when I was small. I've been trying to find him ever since.'

'Ssss . . . ssss . . . sssssksss . . .' the Vart said.

Berniceacedoctor fiddled frantically with the controls

334

of her translator, trying to get a fix on the particular dialect.

'*Ssss . . . sskt . . . ktch. . . . tkcha . . .*'

Almost got it. She adjusted the contextual analyser.

'*Tchk-k k*o away now, Benny, but I want you to know that I love you, and I'll be thinking of you when I'm gone.'

Berniceacedoctor stood facing the alien, open-mouthed, unable to believe what she was hearing. She couldn't feel the ground beneath her feet, or the breeze on her cheek. The world around her seemed to go fuzzy around the edges.

'And look after *sssstchsss* . . . Mummy for me until I come home.'

'Mummy died,' Berniceacedoctor sobbed. 'She died, Daddy. You left me, and you never came home, and she died!'

All self-control was sliding away now, and Berniceace-doctor was a child again, watching from a blast-window as Mummy staggered away through the blazing wreckage of the street, looking for her daughter's toy.

'They said you were a coward!' she screamed at the Vart in the Spacefleet uniform with the row of Conspicu-ous Bravery ribbons pinned down the arm. 'They told me your ship broke formation and ran.'

'It wasn't your fault,' her father said gently. 'Even if you hadn't been scared of the fire, even if you had tried to tell Mummy that you didn't want the doll, she wouldn't have heard you. The blast from the Dalek ship's plasma cannon had stunned her. She didn't know what she was doing.'

Berniceacedoctor sank to her knees, sobbing hysteri-cally.

'But they said you were a coward,' she said again, holding the words like a mantra.

'No,' he said, 'they never did. *You* did, but you weren't talking about me.'

The Vart turned and scrabbled into the crack that led from warmth and light into the darkness. Bernice watched

335

it go, and felt a small area of darkness in her mind that she had always taken for granted dry up and blow away . . .

Ace awoke to find the Doctor standing over her and staring off into the distance. She stretched and, as she did so, fleeting memories touched her brain: images of a mountain, a hospital bed, a doll's head, coasting on a wave of flame, landing at her feet. Looking down at herself, she was relieved to find that everything was intact, where it should be, and recognizably hers.

She stood and looked around. The Mushroom Farm was as placid as the first time she had seen it, and Bernice was lying beneath one of the metal parasols.

'Okay?' Ace asked.

Bernice smiled quizzically. 'I feel . . . fine. No, better than fine, perfect.'

Ace ran a hand through her hair, and took a deep breath. 'Me too,' she said.

Bernice held out a hand. Ace looked at it for a moment, then tentatively touched it. Nothing happened. More confidently, she pulled Bernice to her feet.

Their eyes met. Ace recalled memories that she knew were not hers, and she knew from Bernice's expression that she was finding the same. And somewhere deep down within both of them, a tiny core of alienness sat and smiled at them.

'Doctor?' Ace said.

He turned to look at them, and Ace thought that he looked older, and more tired, than she had ever seen him.

'Doctor, what happened?'

'We succeeded,' he said eventually. 'Together, the strength of the emotions that we dredged up from our respective pasts brought the morphic field machinery back under control.'

'What about Bannen and Mark?' Bernice asked.

The Doctor sighed. 'IMC had already destroyed the feedback control mechanism by putting the torch to the interior of Moloch, but we couldn't have succeeded with-

336

out it. I suspect that if you go back there, you will find that the forest has regrown.'

'You mean – '

'I mean that Trau Bannen and his son will be staying.'

He brushed a smattering of non-existent dust from his lapel. 'Well, Ace,' he said softly, 'did you get what you came for?'

'With Legion dead and IMC legging it, I doubt if there's any way I can get the information to where it would do any good.' She sniffed. 'Can't say I'm sorry. And what about you?'

'How do you mean?' he said carefully.

'I saw you give something to Piper. What was it?'

'I don't know what you're on about, Ace.'

'I may have asked to come here, but I've never known you not to take advantage of a situation. What was it?'

He tried to avoid her gaze, but she kept walking around him until he was forced to look her in the eyes.

'A little concoction of mine,' he said sheepishly. 'To make things easier for myself in a few years time. Or was it a few hundred years ago? No matter.'

'For what?' Bernice asked from the sidelines, but the Doctor just tapped his nose.

'Secrets,' Ace said dismissively. The Doctor scowled.

'I know what it was,' Bernice announced suddenly. 'You tried to tell me about it, back when you were locked up in the conference room. Damn it, I knew there was some kind of subtext to that chat. "Tomorrow's problems I solve yesterday," you said. Yes, and I guess the logical corollary is that yesterday's problems you solve tomorrow. It's got something to do with that Dalek invasion that's coming up – when is it? Twenty-one sixty-three? Twenty-one sixty-two?'

'Twenty-one fifty-eight,' the Doctor said. His face was impassive. The clown had gone. 'You've already noticed the news reports: as the Dalek battlefleet gets closer it destroys any planet which might render aid to Earth. Their biological warfare drones have already started seeding the planet with diseases to weaken any resistance.

When you told me you wanted to "pop back to the year twenty-one fifty-four or so", I decided to set up a little something that would prove useful to a younger version of me, so I knocked together a batch of a highly contagious virus that will confer some small measure of protection on a handful of potential freedom fighters.'

He grimaced. 'I originally put some into Trau Bishop's tea, thinking that he would be returning to Earth sooner than the rest of the Project Eden team, and could spread a little happiness for me. We all know how that worked out. Piper was my next best bet.'

'You always take the complicated way around, don't you?' Ace marvelled. 'You never make it easy on yourself.'

'I prefer the scenic route to the short cut,' he snapped, and walked off towards the door, then paused, and said, 'but don't worry. You may not have to endure my secretive little ways for long.'

'Do what?'

He removed his hat and turned it over in his hands. 'I feel a change in the air,' he muttered darkly, then crammed the hat back on his head and strode off again.

'Well,' he called back over his shoulder, 'are you coming?'

'Are we coming?' Bernice asked Ace.

Ace gazed levelly at the woman, savouring the taste of jealousy that Bernice had left behind her: a dark and bitter envy of the depth of the relationship that still existed between Ace and the Doctor.

Bernice's smile slipped slightly, and Ace wondered what emotional flotsam and jetsam *she* had left behind.

There were depths here that wouldn't be plumbed in a hurry.

'Who else would have us?' she said finally, and walked off after the Doctor, stopping after a few seconds to allow Bernice to catch up.

Side by side, they walked in silence to the Mushroom Farm's entrance. There the Doctor ushered them across the threshold.

He lingered for a moment after they had gone, gazing into the silvery distance. Then, with a grimace, he poked at a metallic parasol with his umbrella. Without a sound, the lights in the chamber began to dim. As the last dregs of light glimmered and died, he turned on his heel and stepped across the melted doors into the darkness of the Base.

At some indeterminate point in time, for time is a meaningless concept when applied to singularities, Alexmark gazed without eyes into the heart of the Angels' temple.

Though what he once would have called an event horizon was no longer present, still the darkness within the singularity was complete.

Through a dancing screen of Angels, he was able to make out . . . something: a pattern, a force. A thing he no longer had the vocabulary to describe.

He looked closer.

Something moved upon the face of the dark.

EPILOGUE

ON THE THIRD DAY . . .

'You cannot fight against the future.'

William Gladstone

The noise of surf on sand was the only hint of the vast ocean that lay before them as they stood, hand in hand, on the headland.

'My father lived here,' Miles said. In the darkness, all that Piper could see of him was the occasional gleam of starlight in his eyes. 'He had a shack down on the beach. He called himself the last of the Tewa. He kept all the traditions going, and he taught them to me, and to Paula.'

A faint chemical tang drifted up from the beach, and Piper was glad that she couldn't see the extent of the pollution. In the dark, with the regular pounding of the waves beneath, and the bright profusion of stars scattered above them like petals in a bowl, the years since she had last seen Earth seemed like a cruel illusion.

'Truth to tell,' Miles continued, 'the Tewa all died out generations before he was born. I think he read about them in a book. But he kept the traditions going, and for that I loved him.'

He paused, and Piper reached into her tunic for a small package. Wordlessly she pressed it into Miles's hand. He tensed as he felt its shape, its weight.

'Piper?'

'I took it from Cheryl's room after Paula died,' she whispered rapidly, before she could think better of it. 'I thought that if you were acting erratically then the Adjudicator might recommend closing Project Eden down. I'm sorry.'

'Too many apologies,' he said quietly, and held the bowl out in front of them. 'Too much weight attached to the past.'

He threw the bowl far, far out over the headland. For a moment Piper thought that she could see it glitter in the starlight, and then it was gone, falling away from them through darkness towards the black sea.

Piper did not hear it break, but she felt Miles relax beside her, and knew that it must have done.

'Only from death do we learn of life,' he whispered, and put his arm around her.

'What does that mean?' she asked.

'It's something Dad used to say.' In the silence, Miles hugged her tight. 'We must live for the future.'

Piper reached into her tunic again, and gently crinkled the small twist of paper that the Doctor had given her in those last moments on Belial. She pulled it from her pocket and unwrapped it. The small grains of powder seemed to glow of their own accord.

'What's that?' Miles asked as she held the paper up.

Piper remembered what the Doctor had told her, and suddenly grinned.

'Hope,' she said, as the powder was carried away from them, like a flurry of sparks, upon the wind.